THE AMBASSADOR'S
DAUGHTER

THE AMBASSADOR'S
DAUGHTER

A NOVEL OF ANCIENT MESOPOTAMIA

ELISABETH ROBERTS CRAFT

Bartleby Press
Washington • Baltimore

Printed in the United States of America

Bartleby Press
9045 Maier Road
Laurel, MD 20723
1-800-953-9929
www.BartlebythePublisher.com

Library of Congress Cataloging-in-Publication Data

Craft, Elisabeth Roberts, 1918-
    The ambassador's daughter : a novel of ancient
Mesopotamia / Elisabeth Roberts Craft.
        p. cm.
    ISBN-13 978-0-910155-64-9
    ISBN-10 0-910155-64-X
    1. Mitanni (Ancient kingdom)—Fiction. 2. Iraq—
History—To 634—Fiction. 3. Courts and courtiers—
Fiction. 4. Fathers and daughters—Fiction. I. Title.

    PS3553.R213A43 2006
    813'.54—dc22   2006012270
                                                      CIP

In memory of Harold Bartz

1

In 1380 BCE, Tushratta was King of the ancient empire of Mitanni, a great empire for approximately two hundred years. It lay on the banks of the Euphrates River in what would be now north central Syria, down into Iraq and Jordan. Landlocked except for the river, its capital, Wassukkanni, developed on a small tributary of the Euphrates. Its people were Hurrian stock, Sematic, overrun by Aryans from the Pakistani area of the Indus River.

Mama, Mama," screamed Kelu, glancing wildly through the rush of morning shoppers. With terrified shrieks, people scattered, plastering themselves against the mudbrick buildings on either side of the pounded earth street or dove into the open doorways of tiny ground-level shops. Kelu pressed her little body against the doorjamb of a bread maker's shop. She turned her frenzied, contorted, face to look at the great, snorting, sweating horses galloping up the slope of the narrow street.

"Mama, mama," she whimpered, again frantically scanning the crowd for her mother. The big horses seemed to be rushing at her. She hid her face, trying to push her head inside the doorjamb.

As the enormous animals pounded by her, Kelu clawed at the wall. A high-pitched scream rising above the throbbing of the flying hooves sent a cold shiver through her. For an instant, she stopped breathing. Something about that scream—her little fists beat against the doorjamb as a silent shriek rose in her throat.

After the fast-moving animals charged past her, Kelu heard the activity in the street erupt into normal pandemonium. She quickly surveyed the road then darted from the wall and raced on skinny legs towards the motionless figure lying in the gutter.

A hairy arm went around her waist from behind, halting her forward motion with such force that the upper part of her body jutted forward, causing her long, blue-black hair to sweep the road dust. Stunned, she hung limply over the arm.

"Don't go over there." The male voice came from somewhere above her, and she felt herself pulled against his naked chest.

"Let me go. Let me go!" screamed Kelu. Squirming around to look at him, she only succeeded in getting his black chest hair in her open mouth and his stubby, meager black beard in her eyes.

"There, there, little one." His big laborer's hand stroked her head and shoulders soothingly.

She flung the back of her head against him, stiffening her torso and sobbing. Her right arm rose slowly, her index finger pointing at the crowd gathered around the fallen woman.

The laborer looked at the finger then his eyes followed its trajectory directly to the woman. He scanned the mix of curious shoppers elbowing each other to see the body. His lips pressed together and worked as he thought. He could always take the girl to his mother while he searched for the father. In this big city! The woman's pale skin, the same golden tan as his own, proclaimed her to be a member of the local people rather than belonging to the dark-skinned ruling overlords. He conjured up visions of himself walking through street after street in the narrow warrens where people lived, loudly calling that he carried a lost child. The prospect horrified him.

A heavily bearded older man, wearing a long, tightly belted dark blue wool robe, extricated himself from the knot around the woman. Glancing first right then left, he spotted the noisily crying child and the youth holding her. Automatically raising his hand to attract their attention, he hastened towards them.

Kelu saw him and cried, "Mama, mama."

"Your mama can't come," the man said, gently stroking her head.

To the youth, he said, "The woman's dead."

Trying to scream and sob at the same time, Kelu choked. The laborer cupped her head in his hand and cautiously pressed it against his chest. "Does anybody know where I take this little girl?"

"Her mother's a slave in the house of Pamba, the Hittite."

"I don't know the place."

"It's a large mudbrick house with wooden decorations on the door lintels and windows. It's just before you reach the great lion gate of the palace complex at the top of the incline." He added, "Kelu can show you." He looked pointedly at the red-eyed, runny-nosed, sobbing little girl. "Can't you, Kelu?"

She turned her head sideways, resting the right side of her face against the laborer's chest and dug one of her small fists into her left eye.

The older man touched her shoulder sympathetically, nodded to the youth, and walked towards an open door to the right of the little group of people.

Pulling his shoulders back, the laborer tipped Kelu away from him. For just an instant, she raised her wet, deep-brown eyes to look at him. "You have to help me, little one. Show me where you live." He set her on the ground, keeping a firm grip on her right arm to prevent her from making any sudden dash to her mother.

"Let me go. Let me go!" She pulled away, trying to free herself.

Ignoring her objections, the youth resolutely turned her body to face uphill, grasped her hand, and took two steps.

Kelu dug in her heels. "Mama, mama!" she yelled, twisting her head around.

"Child, it you don't want to be dragged, which will hurt, you better walk."

"I want my mama," she sobbed. With her free hand, she beat the hand that held her.

He caught the small beating hand and looked down at the thin little body, the cheap, pink wool dress, the bare feet. Through the streaming tears, she glared at him. Shaking his head in frustration, he grabbed both of her shoulders and squatted low enough to be at eye level with her.

Kelu stopped crying and fluttered her eyelashes. The closeness of his big, stubby face startled her. She wondered if the master's heavily bearded face would look like this up close. The man's black eyes looked serious, but kind. She decided she didn't need to be afraid. Immediately, his face started to fade, and the vision of her mother's face reasserted itself. With a shuddering gulp, she started to cry again and struggled to escape from his grasp.

He sighed. "Once we pass the temple and are away from this market section, we'll walk." He scooped her up.

Kelu hung over his shoulder, watching the group congregated around her mother. Tears flooding from her eyes dribbled down his naked back and wet the waistband of his short, dark, green, wool skirt.

As soon as they reached the stretch of private homes clustered around the massive stone wall surrounding the king's palace, he set her down and took her by the hand. He felt nervous. Never had he been so close to the king's palace on its platform. He tried to look at the guards grouped around the gate without their knowing it. He knew they looked at him. The hand holding Kelu trembled slightly. Had she felt it? He glanced down at her then at the wall that encircled the palace.

The wall looked much like the ramparts that enclosed the whole city. He knew that the top of the city's ramparts allowed two horses to race side by side. He doubted that this wall could accommodate more than one horse.

Trying to forget the guards, he squeezed Kelu's hand. "Now, tell me in which of these houses you live."

They walked along slowly. He adjusted his long steps to her short ones. She seemed so tiny walking beside him—straight, shiny black hair like the overlords. That startled him.

"How old are you, Kelu?"

Without answering, she stared straight ahead through water-logged eyes, lost in her own forlorn thoughts.

The youth looked closely at her skin. It reflected the sunlight with a golden glow. Her skin was darker than her mother's. The blood of the overlords. The house of Pamba, the Hittite, wasn't the overlords. He shrugged. He had enough problems at the moment without adding that.

In the high, round-necked dress hanging shapelessly to her knees, Kelu plodded forward. An empty feeling overwhelmed her. She rubbed a wet hand down the side of her pink dress then gave the dress a yank. The cook, the master, and the mistress, the people in her life, were all nice to her, especially the cook, but they weren't mama, her warm, beautiful mama. She stuck out her jaw and fought back fresh tears.

The laborer carefully checked each house they passed, some of stone, some of mudbrick, some with fine wood trim. He whistled inaudibly. These houses cost a lot of silver. He couldn't imagine the amount. He turned expectantly to Kelu.

Stone-faced, looking neither right nor left, she showed no sign of recognizing any of these houses. Every few seconds, she hiccupped.

A short distance from the monumental lion gate and the guards standing around the entrance, he shook his head hopelessly. Surely, though still quite young, the child should know where she lived. Would he have to knock on every door and ask, "Does this little girl belong to you?"

Just as he made up his mind to do that, Kelu said, "Over there," pointing to the large tan-colored house on the left with the fancy carved-wooden triangle over the door. .

Hesitant, feeling uncomfortable, he walked towards the house. Somewhere, there must be a door for the slaves.

Kelu broke from him. Cook. She had to find the cook. She tore around the corner of the house, her legs flying.

Instantly, the youth tailed her. His hand reached out ready to grab her when she dashed through an open door. He stopped abruptly and looked in.

Using a ragged piece of cloth, the big-boned woman on her knees energetically fanned the embers in a corner hearth. Surprise crossed her face as she took in the tumultuous entrance of Kelu and rested her eyes on the laborer.

Kelu flung herself on the woman. "Mama, mama," she cried, tears starting again.

As her arms gathered in the child, the cook looked up at the youth. Her deep gray eyes demanded an explanation.

"Her mother's dead," the laborer blurted.

"Dead!" After a pause to assimilate that, she sank to the floor and gathered Kelu into her lap, cradling her, gently rocking the sobbing girl. "How?"

"Galloping horses in the marketplace. She wasn't quick enough."

"You had better see the master." Still holding Kelu, she managed to get to her feet. "Follow me." She put Kelu down, careful to keep tight hold of her hand. With her other hand, Kelu grabbed the woman's dress, hiding her face in it.

"Kelu," the cook said gently, "you are making it difficult for me to walk. Let go of my dress, but stay close to me and hold my hand."

She opened the door near the hearth. "Watch the fire," she said to the wide-eyed scullery maid who had been standing in a dim corner near the entrance.

The laborer followed behind the cook as they walked through two small, sparsely furnished, yet elegantly carpeted, rooms and then a third simply containing a table and two chairs. He tiptoed through the rooms, afraid to put his weight on the carpets, afraid to look at the furniture, but stared, intrigued by the green mountains, the barren rocks, and the heavy snow that decorated the painted walls.

The cook tapped at the closed door of the third room.

"Come," boomed a male voice.

The young laborer shyly followed the bowing woman into the room and dropped to his knees on the carpet. He shivered as he felt its softness. Raising his eyes a little, he silently gulped. Before him, the plump man, wearing an ankle-length purple wool robe with a high round neck and three-quarter sleeves, sat on a high chair. Large gold loops hung from his ears, a purple skullcap covered most of his tightly curled black hair. His feet, in slippers with curled-up toes, rested side by side on his footstool.

Alert black eyes seemed to peer out of the curly black beard that completely covered his face. The laborer wondered if his beard would ever grow that luxuriously.

Seated near Pamba, in a matching chair, the mistress straightened and said, "What is it, cook. Why is Kelu crying?"

The laborer turned his eyes on the mistress, noting that the fabric of her purple dress had narrow, horizontal pleats and that her dark curly hair was elaborately coifed. Her face struck him as pleasant, though not pretty.

"This man has something to tell you." Bowing, the cook said, "I'll take Kelu back to the kitchen."

Pamba raised his hand, dismissing her.

Drawing Kelu close and bending over her slightly, the cook retreated.

"Her mother is dead," the laborer began, looking directly

at Pamba's wife, Hepit. "She was hit by horses galloping up the road." Using his thumb, he pointed in the direction of the road.

"Killed!" Pamba half rose from his chair.

"From what I could see, the horses' hooves crushed her shoulder and legs after she hit the ground."

"No," cried the woman, covering her eyes with her heavily ringed hand.

"Where is her body?" asked Pamba whose face had drained of color.

"By the side of the road."

Pamba turned to his wife. "Send someone to retrieve Khelpa's body."

Hepit rose and left the room.

"What name do you go by, laborer?"

"Rasi, My Lord."

"Where do you live?"

"Near the south corner of the track where the race horses are trained."

"So the child is on my hands," Pamba mused, his thumb and forefinger stroking his beard.

Rasi knit his brows, not understanding the Hittite's statement.

"You may go," said Pamba. "Another will undoubtedly want to talk to you."

After Rasi left, Pamba sat for a short time with his hand pressing his forehead.

Then he reached for the papyrus roll lying on the round table beside his chair, changed his mind, and let the roll fall. Deep in thought, he stared at nothing until his wife returned.

"You will have to tell Arttarna as soon as he arrives in the city," she said as she seated herself.

"He came back this morning." Pamba's sad eyes met his wife's. "This will crush him."

She nodded, pursing her lips. Suddenly, she gasped. "Wouldn't it be awful if one of his own horsemen struck her?"

Pamba cringed, clutching his chest. "That horseman would be dead before sundown." He sat in silence before saying, "Strange the way things happen. I never thought when King Suppiluliumas sent me here from the great Hittite capital of Hattusas, to be his ambassador to King Tushratta in the Mitannian capital of Wassukkanni that this would happen; that

I would become close friends with a famous roving Mitannian Ambassador and end up housing his mistress. I never expected to get caught up in this kind of domestic tragedy when I agreed to take Khelpa."

"Considering your friendship with Arttarna, you are involved in this. We both are. But he will have to make some decisions now. We cannot keep Kelu or have our slaves responsible for her."

In silence, Hepit studied her folded hands; Pamba fiddled with the papyrus roll on the table. Each thought of Arttarna, his handsome dark-skinned physique, his shoulder-length black hair with its soft wave and sheen, his snapping black eyes, his position as close confidant, indispensable advisor, to Tushratta, King of Mitanni, and his loyalty to him.

Pamba slapped his knee and rose so swiftly that Hepit jumped. "I will prepare myself for a visit to Arttarna," said Pamba.

2

Arttarna lay naked on the narrow bed in his small bed room. The door into his workroom stood slightly ajar in case the messenger from the king knocked. Using scented oil, his slave, Sebi, massaged his right leg.

"That's better. Now do the left leg."

Sebi straightened. Slight in stature, bald and clean-shaven, he moved in silent, floating motion to the other side of the bed. He poured oil into his left palm, slid his hand deftly along the length of Arttarna's left leg and drew it back down, catching the oil as it spread.

After a short silence, broken only by his grunts, Arttarna said, "Now, my shoulders. All night on the back of a horse takes its toll."

The rough blanket thrown over the back of his horse had irritated his inner thighs and the heavy stirrup loop around each of his big toes had rubbed his toes raw. The flat leather piece connecting the loops, lying across the horse's back under the blanket, had bunched, causing his legs to be drawn up uncomfortably. In too much of a hurry to reach Wassukkanni, he had ignored the pain and galloped on. Now, with the strong hands of the slave kneading his shoulders, Arttarna sighed as his body relaxed.

Finally, he said, "I shall bathe now." As he placed his hand on the bathroom door, he said, "Order food laid on the table in my workroom."

In his bathroom, he stood on the waterproofed floor and flexed his muscles in delight as Sebi, his skirt hiked up to avoid the splashing, poured a bucket of warm water over him. Arttarna wiped the stream of water off his face and looked at the row of buckets against the wall. "Use four of them," he said.

Later, dressed in a white, long-sleeved wool robe, a wide crimson sash around his waist, Arttarna opened the door between his tiny sleeping chamber and his workroom. His glance swept around the room. A number of small dishes lay on the oblong sandalwood table that he used for a desk.

The goblet of wine to the right of the dishes reflected the sunlight filtering through the window. At the end of the table, a household slave held a brightly painted pottery pitcher, ready to pour milk over his mush the moment he sat down. Another slave stood by the open door across the room.

Arttarna exhaled in contentment at being home again.

"Send for Khelpa," he said to Sebi who was standing behind him. "Tell her to come to me."

"Yes, Master." Sebi disappeared.

Arttarna sat down and tore a small piece of bread off the chunk in one dish and dipped it into the bowl of spicy lentils. Hearing soft footfalls, he looked up, and his hand stopped short of his mouth.

A tall, dark-skinned, delicate-looking woman stood in the doorway. Her shiny black braid hung to her waist, the hair tight and smooth over her head.

"My lord husband has returned from Nineveh and has not been to see me." The words purred from her unhappy, discontented, mouth.

"I have only been here long enough to bathe and have not even eaten," he said, indicating the food.

"You would have made me happy if you had stopped by our palace suite for a moment, or at least sent to tell me you had returned rather than my hearing it from the whispering of slaves."

He threw up his hands helplessly, not wanting to get into an argument with her.

"You are gone for months. I am alone," she shot at him. "Then when you return—" She saw his eyes shift to the door so stepped sideways and turned. Her eyes met those of Sebi.

"Does the king call?" Arttarna asked Sebi, half hoping Tushratta ordered his presence.

"No, Master. Pamba, the Hittite, awaits your pleasure." Bowing profusely, Sebi backed into the corridor.

A red flush of fury colored the woman's face. Arttarna

knew what she was thinking and didn't care, although the fact that Pamba had come instead of Khelpa surprised him.

"Leave me now," Arttarna said to his wife. "I have business with Pamba."

"About that slave you sleep with instead of your wife?" she spit out.

"That's enough," he commanded. "Go."

She flung her nose into the air with a haughty sniff and swept out of the room.

No sooner had she gone than Sebi appeared in the doorway.

"Bring Pamba to me," said Arttarna, pushing aside the food in spite of his hunger. "And place another chair."

The slave turned and motioned to the figure in the corridor. He then silently placed a chair in front of the desk and bowed himself out of sight.

Arttarna rose to greet Pamba as he walked slowly into the room. "What an unexpected surprise, my friend," he said, his black eyes sparkling. A wisp of a smile poked at the corners of his mouth. The two men embraced.

Pamba noticed the way the sheen on Arttarna's smooth black hair glistened across the top of his head then danced in and out of shadow as his hair fell in soft waves to his shoulders where it played hide and seek with the long gold earrings he wore.

"Don't tell me you carry an urgent message from your king," said Arttarna lightly.

With a wave of his hand, he invited Pamba to sit down and returned to his own seat. "I have hardly reached home before I am honored by your presence."

Pamba uneasily folded his hands in his lap and looked at them.

Arttarna observed him before saying, "Pamba, in spite of any problems between our countries, you and I have been close friends for years. Whatever you have to say to me will not lessen my feelings towards you."

"Arttarna, would that I had that kind of communication."

"Have you come here to speak to me about—" he hesitated—"my slave?"

Pamba nodded without looking at him.

"Khelpa?" The word floated out between them.

"Is dead."

Arttarna gripped the table. An agonized cry exploded into the silence of the room. Then he sat motionless, his breathing rapid.

Covering his face with his hands, he whispered, "How?"

"She was struck by galloping horses in the street."

The hands dropped to the table. "Laggards in my guard force." In a minute, he said, "And the child?"

"She is all right."

"She is with you?"

"Yes." Pamba shrank within himself, bolstering his nerve. Hepit had stated her feelings adamantly. "We can no longer keep her."

"I understand." Trying to come to grips with what had happened, Arttarna sat with his eyes closed. When he looked at Pamba again, he said, "Give me a few days. I cannot make a decision now."

"Yes."

Silence.

"Where is Khelpa's body?"

"We have retrieved it."

"You will give it to me?"

"Of course."

Suddenly Arttarna stood up, causing Pamba to spring to his feet.

"Please, my friend, leave me now. Your news has devastated me. I need to be alone."

"I will await your decision. And if there is anything I can do—" Pamba's voice trailed off.

"Thank you."

Alone, Arttarna sank back onto his chair. His eyes, wide and bulging, swept the ceiling. "How can I live without her?" he moaned. "She was my solace, my companion, my dearest love."

He jumped up and began circling the room, flinging his arms out and calling to Teshub, his god. Slowly, after endlessly pacing, he regained control of himself. He walked in slow motion into the next room, threw himself onto the bed, and turned over on his back. With his thumbs, he pressed his temples, trying to lessen the throbbing that had started.

Ahead of him stretched a dull, gray life devoid of Khelpa's happy laughter. No more would she run her hands through his hair, tweak his earlobes, and kiss the top of his head.

He'd contact the temple she had attended and make arrangements to send her body there to be cremated. He would order beer and wine poured over her bones to cool them off. The bones would then be placed in a silver jar of fine oil, removed from the jar the next day, and laid on a linen cloth on top of a beautiful garment.

Arttarna nodded his head repeatedly as he thought about the funeral. He must order the finest embroidered cloth from the local importer to make the garment placed under the linen. And he would order a sandalwood chair on which to place her bones when they were wrapped in the linen. Around the chair, he would place loaves of bread and a tallow cake.

After the priest conducted the ceremony, he would bury her in an alabaster jar with gold writing. He would spare no expense. And her little daughter would— Her little daughter? His little daughter. He sat up, his back stiff, jerking his head in defiance. The child was his and hers. He had fathered her. He had watched Khelpa's body change over the months of her pregnancy and had hovered near when she gave birth.

Afterwards, the midwife had placed the tiny girl baby in his arms. He remembered looking at the little screwed-up face, the little pale brown body, and had instantly felt love for her. True, he hadn't seen much of her. Kelu never entered the palace. If he happened to be in Pamba's home, Khelpa would bring her to him. But Kelu was shy towards strangers and wouldn't come near him.

Now, all he had left of Khelpa rested in this little girl of, what? She must be five or six. What did she look like? Had her skin darkened? He remembered she had black hair but couldn't remember the shape or color of her eyes. She always focused on the floor when he saw her.

Though Khelpa was his slave, her daughter—his daughter—bore the stamp of the highest society in Mitanni. He flung back his head and set his jaw. He would bring her up appropriately, as befitted a child of his.

Again, grief overwhelmed him. Khelpa had given him the love and affection he had never gotten from the woman his parents had chosen for his wife. That brilliant marriage ceremony turned into disaster the minute the two of them were alone. She spent their wedding night running in circles around the room, yelling for her mother. She wouldn't let him near her.

When her mother finally explained a wife's duties to her, she lay in the bed like a stick. She soon showed her true nature: grasping, cold, interested only in her position in society. As she had given him no children, he had eventually left her bed. But for appearances' sake, she had remained his wife.

"Master."

Arttarna removed his hands from his face and raised his head.

Seeing the distress on his master's face, Sebi trembled, but quickly recovered his poise. "The king requires your presence in his private quarters," he said.

Arttarna stared at the slave, a plan forming in his mind. Quickly adjusting his clothes and forcing a smile on his lips, he hurried from the room.

3

Arttarna entered the ornate royal sitting room and prostrated himself before the king.

"I did not expect to have to send for you, Arttarna," Tushratta scolded. He ran his hand over his dark red wool robe where it covered his knees and tugged at one of his carnelian earrings petulantly. The full mouth in his black beard pouted.

"Forgive your servant, Your Majesty. I could not appear before you smelling of horseflesh."

"I don't mind the smell of horseflesh." Tushratta shifted his position. "Get up, Arttarna. I can't hear you well when you lie on your face. Come sit here beside me."

"Thank you, Your Majesty." As he rose, Arttarna glanced around the room at the gilded furniture and beautiful wall paintings of palace life, and noted how well the king's robe blended with his dark brown skin.

"I have received numerous messages from you on the machinations of my brother Artatama and his son Suttarna in Nineveh."

"Artatama and his son have worked their way into such favor with the Assyrian king that he receives them in court every day."

"Artatama has always been good at working his way into any place where he thought he would benefit."

"He lavishes expensive gifts on the Assyrian king."

"That does not surprise me," said Tushratta with disgust.

"Of course, I am not privy to what they talk about in private, but I have a feeling that it is not to your advantage."

"When was it ever!"

"I do know, though, that he denies your claim to the throne and advances his own, because that is general knowledge in the

Assyrian court." Arttarna looked down at his hands. "I suggest you would be wise, Your Majesty, to recall him from Nineveh."

"To do what here? He is nothing but trouble."

"At the moment, I do not think he can incite Assur-uballit to attack you."

Tushratta stared at Arttarna. "Do you think that is his intention?"

"I do, Your Majesty."

"The Assyrians will not attack me only to give the throne to my brother. Besides, they are no longer powerful."

"Please, Your Majesty, listen to me. They will rise again. Assur-uballit's sons are powerful, warlike, men. In a few years, they will attach Babylon."

Tushratta's eyebrows flew up. "Babylon!"

"You have my word on it."

"Well, I will think about recalling Artatama, but first I have to decide what I will do with him. I do not want him stirring up trouble in the palace." Tushratta shook his head unhappily, remembering that he had ascended the throne after the murder of his older brother. Artatama had been a thorn in his side ever since.

"May I suggest you send him to Egypt, Your Highness? Their king doesn't seem interested in maintaining their borders. That should silence him."

"I do not want to do that."

Arttarna shrugged.

"Amenhotep III is my friend. We are brother kings. He will come to my aid."

"Do not count on that, Your Majesty."

"Well, I still do not want my brother bothering him."

Arttarna changed the subject. "Unfortunately, Assur-uballit is not the only one who might attack us. Suppiluliumas, the Hittite king, may be a greater threat. He is subduing all of the small principalities around us. I suspect that we may be next on his agenda."

"Thank the gods we are on good terms with Egypt."

"My King, Amenhotep III is an old man now. He pays little attention to the countries along this coast that have traditionally depended on the protection of his armies. His son, who will be Amenhotep IV, has only done battle once and that was to chastise Nubia for some minor infraction. I seriously doubt that he would come to your assistance against Suppiluliumas."

"Well, I shall write and remind him that my aunt was married to his father and my sister is married to him. We not only need his help against our enemies, but we need gold. Egypt has much gold."

Arttarna knit his brows. All his warnings had flown to the winds.

"All I can do is try," Tushratta said with finality.

"Your Majesty," said Arttarna, if you will allow me, I have a personal matter."

"Really! That's unusual." Tushratta looked intently at Arttarna before saying, "What is it?"

"Your Majesty, I have a little daughter of five or six years."

Tushratta gasped. "You do? Where have you hidden this child? Your wife, Garadu, never mentions her child. And don't you know her exact age?"

Arttarna dropped his eyes. "The child is not Garadu's."

"So—" Tushratta grinned. "And what do you want me to do?"

"Place my little daughter as an attendant to Princess Tadukhepa, Your Majesty."

The king's jaw jutted forward. At ten, his oldest daughter was at least five years older than Arttarna's child, but he supposed that the age difference wouldn't matter if the girl was obedient and a quick learner.

Arttarna sat with bowed head, tensely gripping the seat edge.

Finally, Tushratta said, "Does Garadu know about this child?"

"She has never mentioned her. If she knew or even guessed, she would have said something."

"Is the mother pushing this idea?"

Arttarna averted his face. "Her mother is dead."

Tushratta pursed his lips and lowered his eyes. "You have plenty of slaves who could take care of her."

"My wife would not allow it. I cannot trust her around Kelu."

Both men were silent.

Arttarna broke it by saying, "Kelu does not know that I am her father."

"Well, I do not want my daughter compromised, Arttarna. The lineage must be impeccable."

"My child has the finest lineage in your realm," said Arttarna stiffly.

Tushratta looked at him, not quite sure he liked that comment.

With bowed head, Arttarna waited.

"If I agree to your request and your child comes as an attendant to my daughter, she will live here. So the fact that she is your child will remain between us. Understand?"

"Yes, Your Majesty."

"My wife will have to see her before any decision is made. We will let you know when to bring her."

"Thank you, Your Majesty." Arttarna slipped to his knees and touched the floor with his forehead.

"You may go."

Walking rapidly, Arttarna took a circuitous route back towards his workroom, choosing the quietest corridors he could find around the crowded court. He ticked off in his mind the many things that needed to be done.

First, he would send a message to the temple Khelpa frequented notifying the priest to be prepared to receive her body for cremation and an alabaster jar for her ashes. In his social class, the dead were cremated. He hoped Khelpa wouldn't mind. He planned to place the jar in his family tomb. Regardless of what anybody else thought, he intended to lie beside her through eternity. He would order her name written in gold on the jar's shoulder. The small, private service held in the tiny temple would fulfill the funeral requirements, and he would have Kelu attend the ceremony with him. Unless Pamba and Hepit came, he and his daughter would be the only ones present.

Second, he would send a message to his wife, announcing that he would supp with her in the late afternoon, adding a request for a spicy soup, whitefish with a tasty sauce, the usual lentils and cucumbers. He wished to retire early.

And lastly, he would visit Pamba. That had been an agony in the back of his mind all day.

After arriving home, Arttarna sent word to his wife about dinner and dispatched Sebi to relay his message to the temple priest. Then, he left the palace by the main gate. Instantly, a number of his personal guards, loitering around the entrance, prostrated themselves in front of him.

"What is your desire, Master?" said the one nearest him.

Had one of these horsemen struck Khelpa? What good would it do to upbraid that man now? "Go to your quarters," he said. "I do not need you tonight." Swiftly, he walked between them and reached Pamba's door.

A slave led him to the room where Pamba and his wife, Hepit, sat at a square table eating yogurt.

"Join us," said Pamba, rising to greet him. He signaled the slave to place a brimming bowl of yogurt before Arttarna.

Arttarna smiled sadly. "I had forgotten that I had not eaten."

Hepit clucked. Turning to the slave, she ordered milk and lentils.

While he ate, Arttarna told Pamba and Hepit what he intended to do with Khelpa's body and about the service he had planned for her.

"I would like to see her," he said as soon as he finished eating.

Pamba rose. "Follow me."

Khelpa lay on the floor of an outdoor shed, a blanket covering her. With a catch in his throat, Arttarna knelt and gently lifted the blanket. Her lovely face held a look of surprise. He ran a trembling hand over her eyes, closing the lids. He caressed her dark brown hair, bent to kiss the unresponsive lips, noting Khelpa's crushed shoulder with its caked blood, and covered her with the blanket.

Rising, he stood over her, desolate, unable to leave her. With supreme effort, he said to Pamba who stood discretely facing the wall, "Send her body to the temple."

After Pamba ordered a slave to fulfill Arttarna's request, he and Arttarna rejoined Hepit at the square table. Arttarna asked to see Kelu.

While they waited for her, Arttarna mentioned that he had appealed to the king to consider Kelu as an attendant to Princess Tadukhepa, the king's eldest daughter.

The door opened. A subdued, unhappy little girl, tightly holding the cook's hand, entered the room. The cook bowed, almost doubling over. Kelu, looking frightened, shifted her tight grip to the cook's clothing.

"She won't let go of me," said the cook.

Arttarna noted his daughter's tawny skin—a beautiful golden color, a mixture of his skin color and the lighter shade of Khelpa's skin. Kelu's features were almost an exact copy of her mother's, but the eyes were his. That pleased him. She would be beautiful.

"Kelu," said Hepit kindly, "Ambassador Arttarna, a high official at the palace, feels badly about what happened this morning. He is going to look after you from now on."

"No." Kelu hid her face in the cook's long wool skirt.

Hepit rose from her chair, took Kelu by the hand, and dragged her towards Arttarna. All the time, Kelu resisted, yelling, "No, no."

Much as he wanted to cuddle his child, Arttarna only smiled at her, trying to look as loving and kind as possible. "You are a very pretty little girl," he said.

She just glanced at him.

"Starting tomorrow, you are to come to me whenever you need something or you just want to talk to somebody."

In response, she clutched Hepit's green wool skirt and hid her face.

"In a few days," Arttarna continued gently, "I am going to take you to see the king. Have you ever heard anybody talk about the king?"

Kelu shook her head, her face hidden in the folds of Hepit's skirt.

"Never mind. However, when we go, I want you to look very pretty. I am going to ask this nice lady to have a new dress made for you, a dress suitable to wear for an audience with the king. Would you like that?"

Kelu drew her face from the skirt to look at her pink, thin wool dress, and slowing raised her eyes to Hepit.

Hepit smiled and nodded her head. "Would you like that, Kelu?"

"Yes," said Kelu almost inaudibly.

"Then you and I will go to see the king," said Arttarna.

Screwing up her face anxiously, Kelu twisted her body around to look at the cook standing by the door.

"It's all right, Kelu. Don't be frightened," said Hepit. "Ambassador Arttarna will bring you right back here afterward and tell us what the king said." Hepit looked at Arttarna for confirmation.

"Yes," he said.

Hepit signaled the cook to take Kelu away.

"Hepit," said Arttarna, "I will have some fine Egyptian linen sent to you. White should appropriately set off Kelu's coloring."

Hepit nodded assent.

Arttarna dropped his eyes. "She is a very pretty child."

"Yes," said Hepit, smiling. "She will blossom under your tutelage."

Suddenly, awareness of the full extent of his responsibility for Kelu overwhelmed Arttarna. His eyes sought the floor.

Sensing his feeling, Hepit said, "The appointment of Kelu as an attendant to Princess Tadukhepa would be the perfect solution."

Pamba broke in. "It would allow you to keep an eye on her without interfering with your duties towards the king and give her wonderful training for her future life in your household."

Arttarna smiled, appreciating their support. "It just remains for the king and queen to approve. A problem might arise if my wife finds out about Kelu. But fortunately, Garadu never goes near the palace nursery."

Arttarna left Pamba's house and went directly to his large palace suite. Oil lamps flickered in one end of the main room where Garadu had placed the small table for dinner. Their light cast dancing shadows on the garden scene painted on the walls, giving the room an intimate, inviting atmosphere. Slaves hovered near the table set with bowls of yogurt, cucumbers, dates, and figs, accompanied by chunks of barley bread and full beer glasses. Hot food would appear the minute he sat down.

He groaned. All he wanted to do was eat and go to sleep in the narrow, solitary bed that he kept in his small workroom suite. Garadu obviously intended to make that difficult for him.

He took the few steps to the table while trying to decide on which side he wanted to sit. The milk and honey pudding caught his attention. Garadu must have asked Cook to make it, knowing it was his favorite.

"Welcome, my husband." Her voice came from the doorway behind him.

He spun around. She wore a scarlet dress that he had not seen before. One sleeve was the standard wrist length; the other bunched above the elbow, making a little puff. And the neck of the dress sloped slightly, adding a bit more fabric to the puff. Her long black braid hung over that shoulder. He almost gulped as his gaze hit the heavy gold belt.

"Do you like my new robe?"

"Yes. It is very becoming. I have not seen that belt before."

"My father gave it to me," she said smugly. "Some men know how to give a woman gifts."

Arttarna caught the barb. Stepping to the table, he said, "How kind of you to arrange my favorite pudding."

"You know I would do anything for you."

He ignored her seductive tone and sat down. Immediately, steaming bowls of soup, fish, lentils, and sauce were set in front of him. He raised the soup bowl to his lips and tasted. Up went an eyebrow. "Perfect," he said.

Garadu slid into the chair near him. "I stood over Cook to make sure the spices were right. These natives do not know how to use our spices properly."

He doubted that statement, but continued. "Did you do the same for the fish sauce?" He dipped a bit of bread into the bowl of sauce and popped the soggy piece into his mouth. His eyes went around the room as he savored the flavors, nodding his head in approval.

Not wanting to appear too pleased with herself, Garadu lowered her eyelids so he couldn't read her eyes and shifted her weight on the chair.

The dinner progressed pleasantly. Arttarna told her about the court fashions in Nineveh and how ugly he thought the queen, at which Garadu giggled in delight.

After the slave placed a bowl of pudding in front of him, Arttarna eagerly pushed some of it into his mouth, using a piece of bread. Closing his eyes, a beatific expression on his face, he gently moved the pudding around the inside of his mouth.

Looking at him, Garadu said, "You will spend the night with me?"

"No, I'm too tired. I rode all night."

"You are always too tired for me, but never too tired to have that slave in your bed."

"You better not say what you know nothing about," he said icily.

She changed her tack. "How am I ever to give you an heir when you refuse to frequent my bed?"

"You gave me no heir when I did frequent your bed as you put it."

"Then perhaps you are the one at fault," she shot back, her voice rising.

Stunned, he stared at her, opened his mouth to speak and stood up, knocking over the chair. "You have forgotten your place," he said and whipped angrily out of the room.

"Damn you," he heard her yell. "I'll show you."

By the gods, rage had almost made him say he had a little daughter. Anger still gnawed at him as he stalked into his work suite. Two of his guards instantly dropped to their knees and fell forward on their faces.

"What is it?" Arttarna sounded irritated and brusque even to himself.

"We found the young fellow you wanted to see, this Rasi."

"And?"

"He lives with his parents over by the racetrack. His father's a carpenter. Two younger sisters and an older brother live at home. The brother, also a carpenter, works with the father."

"Good work. Bring him to me first thing in the morning." Arttarna walked straight past the prostrate men into his bedroom and fell, fully clothed, onto his bed.

Sebi moved silently about the bed, removing with practiced ease the master's clothes. He covered Arttarna with a light blanket and lay down on his own mat at the foot of the bed.

In the morning, well past Arttarna's usual rising time, the worried slave whispered, "Master, are you ill?"

Arttarna blinked, rubbed his eyes, and stretched luxuriously. He smiled up at Sebi. "No. I feel better than I have for a long time, full of energy." Then he drew his brows together as the sorrows of yesterday swarmed across his mind.

Glancing at his carefully folded robe, he said, "I will wear something less elaborate this morning. Put my breakfast on the table. I am expecting the guards to bring in a young laborer."

"Yes, Master." Sebi hurried from the room.

After breakfast, trying to distance himself from dwelling

on Khelpa, Arttarna set to work on his report for the chancellor. He was deep in thought when Sebi announced two guards with the laborer.

Arttarna looked up. The young fellow between the guards acted jittery, his eyes frightened.

"On your knees before the ambassador," snapped one of the guards in military fashion before dropping to the floor. Rasi and the other guard followed suit.

"You may stand up," Arttarna said, looking Rasi over carefully. The youth could be fifteen or sixteen, light skinned, stocky, curly black hair, the beard just starting to grow, intelligent black eyes.

"Do not be afraid," Arttarna said quietly. "I had you brought before me to thank you, not to punish you."

Rasi's tense shoulders relaxed.

"That is better." Arttarna smiled at him. "You answer to the name of Rasi, right?"

"Yes, Ambassador."

"Rasi, yesterday, you took a child home after her mother was killed." With effort, he kept his voice even. "Her father is most grateful and wishes me to tell you that."

"Thank you, sir."

"I have been authorized to ask you if you would like to become one of the caretakers at the royal stables. The lead caretaker is old. He needs a strong young fellow to train."

Rasi gulped. Here in this room, the likes of which he had never seen before, never dreamed of, he, Rasi, was being asked to train as a caretaker of royal horses. He glanced around at the painted walls of blues and greens, galloping brown and black horses, flags flying. He was standing before an aristocrat, a high official, an important person, who was offering him work. But what work! He couldn't believe it. He, Rasi, was to take care of those beautiful great beasts he liked to watch through the cracks in the enclosure of the royal stables. Internally, he fluttered. His heart skipped a beat.

Arttarna waited, tracking all of the expressions that flowed over Rasi's face, from astonishment to anticipation to absolute overwhelming glee.

"It would not be hard work, but constant, so you would be expected to live at the stables. Can you do that?"

Again Rasi gulped, rapidly blinking his eyes.

Arttarna ran his hand over his face, trying to hide his amusement.

Keeping himself under control, with bowed head, Rasi simply said, "I would like that very much." He studied the floor before looking at Arttarna. "When am I to start?"

"Tomorrow morning," answered Arttarna, smiling. "Go home now. Pack whatever you need and say good-bye to your family. Report to the stables of the man Arttarna at dawn. The lead caretaker will expect you."

On his knees, Rasi said, "Thank you, sir. Thank you. Thank you." He bowed his head. "Thank you."

Arttarna motioned to the two guards.

They took their places on either side of Rasi. Each man put his hand under an armpit, lifted him, turned him around, and marched him out of the room.

4

For the next few days, Arttarna spent every minute he could spare at Pamba's home. Anxious to put Kelu at ease, he talked to her, coaxed her onto his lap, played little guessing games with her, did everything he could think of to overcome her shyness. He showed her the fine white linen he had ordered for her new dress, let her feel the fabric, smiled at her when she raised delighted eyes.

Crossing the house towards her sitting room one afternoon, Hepit heard loud, strange noises coming from the family reception room. Without hesitation, she stepped to the door and opened it. Gaping, she broke into fits of laughter.

As soon as she could speak, she said, "Look at you—two adult men who think you affect the running of the world, and here you are on your hands and knees shaking your heads and roaring like the king of beasts, all to entertain a squealing five-year-old." She wiped laughter tears from her eyes.

Pamba looked sheepish. Arttarna grinned. "We have been having a roaring good time," he declared.

"Well, on your feet both of you." She turned to Kelu. "Kelu go put on your new dress. We wish to see how it looks on you."

After Kelu left, Hepit said, "The dress is really lovely."

"Darling child," said Arttarna when Kelu reappeared, "you look beautiful in that little dress."

Kelu smiled shyly and smoothed the front with both hands. That evening, she allowed him to lead her to the mat she slept on in the cook's tiny room and cover her with a lightweight wool blanket.

"I think," Arttarna said to Pamba and Hepit as he prepared to return to the palace, "she will go with me willingly tomorrow and not make a fuss."

"The gods be praised," said Pamba.

"You have done wonders with her," added Hepit. "The gods be with you tomorrow."

Arttarna had been notified by one of the palace slaves that he was to introduce Kelu to the king after his morning audience. At noon of the appointed day, just before the king ended his public audience, Arttarna brought Kelu to the palace.

They walked slowly along the corridor leading to the throne room. Holding Kelu's hand, he talked to her about the bright yellows, reds, and blues that created the people in the paintings on the walls and about the king they were going to visit. Every once in a while her free hand stroked the front of her new dress.

Arttarna watched her. He found this little daughter of his absolutely adorable. Her shiny black hair hung just below her shoulders. Her large, deep brown eyes looked at the world soberly, with a gravity that was uncommon for a child. He hoped one day they would sparkle. Her fine linen dress hung in small pleats from her shoulders to her ankles. Around the high circular neck, Hepit had lovingly embroidered flowers with cream-colored thread. He couldn't imagine that the king would refuse to take Kelu into his household, even though five years younger than the princess.

They stopped before a closed door. Saucer-eyed, Kelu stared at the red-skirted guard standing at attention before the door, a sword at his waist.

"When we enter this room," said Arttarna, "I will drop to my knees. You must do the same."

"Like the cook does before Pamba?"

"Exactly." He smiled at her, delighted to have fathered such a bright child

"King Tushratta expects you, Ambassador Arttarna." With a flourish, the guard opened the door.

At the sight of a bearded king in a glittering robe, sitting on a high chair raised three-quarters of the height of a man above the floor, his feet on a carved wooden stool, Kelu gripped Arttarna's hand as hard as she could. Her gaze shifted to the woman sitting in a chair placed on the floor directly below the king. The woman's long black braid lay gracefully across her chest and ended at the waistline of her pale green wool dress. Winking green gems dangled from her ears. Kelu decided she liked the woman even though she wasn't pretty like her mother.

Halfway across the room, Arttarna fell to his knees, pulling

Kelu down with him, and touched his forehead to the floor. She did the same, making such a tiny bundle in her lovely white dress that Queen Iuni smiled.

"Rise," said the king. "Come forward."

In a loud whispered aside, cupping his hand over his mouth and grinning, the king asked, "Have you figured out how old she is, Arttarna?"

"She is five, Your Majesty."

Arttarna laid both of his hands on Kelu's shoulders and slowly pushed her forward.

She stepped shyly, but held her head up and directly met the king's eyes.

Queen Iuni nodded her head approvingly.

Suddenly, Tushratta smiled. "Do you have any playmates, Kelu?"

"No," Kelu said in a sweet, high-pitched, childish voice.

"Would you like some?"

"I don't know. I don't know what you mean."

Tushratta looked startled. "I mean to play with other little girls like you. Would you like that?"

"Yes," Kelu said after giving the question some thought.

Tushratta turned to his wife. "Take her to Princess Tadukhepa's rooms."

"Yes, My Lord." She rose, smiling at Kelu. "Come with me." She took Kelu's free hand, but Kelu wouldn't let go of Arttarna.

"I guess you better come too, Arttarna."

Queen Iuni led them through the palace. When they reached the children's area at the rear of the king's private quarters, she explained that the first two rooms belonged to Prince Mattiwaza. "The single rooms are for the two younger boys. Tadukhepa lives in the two rooms next to them and is attended by two personal slaves, Alala and Lesser Slave. The younger princesses occupy rooms beyond that."

The queen stepped to the open door of Princess Tadukhepa's suite. Paint had transformed the room into a landscape of beautiful castles and green parks inhabited by princes and princesses. Two little princesses and two slaves were playing attendants to Tadukhepa's queen.

At the entrance of her mother, Princess Tadukhepa instantly

changed from a queen to a little girl in an ankle-length blue wool robe with small gold loops in her ears. Her black braid hung down her back. With a joyous skip, she ran to the queen.

"This is Kelu," said the queen. "She is going to live with you."

The two little girls eyed each other. Tadukhepa noted the light color of Kelu's skin, lighter than her own brown skin, the pretty face, and decided she liked this little girl. The princess walked over and laid a hand on Kelu's shoulder. "You must bow before me," Tadukhepa said, flashing a happy smile.

Kelu did as she had seen the cook do for ordinary household conversation with Hepit. She bowed from her waist, much to the amusement of the queen and Arttarna. Princess Tadukhepa took her hand, and together they ran towards the group across the room, Kelu bobbing up and down, trying to keep up with the older and taller princess.

Queen Iuni turned to Arttarna. "They will get along nicely, it seems."

"Yes, Your Majesty," Arttarna said. "I hope they will develop a strong friendship."

"Let them play for a short time before you take Kelu home."

Deeply bowing, almost doubled over, Arttarna said, "Thank you, Your Majesty."

She led him out to the corridor. "There is a small room nearby that we use for storage." The queen turned to the right. She pointed to the door and indicated that she wanted Arttarna to look at it. "I will order it cleaned tomorrow and have a small bed put in it for Kelu. Tadukhepa's Lesser Slave can sleep at the door."

Arttarna opened the door wide, allowing enough light to enter so that he could see inside. He observed the narrowness of the room, barely deep enough for a small bed. The slave would have to lay her mat in the passageway.

"If Your Majesty pleases," he said, "a drape across here instead of the door would make Kelu feel less isolated. She is used to sleeping in a room with an adult."

"Of course," said the queen, gazing around the small space, "a closed door might frighten the little thing. I will order a drape." She smiled, remembering the tiny, white-clothed form on her knees in the audience chamber.

Queen Iuni half turned. "Bring her back in two days and be prepared to leave her."

"Thank you, Your Majesty." Arttarna bowed, doubling over at the waist and remained that way until the soft sound of the queen's footsteps ceased. Straightening up again, he stepped into Tadukhepa's room. What he saw pleased him. Now, two young princesses, two slaves, and Kelu played handmaidens to Tadukhepa's queen.

"Kelu," he said softly. When she looked at him, he motioned to her to come to him.

"I like it here," she said when she reached him. "Can I stay?"

"Not now. I will bring you back the day after tomorrow and you will live here." He smiled down at her surprised but happy expression. How miraculously this had all fitted together. He said a quick prayer of thanksgiving to Teshub, the great weather god.

Two days later, Arttarna returned to the royal nursery, Kelu dancing happily alongside him. At sight of Tadukhepa eating breakfast at a corner table, Kelu glanced up at Arttarna. After receiving a nod of approval, she ran to the princess.

Tadukhepa grinned. "Bow," she said.

Kelu fell to her knees.

"Rise," said Tadukhepa.

Kelu rose and scrambled onto the chair that thin, light-skinned Lesser Slave placed for her at the table.

Arttarna quickly left the area. Tomorrow morning, he told himself, he would return to see how the two children were getting along.

The news the next morning pleased him. Kelu and Princess Tadukhepa appeared happy with each other's company. Arttarna asked Lesser Slave how Kelu's first night away from home had gone.

"The only thing," said Lesser Slave, "shortly after I lay down on my mat, Kelu crawled in beside me."

Arttarna raised his eyebrows. "And?"

The slave lowered her eyes, "Master," she said, half afraid, "we both slept in her bed."

Arttarna pulled at his lip. "Try to make her sleep alone in her bed. Perhaps leave the curtain open and see if that helps. But do not force her to sleep by herself, at least not until she feels at home."

"Yes, Ambassador Arttarna."

As he returned to his workrooms, his step lightened. A weight had lifted from his shoulders. His daughter would receive the training appropriate to her status. In time, she would take her place in the highest ranks of Mitannian society.

5

Word quickly circulated around the court that a tiny stranger, a beautiful child of five, who was exquisitely clothed, had been appointed as an attendant to Princess Tadukhepa. Complete silence on the subject from the royal household stifled any inquiry. Some of the court ladies tried to sneak into the royal quarters to see the girl, but the palace guards turned them away, saying, "The children are with the king," or, "The children are being counseled on court etiquette." The attempts soon ended.

But, as usual, one determined woman felt capable of trying. Slowly, Garadu walked along the corridor to the queen's audience hall. She scowled. The summons to see the queen inconvenienced her. She had planned to take a lover this afternoon, the handsome ambassador from Assyria. Afterwards, she intended to have that fact carefully leaked to Arttarna. "That will fix him," she thought. "And if I have a child, I'll claim it's his. He won't dare deny it." Glee at the idea consumed her.

Near the queen's chambers, she hesitated. Not a sound reached her from the private quarters of the royal family. She looked around. Could she possibly sneak in to see the princess' new attendant? Yes. She had to see this child.

Swiftly, she veered right, careful to step silently on the polished stone floor. She reached the nursery area. She would take just a quick look, she told herself, then would retrace her steps and go to the queen's audience hall. Prince Mattiwaza darted out from his suite, chased by Prince Shaushtatar, his younger brother, who was angry and screaming. Garadu went to her knees and bowed her head, hiding her face from them. The boys ignored her and dashed into the room opposite. She rose and hurried on to Princess Tadukhepa's rooms.

Two slaves sat in a corner gossiping. Kneeling amid a circle of dolls, Tadukhepa and a younger child were engaged in feeding each doll one by one. A small plate of sweetmeats lay next to each child.

"If you don't like that bit of pudding," Tadukhepa said to one doll, "try this one." She placed a morsel against the doll's mouth. "It's delicious."

The other little girl turned around to see what Tadukhepa was offering the large wooden doll.

Seeing the child's face, Garadu sucked in her breath. Since when had the king's daughter played with slaves? With that light skin, she must be a slave or—Garadu entered the room. "Princess Tadukhepa!" she said, curtsying.

Tadukhepa looked up and smiled.

"How pretty you look, Princess. And you have a new little playmate. When did she come?"

"I don't remember. Some time ago." Tadukhepa shrugged and looked at Kelu. Kelu sat down and looked at Garadu.

"Where did she come from?" Garadu persisted.

The heavier of the two slaves rose, a stern expression on her face. Garadu gave the slave an arrogant stare, daring the woman to order her out. She turned back to Tadukhepa. "Who brought her to you?"

"My mother."

"Just your mother?" Garadu was perplexed. That didn't make sense.

"Well, Ambassador Arttarna came in with Mother."

The realization of who this child was flashed across Garadu's brain. She must be the slave's child. He had palmed her off on the court.

Garadu's hands began to shake. She slid her hands behind her back to hide their tremor. Hardly able to contain her anger, she thought to herself, "The queen, no, the whole court is going to hear about how he made the daughter of a slave the companion to Princess Tadukhepa."

"I'm glad you are so happy, Princess." Garadu bowed from the waist. "I must fly to your mother." With extraordinary effort, she managed to get the words out smoothly. Continuing to bow, she backed out of the room.

Garadu hurried to the queen's chambers. To her annoyance,

the wives of the king's advisors and courtiers packed the queen's audience hall, chattering and pawing over some beautiful linens and jewelry newly arrived from Egypt. Garadu had no chance to talk to the queen in private. Her fury mounted.

As soon as the queen dismissed the ladies from her court, Garadu stormed back to her rooms and flung herself on her bed, where she spent hours trying to decide how to kill the child. Since Arttarna and his guard force had left the city three days earlier, she didn't have to worry about her husband. She could plan and reconnoiter at her leisure until he came back. Perhaps she could manage to kill the child before his return. That might be wisest. The best time to do it would be late in the afternoon, when most of the palace occupants rested.

To carry out that decision, Garadu snuck to the royal nursery late each afternoon, hoping to catch Kelu alone. She'd nod authoritatively to the guard at the royal quarters, implying that she had some business to do there, and then walk serenely ahead. Along the nursery corridor, she would pass some slaves or sometimes one or two of the royal children, running up and down the hall. Nobody paid attention to the court lady purportedly there at the request of the queen. She would slow down when she neared Princess Tadukhepa's rooms, using any pretext—the need to straighten her robe, to clean a spot on her sleeve, or to tend to a sore ankle—to stop and glance inside the princess' suite. Day after day, she saw the same two slaves standing against the wall, the same two girls on the floor in the middle of the room. Often Prince Mattiwaza or Prince Shaushtatar, who was one year younger than Prince Mattiwaza, would play with the two girls.

Garadu fumed. Didn't the slaves ever leave the room or the princess disappear into her bedchamber?

Bored and tired one evening after a long day on the racetrack, where she was breaking in a new brown mare, she decided not to check the royal nursery. What was the use? She sighed and sank wearily into a chair. Maintaining her reputation as a superb horsewoman, one of the few women who rode horses, was tiring. She must have dozed because suddenly she leaped up as if she had seen a vision and scurried to the royal nursery. At Princess Tadukhepa's door, she stopped with a jolt. Kelu sat alone on the floor cradling a doll. Garadu glanced around. No child or slave appeared in the corridor.

Garadu walked directly up to Kelu. "Where is Princess Tadukhepa?" she said sweetly.

Kelu looked up. "She's sick. The slaves are putting her to bed."

Garadu kicked Kelu in the ribs, sending her sprawling.

Kelu, shocked, twisted her head up to look at her.

Garadu grabbed Kelu's arm, yanked her to her feet, made a fist, and struck her in the jaw with it. Kelu reeled into the air before landing on her back a few feet away.

Raging out of control, Garadu rushed at Kelu and kicked her in the hip. Kelu screamed. Prince Mattiwaza dashed into the room.

"What are you doing?" he yelled, seeing her leg pulled back, prepared to strike again. "How dare you kick her?"

Garadu flew from the room as if fire licked at her heels.

Prince Mattiwaza knelt beside Kelu, who was sobbing. "Please don't cry, Kelu." He patted her gingerly on the shoulder.

Kelu's loud wailing brought the two slaves running from the princess' bedroom.

"What happened?" cried Lesser Slave, dropping to the floor beside Kelu. She looked accusingly at the prince.

The warning look he flashed her said, "Don't you dare blame me for this."

She looked down at Kelu, whose red, bruised face was beginning to swell. Alala hurried to the door and called to a slave crossing the corridor. "Ask one of the guards to bring Ambassador Arttarna's slave Sebi here immediately."

"I'll do it myself," said the prince. He jumped from the floor and dashed out the door.

Lesser Slave darted to Kelu's bedroom and returned with a blanket. Gently, she spread it over the weeping child. "Where do you hurt, Kelu?" she asked, her face tight with worry.

"Here," stuttered Kelu between sobs, pointing to her chest, "my side, my face. It hurts everywhere." She moaned loudly and pulled the blanket over her head.

Not knowing what else to do while waiting for Sebi, Lesser Slave stayed on her knees beside Kelu and stroked the top of her head.

The ambassador and Prince Mattiwaza hurried in together, Sebi behind them.

Lesser Slave jumped up. "Ambassador Arttarna," she exclaimed in surprise.

Still disheveled from long hours on horseback, Arttarna sucked in his breath at sight of Kelu. Instantly, he knelt at her side and carefully removed the blanket Kelu held over her face.

Sebi gasped. "She's badly bruised."

"Yes." Arttarna threw the blanket aside to see how much damage the woman had done. It pained him to look at his daughter's crumpled little body. "Kelu, can you straighten out to lie flat?"

Her eyes holding his, she tried and screamed, clutching her ribs.

Arttarna stood up. "Sebi, bundle her in the blanket and lift her carefully. We will take her to my rooms."

He caught the eye of Prince Mattiwaza, who was standing on the other side of Kelu. For an instant, he saw something he couldn't place, but didn't like, in the prince's eyes. Quickly, he bowed slightly to the distraught prince. "I thank you for notifying me of this, My Prince. Fortunately, I had returned to the palace just a quarter of an hour before you came to me. I will take steps to make sure there won't be a second occurrence."

"If it please you, Master," said Sebi, "I'll ask a guard to help me. We'll lay her on another blanket to make a cradle and carry her between us."

"Good. Do that."

Within minutes, Kelu was cautiously lifted onto a second blanket. In single file, the men left the princess' rooms, Sebi and the guard carrying Kelu in the makeshift cradle, Arttarna in the rear so he could keep an eye on each swing of the blanket.

They reached Arttarna's quarters. As the three men passed through his door, he ordered the house slave who had opened it to call the physician.

Sebi and the guard slowly lowered the blanket onto Arttarna's bed.

Sebi gently rearranged the wrapping blanket around her. Several minutes later, the physician arrived. One look at Kelu, and he removed a small bottle from his bag. "Stick out your tongue, Kelu," he said. "I'm going to put a few drops of some medicine on your tongue for you to swallow. It will take the pain away."

She stuck out her tongue as far as she could, holding her swollen jaw with both hands.

The physician dropped a small amount of poppy juice on her tongue. She sucked in, swallowed, and stuck out her tongue again.

He smiled. "I think that's enough." Lifting the blanket off her body, he said, "Point to where it hurts most."

Kelu laid two fingers lightly on her left rib cage. "And here, too," she said, placing her whole hand on her left hip.

Fussing slowly through his bag, waiting for the narcotic to work, the physician watched her. The minute her eyelids started to droop, he gently probed her ribs, then her hip with his fingers.

After he finished his examination, he straightened. His eyes sought those of Ambassador Arttarna who was hovering over her. "Her hip is as badly bruised as is her face," said the physician. "Two of her ribs are broken. I'll strap her chest with bandages to reduce the pain and leave a sedative. She can move about tomorrow if she wants to. But she may prefer to stay in bed. Walking might hurt for a day or two."

"Can you come back tomorrow?"

"Yes, Ambassador. I'll be here in the afternoon. Give the swelling time to go down a little. Have your slaves apply some cold compresses to her jaw. That will help reduce the swelling."

After the physician left, Arttarna told Sebi not to move the sleeping Kelu. "We will leave her on my bed. To be sure nothing more happens tonight, lay a mat for me on the floor next to the bed."

"Yes, Master. And I will lie across the entrance door." Upset over what had happened, Sebi frowned, the lines across his forehead prominent.

Arttarna eyed his slave. "Sebi, I've been thinking this over. The prince told me that the person who attacked Kelu was a lady from the court. I can guess who the lady was, but before I act on my hunch, I need some proof."

Sebi nodded.

The minute he woke in the morning, Arttarna bent over his sleeping child to see how she was. The swelling in her face had reduced somewhat, but all along her jaw and under her eyes, her skin had become discolored and was purple. Anger rose in him.

Sebi bowed as he came into the room. "Master, the head of the royal guard begs you to go immediately to Princess Tadukhepa's rooms."

Non-plussed, Arttarna said, "Bring me a robe quickly."

Dressed, he walked rapidly to the princess' area. The chief palace guard and the princess' two slaves huddled in the doorway of Kelu's bedroom. They parted as Arttarna appeared.

A long dagger stood straight up in the pillow on the bed, having gone through the pillow and into the mat.

"I will take care of this," said Arttarna. Stunned, he drew the weapon from the pillow. Garadu had used the dagger he kept in their palace suite dressing table. This was the proof that she was the one who had attacked Kelu.

"How is the girl?" asked the head of the guards.

"She is asleep in my quarters and will stay there until she gets better."

White with shock and fury, Arttarna left the royal nursery. So, Garadu had guessed Khelpa was the child's mother. She had used his short sword to try to kill Kelu. He pictured her sliding silently through the dark palace corridors. Undoubtedly, she would be wrapped in black. She was good at sneaking around in the dark. But luckily, because of the lack of light in the room, she had not realized that the lump in the bed was only a pillow.

Tight-lipped and angry, he sat down at his desk and summoned Sebi from Kelu's side. "Get Garadu from our large palace suite. I've sent one of the slaves to have her new mare and a horse for you bridled. If she objects to mounting her horse, force her. Then take her to the home of her parents. Leave her there with the understanding that she is never again to cross the threshold of my home."

As soon as Sebi reached the paddock, he sent the stable boy to tell Garadu that her mare was causing trouble. While he waited, he asked Rasi to put a lead on the mare so he could prevent any attempt to escape. Garadu swept into the paddock five steps ahead of the stable boy and stopped abruptly, sizing up the situation.

Sebi asked her politely to mount the mare. Turning red with rage, she refused and screamed invective at him. Rasi picked her up from behind and planted her on the horse. Leaning over, she tried to hit him, but he dodged the blow.

Sebi started at a fast canter, keeping a tight grip on the lead. The mare jerked and broke into a canter. Garadu had to grab her around the neck to keep from falling off. She screamed at Sebi the whole time she wasn't coughing to catch her breath while struggling to get her balance. Once she did, Sebi set a fast pace all the way to her parents' home. The noise of two horses galloping into the open courtyard brought slaves and her parents running out.

Slaves helped the still sputtering and angry Garadu dismount. Her father demanded the meaning of the unceremonial visit.

Sebi said, "Your daughter is from this moment forever in your care."

Garadu screamed, "No, no, he can't do this to me," and fell in a sobbing heap on the stone of the courtyard.

Her father flew into a temper and shook his fists at Sebi. "I will go to the king and ask him to punish Arttarna for dishonoring my family."

Sebi explained that Garadu had attempted to murder a young girl, the ward of the Ambassador.

Garadu jumped up, saying, "Yes, a slave's child." She clapped her hands over her mouth. Her father stared at her. She stood there with lowered eyes, realizing that she had admitted her guilt. Her father gave a huge sigh and looked at the ground for what seemed a long time. When he raised his head, he looked straight at her and said, "Go to your room." He sounded so sad that Sebi felt sorry for him.

Garadu turned, sobbing, and stumbled toward the house. Her father waved a dismissing hand at Sebi.

Sebi guided his horse out of the courtyard and headed for Wassukkanni.

The setting sun neared the horizon by the time Sebi returned to Arttarna's quarters. He found his master sitting on the bed playing a dice game with Kelu, who was propped against five bolsters that formed a nest around her.

"Master," said the slave, "all is accomplished."

"Sebi, we will go into the other room."

Arttarna rose. "I'll return shortly, Kelu," he said, caressing her hair.

Sebi followed him out the door. Once they were in Arttarna's workroom, Arttarna seated himself at his desk. Sebi stood in front of him and told him about Garadu's admission of guilt in front of her father.

Arttarna nodded thoughtfully. "Good. There will be no trouble; they'll keep her."

A smile on his face, he returned to the dice game.

The game hadn't progressed far when Kelu started to slide further and further under the coverlet.

Arttarna watched her and slowed his movements accordingly. The minute her eyelids started to flutter, he scooped up the dice. "I think this can wait until tomorrow," he said.

She nodded sleepily.

With morning light streaming in the small, high window, she wakened. She lay on her back, wondering if she should get up or stay in bed until she got better. Arttarna entered the room.

"May I get up?" she asked.

"Of course, if you want to. I'll help you." He flung aside the blanket. Gently raising her shoulders, he swung her feet off the bed. "Does it hurt?"

"No." She slid down, took three steps, and faced him. "I think I'm all right," she said, amazement in her voice.

He smiled down at her. "Good, but be quiet and rest today. Your face is still badly bruised, and I don't want you moving rapidly yet."

"May I go back to Princess Tadukhepa's?" Then, fear in her eyes, she added, "Will that woman be there?"

"No. She will never come near you again."

Kelu blinked her eyes and screwed up her mouth. "I'm glad."

"Stay here today. Walk around as much as you want, but be careful and stop the minute you feel any pain."

"It hurts a little," she admitted. "Even with all these bandages."

"The physician put those bandages on to help your bones heal."

"Will that take long? When can I go back to Princess Tadukhepa's?"

"If the physician says you are well enough to go back, I'll take you there tomorrow after breakfast."

Walking hand in hand along the palace corridor the next morning, Arttarna looked down at his little daughter in utter astonishment. In his position at court, he exerted authority over many men, yet this wisp of a child had twined herself around his heart until he fluttered like chaff in the wind at her every breath. What would he do when King Tushratta sent him out on a mission to another country again?

"Ambassador Arttarna," she said, looking up at him, "Could I—"

"I may be Ambassador Arttarna to you, Kelu, but I want you to know that your father asked me to be your guardian."

"My guardian?" She looked at him blankly.

They had arrived at the corridor in the children's quarters. "Kelu we'll go into your bedroom and have a talk." He caught her hand and held it, aching to have her call him Father. She would have to keep addressing him as Ambassador Arttarna, but hearing that name on her lips stung him. "I'm her father," he thought, "but she doesn't know that, and I can't tell her who I really am. She might babble it without realizing. And it would quickly get back to the king. After all his kindness to me on Kelu's account, I don't want to risk offending him."

Passing Tadukhepa's suite, he waved at the princess' two slaves, making a gesture of dismissal to indicate that he didn't need them. Then he steered Kelu into her room.

"Now," he said, sitting on the bed and drawing her onto his lap, careful not to jar the bandages on her chest, "you had a mamma who loved you and whom you loved very much."

She nodded her head and tears came to her eyes.

"Your father loved your mamma very much, too."

Her mouth half open, she looked at him, not sure she knew exactly what a father was. Most of the time, Tadukhepa called the king Your Majesty. Occasionally, she called him Father. Was he her father as well as the king? What made him her father? The queen was her mother. Did that make the king her father? It was all very confusing.

"When two people love each other that much, sometimes the gods give them a little boy or girl. The gods gave you to your mother and father. A great deal of the time, your father lives far away. He asked me to take care of you. I will always do that. If you have trouble or are afraid or anything else, you are to come to me. Do you understand?"

"Yes." She nodded her head.

"I love you, Kelu, and I want you to love me."

"I do." She flung her arms around his neck, but then caught her breath as she felt a twinge of pain from her broken ribs, loosened her arms and nestled close to him.

"Be careful," he admonished softly, turning to pudding as his arms closed around her.

"You can call me your guardian." He kissed the top of her head. "Do you think you can do that?"

"I guess so. But I don't like the sound of that word."

"You're right. 'Guardian' does sound cold. How about 'uncle'?"

"Yes, 'Uncle.' I like that word better. I'll call you that from now on."

"Now," he said, rising, "I have to leave. You are not to run or jump. I mean it. The physician will come to see you here and tell the slaves how you are doing, so that they can tell me."

"Will you come to see me?" Her worried little face peered up at him.

"Every few days, I'll send Sebi for you so you can come to my palace suite and eat your evening meal with me. Would you like that?"

"Oh, yes."

His hand caressed her shoulder as they entered Princess Tadukhepa's suite of rooms.

"I'll leave you here," he said, motioning to the two slaves near Tadukhepa's bedroom door.

"Two of her chest bones are broken so don't let her overdo. And that means, she is not to do much. She was so anxious to come back here that the physician agreed. But as you can see, she is badly bruised."

"Poor child." Lesser Slave ran to them, squatted, and drew Kelu toward her. "We'll take good care of her, Ambassador Arttarna."

Still in her nightclothes, Tadukhepa peered from her room, saw Kelu and squealed in delight. Kelu grinned, tried to bow, gasped, then clutched her chest.

"Never mind, Kelu," Tadukhepa said, "wait to bow until you are well."

Arttarna had been gone only a few seconds before Prince Mattiwaza hurried in. "Kelu, I went round to Ambassador Arttarna's rooms to see how you were and his slave said you were here." He planted himself in front of her, squinting at her black, yellow, and purple face. "It looks bad. Does it hurt?"

"Not much except when I try to chew."

He noticed she didn't move her mouth much when she talked.

"Well, I'm glad you're better. I've been worried about you."

She smiled and dropped her eyes shyly.

He hovered over her protectively.

"My Prince," said Alala, deliberately intervening between the two children, "Kelu is not strong yet. Two of her chest bones are broken. Perhaps she should rest now while Princess Tadukhepa dresses."

"Very well," said Prince Mattiwaza, "but I will come see you often, Kelu."

He dawdled out the door, constantly turning to look at her.

A shining-eyed Kelu followed Lesser Slave to her bedroom.

6

Slowly, Kelu became the favorite of the royal children. Tadukhepa's rooms constantly resounded with the children's happy squeals and laughter, their racing around, their noisy games, until the two slaves, wanting to tear their hair out in frustration, sent the little boys to their own quarters.

In the evening, after a light meal, Tadukhepa and Kelu liked to whisper confidences. Sitting close together, Princess Tadukhepa would detail each subtle blooming of womanhood she was experiencing. One minute, she would outline all the newest changes in her body; the next minute, she would become silent and withdrawn.

During her moments of introspection, she would inform Kelu that she was too young to understand the intricacies of womanhood. At other times, Tadukhepa dwelt on her obligations as a princess; her panic at being sent alone to a foreign country; her fears of marriage to an old man.

One day, in a pensive mood, Tadukhepa said, "I am almost twelve. Soon my father will marry me to an important king and send me away." Tears appeared in her eyes. "What will happen to me? My father's sister just disappeared when she married the king of Egypt and became one of his wives. Father doesn't know whether she's dead or alive. He sends her small gifts, but she doesn't reply."

"Perhaps," Kelu said hopefully, "you'll go to a country where you'll be a great queen like your mother."

Tadukhepa brightened. "Do you think so?" She drew circles with her finger on the table as she thought about that. "Maybe you are right, but I don't really know of any country that has a queen like my mother."

"I'll ask my Uncle Arttarna," offered Kelu. "He will know."

Kelu arrived at Arttarna's large palace suite for their twice-weekly meal together full of questions about Tadukhepa's possibilities for a happy marriage and about the royal houses of the countries he knew.

In the empty reception room, she walked to the far corner of the room where they usually ate and examined the small table set for two. Fruit juice lay at her place, beer at Arttarna's. Three little dishes occupied the table's center—lentils, cucumbers in sour cream, and her favorite nuts. She smiled, pulled the chair back and sat down.

Sebi entered, carrying bowls of cold soup. "The master will be here shortly. The king kept him late."

"Sebi, have you ever been married?" Kelu asked as the slave started to place a bowl at her place.

The bowls jostled. "No, Miss."

"I'm worried."

Sebi smiled. "About getting married?"

"No. I'm worried about Tadukhepa."

"Why? Has anything been said about her getting married?"

Before she could answer, Arttarna blew in and quickly sat down. Kelu immediately attacked.

"Are there any countries that have a young, handsome king to marry Tadukhepa so she could be a queen like her mother?"

Part way to the kitchen, Sebi stumbled, but quickly recovered.

Arttarna put down his bowl. The pleasant father-daughter evening he had envisioned disappeared in an instant. "Kelu, Tadukhepa is the reigning princess of Mitanni, one of the world's great powers. Sadly for Tadukhepa, this means that she will be sent to some royal house to cement relations. She has no say in the matter." He hesitated. "Other than the Kingdom of Hatti, I do not know of any royal house that has an unmarried crown prince."

"Then she could be married to an ugly old man." Tears threatened.

"Unfortunately, dear child, that is what happens to lovely young women like Tadukhepa. She has been brought up with that understanding."

"Yes, she understands, but she is still afraid."

Arttarna was silent, wondering how to reassure his daughter.

Sebi entered the room carrying steaming fish.

"Where could Tadukhepa go?" Kelu pressed her question, her voice quivering.

Arttarna sighed. "Kelu, to be an important queen like Queen Iuni, Tadukhepa would have to be the first wife of the crown prince. And as I said, Hatti is the only country that has an eligible crown prince at the moment."

Kelu took a mouthful of fish in spicy sauce and pushed the lentils around in her bowl.

Arttarna watched her then his eyes swept over her little body. He saw no signs of maturation. "Are you and Princess Tadukhepa discussing the changes in her being?"

Kelu blushed. "Yes."

"You are only six. Well, going on seven. You still have four more years before any of that happens to you," Arttarna said with a sense of relief that she was finding out some of these things without involving him.

"Will I be sent away, too?" She sounded fearful.

"No, of course not. Even though you live in the royal nursery, you are not royal. Nor am I royal."

Arttarna looked at her thoughtfully. "Someday, the father of an eligible young man will ask me to let you be his son's wife. I will consider the family and the young man. He will have to be from the aristocracy here in our city. And that means people who look like me, people who have dark skin and smooth black hair."

Remembering his own unhappy experience, he added, "I may even let you have some say in the matter."

"Prince Mattiwaza said he wished I could be his wife."

Arttarna looked startled. "Kelu, don't let that go to your head. Prince Mattiwaza is ten. He will marry a foreign princess to strengthen our country's diplomatic relations."

"The same as Princess Tadukhepa?"

"That's right, except that the young woman he marries will come here to live. He will not be sent away like the princess."

Kelu's face fell.

"My dear child, you have learned many valuable lessons by being an attendant to Princess Tadukhepa. Before too long, they will come in handy. I expect you to travel with me the next time I leave on an extended stay, not like the short trips this past year. When that happens, I expect you to be mistress of my home."

"But I'm too young."

"Yes, you are right. But you are almost seven," Arttarna explained patiently. "I'm talking about the future. The minute Princess Tadukhepa gets married and leaves Mitanni, you will come here to live." He tapped his forefinger on the table, and then stared at the wall without seeing it, preoccupied by the thought of what Kelu would need when she became the mistress of his household. "I must buy a suitable woman for you," he said finally.

"Like the slaves Princess Tadukhepa has?"

"Yes."

Kelu considered the idea. "I'd like a slave of my own, Uncle, rather than having one of Princess Tadukhepa's slaves take care of me."

The day after Tadukhepa turned twelve, the slave Alala fluttered up to the princess where she sat tête-à-tête with Kelu.

"Princess, your father has ordered you to appear before him. We must change your clothes immediately."

Tadukhepa rose slowly, her face taut, her eyes frightened. "Something important is going to happen, Kelu. I know it. I'm afraid."

Kelu jumped to her feet. "I'll come with you as far as I can."

Tadukhepa hugged her and headed rapidly for her bed-room, followed by the flustered slave.

Kelu squealed and clapped her hands when Tadukhepa emerged in her red wool dress with gold threads. "You look beautiful in that dress. And your black hair hangs nicely."

The slave said, "You can only come as far as the entrance to the court, Kelu."

Kelu held Princess Tadukhepa's hand tightly as they walked along. At the big wooden door to the formal audience hall, Alala put her restraining arm across Kelu's shoulders and gave Tadukhepa a gentle push. The tall guard who stood at the door bowed and swung the door open.

"We will wait here," said the slave. She stood motionless while the door was open and the court could see her. When the guard shut the door behind Tadukhepa, Alala relaxed, led Kelu a few steps away, and leaned against the wall.

Kelu did the same. "Do you think Princess Tadukhepa will be long, Alala?"

The slave shrugged. "I don't know."

"What do you think is happening?"

"I don't know that either, Kelu. I can only guess, which is the same as the princess guesses. And you know what that is."

Kelu puckered her brow and looked at the big wooden doors. After a while, she began restlessly slapping her lower back against the wall.

The slave glanced sideways at her, but said nothing.

"They are taking a long time," observed Kelu.

"When the king is finished, she will come out."

Shortly thereafter, the door opened. Eyes downcast and cheeks flushed, Tadukhepa slowly emerged. She looked around, saw Alala, and ran to her. "Alala," she gasped, throwing her arms around the woman, "I'm being sent to Egypt to become the wife of King Amenhotep III." She started to cry.

"Shush, shush, Princess, don't cry here where the court can see you," cautioned Alala. She folded the girl into her arms and started quickly towards their own quarters. "Come along, Kelu."

Once there, Tadukhepa sat down on a chair while Kelu sat on the floor in front of her. Alala and Lesser Slave stood behind Kelu.

"My father sat on his throne, mother on a chair below him," Tadukhepa began. "Our chancellor, with two strangers next to him, stood in front of father. After I bowed properly to each person present, father called me forward and introduced me to the two men. One man was the ambassador from Egypt and the other was a special messenger from the Egyptian king, a man named Meni."

She hesitated and swallowed.

"Father said, 'Amenhotep III, the great king of Egypt, has asked for you to be his wife.' I was so upset, I trembled. I knew that the Egyptian king was old and ugly. My Aunt Gilukhepa, father's sister, is married to him."

She brushed a tear from her cheek.

"I guess Meni looked at me approvingly because father said, 'Meni rejoices now that he has seen you, and he will return to Egypt with my letter of consent.' After that, Meni beckoned to a few men that I hadn't seen. They were standing in a row against the wall with packages of all shapes and sizes in their hands. They marched forward in single file and fell on their knees before my parents. Then one at a time, they presented the gifts they had brought from the king of Egypt to my parents." Tadukhepa glowed and hid her face with her hands. "The most beautiful necklaces of gold, turquoise, and carnelian for me and mother," she mumbled, "lovely alabaster bowls and lamps. And gold." She dropped her hands into her lap. "That was good because father needs gold for his coffers. I could tell that he was very pleased."

She hesitated, thinking about her father.

"Then Meni said, 'Your Majesty, I will return and accompany your daughter to Egypt.' After he said that, my father told me I could leave."

Rather tearfully, Tadukhepa looked from one to the other and said, "Alala, do you think my father would let you come with me?"

"I think he might if you ask him. After all, the king bought me for you. He will certainly give you other personal attendants when you go to Egypt. Princess Gilukhepa had three hundred and seventeen attendants when she went to Egypt to marry the king."

The next morning, while the princess and Kelu hungrily devoured barley cooked to a soupy milk mush, flat bread with butter, honey and cheese, a platter of fish in the usual spicy sauce, and pomegranates, the queen arrived.

Alala and Lesser Slave dropped onto their faces.

"Rise," Queen Iuni said crisply, heading for the table where Tadukhepa and Kelu sat. Both girls slid slowly from their chairs and bowed deeply.

"Finish your breakfast quickly, Tadukhepa. Slaves from the Egyptian court are on their way here now to fit you for a new wardrobe."

Tadukhepa stepped forward. Her face taut and anxious, she grasped the queen's orange wool robe. "Mother, I want Alala to come with me to Egypt. Can I have her?" she begged.

Queen Iuni looked into the panicky, frightened eyes raised to hers, and her heart skipped a beat. Her sweet child would need the comfort of a familiar face to bolster her spirits as she stood alone among all those strangers.

"Yes, Tadukhepa, you may take Alala."

"Thank you, Mother." Tadukhepa went down on one knee and kissed her mother's hand.

With her other hand, the queen stroked her daughter's hair. "Come now, you have a busy day ahead of you."

Kelu watched the queen and Tadukhepa intently, her eyes glistening. Before any memories of the warm caresses of her mother brought tears, they heard a soft knock at the door.

Silently, the Egyptian slaves entered the princess' suite, carrying rolls of fabric, alabaster boxes, and tailoring equipment. The men and women slaves bowed as they made a circle around the princess.

Kelu gasped and stared at the dune-colored short linen skirts. They wore nothing more. She looked at the queen and back at the circulating slaves.

"Alala, remove this table of food," ordered the queen.

A heavy woman with dark skin, kinky hair, and thick lips knelt before Queen Iuni and Tadukhepa. "Your Majesty, my name is Ronpe. I have been delegated to supervise the making of a wardrobe suitable for your daughter's position as the wife of our illustrious king. If it please Your Majesty, we will begin immediately."

"You may begin," said Queen Iuni. "I will return later to see how you are progressing." She walked sedately to the door and disappeared.

Instantly, the room became a flurry of activity. Slaves threw rolls of cloth onto the floor, allowing the fabric to spin out. Others rushed at Tadukhepa with long measuring sticks. Still others crawled around the floor, handling the fabric.

"Let me help you take your dress off, Princess," Ronpe said to Tadukhepa.

"Right here in front of everybody?"

"Of course. How do you think the tailors can fit you if you don't remove your dress?" Ronpe stooped, caught the hem of Tadukhepa's blue robe and straightened her arms, lifting the dress up.

Tadukhepa sucked in her breath. "No." She tried to pull the dress down.

"Princess, please. Let them do their job. They want you to look beautiful when you appear before King Amenhotep III."

Tadukhepa let go of her dress. She hung her head and looked down at the floor, her lips tight together.

The male slaves measured and poked her. A muscular, bronze-colored slave said, "She needs less fabric here under the arms. And we need to lengthen the waist." Without touching Tadukhepa, the older of the two slaves ran his hand from her bust area to the tops of her legs.

Tadukhepa raised an eyebrow. They treated her as if she were a stuffed doll.

"Princess," exclaimed Kelu, "this is the fabric you are going to wear when you meet the king." She held up the loose end of fabric spilling from a roll of rich, deep red, almost gossamer wool.

"How do you know?" said Tadukhepa, staring intently at the most luscious fabric she had ever seen.

"I heard Ronpe tell that man going into your bedroom."

Tadukhepa edged over to the red wool and pulled it up across her body.

"Oh, how beautiful it makes you look," sighed Kelu.

Starting to enjoy the attention brought on by her new status, Tadukhepa smiled shyly. A long, sheer, pleated, white linen dress fell in folds around her as a slave placed it over her shoulders. "But there's nothing under it," she sputtered.

"That's the style at the Egyptian court, My Princess. Your aunt slipped it in with the gifts so you would know what the royal women wear."

"How sweet of Aunt Gilukhepa." Tadukhepa fondled the fine linen fabric.

The tailor stuck a big broach in his mouth as he fussed with the gown's waistline. "You wear the broach here." He gathered a handful of fabric and anchored it just below her breasts.

Tadukhepa caught her breath, every nerve tense. But she controlled herself.

"You, slave," yelled Ronpe, "how dare you touch the princess like that?"

Ronpe dropped to her knees before Tadukhepa. "Please, Your Highness," she implored, "don't report him. He's a good tailor, but from a rural tribe and hasn't been fully trained yet."

Mollified, Tadukhepa nodded graciously.

An hour later, Queen Iuni returned. She walked up to Tadukhepa and placed her hand on her daughter's shoulder. "You look lovely in that yellow wool. It's so thin, it drapes nicely." She smiled at Tadukhepa and touched her arm affectionately. "I see," she glanced around, "that the work goes well. So I will visit you tomorrow."

She again smiled at Tadukhepa, turned and said, "Continue," to Ronpe before leaving the room.

When the light began to dim, Ronpe straightened and looked around. Two tailors were holding up needles, trying to thread them in the dim light. She sighed and dismissed the slaves from the princess' quarters for the night. "We will start at the same time tomorrow."

The Egyptian slaves bowed and withdrew. Tadukhepa and Kelu stood alone in the middle of the room with their two slaves. Giggling and tired, they fell into each other's arms.

"It's so exciting," exclaimed the princess. "Can you imagine having all those beautiful clothes? But with nothing underneath! I'm not sure I can do that. When I get to Egypt, I'll have to hunt for my aunt right away and discuss it with her." Tadukhepa paused for breath and sank into a chair. "And to think that all of this activity will continue until the messenger from Egypt returns."

She looked at the glowing Kelu sitting on the floor in front of her. "I'm going to have the tailors make some clothes for you, too, Kelu. We can practice walking around in them."

"Without anything underneath?" giggled Kelu.

"No. I think I'll wear something underneath."

Day after day, the work went forward. Ronpe directed the tailors to make two little dresses for Kelu. The girls wore the new clothes to eat their meals, to walk up and down the corridor of the princess' quarters, to play court in their room, to do everything except wear them to bed.

The queen came regularly to see how the work proceeded. "I shall miss you, my daughter," Queen Iuni said one day while she stroked Tadukhepa's silky black hair.

"Even with Father's sister there, I'll feel so alone in Egypt, Mother. They will all be strangers."

"You will soon get to know the people of the court. But remember, you can send me long letters, telling me all about the people you meet and how you like the king." She continued to stroke Tadukhepa's hair.

Suddenly, Tadukhepa began to cry. "I'm afraid."

The queen gathered her close and rocked her. "There, there. You will have Alala."

"Yes, Princess," the slave said, "I'll be with you all the time."

After the queen left, Tadukhepa and Kelu sat together, eating lentil stew with roast mutton. Tadukhepa laid down her scooping bread, turned to Kelu, and said, "You will come with me."

Kelu's mouth dropped open. She deliberately laid down her bread and said, "No."

"I command you. I'm the queen of Egypt."

"No." Kelu wagged her head from side to side, and started to cry.

Princess," said Alala from her squatting position against the wall, "Kelu is too young. Who will take care of her?"

"You."

"I take care of you, Princess."

"Then we will buy a slave in Egypt to take care of Kelu." Tadukhepa flung up her head. "I demand it."

Kelu jumped up from the table and ran sobbing to her room. She threw herself down on her stomach and buried her head in her arms.

Moments later, Lesser Slave entered and sat down on the bed beside Kelu. "I don't think, Princess Tadukhepa can order you to go with her, Kelu, so don't cry." She patted Kelu's shoulders.

"I want to see my Uncle Arttarna." Kelu sat up and wiped away her tears. "I'm going to go tell him what Princess Tadukhepa said." She scrambled off the bed, her face set in determined lines.

The slave said, "Yes, he should know about this."

Kelu ran along the corridor and out the door of the nursery.

Tadukhepa left the table where she had been diddling with her food to face Lesser Slave leaving Kelu's sleeping area. "Where did she go?" demanded Tadukhepa.

"To Ambassador Arttarna."

"How dare she! That won't do her any good." Tadukhepa's face darkened in anger. "I have half a mind to send you after her."

"As you wish, Princess." The slave started towards the door.

"No. Don't go. She'll come back." Tadukhepa's nose went up. "Maybe Ambassador Arttarna will come with her. I'll tell him it is my order."

Alala, behind Tadukhepa, raised her eyebrows and shrugged

her shoulders at Lesser Slave, much as to say, "What has gotten into the child?"

Tadukhepa stamped back to the table and continued playing with her food.

At the door of Arttarna's suite, the guard stopped Kelu.

"Master is having a massage then he's going to the king's chambers," the guard informed her.

Panicky, Kelu puckered up her face, tears forming at the corners of her eyes. She'd just stay here in the corridor all night. She sniffled and rubbed her nose, smearing her face with sniffles. Then she flung herself against the door and struck it with her fists.

"Little Miss, Little Miss," said the big guard, softening.

He opened the door and Kelu bolted into the room, shrieking, "Uncle, Uncle."

Sebi came running from the back room, Arttarna close behind him, a large piece of blue fabric wrapped around his waist.

Kelu threw herself onto Arttarna. "I don't want to go," she sobbed.

Arttarna sat down and pulled the blue fabric up over his knees and shoulders before drawing Kelu onto his lap. "Now, dear child, tell me what the problem is. Where don't you want to go?"

"To Egypt."

"To Egypt!" he exclaimed, startled. "What do you mean?"

"Princess Tadukdhepa has commanded me to go with her. She said I had to go because she was queen of Egypt." Kelu choked back tears.

"My dear Kelu, Princess Tadukhepa is not queen of Egypt yet. Besides, Amenhotep III already has a queen. Princess Tadukhepa will only be a minor wife. She does not have the authority to command you."

He set her down on the floor. "Kelu, I have been ordered to attend the king's banquet so I must dress. But while I am there, I will talk to His Majesty about what Princess Tadukhepa said to you. I am sure he will tell her that she cannot do that. In the meantime, Sebi will make up a bed for you here and stay with you. Is that all right?"

Kelu slowly nodded her head.

"You sit here in my chair while I go into the other room and dress. Then as soon as I have gone to the audience hall, Sebi will take care of you." He studied her. "I think tomorrow would be a good time to buy you a slave." He picked her up, kissed her, and settled her in his chair.

At breakfast, Arttarna said, "As I promised, I spoke to King Tushratta last night about what Tadukhepa said to you."

Kelu's cautious eyes met his.

He smiled. "The king laughed and said that her new status had gone to her head. He will speak to her and tell her that you will not be going to Egypt."

Kelu visibly relaxed.

Patting her hand, Arttarna said, "Shall we go?"

They left the palace grounds through the massive lion gate, taking the road that led to the center of the city. Kelu skipped along, delighted with the exquisite clear day, the blue sky, and the sun. Her steps slowed as they passed the small temple where she had gone to her mother's funeral service. Next, she noticeably slowed again as they passed the spot where the horses had struck Khelpa. She carefully examined the ditch where her mother had lain.

Arttarna looked sharply at her then understood why she was lagging behind. So this was the exact spot where Khelpa had been struck. He clasped Kelu's hand, an ache in his chest.

From the city center, they turned right and exited by the western gate, headed for the slave market near the racetrack. After purchasing a slave, Arttarna intended to discuss his mares with Rasi, his caretaker, and perhaps put Kelu on one. Three of his mares had fouled, and he wanted to look over the colts.

"We are almost at the slave market, Kelu. It may be crowded, so stay close to me. I do not want you to get lost."

"Yes, Uncle Arttarna." She moved nearer to him so she could clutch the fullness of his yellow wool robe.

He smiled down at her. "I want to find a woman who is old enough so she can mother you, but also young enough to be good company for you."

Kelu smiled. "I'd like that."

"If you see someone you think you would like to have live with us, tell me, and I will talk to her."

"Yes, I will."

They edged their way through the slave market, past the

male section where slave owners and well-dressed men haggled over muscular young males, finally reaching the area where the women were being sold. They saw a beautiful young naked girl standing disconsolately on a small raised platform. Arttarna's eye flicked over her. Pretty, but a sulky mouth and too young.

Kelu looked intently at the girl. Scorn in her eyes, the girl looked back. Kelu tightened her hold on Arttarna's robe.

Slowly, they walked along. Every once in a while, near a woman he thought suitable, Arttarna looked down at Kelu. She showed no reaction. They came to the end. Puzzled and somewhat irritated, he said, "Well?"

Kelu looked up at him with confidence. "I like the one back there on the left." She used her finger to point. "The fourth one back. She smiled at me."

Arttarna tried to mask his surprise and pleasure at the way Kelu had handled herself. She had looked over all the prospects before making a decision. He remembered the woman. Maybe eighteen. Not particularly pretty, but she had a pleasant, intelligent face. Light skinned, well proportioned, slightly on the plump side, probably a Canaanite captured in one of the Hittite raids along the coast.

Arttarna dickered with her owner while the young woman and Kelu stared at each other.

"What's your name?" The girl smiled at Kelu.

"Kelu. What's yours?"

"Eshtar."

"My uncle is buying you for me. I don't have anybody."

Eshtar blinked. The family must be extremely wealthy if this child was being given a slave. She appraised Arttarna covertly. His dark skin proclaimed him one of the overlords, and he handled himself with aplomb.

"Take her to the palace and ask for Sebi, my personal slave," Arttarna directed the slave owner.

"Yes, Ambassador Arttarna." The man bowed and groveled.

"Come, Kelu." Arttarna passed his new possession without a glance.

They exited the slave market and headed for the racetrack.

At the paddock, Rasi bowed to Ambassador Arttarna and smiled at Kelu. "How are you, Young Mistress?"

"I'm fine, Rasi." Kelu beamed at him.

"Have we got a small-boned young mare that would be right for a small-boned little girl?"

"I do."

Seeing Kelu jump up and down, Arttarna grinned.

"Oh Uncle," she squealed. "You mean a little horse of my own? Whenever I ride with Tadukhepa, I have to use one of the mares out of the royal stable, and not always the same one."

"There are two, Master, either one of which might do nicely," Rasi informed Arttarna.

"Let us have a look."

Arttarna, along with Kelu, sauntered by the stalls, commenting on the fine horseflesh. Rasi stopped in front of a quiet little mare being rubbed down. He laid his hand on the horse's shiny neck and said to the boy grooming her, "Bring me the black filly with the white diamond on her forehead."

As the boy ran off, he continued, "This little mare has a sweet disposition, but she's not as fast as the other one."

"Rasi," Arttarna interjected, "swiftness isn't an issue here. I am more concerned about Kelu's safety."

The stable boy approached, leading a beautiful black mare who clipped along spiritedly on her little feet.

"Oh!" Kelu exclaimed, running up to the filly that nuzzled her with a velvety nose.

"I think the decision is made, Rasi," laughed Arttarna. "This little mare belongs to Kelu, and you will train her accordingly."

"With pleasure, Master."

"May I go for a ride now, Uncle?" Kelu raised an excited face.

"No, Kelu. After Princess Tadukhepa leaves, you will have plenty of time to try her out."

"Yes, Uncle." Kelu meekly returned to his side.

Feeling subdued, Kelu walked thoughtfully back to the palace. She had responsibilities now—a slave and a horse of her own.

"What's troubling you, Kelu?"

"I was thinking about my small room. Eshtar will have to put her mat in the corridor the way Lesser Slave does rather than at the foot of my bed."

"No matter where she places her mat, she is to accompany

you the way Sebi accompanies me. If you want her to do something for you, she will do it. For example, if you want to drink
some juice, send her to get it for you." He paused, then said
with emphasis, "You are to treat her well, Kelu. That is my first
principle with slaves."

"Yes, Uncle." She squared her shoulders. She would treat
Eshtar exactly the way she saw Uncle Arttarna treat Sebi.

Kelu couldn't help smiling with pleasure at the thought of
her new acquisitions.

"Now," said Arttarna when they reached his palace suite,
"You had best take your slave and go back to Princess Tadukhepa.
She will be leaving for Egypt soon. I think you should be spend-
ing your time with her."

"Yes, Uncle."

From where he stood against the wall, Sebi said, "Eshtar is
in your room in the princess' suite, Little Mistress."

Kelu turned and walked quickly across the room towards
the door.

Arttarna watched her go. In the space of the morning, his
little daughter had matured a bit. What a joy she was to him.

At the royal nursery, Kelu went directly to her closet bedroom. She found Eshtar sitting upright on the bed.

On seeing Kelu, Eshtar immediately jumped to her feet.

Kelu smiled at her. "We must stay here with Princess
Tadukhepa until she leaves for Egypt."

In amazement, Eshtar's eyes widened. What had she fallen
into with this pretty little girl?

Kelu interpreted Eshtar's reaction as fear. Trying to reassure the young woman, she said, "You must lay your mat right
outside the door. There isn't space at the foot of my bed. But
that's only for a short time. Once I move back to my Uncle
Arttarna's suite, you will sleep at the foot of my bed."

Kelu lifted her chin. She owned this woman. She had complete control over another human being. She must remember to
behave towards Eshtar as Uncle Arttarna behaved towards Sebi.

"Follow me," she said. "We will go to Princess Tadukhepa
now."

On entering Princess Tadukhepa's room, Kelu went down
on one knee, her head bowed. Eshtar on all fours, dropped her
head to the floor.

As usual, Princess Tadukhepa's suite was full of slaves, tailors, fabric, and noise. Tadukhepa stood on a footstool in the middle of the room.

"Rise, dear friend," Tadukhepa said, extending her arm towards Kelu. "I missed you." She looked at Eshtar. "Is this slave yours?"

"Yes. Uncle Arttarna bought her for me."

"Stand up, slave," said the princess.

"Eshtar will take care of me," said Kelu. She glanced at Lesser Slave and saw her face fall. "Along with Lesser Slave," she added quickly.

"Very well," Tadukhepa said. "My slave, Alala, will show you around my quarters and instruct you on the rules here."

Alala beckoned with her index finger. Eshtar followed her into Tadukhepa's empty, quiet bedroom where they could talk.

Tadukhepa never again brought up the subject of taking Kelu to Egypt, though Kelu remained apprehensive. She was delighted to have Kelu with her during the last of her time in Mitanni.

The flurry of new clothes and collection of dowry receded and activity in the princess' suite returned to near normal. Nevertheless, Tadukhepa remained very aware of her new position. Occasionally, at some childish suggestion by the other children, she would say, "I can't do that any more. I'm a married woman, queen of Egypt."

Queen Iuni visited Tadukhepa and Kelu one morning as they were deciding what to do with Tadukhepa's dolls now that she no longer played with them.

Forgetting to bow, Tadukhepa ran to her mother to hug her. The queen held her close.

"The Egyptian king is objecting to the bride price your father is demanding. When that question is resolved, Meni will come back here to escort you to Egypt."

Tadukhepa shrugged and returned to her task of figuring out what to do with her dolls. "I think I'll give them to you and to my sisters," she said to Kelu. "Until Meni comes back to Wassukkanni, I will go about my preparations to be queen of Egypt."

Five months later, Meni returned to Wassukkanni, capital of Mitanni, to collect Tadukhepa and her dowry. King Tushratta had the dowry listed on two clay tablets. He ordered them packed in the elegant chariot in which Tadukhepa would travel to Thebes, the capital of Egypt.

Standing in the palace courtyard beside Arttarna, King Tushratta, Queen Iuni, Prince Mattiwaza, Prince Shaushtatar and the younger royal children, along with members of the court, Kelu cried uncontrollably as she waved good-bye to Tadukhepa. The luxurious equipage, carrying the princess, Alala, and Lesser Slave, rolled through the palace gate. Meni's chariot followed Tadukhepa's. Three hundred and forty-five Mitannian men and women who would take up their residence with Tadukhepa in Egypt walked after Meni's chariot.

7

After Tadukhepa's chariot disappeared through the lion
gate, Arttarna took Kelu's elbow and made his way
back into the palace through the crowd that had gathered to send the princess off. He turned to speak to Eshtar, who
followed behind them. "See that all Kelu's belongings are immediately transferred to my formal suite of rooms."

"Yes, Master."

"Kelu, come with me."

The minute they entered the reception room of Arttarna's
large palace suite, Sebi dropped onto one knee. "All is in readi-
ness, Master."

"Good. Take Kelu to the room she is to occupy, then go
help Eshtar bring Kelu's things back from the royal nursery."

Kelu followed Sebi, stopping every other second to look at
the rosy hue of the people painted on the walls. Her uncle must
have had the walls repainted in preparation for their moving
into the large suite. Her own room brought a gasp of delight.
She turned completely around, to make sure she didn't miss any
of the bright flowers painted on the pale green walls.

"I'll be sleeping in a flower garden, Sebi."

Her head bobbed in approval when she saw the bed resting
against one wall. Plenty of space remained at the foot of the bed
for Eshtar's mat.

"Oh, a corner table for all of the lovely toiletries the
princess has given me. And the table even has a matching stool."
She sighed her happiness. "This room makes me feel like a
princess."

Sebi smiled. She always expressed such delight with any
little thing he did for her that doing it gave him joy. He hurried
away to go help Eshtar in the royal nursery.

Kelu sat down on the stool to wait for Eshtar and Sebi to return with her things.

The two slaves staggered in, loaded down with clothes, toiletries, and Kelu's personal belongings. Eshtar also carried the alabaster lamp that Princess Tadukhepa had given Kelu on the eve of her departure. Sebi deposited his load on the bed and disappeared.

Kelu watched as Eshtar laid the toiletries on the table. She picked up the mirror and brushed her hand gently across the mirror's back. "This has the royal seal on it. And the comb has a little handle." She picked up the comb with her other hand. Holding the mirror in front of her, she combed her hair.

Turning sober eyes on Eshtar, she said, "Princess Tadukhepa is my friend. I am going to miss her."

"I'm sure you will, Kelu, but you are going to be a busy girl now in this lovely suite of rooms. Ambassador Arttarna has instructed me to take you to the home of Pamba, the Hittite, tomorrow. His wife will spend some time—" Eshtar swallowed her surprise as Kelu's face lit up and she clapped her hands in delight.

Eshtar continued, "She will be teaching you how to run a household and how to conduct yourself as the mistress of the house."

"Just the way Ronpe instructed Tadukhepa how she was supposed to behave in the Egyptian court?"

"Something like that, yes," said Eshtar, smiling.

"What else?"

"Rasi is going to give you special riding lessons. Your uncle wants you to be an expert rider." She didn't tell Kelu that Rasi had been instructed to give her lessons, too. Even though few women rode, the master wanted them both to be proficient horsewomen. She couldn't figure out why. And she wasn't sure she liked the idea. She had confided her feeling to Sebi. All he had said was, "The master has a reason."

Sebi appeared in the doorway. "Little Mistress, the master wishes you to join him in the audience room."

"Your mat goes there, Eshtar." Kelu pointed to the floor at the foot of the bed and trotted after Sebi.

"Kelu," said Arttarna when she stood in front of him, "I have received a message from King Tushratta about you."

"Me!" exclaimed Kelu, opening her eyes wide.

"Yes, you." Arttarna laughed, stretched out his hand and drew her onto his knee. "It seems that the king's children are upset now that you don't live in the nursery anymore. They have asked him if you could play with them every afternoon, the way you all played together when Princess Tadukhepa was still here. King Tushratta sent a guard to me with their request."

"Playing with them is fun," Kelu said primly, "but I'm grown up now. I'll be going to Hepit's every day."

Arttarna tried not to smile. "True, you are quite a young lady now that you are almost eight. However, when the king makes a request, even though it is phrased more in terms of a favor than a command, you do what he asks. Hepit and Eshtar will help you schedule your time so you can go to the palace nursery in the afternoons."

"And that reminds me, Kelu." The change in his voice made her sit up straight.

"I have something to tell you that makes me sad." He pulled her against him so she could nestle in the crook of his arm. "For the last two years I have been able to stay here in Wassukkanni. Inevitably, that couldn't last because, normally, I am posted to other countries for long periods of time. Now I'm being called on to do service abroad again. King Tushratta has asked me to make a quick trip to Assyria."

"I'm going with you, aren't I?"

"Not this time, Kelu. I'll only be away for a few months, but it's important I go. I'll leave sometime within the next few days, depending on when the news we expect arrives. As soon as the king receives it, he will send for me. So it may happen very suddenly."

"Uncle, I don't want to be left here alone," Kelu whimpered, pressing her face into his chest.

"Kelu, when you lived with Princess Tadukhepa, you didn't see me all the time. Think of it that way. You will live here with Eshtar and Sebi—I'm going to leave Sebi here—and all the others. You will play with the royal children the way you always have, and you are also going to be taking riding lessons from Rasi. That will be different and exciting. Your mornings will be spent with Hepit. So you see, you have a lot to learn and too much to do to miss me inconsolably."

Kelu bit her lip and blinked hard, but didn't cry.

"Hepit will teach you how to run a large house. I now have slaves doing some of the tasks you will be expected to do in the future when you run my household. You will be able to do them yourself soon. By the time the king asks me to go to some new country for a long stay, Hepit will have taught you all those skills, and you will travel there with me and run my house. One day you will marry and have your own home to run, too. So you need to know how to do it properly."

"Will Tadukhepa do that in Egypt?"

"I doubt that very much. The King of Egypt has many, many wives. Princess Tadukhepa is only one of them. The new king, Amenhotep IV, has several wives as well. And he also has a very beautiful principal wife. What all the other wives do, I don't know."

He explained that the wives of the Egyptian king were essentially hostages. "The king marries them to ensure that their father or their brother, whichever relative of theirs sits on the throne, won't make war with Egypt or join in an alliance against it."

"Does King Tushratta have many wives?"

Arttarna scowled. How did they get off on this tangent? "No, not many."

"Does Queen Iuni run the palace the way I will run your house someday?"

"Yes. That may surprise you, but she is very busy. Not only does she oversee all the work that goes on here, but she also plays a role in affairs of state. Actually, the king's other wives help the queen with the palace work, too."

He kissed the top of her head and pushed her off his lap. "Are you going to play in the royal nursery today?"

Kelu nodded. "Yes."

"Then get Eshtar and run along. I will see you at dinner."

By the time Kelu had dressed and had eaten breakfast early the next morning, she was summoned to go to Hepit's house.

Hepit's slave stood timidly at the bedroom door. "Mistress waits," she said.

"I'm ready," said Kelu.

Her head held high, Kelu walked sedately across the palace

courtyard and through the lion gate. The guards jumped aside and stood at attention as the small, confident figure, followed by Eshtar and Hepit's slave, passed by them without a glance.

Kelu walked straight up to the house's formal entrance. As if by magic, the door opened. Hepit stood waiting inside the entryway. Casting all solemn, lady-like behavior aside, Kelu ran smiling up to Hepit.

"My dear Kelu," said Hepit, taking her by both shoulders and gazing at her, "how lovely you look in that yellow robe and how you have grown. I'm to teach a charming young lady rather than the tear-stained little girl I last saw."

"Eshtar," said Hepit, looking over Kelu's head, "go with my slave to the kitchen."

Hepit took Kelu's hand. "Come along. You have much to learn."

She led Kelu to the back of the house. "We are going to start with weaving. Do you remember the weaving rooms? Your mother worked there some."

"I don't think so."

"Well, anyway, today, that is what you will do first. I have asked my best weaver to teach you. In the future, when you run your own household, you will not be expected to do the weaving yourself, but in order to supervise a roomful of weavers, you need to know how it's done."

They entered a large, square room full of upright looms. Kelu gasped as memories started flooding back. Her eyes automatically sought the third loom in the string of looms along the left wall.

Hepit quickly maneuvered Kelu to the first loom along the right wall. The old, white-haired woman standing there, smiled at her.

Kelu had trouble keeping her eyes off the gaps in the woman's teeth.

"She will teach you for a short time each morning, maybe for the next six mornings. We'll see how you get on," said Hepit.

"Take her now," Hepit told the slave. "I'll come back soon."

Kelu watched Hepit walk to the back of the room and exit out the door. The slave touched Kelu's arm to draw her attention back to the loom. "Stand here where I am so you can handle the threads." She moved aside. Shyly and with some hesitation, Kelu stepped in front of the loom.

"Don't worry," said the old woman. "If you mess up any of the threads, we'll rip them out and start over."

Slowly, Kelu mimicked what the slave did. A minute later, she stopped. "I messed it up," she said

The slave smiled. "Just rip it out."

After three more tries, Kelu wove a whole line. "There," she said, turning shining eyes on the slave.

"Good." The slave patted Kelu's arm. "Now I'll show you what to do next."

On her return, Hepit stood quietly at the rear entrance to observe Kelu's progress. She smiled. How intent the child was. After a few minutes, Hepit walked up to the front of the room, to stand beside her.

"Very good, Kelu," she said. "You are doing well on your first lesson." Hepit nodded to the slave and led Kelu from the room.

"This morning," said Hepit, as they walked towards the front of the house, "most of the women are weaving wool for the slaves' clothing. Perhaps tomorrow, they will weave blankets. Every bit of fabric we use in this house is woven in that room. In your home when you marry, you will have to set up a weaving room and tell the slaves each day what they are to weave. So you'll have to know how much thread and yarn you will need and keep a sufficient supply of them on hand."

"Does my uncle have a weaving room?"

Hepit's eyebrows flew up at the word "uncle."

Well, that is his business, she mused. Someday, he'll have to tell her the truth.

"No," she said, "he doesn't have slaves who do weaving just for him. All of his bedding and clothing are woven by slaves who are in the palace weaving room."

Kelu decided she would find out about the palace's weaving room the minute she returned.

Hepit told her that, besides becoming familiar with weaving, she would have many other household tasks to learn. "You will need a house staff to keep the rooms picked up, to make the beds, to roll up the mats, whatever needs to be done." She opened a door to the front room. Kelu remembered the room where Pamba and Hepit had their chairs. Two slaves were straightening up the chairs and brushing them off. "You will have to supervise the slaves who do the housecleaning. These two slaves," she added, "keep the reception room clean. You must see that this is done or have a head slave who sees to it. Sebi does it for your—" Hepit bit her tongue before the word "father" burst out—"uncle."

"Eshtar takes care of my room," Kelu announced.

Hepit smiled. "We will go to the kitchen now so you can speak to the cook. She was delighted when I told her you would be coming each morning."

"She was always good to me," Kelu said simply.

Hepit put an arm across Kelu's shoulder, giving her a gentle hug. "Eshtar is waiting for you in the kitchen. That will be all for today." Hepit stopped at the kitchen door. "I'll see you tomorrow morning."

Hepit turned on her heel. Kelu waited until Hepit disappeared, opened the door, and ran to the cook. "Cook," she cried, her eyes moist.

"Oh, my sweet baby!" The cook drew Kelu into her arms and rocked her before leaning back to look at her. "You've grown, my lovely girl."

Kelu smiled happily.

Soon, Kelu and Eshtar returned to Arttarna's quarters in the palace. A subdued, but pleased, Kelu sat down to eat her lunch, which Eshtar served her at a small table placed in a corner of the audience room. "Eshtar," Kelu said as she picked up a burnished red clay pitcher full of milk, "I want to see the palace weaving room."

"I'll find out where it is for you, but as soon as you're finished eating, you have to go play with the royal children."

"Oh, that's right. I'll hurry." Kelu popped a large piece of pork ladened with spicy sauce into her mouth. She sneezed, grabbed the drinking bowl, and sucked in some of the milk from the bowl to cool her mouth.

"You don't have to hurry that much, Kelu," said Eshtar. "That was a lot of spice."

"I think I've eaten enough. I'll just have some dates."

"All right. But that's really fresh goat's milk. Drink some more."

After drinking a little more, Kelu set the bowl down and stood up decisively. "I'm ready." She hurried along the corridors leading to the palace nursery, Eshtar at her heels.

To Kelu's delight, Prince Mattiwaza stood at the door of Princess Tadukhepa's old audience room poking his youngest brother, who squealed in anticipation each time the finger came near, but waited expectantly for each new assault.

Their game stopped when they saw Kelu, followed by Eshtar. Prince Mattiwaza grinned broadly at her. From the door of his room, Prince Shaushtatar bellowed, "Kelu's here." He ran to her, a big smile on his face. Kelu smiled back. She liked Prince Shaushtatar; he was fun.

The nursery erupted. Kelu walked into the reception room, followed by the others. The princes' little brothers and sisters came running into the room. Even a slave appeared with the newest royal baby to introduce the baby to Kelu. Everybody swarmed around her. In seconds, a game of tag began.

"You chase me," yelled one of the little princesses at Kelu. "All right." Kelu darted towards her.

"Me, too," cried her little sister.

Kelu laughed and lunged at the small girl who squealed and scampered to her slave.

Mattiwaza yelled, "Look out," and started for Kelu.

She quickly ran from him and circled around the room, Prince Mattiwaza after her. Panting, he caught her, his arms encircling her waist. Embarrassed, he let his arms drop. Kelu blushed, spun away, and ran toward Shaushtatar. He hooted and spurted away. He easily outdistanced her, turned and laughed. She made a face at him and swerved, running after one of the little girls.

Eshtar observed the encounter and decided she didn't like the emotion Prince Mattiwaza betrayed. She made a mental note to try to prevent any further physical contact.

For the rest of the afternoon, Prince Mattiwaza kept his distance. Eshtar watched him closely, realizing that he was aware of every move Kelu made.

At breakfast a few days later, Kelu suddenly said, "My uncle has gone, hasn't he?"

"He left sometime during the night for Assyria." Eshtar

found it interesting that Kelu sensed the departure of Ambassador Arttarna.

Between her lessons at Hepit's, her playtime at the royal nursery, and riding her horse under Rasi's tutelage, Kelu didn't have much time to fret about Arttarna's absence. She quickly learned how to do the weaving, grappled with how to manage household finances, a much more frustrating subject for her, and became adept at understanding food preparation and keeping pottery jars in the storage house full and well supplied.

Hepit insisted that she learn how to read and write a few numbers plus words like wheat and barley, basic words for her supplies. "You need to make lists for yourself so you can keep track of what you have ordered and how much you have ordered. A lot of ladies don't have records, but I find it useful."

Hepit's cook taught her how to plan menus. Most of the time, the cook agreed with her choices, though once in a while she did object to Kelu's heavy preference for sweets.

In the late afternoons, Rasi taught her how to be a better horseback rider. Her proficiency at it improved, but not rapidly. She complained to Eshtar that the demands of the royal children took up too much of her time.

Eshtar simply said, "You have to play with the children."

"I don't want to go there every day. I want to ride my horse."

Eshtar wondered if Kelu's reluctance to play with the royal children had anything to do with the presence of Prince Mattiwaza. But she also sensed, whenever she saw the two children together, that Kelu liked having his attention.

"You have no choice." Eshtar, closed the subject.

Day after day, life for Kelu progressed along the same busy path. She learned housekeeping with Hepit, horseback riding with Rasi, and played with the children in the royal nursery.

Nearly six months had passed when Hepit told Kelu she had completed her schooling in how to run a large house. "Unhappily, this is also going to be our good-bye as well, Kelu."

"Why?" Kelu's face began to pucker up.

"Because, my dear, our king has called us back to Hattusas, our capital."

"Then I won't ever see you again."

"Probably not."

Throwing her arms around Hepit, Kelu clung to her and buried her face in Hepit's dress.

To soothe Kelu and calm her own sorrow about leaving, Hepit stoked Kelu's hair then disengaged herself. "I hope you will use your skills to make your uncle proud of you," she said, smiling, kissed Kelu, and sent her back to the palace.

From then on, Kelu spent every morning with Rasi, but still had to play with the royal children in the afternoon. She began to feel constrained by her visits to the palace nursery. She felt grown up, ready to do the things she had been taught. She spread her wings in her suite of rooms as much as possible and walked around the palace to see where the different domestic activities took place. Occasionally, she met the queen, who smiled at her and commended her interest.

Weeks went by. Eshtar also became bored with the playtime hours. One afternoon, she suddenly realized that Kelu was not in the room, nor was Prince Mattiwaza. Jumping to her feet, she ran to the door and frantically looked up and down the corridor. Faint noises came from the tiny room where Kelu had once slept. She listened. Yes, it was Kelu's voice.

In three steps, she reached the door and yanked it open. Light flooding into the room surprised Kelu and the prince. Standing close together, their arms around each other, their two heads swiveled to face her.

Eshtar swallowed hard, bent her knee, bowed her head, and said, "Please, Mistress, Rasi will be waiting for you with your horse."

Pointedly ignoring Eshtar, Prince Mattiwaza turned to look at Kelu. "Do you always ride in the late afternoon?"

"Sometimes," she answered.

Blushing deeply, Kelu moved away from Prince Mattiwaza. Her eyes met those of Eshtar for an instant as the two of them exited the room together. The formality with which Eshtar had addressed her and the disapproval in Eshtar's face sobered Kelu. Looking neither right nor left, she walked out of the nursery, hurried along the palace corridors to Arttarna's suite, and went into her bedroom. There, she turned around to face her slave.

"Eshtar," she said defensively, "Prince Mattiwaza says he

loves me. He wants me to be his wife. And I want to be his wife."

"Kelu, you are too young now to be anybody's wife. Prince Mattiwaza shouldn't have taken you into that room. And you were wrong to go there with him. I may be your slave, but I'll tell you bluntly that I don't condone what you did. I intend to discuss it with your uncle when he gets back."

Kelu frowned. "You are my slave, Eshtar, and I am asking you not to say anything to him."

"I am also older than you are, and it's my job to look after you, as well as to do your bidding."

Kelu started to cry. Eshtar took her in her arms. "Dear child, you are both too young. Please believe me. In a few years, there will be a big change in your life. I expect lots of men will want to marry you. But Ambassador Arttarna will have to deal with that."

Eshtar hadn't liked the prince's question about whether Kelu always went horseback riding in the afternoon. After she had calmed Kelu down, she went to the stables to tell Rasi to be on the lookout for the prince and keep him away from Kelu.

Two days later, Rasi brought Kelu back to the palace early. She went directly to her bedroom and shut the door, leaving Rasi and Eshtar in the reception room. Eshtar looked at him quizzically.

He said, "Prince Mattiwaza rode up to us as I was teaching Kelu how to jump a small ditch and demanded that I release her from her lesson so they could go riding together. I begged off, saying I had orders from Ambassador Arttarna never to let Kelu ride without me. He threatened me with insubordination and refused to leave us. That is why I thought it best to cut the lesson short and bring her back to you."

After Rasi left, Eshtar went to Kelu's bedroom. As soon as she entered, Kelu scrambled off the bed and wrapped her arms around Eshtar, saying, "I'm scared."

Trying to think what to do, Eshtar led her back to the bed, sat down, and cuddled her.

After a while, Eshtar said, "I have thought of a plan. I intend to request an urgent audience with Queen Iuni. So please stay here tomorrow and supervise the housekeeping while I go to see the Queen."

Kelu stared at Eshtar. "Aren't you scared to do that?"

"Yes, Kelu, I am very much afraid." Eshtar looked at the floor, her face half hidden. "But I don't know what else to do. The prince's attentions to you have got to stop. So pray to your Teshub tonight that I meet with success."

8

Arttarna and his guard force cantered up to the massive limestone wall surrounding the Assyrian city of Nineveh, slowed their horses, passed through the gate with its great winged lions then walked the horses through the many twisting and turning streets, little and muddy, just like Wassukkanni.

Slowly, they approached Assur-uballit's palace on its platform built on top of another platform. The construction never failed to amaze Arttarna. Steps led from the ground to the first platform then up to the second platform. Formidable walls built of great stone blocks surrounded the palace. Nearly three times as wide as the ramparts around King Tushratta's palace, three chariots, side by side, could race along the top of this wall. Square towers punctuated the huge stone walls at regular intervals, and two enormous sculpted lions with wings and human heads guarded every gate. The large room built into the wall of each of the four entrances served as headquarters for the soldiers who protected Nineveh.

Assur-uballit's outer court, called the court of Assembly, measured three hundred fifty feet by one hundred sixty feet, sizably bigger than the court at King Tushratta's palace. Exquisitely carved and painted alabaster slabs paneled the open, outdoor Court of Assembly. The slabs and all the lime plaster walls of the building, even the separate women's quarters, were painted with beautiful scenes of palace life, the surrounding countryside, and the Tigris River. Great human-headed animals, lions and sometimes eagles decorated every door in the palace.

Once inside the palace, an official escorted Arttarna to the elegant room he would occupy while in Nineveh. The official suggested that he join the parade in the morning. Arttarna thanked him, knowing that this was an order.

He slipped into line in the morning with the other ambassadors just as the parade was starting. Arttarna's eyes sought the figure of the king. King Assur-uballit stood at the head of the forming line. A huge man, he reminded Arttarna of a great bull. His beard, all done in tight curls, reached his chest, and his hair was done in the same style. Descending in layers of curls from under his hat, each row of curls became smaller as the layers fell to his shoulders. Long earrings dangled from his ears. Rings covered his hands. And he wore gold bracelets around his upper arms. With his immaculate, short-sleeved wool robe, he wore a wide, lighter colored fabric band around his waist that blended with the color of his robe. A long fringe, ending in beads that jangled when he walked, surrounded the bottom of the robe.

Arttarna shuddered. This king overdid his dress. It became garish. His parade, too, in Arttarna's opinion, became pompous. He found the king unappealing, his appearance nothing but affectation.

Each time Assur-uballit moved, two eunuchs followed him, one to hold a fly-flapper over him, the other to hold his scepter, as well as a bow and a quiver. Whenever he walked to the palace court or to the outer court, a whole procession of dignitaries walked down the palace's narrow passageway behind him in two lines—princes, governors, captains, judges, treasurers, councilors, sheriffs, and rulers from every province in Assyria—headed by an officer from the Court of Assembly.

Arttarna caught sight of King Tushratta's brother Artatama and his son Suttarna standing at the end of the procession.

The parade reached the outer court. The line of dignitaries spread out, to stand around the court while King Assur-uballit conducted the country's business and heard the requests of petitioners.

His Majesty greeted Arttarna graciously when he presented his credentials. For weeks, the king smiled at him and offered special favors the same as he did to Artatama and Suttarna. But after two months, he perceptibly cooled towards him. Arttarna began to feel exceedingly uncomfortable in the king's presence, suspecting that Tushratta's brother and nephew were plotting against Mitanni. Always in attendance at court, they seemed to have gained the king's ear. Arttarna quickly came to understand that their machinations were behind Assur-uballit's treatment of him.

One evening three months later, while leaving the Court of Assembly, a Babylonian whom Arttarna knew casually, walked slowly past him and, without turning his head to draw attention to them, whispered, "Leave the city tonight, quickly." The faint sound floated by him.

Arttarna immediately recognized danger. He sent his guard force out of the city on a moment's notice and left himself just as the city gates were closing.

He met up with the guard force anxiously waiting a short distance away on the road to Mitanni. Arttarna galloped up and yelled, "We go home as fast as possible," and galloped away, the guard force quickly catching up with him.

During the night, Arttarna and his guard force returned to Wassukkanni. Unlike his usual vigorous, commanding self, he felt completely worn-out, disturbed by the news he was bringing back from Assyria. He had to tell King Tushratta about leaving Nineveh the way he did. He shivered. Right now, he had to get some sleep before reporting to the king.

In the morning, an excited little girl raced across the reception room when she saw him and jumped into his arms. "Uncle, you're back."

He crushed her to him, her love releasing the fatigue, the tension, the overwhelming depression that numbed him.

"Have you been a good girl, Kelu?"

She tightened her hold on his neck for a few seconds, deliberating, then leaned her head back to look at him. "Yes and no," she replied.

"What do you mean by that?"

"I learned a lot at Hepit's. Hepit even told me that I'd learned so much that she couldn't teach me anything more." She announced gleefully, "I know how to do menus now, too."

"Oh, you do!" He smiled, impressed, but at the same time wondered of what his young daughter's meals would consist. He knew how much she liked sweets.

"And right after she dismissed me, she told me that their king had ordered them back to their capital."

That news surprised him. Possible reasons for the recall swirled through his mind. Later, he'd ask Sebi what he knew about it.

"Now tell me the 'no' part."

"Eshtar is upset with me because of Prince Mattiwaza. She is going to ask the queen for an audience today on account of his constant attention to me." She hung her head. "Prince Mattiwaza says he wants to marry me."

Arttarna frowned and set her down. "Tell Eshtar I will handle this myself. There is no need for her to see the queen."

He drew his hand across his forehead. "I suspect you are part of the trouble, my little minx, but I've told you before that Prince Mattiwaza is not for you." His eyes bore into her. "I mean that, Kelu. I'll see to it that his attentions stop, but you are not to encourage him in any way. Do you understand?"

"Yes, Uncle."

"I forbid you to play with the royal children, at least not until I straighten all of this out. I have sent Sebi to ask the king if he will grant me an immediate urgent audience, so run along now. Tell Eshtar I'll talk to her as soon as I come back."

She bowed and hurried off to give his message to Eshtar.

Arttarna waited for Sebi to return. He dreaded the session with Tushratta. It would not be pleasant.

The slave appeared at the door. "Master, King Tushratta is eating breakfast with the queen, but he will see you privately as soon as you arrive in his audience chamber."

"Very good." Arttarna spun around and headed for his bedroom. "Prepare my court robe immediately."

Arttarna slipped the dark blue wool robe over his head and Sebi tied the gold encrusted dark blue waistband so that it draped nicely in the rear. Arttarna added gold earrings and a medallion on a heavy gold chain around his neck. He had overdone his ceremonial robing this morning for the private audience with King Tushratta, but he didn't care. The elegance helped bolster his spirits for the coming interview.

Walking quickly along the corridor, Arttarna kept his eyes down, concentrating on what he would say to the king. As he neared Tushratta's audience hall, the guard who stood at the entrance jumped to open the door. Inside, Arttarna walked directly across the room and reached the king's private quarters.

"Tell the king that Ambassador Arttarna awaits his pleasure," he said to the guard who stood rigidly at that door.

"Yes, Ambassador."

Holding his sword still so that it wouldn't swing as he moved, the guard swiftly turned and disappeared inside.

Arttarna breathed deeply trying to calm himself.

"The king will see you," said the guard, pulling the door wide open. Arttarna stepped inside and instantly dropped to his hands and knees before the king.

"Rise," said Tushratta, giving Arttarna a sharp look. "I can see from your expression that all is not well."

"No, Your Majesty. The situation in Assyria is explosive. And only because of a clandestine warning am I here to tell you that."

"That bad!" Not taking his eyes from Arttarna, he called, "Guard, bring a chair and place it right here in front of me." He pointed.

After seating himself, Arttarna continued, "I expect that your brother Artatama and his son Suttarna are plotting to start a war against you."

"War!" yelled Tushratta, leaning forward in his chair. "Where is your proof?"

"I cannot account for the king's behavior in any other way. Your brother and nephew are always in attendance at court, doing their best to gain the king's trust. They plot against you. I escaped with my life only because of the secret warning I received. They planned to flay me alive and hang my head on the wall."

"They would murder my representative!" Tushratta roared. "This is treason." He grabbed his beard and leaped from his throne.

Arttarna slid off the chair and bowed his head on the floor. "Please, Your Majesty, hear me out. Fortunately, I am here with you."

Well, that shocks me. I don't like it one bit." Tushratta settled back on his throne. "Continue."

"Your brother and nephew are pushing Assur-uballit to fight a war against you, but Assur-uballit, at least for now, can't make a decision one way or the other. He is a weak man, who shilly-shallies about making decisions. He wants to fight a war against you, but he's afraid of what Suppiluliumas, King of the Hittites, might do. So I don't think war is inevitable at the moment."

"Speaking of King Suppiluliumas, he is up to something. He

recalled Pamba to Hattusas unexpectedly. Pamba and his wife left while you were gone."

"It might be worthwhile to discover the Hittite king's intentions."

"Worry about Suppiluliumas' intentions would, I suspect, make Assur-uballit hesitate before attacking me."

"Even though Assur-uballit may not start a war for a while, Your Majesty, it might be good to put some spies in Nineveh to keep track of him and Artatama."

Tushratta nodded. "I'll do that. I think I'll send some spies to Nineveh today and have them report back to me."

"Good idea." Arttarna smiled, pleased at Tushratta's decision.

Tushratta remained silent, going over in his mind how his country could prepare itself for war.

Arttarna watched and waited.

Finally, Tushratta said, "You may go. I'll think over what you have said and will contact you if I need any more details."

Arttarna put out his hand in supplication.

"You have something else to say?"

"Yes. Kelu told me fleetingly this morning that her slave intends to seek an audience with Queen Iuni today."

Tushratta's eyebrows went up.

"It seems that Prince Mattiwaza is enamored with Kelu. As yet, I do not know all the details."

"That is outrageous." The king brought the royal fist down on the royal knee. "My son knows where his duties lie, and I expect him to abide by my wishes."

"Guard," he yelled.

The door opened. A young guard in a straight knee-length skirt, a sword buckled to his side, entered the room and dropped to the floor before the king.

"Send Prince Mattiwaza to me."

As the man jumped to his feet and started backing out, the king said, "No. Don't do that yet. Wait outside until I order you to call for him."

After the guard left, he turned to Arttarna. "Kelu is, what, eight, nine, now?"

"Nearly nine."

With his head turned to the side, the king thought over what might be best for him to do. If he roughly lectured

Mattiwaza, he would anger the boy further. For some reason, lately, Mattiwaza seemed to resent every suggestion he made to him. He didn't know why. And scolding Mattiwaza wouldn't solve the basic problem.

On the other hand, he could send Arttarna abroad again. He hated to do that. He needed Arttarna with him. But, on the other hand, his considerable diplomatic skills would be extremely helpful among the Hittites.

When his gaze returned to Arttarna, he said, "While I hate to lose your counsel and judgment on situations in the realms of my neighbors, it might be wise to send you abroad for an extended period of time. Hattusas, I think, where you will try to find out the extent of their army and any plans to attack. Of course, look into their trade relations with other countries, the government activity, and all the other things you always do as my special ambassador."

He scratched his cheek.

"And take your daughter with you."

9

A cold wind blew through the mountain pass, swirling the snowflakes. Miserable, tired, and wet, nine-year old Kelu clung to the neck of her sweet-tempered little black horse, rather than controlling her with the reins. Mountains, mountains, nothing but mountains, for days. The mountains covered with trees, the trees covered with snow, all so cold, cold, cold. The awful part was that she had to live here in this miserable place. She shivered, unable to control it.

For days and days, until Kelu had lost count, her uncle had led their group, consisting of Sebi, Eshtar, Rasi, Cook, and eight guards. The guards rode behind the family and servants and cared for the ten donkeys carrying the household effects. All the heavy pieces had gone with the guards sent ahead to find a house in Hattusas, the capital of the Hittite Empire, and ready it for their arrival. Occasionally, they had traveled alone. Most of the time, they had joined merchants along the trade routes between Wassukanni and Hattusas. The road seemed endless.

Kelu's horse stepped gingerly in the deepening snow, following close behind Arttarna's big stallion. Suddenly, the stallion stopped. Kelu almost pitched over the mare's head when she abruptly halted.

Arttarna swiveled around in his saddle and yelled to make himself heard against the wind. "Kelu, move up here alongside me."

With a slight kick, Kelu drew the reins to the right. The little mare stepped beside Arttarna's dark brown stallion.

"See those buildings rising on the ridge across the valley?" He pointed slightly to the right.

Kelu squinted. Everything looked gray and blurry through the snowflakes. As she stared, the rocks in the distance took the shape of a wall with the occasional building towering above.

"We will be there shortly, as soon as we cross the bridge over the Halys River." Arttarna snapped the reins on the neck of his horse and moved slowly away from Kelu, letting her fall back into line.

Standing up in his toe stirrups, Arttarna beckoned to the captain of his guard force.

The man drew alongside. "Yes, Master?"

"Ride ahead and alert our guards in Hattusas that we are approaching. Someone will be at the main gate."

The captain cautiously trotted ahead and disappeared.

The minute the horses walked through the main gate of Hattusas, one of the guard force left the shadows of the inner gate and guided his mount to Arttarna's side. "Master, your house is a little distance past all these small temples." He pointed to the mass of little temples.

Arttarna glanced around. Tiny stone and mudbrick temples dotted the landscape right up to the top of the rise upon which stood the royal buildings. "Do the Hittites have a temple for every god?" he exclaimed in amazement.

"Just about." The guard laughed. He kicked his horse into a walk and led the tired, cold caravan from Mitanni along the main street of Hattusas.

As they crested the hill, King Suppiluliumas' palace and the large temple, almost hidden by the stout stone wall, came into view. Soldiers stood guard at the wall's entrance. All around the safety of the wall, private homes nestled like baby animals around their mother. Bright, flickering light of roaring fires showed through the snowflakes as doors opened and closed.

One door, slightly ajar, strongly reflected the dancing orange light. The guard headed straight for that door.

The moment they stopped in front of the long, low house, Rasi jumped down from his horse and raced to help chilled and tired Kelu from her horse.

Eshtar also dismounted and ran to Kelu where she sat numb and crying.

"She's stiff with cold," said Rasi, lifting her down from the black mare. With long, rapid strides, carrying Kelu, he reached the great fire at one end of the long reception room and set her on the floor near the blaze.

Cook rushed in yelling, "Where's the kitchen? Kelu needs something hot in her stomach."

"Come on," said one of the guards, "I'll show you. It's through that small corner door at the other end of the room from the fire."

Cook ran towards the door.

"It's in another building," said the guard, running right behind Cook.

"I assume you guards stocked the kitchen."

"Of course. Don't we always?"

They passed through the door, slamming it shut behind them.

On her knees, Esthar pulled the damp hood from Kelu's head and was pulling the coat sleeve from one arm when Arttarna reached them.

He took one look at his shivering, crying daughter, turned, and motion to a house slave. "Bring us some blankets and hot broth." The sharp snap of his fingers made the slave jump and run from the room.

"I have glanced quickly over the house," he said to Eshtar. "Through that door in the middle of the wall opposite the entrance door, there is a step down into a small, square room. On either end, there is a bedroom. You and Kelu will occupy one; I shall occupy the other."

He looked around as Sebi approached them, carrying a bowl of steaming broth, followed by the house slave, balancing a stack of blankets in his arms.

Arttarna dropped his own wet coat on the floor and took one of the blankets from the pile. He shook it open, knelt beside Kelu, and wrapped her securely within its warmth. Gathering her tightly into his arms, he picked her up and sat down in the chair one of the guards placed near the fire.

Eshtar took the small cup Sebi handed her and dipped it into the bowl of hot broth. Kneeling beside the chair, she said, "Sip, Kelu," and held the cup to Kelu's lips.

Arttarna shifted Kelu's head close to the cup. Kelu took a tiny sip, closed her eyes, and sighed.

"I'm so cold," she said.

"Drink some more." Arttarna raised her up so that she faced Eshtar, her wrapped body leaning against him.

After she had consumed all of the broth in the cup, she extricated her right arm from under the blanket and, reaching for the cup, proffered it to Sebi for more.

Arttarna smiled. "Well, my dear, I am glad to see that you are feeling better now."

She shuddered. "Is this country always so cold?"

"I do not know!"

Noise at the door made Arttarna look up.

"Master," said Sebi from the door, "Pamba has come to see you."

Arttarna gently pushed Kelu into Eshtar's arms, rose and hurried to the door. "Enter, my friend." The two men joyously embraced.

"Come sit by the fire," said Arttarna, drawing Pamba towards the large hearth. He motioned for Eshtar to take Kelu out of the room and signaled Sebi for another chair.

Eshtar helped Kelu up, the blanket still tightly draped around her. "Kelu, let's go your bedroom. It will be warm by now."

As she passed by Pamba, Kelu went down awkwardly on one knee, trying to loosen the blanket at the same time.

"Kelu," exclaimed Pamba, placing two fingers under her chin and raising her face up towards him, "how you have grown in the year or more since I have seen you."

"Yes, Master," Kelu said, lavishing a beautiful, sparkling smile on him.

Pamba gazed at her in amazement. "I expect we shall see each other often now that you are settling here in Hattusas."

He turned to Arttarna. The two men walked slowly towards the chairs. "Your daughter, my friend, is turning into a spectacular beauty. She has such a dazzling smile."

"Thanks to your wife, she has become adept at running my household. Hepit did an excellent job of teaching her. I'm pleased with that. I'm not so pleased with the extraordinary beauty. She is rapidly reaching the age when she will attract suitors. Already, she has had trouble with Mattiwaza."

"The young prince of Mitanni?" Pamba's body pitched slightly forward in surprise.

"I explained to her that the prince had to marry for political reasons, and then I asked the king to speak to the prince. The prince's attentions stopped. But I have a feeling that Kelu still dreams of him."

"She will forget him as soon as she starts taking part in the life here."

Silence while Pamba gazed deeply into the flames. "King Suppiluliumas expected to accept your credentials as ambassador tomorrow, but both he and the queen are too distraught to receive anyone. The crown prince died this morning. He was not feeling well when he and Their Majesties returned from Gursamassa. The king insisted on taking the crown prince to Gursamassa because that city has some of the most important festivals in Hatti. And it is necessary for the king to participate."

Pamba screwed up his mouth and shook his head.

"The queen, who is a particularly strong and outspoken woman, is blaming the king for the boy's death. She claims that their son, the crown prince, was not feeling well before they left Hattusas.

"Since the boy next in line for the throne is chronically ill, it will probably be Mursilis, their third son, who will become crown prince. It is well known in court circles that the queen does not favor him. So there will be problems." Pamba raised one hand helplessly and let it drop.

Arttarna made snapping sounds with his teeth. "How long will the funeral ceremonies for the crown prince last?"

"At least thirteen days, unless the queen forces the king to declare that the period of mourning has to go on for the full forty days allowed for royalty. His body will be cremated tomorrow. The day after that, the old women will collect his bones from the fire and pour jugs of beer over them. Then the women will throw wine and water onto the flames to extinguish them."

He shifted his chair a fraction away from the fire.

"From that point on, the ritual shifts to the great temple in the center of the city and then to the royal burial gallery. His burial takes place on the eighth day. After that, the rituals are of a more general nature such as prayers and music."

"So the king will not be able to see me officially for at least thirteen days?"

"That is right. But the king might ask you to participate in some of the funeral services."

"I'd like that. I hear that the rock sculptures leading to the most sacred grove are magnificent."

"They are, and an invitation would be a great honor. Other than members of the royal family, very few people are invited because the space in the burial gallery is so small. However, he considers his relationship with Mitanni of utmost importance."

Not sure just how important Mitanni's friendship was to the Hittite king, Arttarna bowed his head in acknowledgment.

"King Suppiluliumas takes religious festivals seriously, so seriously that if one occurs during the summer campaigns, he either has to suspend the fighting or hand the army over to one of his generals and come home to attend the festival."

"I cannot imagine King Tushratta doing that."

"If King Suppiluliumas did not come back to attend these festivals," said Pamba, "there might be rumblings against his throne."

Both men were silent, knowing that King Tushratta didn't take his army to the field every spring, either.

Arttarna recalled the time Suppiluliumas attacked Mitanni. Tushratta handled it by just fading away. Suppiluliumas couldn't find him. The Hittite king ended up sacking Wassukkanni, but without King Tushratta there to surrender, no power changed hands. Arttarna wondered when Suppiluliumas' next foray into Mitanni might take place and if Tushratta's alliance with Egypt would hold up. He intended to find out just how formidable Suppiluliumas' army had become.

After Pamba left, Arttarna rapped on Kelu's door and heard Eshtar's voice call, "Enter." He found his daughter and Eshtar sitting before a bright fire, eating a thick beef stew.

"Obviously, you have recovered, Kelu," said Arttarna, smiling.

"Yes. Eshtar and I are already settled. Sebi hung that piece of fabric up to hide our clothes." She flung her hand out expansively towards the curtain, looking at Arttarna with sparkling eyes.

"I am pleased that Sebi has made you happy."

He noted that Kelu had placed her bed just where it should be against the wall and that Eshtar had placed her mat at the foot of the bed.

He smiled at Eshtar. What a find. She had turned into the perfect companion for Kelu.

"And did you know," Kelu tilted her head importantly, "that the kitchen is in a separate little house right next to ours and that it also contains the slaves' quarters?"

"No. He raised his eyebrows. "Really?"

"Yes." She grinned, pleased with herself. "Rasi and your guards are housed in a nearby alley. And the horses are stabled there, too."

"Well, I will talk to Sebi and investigate all that in the morning. So I shall seek out my own quarters now and see what Sebi has done to make that comfortable."

In his room, Arttarna looked around approvingly. Sebi had created a makeshift desk from a rectangular table and a straight-backed cane chair. He had also fashioned a cozy sitting area by placing a slightly concave chair near the fire.

"Sebi," said Arttarna to the slave squatting silently in the corner, "As usual, you have arranged everything to my satisfaction. You have also pleased Kelu." Arttarna turned his attention to the food on the table. "I think we are going to be happy here."

10

Well bundled in heavy wool, the next morning Arttarna stood in the street observing his new home. Long and low, stone formed about two big hand spreads of the foundation, the rest being mudbrick. From the inside, wooden beams supported the wooden roof. The painted walls of the entrance room showed a bit of artistry. They looked like a sunny summer forest with a blue sky above and colorful flowers below the trees. Even the occasional bird flew among the branches. Thinking about the painted walls, Arttarna grinned. That sunny scene helped take the chill off the room.

Satisfied with the house, he walked towards the close by main temple. Priests already moved about in the temple, intent on the routine daily care of the bodily needs of Arinna, the sun goddess. Each morning, she had a bath, a clean dress put on her, and her breakfast placed before her.

Arttarna observed that, as in his house, massive stone blocks formed the foundation of the temple, mudbrick and wood the structure. He crossed the threshold, entering a large paved court-yard. The temple walls that surrounded him on three sides had floor-length windows. He had never seen floor-length windows before. They must give a lot of light to the rooms, which would be practical in this dark northern climate. He found himself nodding in approval.

On his left, after passing through two rooms, he reached the statue of Arinna. Made of basalt, it sparkled pristinely as the morning light struck the polished stone. How strange to find their major goddess on the left rather than in a direct line with the entrance.

After offering oblations to Teshub, the weather god, he left the temple and walked the short distance to the tremendous mound that formed the palace base.

The way that platform angled upward fascinated him. It made perfect sense to have the palace complex rise up the hillside to become the highest point in the city. He could just make out the tops of a number of buildings above the stout stone wall that surrounded the palace. A ramp led up to the palace's entranceway, a great lion gate flanked by observation towers.

Arttarna let out a soft whistle. Suppiluliumas maintained quite a fortress for his home.

Turning, he glanced over the white-roofed houses, yesterday's snow glistening in the sunlight. With a happy little laugh, he realized that the snow under his feet made a crunching sound with each step he took. Humming a well-known tune, he turned his steps towards home and a hot breakfast.

Midmorning, three no-nonsense raps sounded on the entrance door. Sebi ran to open it. A royal messenger, dressed in a long red wool robe that peeked from beneath the heavy black wool coat, faced him. The man carried a royal staff. Alert black eyes gleamed from the heavily bearded young face. A clay envelope lay in his extended open hand.

"The King of Hatti addresses this message to the ambassador." With precision, the messenger handed the envelope to Sebi, turned in one rigid motion, and marched away.

As he softly closed the door, Sebi examined the small envelope. The king's royal seal inscribed on the envelope made the message official.

Carrying the letter gingerly, Sebi hurried to Arttarna.

One hand shading his eyes, Arttarna sat at his desk, writing.

"Master, the king's messenger has brought you this letter."

Arttarna laid down his stylus. "The Hittite king wastes no time. Break the envelope for me."

Sebi deftly broke the thin clay surrounding the letter and handed the small clay tablet to his master.

After rapidly scanning the letter, Arttarna let out an appreciative grunt. Rising, he carried it to Kelu's bedroom.

Kelu sat before the fire discussing menus and supplies with Cook.

"Kelu," said Arttarna, "you have received an invitation from the queen."

"I have?" Kelu's voice rose to a gleeful squeak.

Arttarna laughed. "Here, read it for yourself." He offered the bit of clay.

Kelu studied the letter intently for several minutes, her hand clapped over her mouth in astonishment. Then she raised sparkling eyes to Arttarna. "The queen has invited me to go to the ceremony?"

"Yes, we are both invited. As the letter says, you are to walk in the queen's retinue with the young, minor female royalty."

In her excitement, she jumped from the chair and flung her arms around Arttarna, burying her flushed face in his green woolen robe.

With a deep laugh, he released her. "Be careful of the letter, Kelu."

"Oh, I forgot." She opened her hand. The small tablet lay in her palm, some of the edges damaged, but not seriously.

"The king's potters fire their clay well," he commented.

His hand on her arm, he guided Kelu back to her seat.

"I'll call upon Pamba to find out what kind of clothes you should wear. There is no time to waste as the ceremony takes place two days hence. I think it best that you have something new of good wool and a warm cloak. I imagine the walk will be long and slow."

Sebi, he called as he left her, "I go to Pamba."

For the rest of the morning, Kelu had difficulty keeping her mind on her household chores. Cook had to prompt her continually on the incompatibility of the dishes she was ordering.

Finally, Eshtar broke in. "Kelu," she said, "you have given Cook plenty of suggestions. Why not let him put them together for you?"

"Good idea," said Kelu. Turning to Cook, she said, "Will you do that?"

"Yes, Mistress." Head lowered, he quickly backed out.

Smugly pleased, Arttarna returned with two tailors, one laden with an armful of dark green wool, the other struggling under a load of soft leather and fur.

Kelu watched them, flabbergasted, as they dropped the bundles of fur, wool, and soft black leather at her feet.

Arttarna grinned at her open-mouthed expression. "You are to have a long-sleeved, round-necked, floor-length dress out of the green wool. It is of good weight and will keep you warm."

"And the leather is for a cloak?"

"Yes, lined with the fur."

Her delighted expression made all his efforts worthwhile.

"I have never had anything so beautiful," she said, stroking the fur.

She looked at him. "What will you wear?"

"For the service, I will wear my official ambassador's robe, but I also will have a warm cloak made."

He addressed the tailors. "When you finish here, come to my room to measure me for the cloak."

After the tailors had gone, Arttarna walked slowly to Kelu's door, his head bowed, deep in thought, nervous, but intent on discussing with her that which he had been thinking about ever since they left Mitanni. He rapped on her door.

Eshtar opened it a crack and peered out. Instantly, she stepped aside and opened the door wide.

"Leave us," he said as he entered.

She bowed her head and slipped out, happy to have time to gossip with Sebi.

Arttarna closed the door.

"Kelu," he said, "I have something personal to say to you. Sit down on the bed. I will use the chair."

With a puzzled frown, she sat on the edge of the bed. He drew the chair in front of her and quickly sat down.

"Is something wrong, Uncle?" Her anxious eyes searched his face.

"In a way, yes. It's this 'uncle.' I do not want you to call me 'uncle' anymore."

"But I thought you liked me to call you that."

"Yes, I did while we were in Wassukkanni, but now that we will be here for several years, I would prefer that you call me 'father.'"

"Father" came out of Kelu almost inaudibly on a breath. She looked at him in shock. After a pause, she said, "I've wanted to call you father so much, even if you aren't really my father." She started to get up, but he stopped her, brushed his hand across his face, and looked squarely into her eyes.

"But, Kelu," he said, "I am your father."

At that, she jumped to her feet. "You are?" she almost shouted. "But why didn't you tell me before?"

He held up his hand and turned away his hurt face.

Kelu slumped back down on the bed, her brows drawn together, her eyelids lowered.

Looking at his hands gripped together in his lap, he said, "The king knows. I had to tell him when I asked him to take you. He asked me to keep it secret. Even though that broke my heart, I did as he requested."

"Does Pamba know?" she said quietly.

"Of course. Both Pamba and Hepit know because you and your mother lived with them." Arttarna covered his face with his hands. "I love you so much, Kelu. I hope you can forgive me."

She didn't answer at first. Tears streamed down her face. Finally, she whispered, "I love you, too."

He caught her and crushed her to his chest, repeatedly gulping to control his own emotions while she wept.

In silence, they sat, their arms wrapped around each other, adjusting to their new relationship as father and daughter.

"Now, my darling," he said, easing her off his lap, "I must get back to writing my report to King Tushratta. I'll join you later."

"Yes, FATHER." She smiled up at him.

He returned her smile, kissed her, and left her. Before entering his room, he summoned Eshtar to return to Kelu.

Kelu sat on her bed, savoring the joy of knowing that she had this wonderful father. Once or twice some questions about her mother crossed her mind. Somehow, right now, she didn't want to think about that.

11

The sun peeped over the horizon in a great orange arc. The answering sky replaced the fading gray with a blue of awesome clarity and depth. The air sparkled and tingled with millions of specks of light that danced in the plunging cold.

Snug in the folds of her new black leather and fur coat, Kelu took her place beside her father for the walk to the great temple, proud that his leather and fur cloak matched her own. In front of Pamba's house, Pamba and Hepit joined them.

Pamba fell in beside Arttarna while Kelu gave Hepit a hug and took her hand to walk closely behind the men.

"My Lady," said Kelu, "my father bought a small chariot for us to use for the funeral procession today. We tried it out yesterday. Father drove and I clung on behind him."

Hepit eyed her curiously. Arttarna must have finally told her of their relationship.

They walked on in silence. Kelu sensed Hepit's curiosity, but didn't want to elaborate just then.

In approaching the great temple, Pamba said, "When we get inside, we will stand in the courtyard with the other officials."

Uneasy with the silent, strange crowd in their heavy cloaks quickly filling the courtyard, Kelu mustered all of her courage not to grab hold of Arttarna's cloak, but nearly stepped on the back of his shoe with each step in her urge to stay close to him. The second the two men stopped, she planted herself at his side.

Arttarna looked down at her, put his steadying arm around her shoulders, and turned his attention to the ceremony.

From where they stood, they could see King Suppiluliumas and his wife, Queen Henti. The king looked solid, a big man. His black beard was carefully curled and his sculpted black shoulder-length curls showed below his tall jeweled hat. The queen, well bundled in fur, also looked big, though not as solidly built. Her severe profile emphasized her long nose.

One look at her, and Arttarna understood her reputation as a grasping woman, determined to get her own way. He could tell that the king was clenching his teeth to control his emotions. The queen kept surreptitiously brushing her cheek. How difficult it must be for them to sit there in front of the crowd in the temple, trying not to break down in tears. He felt sorry for them.

The king and queen sat on thrones that faced the statue of their goddess. Standing in the middle of the small room, she glittered as the morning light shown directly on her.

In front of the royal couple, an exquisite red wool garment embroidered with gold thread lay on an intricately carved chair. A bundle of linen rested on top of the garment. The prince's bones rested within the tight folds of the linen.

Three men brought out a table, placing it between the chair and the royal couple. With great ceremony, they laid hot loaves of bread and steaming food dishes on the table. Having done that, they presented a platter containing other hot loaves of bread to the king and queen. Each took a loaf, broke it, and put it back on the platter.

Next, the cooks and table-men lifted the steaming dishes up from the table, offering them first to the king and queen then to the members of the royal family and to the soul of the prince. Following the serving of the dishes, they offered beer three times to the king and queen, three times to the royal family, then three times to the soul of the prince.

Next, four old women came out of the temple. They walked in lock step, one behind the other, from the temple entrance to the carved chair, picked up the bundle containing the bones and the elegant garment, and marched sedately into the goddess' small room. The king and queen followed slowly.

"We might as well start walking to our chariots," said Pamba to Arttarna. "Is Rasi bringing yours?"

"Yes."

"Presenting the bones to the goddess is a private service. When Their Majesties come out, the old women will be carrying the prince's bones as well as his ashes, which will be transported to the sacred burial place."

Arttarna and Kelu followed Pamba and Hepit out of the courtyard. Others already moved in a steady stream out of the temple grounds. Two richly caparisoned horses, each hitched to an elegantly draped chariot, stood quietly outside the temple door. A rigidly erect, liveried groom waited in front of each chariot, holding the horse's bridle.

"For the royal couple, I presume," said Arttarna.

"Yes," answered Pamba.

Glancing around, Arttarna spotted Rasi standing beside his new horse-drawn chariot.

"Follow us," said Pamba as they reached the chariots. "I'll have my groom watch over our horses while we are inside the sanctuary."

"Very well."

Pamba stepped into his chariot. Hepit stepped in after him, and the groom clung on behind.

Motioning dismissal to Rasi, Arttarna climbed into his chariot. Kelu executed a gay little leap, landing behind her father.

"Are you holding on tight?" he asked, looking around at her.

"Yes," she answered, standing close to him, clutching the sides of the chariot.

They moved slowly into line with the small group of official guests invited to the sanctuary. Moments later, the crowds in the street fell to the ground as the king and queen, standing tall in their chariots, passed them.

Once the royal couple reached the head of the line, the procession of chariots set out, moving smartly towards the sanctuary. They rattled across the wood-plank bridge over the Halys River, drawing a frightened gasp from Kelu.

"Just hold on, Kelu. You are not going to fall into the river," Arttarna said without turning his head.

Nearing the sanctuary, the procession slowed as the chariots' drivers jockeyed for prime space to park their chariots. Pamba quickly appropriated two good spots and tossed the chariot's reins to his groom, who had jumped off the rear step and run around to the horse's head. Arttarna handed over his reins, glancing with pride at his new plaything.

Pamba, Hepit, Kelu and Arttarna walked gravely towards the detached gateway, through the shrine vestibule, to an open

courtyard, and entered the sanctuary. Arttarna stopped capti-
vated by the row of rock-cut Hittite warriors marching along
the massive slab of rock in single file.

Pamba laughed softly.

"Oh! Look at that," whispered Kelu, pointing to more rock
carvings.

"These represent all the local deities," said Pamba.

"For the sake of Hatti and King Suppiluliumas," said Arttarna
in a serious tone, belied by the twinkle in his eyes, "do you have
a fine sculpture of the great Teshub?"

"How could we not!" said Pamba, responding in the same
vein. "Teshub, the weather god, and his consort, Hebat, are
both represented."

Seconds later, he said, "Arttarna, there is your Teshub, about
twice life size, a lion skin over his shoulders, a sword through
his belt, the five horns of a major god in his cap, and boots with
turned up toes. As you can see, he raised one hand."

"He is not only impressive, but overwhelming," said
Arttarna, bowing his head as he passed the high-relief sculpture.

The procession of mourners veered off to the right towards
the royal burial grounds.

"Unfortunately, we won't be going through the larger gallery," said Pamba. "The smaller gallery is the one that contains
the royal family's burial place." He gestured towards the path-
way for the main gallery. "More than one hundred gods are
represented along that rock wall."

They walked into the smaller of the two galleries. That led
into a tiny open-air square with a small stone building in one
corner. Having arrived first, the king and queen sat on thrones
placed in the center of the square. The small number of honored
guests stood in a semicircle behind them. Hepit joined the court
women on the right.

Arttarna noticed two middle-aged women organizing a bevy
of young girls across the semicircle.

"Pamba, does Kelu belong with that group of girls?"

"Yes. I will take her over and introduce her to the two
ladies standing in front." He beckoned to Kelu. "Come along,
Kelu."

"Madam," said Pamba, approaching the plumper of the two
women, "I wish to present Kelu, the ward of the Ambassador

from Mitanni." He placed his hand on Kelu's back and gave her a gentle push forward.

"Oh, yes," said the woman, smiling. "We have been expecting Kelu."

Pamba bowed and started back to Arttarna.

"Follow me quickly, Kelu," said the woman, "as the ceremony is about to begin." She swiftly led Kelu to the rear of the group of girls, introducing her to the princesses as she went.

Kelu barely had time to greet the other girls before loud clapping by four white-robed court officials, standing in a line before the king and queen, announced the start of the ceremony. Total silence fell. All eyes turned to the four men.

"Let the service and play begin," they said in unison.

Two palace servants and a bodyguard stepped into place before the king. Other palace servants and members of the aristocracy assembled behind the king. Three musicians played a selection standing before the king, then walked around behind the king and played another selection while standing behind him. At the same time, priests wearing yellow garments moved to the king's side. They held their hands palms up and turned around and around in place.

At the end of the musical selection, the king and queen went into the little temple. The mourners waited in absolute silence until Their Royal Majesties had exited the temple and sat down. A palace servant handed a golden cloth to the king. He folded the cloth and hung it over his left wrist.

The king and queen washed their hands in golden basins of water. The chief of the palace servants handed each of them a dry cloth. They dried their hands and handed the cloths back. The king took the golden cloth from his wrist and returned it to the chief of servants.

At this signal, the verger began to walk stiffly to the rear, as if marching. He stood behind the assembled guests and waited for the master of ceremonies to start the play, which was the second half of the ceremony.

In a loud, theatrical voice, the master of ceremonies said to the king, "They are ready."

The king answered, "Let them be brought forth."

The master of ceremonies walked to the back, where the verger stood, and said, "They are ready, they are ready."

The singers, carrying lutes, took their positions in the front of the chamber, at the side of the king. The cooks brought in dishes of water and meat. All the people standing in ritual places in front of the king started to dance. Slowly, they pirouetted, slid from place to place within a circle, stepped in and out of the circle, repeated the steps, and separated, some to the right of the royal family, some to the left, becoming spectators.

Two groups of young men entered the open-air burial chamber, one group from each side. The high priest intoned that the soldiers who would take part in the battle had arrived. The men who held copper weapons represented the Hittites, while the men who carried reed weapons played the enemies. The two groups began to reenact an historic battle fought on the coast by the Great Green Sea. The victory had added much territory to Hatti.

At the end of the symbolic battle, the performers who played the Hittites had vanquished their enemies. The area in front of the king and queen was strewn with the bodies of the defeated enemy.

Two of the Hittite soldiers picked up the body of one of the enemy performers, raised it above their heads and proclaimed in loud voices, "We dedicate this dead man to Teshub in thankfulness for giving us the victory."

Whereupon, all the performers knelt before the king and queen as great applause erupted from the audience.

The ceremony at an end, Arttarna, Pamba and Hepit slowly followed the crowd out of the burial chamber, going past the minuscule housing reserved for the priests who cared for the sanctuary.

Pamba turned to Arttarna. "That play is unique. It is only acted in the autumn in honor of the god Yarris. I am amazed to see it presented at funeral rites, even if it is for the crown prince. It must be at the queen's insistence. The play was a favorite of the prince." Pamba scowled. "I can think of no other reason."

Arttarna shrugged and turned to make sure Kelu followed them. He saw her a short distance behind them in animated conversation with a tall, slender, golden-skinned girl. He beckoned when she glanced in his direction.

Reaching his side, she raised her flushed, excited face. "I

met the Egyptian ambassador's daughter. We hope to see each other again."

Arttarna smiled at her. "That is an excellent idea. You should be socializing with the appropriate young women here in Hattusas."

Weeks later, Arttarna paced his room in annoyance. The funeral rites went on and on. The queen was using her power to force the full forty days of mourning. He still hadn't been presented at court. Though disturbed by the delay, Arttarna had not been idle. He had explored the city and its surroundings thoroughly. In general, he found an agricultural society, which he had expected. Mainly, the Hittites grew barley and emmerwheat, which they used to make flour, bread, and beer. Grapes, both for the table and wine production, grew in large quantities. These, along with corn and oil from the almond trees, represented the staples.

In prayerful rotation, the gods were implored to lend their blessing for the corn, wine and oil. He had seen peas, beans, and a little flax. Mining of copper and silver for export helped make the country rich and silver currency plentiful.

From what Arttarna could ascertain, the Assyrians purchased copper voraciously, probably using it to make bronze. The Hittites also used copper extensively to manufacture their weapons and household utensils. International trade flourished.

The people husbanded the same animals as the Mitannians: horses, donkeys, mules, sheep, goats, oxen, and cows.

Hidden in dense, now snow-covered, mountain forests, no city closer than a three-day journey, the capital wallowed in wealth. Yet, Hattusas bristled with military equipment and soldiers.

Arttarna spent day after day examining the city's wall. No army had yet succeeded in scaling those ramparts. The mammoth main wall and projecting towers at one hundred feet intervals, an inner and outer shell of masonry, formed a series of rectangular spaces between the shells which the architect had ordered filled with rubble to make the walls more impenetrable.

The construction of the three main gates intrigued Arttarna even more than the architecture of the walls. Huge blocks of masonry flanked each gate. A steep ramp ran along the outer wall, at the top of which the road abruptly dropped to a narrow lane between the wall's projecting towers. The first gate was set back from the front of the wall while the second was flush with the city-side surface of the inner wall.

Also, a tunnel used for surprise sorties had been constructed under the ramparts. Arttarna intended to tell King Tushratta about that tunnel in his next letter. He decided he better also make a drawing of it for the king.

He still didn't know the exact strength of the army. Attempting to find that out had caused him some trouble. One day, while walking along the top of the city's wall and counting to himself the number of soldiers stationed there, a soldier had placed a sword tip against his chest. Quick thinking and presenting a calm demeanor had enabled him to leave unharmed.

In the meantime, while Arttarna investigated the city, Kelu barely had time for her duties as mistress of his home. The fact that she had so many social engagements pleased him. She was starting to meet women of importance and soon would be a great asset to him for gathering information.

One evening, as Arttarna paced his room, frustrated because he still hadn't presented his credentials to the king, Kelu knocked on his door and burst into his room.

"Well, what great news brings you flying in here like this?"

"The king has just officially ended the mourning for his son."

"How did you hear that?"

"The Assyrian ambassador came home from court while I was bidding good-bye to his wife and daughter. He said that the king announced in full court that the mourning for his son officially ended at that moment."

"You do bring good news, my dear. Probably in the next few days, I shall be ordered to present my credentials."

"I thought that's what the news meant." She hugged him and bounced out of the room.

An adoring smile on his lips, he shook his head, thinking of the contradictions in his daughter's character. In many ways, she still behaved like a child. In other ways, such as her quick grasp of the implications of King Suppiluliumas' announcement, she had matured beyond her nine years.

In the morning, a royal guard appeared at the front door, requesting Arttarna's presence at court in the afternoon. The summons left him little time to prepare, not that he needed time. He had been ready to present his credentials to the king for days.

Just before he left for the court, Kelu inspected him. "In your dark blue, gold embroidered, court robes and your new cloak, you look so handsome, father." She clapped her hands in delight. "You will make a great impression on the king."

He laughed. "That remains to be seen."

Along with many others, Arttarna walked slowly up the ramp that led to the outer gate of the mudbrick wall surrounding the palace. Once inside, he followed the red flagstone pavement leading to the lower courtyard, a three-story building on its own platform. Then, a line of basalt-sculpted lions indicated the way to the huge courtyard where the king held court.

Arttarna allowed himself to get lost in the crowd so that he could assess the situation. From the size of the group, many people would be presented to the king. He glanced up at the royal platform. King Suppiluliumas sat regally on his throne, his feet on a gilded stool. In one arm, he cradled a mace, the other rested on the arm of the throne. The red robe he wore, liberally covered with gold embroidery, set off his black beard and intricately curled black hair. Long gold earrings dangled from his earlobes and a heavy gold bracelet circled his upper left arm.

In spite of the severity of the king's expression, Arttarna thought he detected a twinkle in the royal eye. This king must have a sense of humor. He wondered if he could portray, while lying on his face in front of the throne, an interest in the lighter side of court life. The king might appreciate release from the rigidity of the proceedings.

To his surprise, a young prince from Assyria was called first. Arttarna looked sharply at the boy. Good. He didn't recognize him. He must be a minor prince. Luckily, he would have no knowledge of the way he himself had been treated in Assyria.

Arttarna heard his name called.

"Arttarna, Ambassador from Mitanni, step forward," said the king's majordomo, a heavy, elderly, white-haired man.

Quickly, Arttarna extricated himself from the press of people. With bowed head, he walked to the spot in front of the royal platform indicated by the majordomo and fell on his face before the King of Hatti. As he went down, he allowed a small smile of pleasure to cross his face in hopes that the king would recognize its meaning.

"King Tushratta sends a well-known expert diplomat to me. You are welcome, Ambassador Arttarna. I would see you often in my court."

Arttarna raised his face from the floor, but did not look up. "Thank you, Your Majesty. My great desire is to garner the pleasure of being in your presence."

"You speak well. We will enjoy your participation in our court."

In the silence that followed, Arttarna lay quietly, waiting to be dismissed.

"I understand that you have a lively, attractive young daughter."

Arttarna's heart stood still. What did that statement mean?

"My young princesses are pestering me to allow her presence in their quarters. Now that I have received you, my daughters may get their wish."

"You are most gracious, Your Majesty."

"You may go." The king motioned to his majordomo. "Next."

Arttarna rose. With multiple bows, he backed away, melted into the crowd, and let out his breath. At last, the ordeal was over. Suppiluliumas apparently understood his little smile. He had offered an open invitation. While flattering to himself, Arttarna didn't like the comments about Kelu. For her own sake, he didn't want her to be too frequent a visitor at the palace.

12

The vicious cold winter melted into a lovely spring. At the sign of the first blossoms, King Suppiluliumas sent requests for prayer to the priests of Teshub. "Offer them sweet incense. Beg the gods to reveal which day this spring we should convoke the army and which day would be most propitious to begin the campaign."

The moment the priests proclaimed the omens favorable to summon his army, royal messengers spread out all over the country, visiting every town, village, and hamlet the length and breadth of the mountainous empire.

"Hear the date and place where you are to meet your king for the spring campaign," they cried from the steps of the main temples, then ordered the priests to see that the men obeyed.

On the designated day for the start of the military campaign, courtiers trotted on horseback through the glittering morning sun to the great field beyond the city limits to cheer their troops as they departed.

Women and children lined the borders of the field. Some women daubed at tears, others waved gaily. Occasionally a child ran to an infantryman, demanding a last kiss. Men yelled encouragement back to the women.

Arttarna moved about the field until he found an excellent vantage point, both to see the king and to judge the strength of the Hittite military. With great care, he observed the chariots, the swift, horse-drawn centerpiece of Hittite military superiority. Spoke wheels. Well, yes, he knew that. The curved knives attached to the spokes dealt a deadly blow to anything crossing their path. Only backward countries still used donkeys and solid-wheeled chariots.

In Mitanni, the soldiers had long ago switched to horses

and had just started to substitute spoke wheels for the solid wooden wheels. Large Hittite chariots held three men instead of the usual two. Hummm. He thought that was a new concept. The third man acted as another soldier. And when the battle turned to hand-to-had fighting, he shifted the balance of power in favor of the Hittites.

Amid great whoops and wild cheers from the assembled army, a slowly trotting white stallion pulled the king's chariot onto the field. Drawn up to his full height in the back of the chariot, Suppiluliumas waved as men jumped out of the way of the stallion. The driver drew the horse to a halt in the center of the field.

Suppiluliumas, dressed in the short leather tunic and military helmet of the army, stepped from the chariot to greet his commanding generals. After that, he stepped back into his chariot and, standing tall, he raised his hand for silence. With bowed head, he prayed aloud to Teshub, the storm god, and to Arinna, the sun goddess, asking them to grant his army victory in the spring campaign, and keep his troops safe.

He raised his head. His arm shot out, pointing straight ahead.

The cheers rose to a crescendo, pennants waved, screaming women jumped up and down, children raced alongside.

Emotionally moved by the enthusiasm of the crowd, Arttarna watched the army go. He tried to calculate the size of the Hittite force. Every healthy man in the country must be in the army. The chariots went first, the horses prancing, the three men waving. Arttarna swelled with pride. A Mitannian horseman had originally taught the Hittites how to train and ride their horses. With a rye smile, he admitted to himself that the skill taught by the Mitannians could be used against their own military.

After them came the proudly marching infantry in their short belted tunics. Each man wore a pointy bronze helmet with earflaps and carried a short sword at his waist and a battle-ax in his hand.

With the young men gone to war, Kelu didn't find the social life quite as exciting as it had been. She still saw the young daughters and wives of the ambassadors who were stationed in Hattusas. But even they lost their interest in parties.

Therefore, hearing a knock on the front door one morning, curious, Kelu snuck to where she could listen.

Sebi opened the door.

The palace messenger standing there said, "The young mistress is ordered to present herself at the rooms of Princess Puduhepa his afternoon. A palace slave will arrive to escort her." The messenger walked away, and Sebi shut the door.

"Father," yelled Kelu, running towards Arttarna's bedroom door.

"What is the matter?" Arttarna jerked his door open so fast that Kelu had to grab the doorjamb to keep from crashing into him.

He looked at her. "From the sound of your voice, I thought you had met some dire disaster."

"No. On the contrary, Princess Puduhepa, the oldest princess, has ordered me to visit her this afternoon."

To Arttarna, she sounded self-satisfied. Amused, he said, "Really?"

He glanced away and ran his hand through his hair. "This afternoon, you will go to the building within the royal compound farthest from the entrance gate, the royal residence. I have only been to the largest building, the royal courtyard with the huge storeroom in the pillared basement below. The king keeps copies of all his letters and contracts with other countries in that storeroom. You will never see those records as I will never see the royal residence."

He looked her up and down. "You are a beautiful girl, Kelu, and you are also smart. As you get to know the princess and the royal family, always conduct yourself properly. If you become a regular guest at the palace, you can be another set of eyes and ears for me."

Soberly, Kelu looked him in the eye. "I will, father." She hesitated before saying, "I would really, really like to help you."

Arttarna folded her in his arms.

By the time the campaigning season ended and the victorious troops returned to Hattusas, Kelu had so ingrained herself with the whole female population of the palace that she found herself constantly in demand. The youngest princess clung to Kelu in adoration until her older sisters pushed her away. The queen herself often came to the princesses' part of the palace when she knew Kelu would be present. Some of the young princes began organizing outdoor picnics and plays to which Kelu and the princesses were invited.

These activities filled Arttarna with misgiving. The picnics and open-air plays would stop with the coming of the cold weather; however, if the princes started thinking up pretexts such as games and indoor performances, he would devise some means to ward off trouble. Kelu had not yet become a woman.

Winter appeared early with a treacherous snowstorm that caught many without shelter. Caravans dragged in with stories of frostbite, starvation, and death along the mountain trails.

As the cold deepened, Arttarna and Kelu spent evenings before the great fire in their entrance room, discussing what they heard or saw at the palace. Arttarna told her what he had learned of Hatti, its government, and its courts.

"These people have laws on homicide, assault & battery, slaves, sanitation, marriage, and theft plus dues on land tenure, magical contamination, and arson. And that is only the beginning."

Kelu's mouth dropped open. "I can't believe that."

"It's true. Most cases go before the aldermen first. Incidentally, that's an organ of the people. Our king should take notice of that. If the aldermen consider a case very serious, they will pass it on to an officer of the king. Cases of sorcery require the decision of the king. And there are severe punishments for anybody who violates the judgment of the king"

"There must be a lot of crime here if they need all those laws."

"No, Kelu, probably no more crime than we have in Mitanni. They just have a large legal section they have to keep busy."

"Oh, Father," Kelu chided, laughing.

Arttarna laughed, too.

"It is getting late, Kelu. That reminds me—Eshtar!" He turned to where she sat. apart from father and daughter, but still close enough to the hearth to enjoy the heat of the fire.

"I want to have a few words with you."

"Yes, Master." She put down her handwork.

Kelu looked worried, wondering what she had done wrong that he needed to speak to Eshtar about.

"Do not worry, Kelu." Arttarna smiled comfortingly. "Occasionally, I do confer with Eshtar. So go along to your room."

After Kelu left, Eshtar moved over to stand beside him.

"Kelu's body is changing," said Arttarna. "She looks different. Do you think her time has come?"

"It could happen soon." Eshtar bit her lip. "I've been reducing her activity a little. I don't want her to suffer any stress right now."

"Excellent. Obviously, you are on top of the situation."

Eshtar bowed and backed away, withdrawing from the room.

Arttarna paced up and down. Once Kelu reached womanhood, he felt sure men would be chasing after her. He knew that one day a man would take her for his bride. He prayed to Teshub and Hebat that her husband would be worthy and of his own nationality, not a prince who would keep her in a palace far from him. She had already mentioned one Hittite prince who paid her too much attention. That unnerved him. He needed to speak to her about it.

The next morning, he asked her to come to his room. "Sit down, Kelu. I want to ask you about Prince Zidantas. From what you say about his attentions, I am concerned and want to hear more about him. Why does he make you uncomfortable?"

She squirmed in her chair. "Whenever the young princes join us in the ladies' quarters of the palace, Prince Zidantas rushes over to me and sits close. He grins at me, and he makes comments about my robe, my jewels, my manners, my smile, everything. I hate him," she said with passion.

"Do you know where he stands in the royal line?"

"Yes. I asked Princess Puduhepa about all the princes to cover my interest in Prince Zidantas."

"Good thinking."

"He is just a minor prince. His mother is one of the king's concubines." She sneered.

"Kelu," said Arttarna, pursing his lips, "Do not sneer. Many a fine minor prince could offer you a better marriage than your position warrants."

She blushed and bowed her head.

After this exchange, he decided to go to court and request an audience with King Suppiluliumas.

As he walked towards the palace, he pulled his fur cloak

tightly around him. Already, more than a year had passed since their arrival in Hattusas on a day just as snowy as today. The time had passed quickly. But he couldn't think of much that he had done as ambassador that was of any importance to show for all the time he had already spent in the city.

He entered the royal courtyard, glanced around, and walked to the side where the petitioners stood. There, remaining quiet and holding he head bowed, Arttarna waited.

"Arttarna," King Suppiluliumas boomed, "it has been a while since you have appeared in court. Come forward." Seated on a low dais in his tall-backed chair on its high square, solid, lower portion with the square footstool in front of him, Suppiluliumas beckoned to Arttarna.

Walking towards the king, Arttarna wondered if the king climbed awkwardly onto the footstool to turn around and sit in the chair or if some court lackey placed a wooden step for him to step onto before stepping onto the footstool. He prostrated himself before the king.

"Come, come," said Suppiluliumas. "Rise." He waited until Arttarna had risen before saying, "What brings you here?"

"My daughter, Your Majesty."

A surprised expression on his face, Suppiluliumas said, "Your daughter?"

"She often visits the royal princesses, Your Majesty. Many times, some of the royal princes are in attendance. Kelu is about at the point where she will be taking particular interest in young men, and I do not want her getting any ideas."

Suppiluliumas flung his head back and laughed before saying, "The idea of a union with one of my minor sons pleases me. She is a charming, well-brought-up young lady from a fine aristocratic family. Now that you bring the subject to my attention, I might consider it." He smiled broadly, the interview at an end.

Stunned, Arttarna left the court. His meeting with the king had had the opposite effect from what he had intended. Sick at heart, he started to walk home slowly. As a last resort, if he whispered to the king that her mother had been a slave, Suppiluliumas might take her anyway as a concubine. That would destroy Kelu.

He dragged himself home, told Sebi to bring him some wine, and shut himself in his room.

For a long time, he sat by the fire and fought with himself, argued with himself, trying to come to an acceptance of the situation. He didn't see how he could prevent the prince she hated from taking his adored child.

Still, Kelu had not yet reached womanhood. Once she did, how long would he be able to stave off the king if Zidantas told his father that he wanted to marry her? He didn't know how long it would be before she became marriageable. Certainly not long. Probably nothing would happen, though, until after the king returned from his upcoming spring campaign.

Finally steeling himself to face whatever came, he left his room. As he reached the main room, he snorted. Never had he been in this state. Even after Khelpa's death, he had somehow faced the loneliness.

Fortunately, Kelu kept to her room that night. He didn't have to watch her and listen to her girlish chatter, his love for her turning a knife in his soft stomach area.

As Arttarna surmised, nothing more than the prince's constant attention happened while Suppiluliumas was away conducting his spring campaign. He watched Kelu as her body changed and she continued to mature. She became more beautiful than ever.

One sparkling day in late summer, after the return of the troops, Arttarna and Kelu, joking and laughing, returned from an evening at the home of the Egyptian ambassador. Bowing, Sebi opened the door for them.

Walking into the middle of the room, Arttarna said, "What is it, Sebi?"

Sebi shut the door carefully before answering. "King Suppiluliumas has presented a gold necklace to Young Mistress," he said, holding up the heavy, glittering chain.

Instantly, the joy in their faces vanished. Both knew what the necklace meant.

"And?" said Arttarna, his face a mask.

"No, no." Kelu hid her suddenly bloodless face in her father's side.

Sebi's sad eyes met those of his master. "For Prince Zidantas," he said softly. One index finger moved in the direction of Kelu. "For Kelu and Prince Zidantas," he said.

"I will not marry him," screamed Kelu. She covered her face with her hands. "I won't. I hate him."

"Darling, darling child." Arttarna pulled her close and held her.

She shuddered, exploding into sobs.

Motioning Sebi away, he picked up Kelu and carried her to the chair where he usually sat. He settled himself as comfortably as possible, cradling her, and letting her weep. The gasping and hiccoughing went on and on. Tears occasionally formed in his own eyes, but he shook them away. Numbness settled on his soul.

In the small room between the two bedrooms, Eshtar and Sebi discussed the situation. Eshtar's usually pleasant expression was drawn in anger. "It's absolutely wrong," she announced, stamping her foot, "That lovely child shouldn't be forced into that kind of a marriage."

"The master will do what he can," said Sebi. "There's nothing we can do."

"Yes there is. We can comfort her." Eshtar hurried to the kitchen for a small bowl of cool water and a rag. Carrying these, she entered the main room and knelt beside Arttarna. He shifted Kelu slightly in his arms so that he could tilt her face up towards Eshtar.

Eshtar caught her breath. Kelu's face was red and swollen, her eyes closed shut. Leaning over, Eshtar gently wiped Kelu's forehead, one puffy eye and cheek then the other, making a soft clucking sound at the same time.

Sebi silently appeared beside Eshtar with more water in a larger bowl. Eshtar dipped the cloth, wrung it out, and wiped Kelu's eyes and cheeks carefully.

After a number of such ministrations, Kelu heaved a great stuttering sigh and opened her eyes. Her glance went from Arttarna's worried face to Eshtar's, to Sebi's. Finally, she touched Arttarna's cheek. "I will try to control myself, Father."

He blinked rapidly and looked away, afraid he might break down, too.

"Kelu," he said when he was sure he had control of himself, "I will negotiate as long an interval as the king will allow before I sign the final contract. There is nothing more I can do without causing an international incident."

Arttarna knew he couldn't possibly get the king to extend the time past winter. Delaying it any later would mean that the preparations and festivities would extend into the spring campaign.

Arttarna met the king with misgivings. Immediately, Suppiluliumas announced that he intended to have the contract signed in ten days.

"Please, Your Majesty," said Arttarna, "we cannot possibly be ready in ten days." He added, "Kelu has some ideas about when she would like to get married."

"When is that, if you do not mind my asking?" His sarcastic tone let Arttarna know that Kelu had no business suggesting her marriage date.

Arttarna bowed, humiliating himself before the Hittite king. "Her favorite time of year is midwinter. She had hoped to marry on a cold, white, crystal-clear day, to match the white gown she intends to wear."

Suppiluliumas thought that over. "White for purity."

"Yes, Your Majesty."

"I do not like it one bit, you understand, but if the day means that much to Kelu, I designate the first pure-white, sunny, cloudless day during January and February for the signing of the marriage contract." He slapped the arm of his throne. "Scribe, broadcast the news."

Arttarna backed out of the king's presence, bowing, and hurried home. At least half a year would elapse before Kelu would have to enter the Hittite royal family. Despite his relief that he had gained some time, his chest hurt at the thought of losing her.

On hearing the news, Kelu said nothing. She bowed her head in acceptance. She knew her father had achieved the best terms he could. The bitter tears, the fantasies of running away, killing herself, she relegated to the past. However, the minute the news was broadcast, the complaints started.

She complained about the prince to Eshtar.

"He forces me to do things I do not want to do."

"Such as what?"

"Well, making me stand in the pelting rain. I was wet through to my skin and starting to shiver. He just laughed at me. His older brother, Prince Mursilis, saw us and yelled at him. He took me to his sister's apartment."

Eshtar reported the conversation to Arttarna. "He bullies her. Kelu is afraid of him, Master."

Arttarna brought the prince's strange behavior to the attention of the queen.

She dismissed the behavior. "He's just flaunting his power, trying to dominate. He'll get over it."

Arttarna walked home in a sullen mood. Now, he not only feared for Kelu's happiness, he feared for her safety. He had seen the prince just once when all the young princes attended a public session at the request of the king. He didn't stand out particularly. All of them had curly black hair, black eyes, and were well built except for the sickly eldest. But what Arttarna remembered most was the way Prince Zidantas held himself. He would brook no opposition to his demands. Arttarna decided that the prince was trying to break Kelu's spirit and make her totally subservient to him. His blood boiled.

While the beautiful late summer weather held, Prince Zidantas demanded that Kelu ride with him in the mornings. On his horse, he performed dangerous tricks at breakneck speed and ordered her to do the same. Sometimes, she tried, but almost always failed. He laughed uproariously each time she failed.

After that, Kelu stopped trying, letting him have his laughter at her expense. The pell-mell racing on the royal horses he forced her to ride frightened her, and she began to fear him.

She confided her fears to Rasi when she visited her father's stables to see her little black mare. She talked to the horse, intending Rasi to overhear.

Concerned for her safety, Rasi started to ride in the group of attendants who followed the pair.

One autumn day, when the prince ordered Kelu to ride a fiery, half-broken in young stallion, Rasi whispered to her, "Kelu, sit low and keep a tight rein on the horse. Try not to let him have his head. If I see you're in trouble, I'll come help you no matter what the prince says."

Rasi watched the two of them leave, riding fast, before quickly mounting his own horse. He rapidly outdistanced the attendants riding in a pack.

The prince galloped ahead, showing off. "Come on Kelu," he yelled. "Don't be such a scaredy, stupid female. I'll force you to ride well and keep up with me."

Her young horse pranced in his gallop, recognizing the flung dare in the voice.

Kelu lowered her head and yanked on the reins, slowing the wild horse against his will.

She heard a high, frightened equestrian scream. She looked up, startled. Why that scream?

Prince Zidantas' horse, flying mane, head flung up, eyes bulging, bucked upright in terror. Prince Zidantas lay on the ground. The horse, still screaming, bolted and started to gallop fitfully back towards the royal stables. Kelu's fiery mount started to buck.

Rasi kicked his horse into a gallop. Glancing to his right, he saw another rider headed straight for Kelu in a collision course with him. The man appeared intent on Kelu, unaware of Rasi or anyone else.

Rasi readjusted his course. He barely brushed the other horse and rider, but enough to confuse the man who dropped back then galloped away.

Without slackening his speed, Rasi swerved and reached Kelu's side. "Let go the reins and loosen your toe stirrups," he yelled, leaned over and grabbed her. Literally throwing her in front of him, he turned the horse and galloped towards Arttarna's stables, keeping a tight hold on Kelu.

At their stables, he jumped down and helped her off the horse. "Are you able to walk home, Mistress?"

"I think so. I'm shaking."

"We'll go slowly. I intend to speak to your father about this."

Kelu half-smiled, appreciating the anger in Rasi's voice.

"Take that horse I rode back to the royal stables," he yelled at the stable boy as he led Kelu away.

Arttarna sat by the fireplace in their entrance room. A small fire burned just enough to take off the morning chill. He turned his head when Kelu entered, followed by Rasi.

"Father, Father," Kelu ran up to him, fell to her knees, and buried her face in his lap.

"What's the matter?" he exploded fearfully, lifting her face to look at her. "You're pale."

His glance shifted to Rasi. "What happened?"

"From what I could see," Rasi said, "a small wild animal sprang up almost right under the hooves of Prince Zidantas' horse, scaring the animal. The crazy, half-brained animal screamed and reared wildly. The prince must not have had complete control of the reins because he first pitched forward then tumbled backwards, falling to the ground headfirst. I saw nothing further because at that point, I grabbed Young Mistress. The prince had forced her to ride a horse that wasn't completely broken in. The whole situation was dangerous, Master. That boy is no good."

Arttarna nodded. "I know, Rasi. I am going to see what I can do to put a stop to these horseback rides."

He looked around. "Sebi, go to the palace and find out how the prince is."

He stroked Kelu's head. "You need to go to bed and rest."

"Send Eshtar to me," he said to Rasi.

Rasi stood motionless with bowed head. "There is more, Master."

"Well?"

"A man I've never seen before came riding up towards Kelu. I had the strong impression that he meant to harm mistress. Fortunately, I got to her first." Rasi scowled.

Arttarna looked away, his face still, unpleasant associations surfacing in his mind. "What did he look like? Would you recognize him again?"

"I think I might recognize him, Master, but I'm not sure. He looked like all the other stable boys." Rasi was silent, thinking. "I've never seen him around the stables before."

"Call Eshtar."

Rasi hurried from the room.

"Kelu, we'll find out how badly the prince is hurt first then we'll decide what we must do to put a stop to these rides." He gritted his teeth. "No matter what the queen says, the boy is going to change his tactics or I am going to create an international incident."

Rasi returned with Eshtar.

"You wish to see me, Master?" Eshtar knelt at his side. Rasi hung in the background.

"Put Kelu to bed. I want her to spend the rest of the day resting."

He turned to Rasi. "Thank you, Rasi. You may go. This kind of thing will never happen again."

Rasi's head bobbed up and down in agreement as he backed towards the kitchen door.

Alone, Arttarna stormed about the room. He would have to face King Suppiluliumas and tell him bluntly that the marriage was called off, the gifts returned. The king could ask for his resignation as ambassador if he wanted to, but before that he would whisk Kelu back to Mitanni with Eshtar and Sebi. He'd do without Sebi until he got home himself. He had had enough of putting her through this agony.

The door quietly opened. Sebi entered, gave Arttarna an amazed look, closed the door and fell on his knees.

From the end of the room, where he had stopped his storming walk when the door opened, Arttarna watched in surprise.

Keeping his facedown position, Sebi almost shouted, "The prince is dead."

He raised his head.

In silence, master and slave simply stared at each other in relief.

Finally, Arttarna said, "I'll go tell my daughter."

His face shining like the sun, Arttarna walked through the door to the bedrooms.

Only then did Sebi rise and shoot his arms into the air in an ecstatic gesture of joy.

13

Arttarna knocked softly on Kelu's door.

"Enter," came Eshtar's voice.

He found Kelu lying on the bed. Eshtar knelt on the floor beside her. Kelu raised the arm thrown across her eyes to look at her father. Seeing his big smile, she pushed herself up on her elbows, her face eager, questioning.

"Prince Zidantas is dead," he said.

She flopped back on the bed. Her chest heaved up then relaxed in a big sigh. "Thanks to the gods."

"I do not know what the king's decision will be, Kelu, but at least you will not have to marry Prince Zidantas."

"What do you mean, the king's decision? I'm free now."

"Not yet, I am afraid. The king could still demand that you marry one of his other sons."

"No, Father, please." Kelu sat up.

"We will have to wait and see. If I think it inevitable, I will send you back to Mitanni with Eshtar and Sebi before he makes his demand."

He eyed her sternly. "In the meantime, we have a good number of days concerned with the funeral and aftermath to get through before the subject of any further marriage can be broached. You will have to look and act distraught at all times, and I mean at all times, when you are in public. Having anybody discover that you are overjoyed would be dangerous."

He narrowed his eyes. "Do you understand what I am saying?"

"Yes, Father, I do."

"All right. I will leave you to get yourself in the proper mood." He turned and left the room.

Kelu looked at Eshtar. "What should I do?" Her brows contracted into worry lines.

"There must be someplace where the ladies buy cosmetics. I'll go find it. You stay right where you are until I come back." Eshtar hurried out of the room, closing the door behind her.

Kelu leaned back and shut her eyes, completely relaxed.

Eshtar returned, carrying extra kohl, powered lime, and powered raw sienna of a deep red color. Laying her purchases in a row on Kelu's dressing table, she said, "Come sit here."

With meticulous care, Eshtar worked the white plaster into the skin of Kelu's face and neck. Using the raw sienna, she smeared it around Kelu's eyes, working in dabs of kohl until Kelu looked as if she had spent hours crying.

Finally, Eshtar said, "I think that will do, Kelu. Lie down and rest now."

As expected, by noon, Kelu received notice from the palace that the contracted bride of Prince Zidantas must appear at his cremation. The ritual burning of the prince's body would take place at sundown in the underground chambers of the main temple. The proper attire, a dark blue, high-necked, long-sleeved robe, arrived with the order to appear.

Dressed in the dark blue garment, looking very pale and red-eyed, Kelu arrived at the temple, accompanied by Arttarna. A royal guard escorted them below ground into the warm, square stone vault. Two thrones, as well as a number of chairs, had been placed in three rows in front of the large oven. The royal guard took Kelu to the chair right next to the prince's mother, who sat next to Queen Henti.

The queen scanned Kelu's face intently before giving an almost imperceptible nod and turning her attention to the priests.

The young prince's mother sat unmoving. A constant flood of tears poured from her eyes, forming large wet spots on her dark blue robe.

Arttarna found himself placed in the front row of ambassadors. He noticed Pamba standing among the Hittite aristocracy. Their eyes met and each looked away.

The priests droned on and on. Tired, Kelu hung her head as if grieving and shut her eyes. After a while, she raised her head. She hoped she hadn't jerked in her sleep. Surreptitiously, she glanced at the queen. But both the queen and the prince's mother seemed to be so caught up in their own grief that they paid no attention to her.

Finally, the service ended. During the entire walk home, Kelu held her father's hand tightly.

"You did well, Kelu."

"I'm glad you were there."

They walked on in silence.

The following day, Kelu again sat next to Prince Zidantas' mother on the main floor of the temple while the old women performed the ceremony of collecting the bones and putting them in a silver jar with fine oil, followed by all the other rituals customarily performed on the second day.

The third day, she sat pale and red-eyed, numb with boredom. She even managed a tear or two when she knew the royal couple were watching her.

At last, the worst ended. Through the thirteenth day, she attended rituals of a more general nature, becoming thoroughly bored with the whole process. Twice, both Kelu and her father were asked to participate in part of the ritual. During one part, Kelu gallantly shed some tears and allowed Prince Zidantas' mother to comfort her. Even the queen leaned over and gave her a few supportive pats.

The king refused to permit the mourning to continue after the fourteenth day when the spirit of the prince, alive in his ashes, was laid to rest in his niche in the royal tombs.

That night, Kelu heaved a great sigh of relief as she settled happily into the chair Sebi placed for her in front of the entrance room fire.

"You carried yourself extremely well, Kelu." Arttarna smiled at her. "I am proud of you."

She blushed.

"Be careful, though. However, as you go into public places now, you don't need the pale face and red eyes, but you need to appear sad."

"Eshtar was a marvel with the makeup. Everybody thought my tears were for grief. Actually, they were from boredom." Kelu laughed in delight at the memory of her performance and the queen's supportive pats.

Winter's cold, ice, and snow quickly followed the funeral

so the mourning intended bride of Zidantas didn't receive as many social invitations as usual. Kelu and Arttarna spent more time together. To her delight, he taught her to act as his secretary, having her write some of his simple letters to Queen Iuni.

Occasionally, in court, King Suppiluliumas asked Arttarna how his daughter fared, but said nothing more. Starting to feel uneasy about the king's behavior, he asked Kelu to repeat the lineage of the royal princes, telling him what their relationship was to Queen Henti. From her recital, no prince seemed far enough removed from the queen's ancestral line to make Kelu an acceptable royal wife. He stewed. He knew something was afoot.

While he sat at his desk one morning, fretting about his inability to recognize what the king intended to do, Sebi entered and handed him a letter from King Tushratta. In the letter, Tushratta ordered him to transfer his sphere of activity to the Minoan Court at Knossos. The Minoan Court! He had no knowledge of the Minoans. He knew of them, naturally, but little else. They lived on a big island in the Great Green Sea. Just what was he supposed to do there?

In his next communication, Tushratta elaborated on the reason for the transfer. It had come to his attention, he wrote, that the Minoan king was seriously courting the king of Egypt. That made him nervous. *I want you to find out whether this new alliance would change Mitanni's close relationship with Egypt. The day might come when I will need Egypt's arms against Hatti. I have to be sure that I can count on Amenhotep IV, or, as he now styles himself, Akhenaten, the young king of Egypt, if Suppiluliumas tries to attack Mitanni.*

The Hittite king had already conquered several small kingdoms around the perimeters of Mitanni. And Tushratta still had vivid memories of the time Suppiluliumas invaded Wassukkanni. That onslaught wasn't successful, but the next time might be different.

During one of Pamba's frequent visits to Arttarna's home to talk undisturbed, Arttarna told him that he would be moving to Knossos in late spring.

"It will probably be after King Suppiluliumas leaves on his annual military campaign."

"He will be sorry to lose you. Every time he sees you in court, his expression brightens."

Arttarna laughed. "Maybe, but since the disaster with Zidantas, he has been more reserved."

"That is not against you. The queen is hounding him to marry Kelu to another of the young princes. She has not been specific about which one. The king want to be sure of his politics before committing himself."

"You mean whether he needs a foreign marriage to cement relationships?"

"Exactly. But the queen is being forceful. She is smitten with your daughter."

Intense silence followed. His hands gripping each other, Arttarna dropped his head.

Pamba stared at him. "My friend, I am confused. Marrying one of the young princes would be an excellent match for Kelu, better than most young women of perfect aristocratic lineage could achieve. Considering how deeply she cared for Prince Zidantas, I would think she would be amenable to marrying another prince. And for a young woman of her background—"

Arttarna cringed. "You are right," he said forcefully, realizing that he had to be careful in what he said to Pamba about Prince Zidantas. He had no fear that Pamba would divulge Kelu's background, but as a Hittite, Pamba might be offended if he found out how much she hated Zidantas.

"Marrying one of the princes would be a great match for Kelu. However at the moment, she is so hurt by everything that has happened, she needs time to recover. I do not want to push her. And there is another reason that I am half-embarrassed to admit to you. I know that one day she will marry and take up a new life. But right now, I cannot face that. Married to a Hittite prince, I would lose her forever."

Arttarna shook his head and gazed into the fire. "I am supposed to be a strong man, but I am worse than a limp cat when it comes to my daughter."

"Well," said Pamba slowly, keeping his eyes fixed on the fire, "I sympathize with you. She is such an attractive young woman that many well-positioned men will request her hand in marriage. You have a hard decision ahead of you." Pamba sighed.

They spoke of other things.

That night, Arttarna lay sleepless. Pamba's revelation meant he might need to change his plans. Should he send Kelu to Mitanni immediately and have her brought to him in Knossos? If he kept her with him in Hattusas, which is what he wanted to do, he might be inviting trouble. On the other hand, he now had a pretext to have her stay away from the royal family.

Grieving for Zidantas would make it possible for her to remain out of the social circle here. He would not tell the king of his departure until just before he left on campaign. That way, the queen wouldn't have time to push him into a decision. Arttarna decided that he would attend court as usual, but try to avoid any discussions with Suppiluliumas. His mind went round and round about what to do.

Winter dragged on longer than usual. Suppiluliumas began to fuss. The cold weather frustrated his plans. The whole royal family contracted colds that lingered. His stuffy nose made the king grumpy, and the queen kept to her rooms, rarely appearing in court. One of the dowagers became quite ill with a fever. The queen didn't have time to think about Kelu.

Arttarna decided not to send her to Mitanni.

As the snow melted and the weather softened, Suppiluiumas' plans turned to action. Full of energy, he roamed constantly about the palace, followed by his entire court, issuing new orders as he went up and down the corridors.

Arttarna chose his moment well. Suppiluliumas scheduled a meeting with his generals right after the morning session at court with the intention of keeping the court session short. Arttarna stood with those having a plea.

"We will hear nothing that takes a long time." Suppiluliumas sat fidgeting and twisting nervously on his throne.

At his turn, Arttarna dropped face down on the floor and said, "Your Majesty, my master, King Tushratta, has ordered me to go to Knossos. In sorrow, I leave your beautiful city soon after you start on campaign."

For some seconds, the king sat pulling his beard and staring at the prostrate body of Arttarna. At last, in an aggrieved voice, he said., "We are sincerely sorry to lose you. As a sign of our friendship, we will order our son Telipinus, Chief Priest in the kingdom of Kizzuwadna on the southern coast, to give you hospitality while you await a ship to Knossos."

Artarna repeatedly touched his forehead to the floor in thanks.

Pamba came by that evening. "I heard in court that you told the king you were leaving. Apparently he is delighted that he does not have to make a decision about Kelu. And the queen is too worn out at the moment to think about her. That is why he is so anxious to have his son host you."

Pamba continued. "Officially, Telipinus is in Kizzuwadna as great priest. In truth, he controls Kizzuwadna's king, preventing any move by the king towards independence."

Arttarna raised his eyes to the ceiling in thanksgiving.

Within a day, Arttarna received a note from King Suppiluliumas saying that he had ordered his son Telipinus, Great Priest of Kizzuwadna, to house the ambassador from Mitanni and his attendants.

A message also arrived from Telipinus inviting him to stay in his palace on the coast as long as necessary.

Perfect, reflected Arttarna. As ships sailing up the coast stopped at Kizzuwadna before going to the great grain port of Ura and beyond, he expected to find ships headed for Knossos.

As the days went by, Arttarna attended court, trying to judge exactly when Suppiluliumas would start his campaign and warned his household of imminent departure. Most of his guard force, he sent back to Wassukkanni with orders to await further communication. The minute the king announced the departure date for the troops, he would sell his local slaves, take six days for his obligatory round of good-bye visits, and leave the city. For six days, he could manage with his remaining staff of four guards, Eshtar, Sebi, Rasi, and Cook to run his establishment. He just wanted their departure to be seamless.

As travelers, he and his few people could attach themselves to some caravan of merchants plying the trade routes that crossed Hattusas. Nights, they would stay in the caravanserai along with the traders and their animals.

Pamba looked anxious the night he stopped by. "Arttarna," he said, "I think it would be wise if you left Hattusas immediately after the king leaves."

"Why? What makes you say that?"

"I don't know why. I just think you should go as soon as possible. I feel uneasy about what the queen will do. You know how headstrong she is when she has decided on a course of action against the king's wishes."

"Yes." Arttarna breathed heavily. "It will be difficult to get my affairs in order in that short time, but I will take your advice, Pamba."

Suddenly, Suppiluliumas announced the date for the troops to depart. The spring campaign had begun. Two days hence! Arttarna scratched his head. Two days! Not much time.

The following morning, he sold his local slaves. After that, he called together his four remaining guards and ordered them to take the household goods and their personal effects out of the central city under cover of darkness and to set out for Mitanni with the morning light.

"When you arrive in Wassukkanni, tell the other guards to leave immediately for Knossos and find me some suitable accommodations."

Later, looking around the emptied house, he felt already on the road to Kizzuwanda and the sea. He told Kelu and his remaining staff to be prepared to leave at a moment's notice and swore them to absolutely secrecy.

Kelu worked herself into jittery excitement at the idea of a clandestine exit from Hattusas. Arttarna had ordered her not to leave the house under any circumstances. She didn't dare to even poke her nose outside. He made sure that Sebi and Eshtar understood his order.

As usual, the court turned out to see the king leave Hattusas at the head of his army. Pamba and Arttarna stood side by side as pennants waved and drums beat.

Looking straight ahead at the marching troops, Arttarna said softly, "We will probably never meet again, Pamba. Your company has meant much to me. I shall miss you."

"Agreed, we shall probably not meet again. I, too, have found much pleasure in your friendship." Pamba walked away to speculate on the king's military goal with some of his Hittite friends.

Arttarna walked slowly home, keeping a deliberate, leisurely pace. Sebi opened the door. "Sebi," he said, "go to the stable and get Rasi."

He paced the floor, waiting for them to arrive. An abrupt

pounding on the front door sent Kelu and Eshtar scurrying for the bedroom.

Drawing himself up to his full height and looking as authoritative as possible, Arttarna opened the door. A royal messenger stood before him.

"Her Royal Highness, Queen Henti, orders Kelu, daughter of the ambassador from Mitanni, to appear before her at noon tomorrow."

Arttarna solemnly nodded his head.

The messenger handed him a small clay tablet containing the order in writing, turned and walked smartly away.

"Sebi," Arttarna said when he realized that the two men had come, "call Kelu and Eshtar."

"Rasi, you get Cook."

"Thanks to the gods," he murmured, "I have rid the house of servants, slaves, furniture, and all I cannot carry with me."

Once his small staff stood in front of him, Arttarna said, "There is a change of plan. It means immediate action."

He continued, "Rasi, have my horse and Kelu's mare ready for us. Leave two horses for Sebi and Eshtar then take the four remaining horses out the city's main gate, as unobtrusively as possible." Turning to Cook, he said, "You go with Rasi and help him. Take with you your personal belongings and any of the general things you can carry. Put blankets on all the horses. Hide clothing under them. You are traders here. Go to the caravanserai area outside the city and make arrangements for six people to sleep tonight."

He pulled at his lip, thinking. "Cook, you stay at the caravanserai with the horses and keep watch over our belongings at the place where we will sleep."

"Rasi, you wait for the four of us at the road coming from Hattusas near the caravanserai."

He turned to Sebi. "Sebi, you and Eshtar each take one of the horses and load whatever you can carry. We must divide what is left among us. Make sure to leave the stable in enough time to get to the outskirts of the city and pass through the main gate a little before sundown. Meet Rasi on the road from Hattusas. I will leave with Kelu at dusk, just before the gate closes. The three of you wait for us."

From under his lids, Sebi glanced sideways at Eshtar and

met her glance doing the same thing. Both quickly looked straight ahead.

"That is all." Arttarna looked at each one of them in turn. "May the gods go with us."

With sober, anxious faces, they dispersed to carry out their assigned tasks.

Between them, Kelu and Eshtar put on all their clothes and divided Kelu's jewelry. That consisted mainly of what Prince Zidantas had given her. Fortunately, many of the valuable presents the queen had given her had already gone with the four guards to Wassukkanani. Kelu put the gold chain Arttarna had given her so many years ago around her neck. Eshtar put Kelu's other gold necklace as well as the string of carnelian and lapis lazuli around her own neck, planning to hide them with her cloak.

Later, Sebi came to Arttarna. "Master, all is well. I spent a little time shopping around the main gate. I saw Rasi and Cook ride through. Nobody paid any attention to them."

"Well done, Sebi." Arttarna smiled at him. "You and Eshtar go next. Are you ready?"

"Yes, Master. Eshtar and I have divided the remainder of the household goods."

"Leave a few for me plus blankets. Remember, we are traders."

Kelu hugged Eshtar. "We will see you shortly."

Arttarna and Kelu watched them leave the house then stood looking at each other.

"There being no place to sit, Kelu, let us sit on the floor." They sat face to face in silence.

Finally, Arttarna said, "I think until after we pass through the gate, I'll take you up in front of me as if you were a child. That way, we can keep your face hidden in case there are any questions tomorrow about a young woman."

"What has happened, Father?" Kelu burst out. "Something must have happened." She leaned towards him.

"Yes. You are ordered to appear before the queen at noon tomorrow."

Kelu groaned and covered her face with her hands.

Arttarna put his index finger on the back of one hand. "It is all right, Kelu. We will be gone before she finds out." He retrieved his finger. "Shall we go?"

"Yes."

Wrapped carefully in her cloak, Kelu followed her father from the back of the house through the kitchen and into the stables. Light still sifted down from the sky onto the beaten-earth road, leaving the corners dark. Arttarna put the lead rein on Kelu's mare, assisted Kelu onto the back of his horse and mounted behind her.

"Now, Kelu, curl up as best you can against me so you look small. I want any of the Hittite guards who see us to think that you are a child. After we leave the gate area sufficiently, you can ride your mare. We must get as far away as possible in case the queen sends soldiers after us. By the day after tomorrow, we should be out of danger."

The guard at the gate was busily urging the last stragglers through when Arttarna and Kelu reached it. "Get that stuff out of the way of the horses," the guard yelled at an old man who had dropped a load of pots and pans off a donkey just as Arttarna rode up.

The guard grabbed the donkey's reins and pulled the animal to the side.

Slowly, Arttarna guided his horses around the mess and walked his stallion down the embankment on the other side of the main gate. On reaching lower ground, he trotted the horses until he reached the small clump of trees he had in mind.

"These trees will hide us from being seen from the gate, Kelu." After he helped her onto her mare, they galloped off into the deepening dusk.

Rasi, Sebi, and Eshtar waited exactly where he had told them to wait. With relief all around, Rasi led them to the caravanserai, a solid mudbrick building secured by a heavy door. Sturdy pillars divided the interior of what had been an open-air courtyard into squares of pounded earth. Groups of men and animals occupied most of the squares.

Rasi led them to the earthen square where Cook, looking unhappy, stood surveying the cold supper he had spread out on one of the blankets. Three oil lamps lit the meager repast. He had taken what food he could pack with him, but it didn't amount to much of a meal.

Kelu wrinkled her nose at the food.

"Eat," commanded her father.

"It's the stench of the animals in the square next to us. It makes me sick."

"Get over that. These people may not like the smell of our horses."

Kelu dropped her eyes and picked up some bread.

Once they finished eating, Arttarna addressed them all. "Now," he said, "I will tell you why we left so abruptly." He hesitated. Cook stopped picking up the remaining food. The others froze where they were.

"The queen demanded Kelu."

"No," cried Eshtar, pulling Kelu close.

"So we leave here at dawn." He looked each one in the eye, and each one nodded agreement.

He then told them where to set their blankets on the ground. "Kelu, you and Eshtar will sleep between Sebi and me." He rose and indicated to Kelu and Eshtar where they were to lie. "Rasi, you and Cook take the top and bottom spots."

Sebi woke first. He could hear others in the big room starting to stir. He walked noiselessly to the door of the caravanserai, opened it a crack, and looked up at the sky. The stars were beginning to fade, but no light lined the horizon yet. Dawn would break soon. He turned back to wake the others.

"The first bit of light will appear at any moment, Master," said Sebi, hearing Arttarna stir. He gently kicked Rasi's foot.

"Ooooh," Rasi groaned and shook himself.

That roused the others.

The light had become a long widening golden brightness as they galloped off.

"The sun will rise behind us until we turn south," said Arttarna, leading the way along the road to the sea.

Arttarna's tired, dirty band rode into the great priest's palace courtyard at Kizzuwadna on the banks of the Pyramus River. Slowly, Arttarna dismounted, glad to be off his horse.

The front door swung open. A large, impressive-looking man dressed in scarlet, stepped out, to stand on the edge of a slight stone rise surrounded by men-at-arms.

Arttarna moved forward and bowed from the waist. "I am Arttarna, the Ambassador from Mitanni, here at the invitation of King Suppiluliumas and of his son, the great priest."

"Our great priest extends welcome," said the man. "He has journeyed here from his palace in the capital of Kizzzuwadna specially to receive you, and he brought four of his wife's women to care for your daughter."

"I am humbled at his generosity and offer my deepest thanks."

"Follow me, Ambassador. I will take you to the great priest. The rest of your party is to wait in the open court."

Arttarna motioned to the others to follow and walked inside the front door. Kelu skittered across the intervening ground to walk right behind her father. Eshtar hurried to catch up with her. Sebi, Rasi, and Cook hung back, but followed the other three into the palace. The men-at-arms closed in behind them.

In the square, open court, people walked about, stood in groups talking, or waited quietly for an audience with Telipinus. In front of the great priest, Arttarna dropped onto his knees.

Telipinus, dressed in purple and bejeweled with curled hair and beard, sat on a throne exactly like his father's. Rather pompously, he said, "I am Telipinum, Great Priest of Kizzzuwadna. My father, King Suppliuliumas of Hatti, sent word of your coming. You and your people are welcome here for as long as it takes you to find a ship leaving for Knossos."

"I greatly appreciate your hospitality," said Arttarna from his position on the floor.

"You may rise."

Arttarna stood, but maintained a humble stance.

"My Master-of-Household will show you to the rooms I have designated for you and your immediate servants. One of my wife's slaves will take your daughter and her woman to my wife's quarters. I will expect you at the banquet later."

Telipinus turned to the master-of-household who stood on his right. "Take these people to their accommodations."

A woman approached Kelu, bowed and said, "Come with me, My Lady."

Kelu glanced at Eshtar and followed the woman, Eshtar right behind her.

The master-of-household bowed and motioned to Arttarna to follow him. Arttarna bowed deeply before Telipinus and left the court, accompanied by his men.

With the barely risen sun the following morning, Arttarna

prowled the port. Ships jostled each other in the available spaces on the jetty. Other ships lay at anchor in the harbor entrance, waiting to unload their cargo. Men ran back and forth along the dock, and sailors yelled at each other in frenzied activity. Slaves shuffled jars of grain, so large that it took two to carry one jar.

In response to Arttarna's queries of ships' captains about their destinations, the answers came back: Sidon, Tyre, Prelusium, Troy, everywhere but Knossos. The following day, he sent Sebi out.

Five days passed before a ship arrived from Tyre, headed for Knossos after two days of cargo exchange. Arttarna arranged passage for six people with the captain and argued with him over the horses. The captain adamantly refused to take more than four. "They take up too much space. I have cargo to pack."

Arttarna paid him well, but still had to leave four horses behind. He fumed. "I will have to give them to Telipinus," he said to Rasi. "I hate to do that because I do not know what I will find in Knossos. We might need them."

Late the next day, another ship arrived, heading for Knossos after a fifteen-day layover in Kizzuwadna's port city. Arttarna persuaded that boat's captain to transport his four remaining horses and hired a man to care for them until they were put aboard.

With a relieved sigh, he waited for morning.

14

Arttarna swung up the gangplank, trailed by a flushed and bouncing Kelu.

Behind her, Eshtar frowned. Her young mistress had become a bit cocky, not even holding onto the rails.

Cook, following Eshtar, held his head high. He planned to perform his job of feeding the master and his servants with elegance, even if they were aboard a ship.

Rasi, coming up the gangplank behind Cook, knew he faced life in the hold with the master's four prized horses. So be it, he would do his job expertly.

Once on deck, Arttarna turned and watched Kelu and his servants cross the gangplank. Knowing that they were going to spend the next few days on the strange Great Green Sea affected them all. Their reaction to boarding the vessel showed it.

"Kelu," said Eshtar, poking her in the back, "calm down. You are jumping around like a young colt."

"But I have never been on a ship before." Kelu flung her long, shiny black braid back and danced up the gangplank. "Oh." She grabbed the rail as the ship rocked, making the gangplank shake.

"See." Eshtar smiled smugly at her.

Kelu held the rail tightly until Arttarna ordered her to jump off the plank to the deck.

He motioned to her from the opposite ship's rail. "Come over here until the sailors finish arranging our accommodations."

She ran to him. "You said we were each to have a little hut."

"We are. The sailors are tying them down on deck now, one right next to the other. You can see them there in the back of the ship."

She squinted disapprovingly. "They are kind of small."

"You will have enough room to sleep comfortably, Kelu," he replied tersely.

"Can Eshtar sleep in there, too?"

"Probably not. She will have to sleep on deck at your door."

"I don't like her being alone on deck."

"She will not be alone. Sebi will be in front of my hut. Rasi and Cook will be nearby."

"Rasi doesn't need to sleep in the hold?"

"No. The horses sleep at night so he can come up on deck."

Satisfied, Kelu turned to gaze at the buildings on the wharf, the high palace and surrounding houses. "This is a big city. I had no idea."

"You rode your horse through the noble section of the town on the way to the palace when we arrived and came here this morning in a closed cart. No wonder you have little sense of the city. It's a big city, a famous city. That's why King Suppiluliumas made his son great priest of this country. Telipinus controls Kizzuwadna on behalf of his father."

"Telipinus is very handsome."

"That is enough of that, Kelu. I do not want any more comments on Hittite princes. Besides, I thought you had given up young men after what you have been through recently."

"Not men in general, Father. Only one, Zidantas."

"Well, that puts things in a different light." Arttarna scratched his head, envisioning the trouble ahead.

Kelu pointed across the water. "I though we were going to sail on a great sea. I can see the other side of this water."

"This is not the Great Green Sea. We are moored on the Pyramus River. After we lift anchor, we will sail out the mouth of the river into the Great Green Sea."

"Will I be able to see that?"

"I don't know. We might not reach the sea until tonight."

Kelu bit down on her lower lip, turning over in her mind the possibility that she might miss her first glimpse of the sea. "I'll ask the captain," she announced, all motion as she flitted off.

Arttarna watched her go, the love in his eyes dominated by unease.

After talking to the captain, Kelu settled cross-legged on the deck in the special place the captain suggested to watch the water change as the ship left the land mass and ventured into the Great Green Sea.

Off and on during the morning, Arttarna returned to the ship's rail to watch the land and the river. The sea interested him as much as it did Kelu. His spirits jumped when he saw choppy water replace the calmness of the river and the land start to fall away. He turned to see how Kelu was reacting.

Hurrying to her, he shook his head in amazement. How could she have fallen asleep when she was so excited about seeing the Great Green Sea?

"Kelu," he said softly. Then as she stirred, he said, "We have just left the river."

Kelu sprang to her feet and grabbed the railing, looking forward, backward, at the water, at her father.

"Why didn't you wake me?" she asked him accusingly.

"I did not realize you had gone to sleep."

He told her to look carefully behind them. "You can see where the river rushes into the sea. The color of the water changes."

She watched the shoreline recede for several minutes in silence, feeling the ship rock more than before. "The water is rougher here. The sea isn't as smooth as the river."

The boat rocked pleasantly all night. In the morning, the breeze whipped up white caps as far as she could see and became stronger as the day progressed.

Late in the afternoon, a sailor rushed up to the captain where he stood talking to Arttarna. "Captain," he gasped, "we see yellow in the sky just above the horizon in the distant left."

The captain whirled on the sailor. "Yellow!"

"Yes, Captain."

"I'll have a look." The two men ran forward, leaving a curious and disturbed Arttarna.

He peered at the left horizon. He didn't see any yellow.

Soon, the captain returned. "We have changed course to try to avoid the storm that colors the distant sky. It would be best if you keep your daughter inside her hut and you stay in your own. Keep your personal slave with you, but the rest will have to stay with the horses in the hold."

Arttarna glanced sharply at the bright blue sky. He wiggled his shoulders indifferently and called Kelu from the rail on the forward deck.

"The captain thinks a bad storm is brewing and suggests we stay inside our huts," he said when she reached him.

Her eyes widened. "A bad storm here on the sea?" A shudder passed down her spine.

Arttarna patted her shoulder. "He is not sure yet, but stay in your hut until we hear otherwise I have to send Rasi and Cook to the hold. Eshtar will stay with you, and Sebi will be with me."

Ever obedient to his wishes, Kelu hurried to her hut and looked around. Her mat fit snugly. She saw no way to use Eshtar's mat. She flopped full length on the mat.

Eshtar entered and closed the door. "The wind is rising."

Kelu scrambled into a sitting position. "Sit beside me. I'm afraid of the storm."

"You know what storms are like in Hattusas—wind and hard rain. That's nothing to fear." Eshtar bent down to sit next to Kelu. The ship pitched unexpectedly, and she fell across Kelu. "Oh, my! Did I hurt you?"

"No." Kelu moved close to her. They sat in silence.

The ship started to pitch more violently. Kelu stifled a scream and threw herself onto Eshtar. They sat wrapped in each other's arms as the pitching became more frequent. They could hear small objects banging around on the deck.

Suddenly, Eshtar said, "I don't feel very well."

Kelu raised her head to look at her. "Your face is green."

"I'm going to throw up." Eshtar leaped up to get to the door, but vomited and fell across the mat.

Trembling in fear, Kelu lay down on the lower portion of the mat.

The violent pitching repeatedly threw her against the heavy, coarse fabric of the hut. She tried to roll some of the mat against the wall to soften the pounding she suffered. She noticed Eshtar, looking awful, pull herself into a corner and curl up.

Water began to splash against the hut and seep under the walls. In a feeble, shaky voice, Kelu began to repeat all the prayers that she knew to Teshub, the storm god.

Hours went by. Blackness descended. Water splashed around

the hut. Groans came from somewhere. From where, she couldn't tell. She dozed. Feeling bruised and sore, she opened her eyes. She could barely make out Eshtar slumped against the hut wall. The ship's motion had not abated.

Kelu put her hand down on the mat to steady herself. "Ugg." She quickly withdrew her dripping hand from the cold, sopping mat.

"I'm going to my father." She addressed the torped Eshtar.

Between the rocking of the ship and slipperiness of the mat, Kelu had trouble reaching the door. Once there, she managed to open it enough to crawl out. The wind caught the door, banging it shut behind her.

In the dim light and the pouring rain, Arttarna's hut looked far away. Unable to stand against the buffeting wind, she started to crawl towards his hut. A surge of water washed over her, knocking her against her own hut. The ship creaked in agony. Determination gripped her. If they were going to die, she intended to die with her father. She reached his door.

Bracing herself against the doorpost, she raised herself onto her knees and knocked on the door. "Father, Father," she called above the howling wind.

No answer came. She called again. Finally, perspiring and panicky, dripping hair and wet clothes, she turned the doorknob and yanked.

The door opened enough for her to see Sebi's head. Just beyond his head, wet wool lay plastered over her father's legs.

The ship bucked, sending her sprawling and coughing in sloshing water. The door snapped shut. Regaining her balance, she again turned the knob and yanked hard, quickly inserting her head and shoulders inside the hut in case the door swung shut again.

She could barely make out the upper part of her father's body at the opposite end of the wet mat. Both bodies lay in water. She looked sharply in the faint light to make sure their faces remained above the waterline. Her father looked as awful as Eshtar and Sebi.

The smell of vomit pervaded the room. Wind rushing in along with a lot of rain and splashing water caught the door and opened it wide. Struggling, she managed to pull it shut then found herself in complete darkness, wedged against the door.

Knowing that Arttarna's head was to her left, she wiggled in that direction, bracing against the side of the hut and using the small space left by Sebi's legs. Eventually, after nervously inching along, she bumped into the end of the hut. Stretching out her arm, she cautiously, experimentally, dropped her fingers where she thought her father's head would be.

Hair. She put her whole hand down, holding her breath. More hair, thick hair. She sighed in relief. Moving her hand down, she found his forehead, his eyes and nose, her hand a feather moving over his features.

Dipping her hand in the water, she passed it over his face and repeated the motion. He groaned once. He lived. Hot tears streamed down her cheeks. Overjoyed, she touched his face again.

She leaned back against the wall of the fabric, resting. Reaching over as she had been doing strained her muscles, making her back ache.

"Father, it's Kelu," she whispered. He didn't respond. Again, she started to bathe his face. Crying, she kissed her fingers and laid them on his forehead. Then, she crawled over Sebi's legs and pushed them away so that she could sit with her hand on her father's head to await a watery death.

The roaring of the wind, the surging water, and the creaking ship played a mournful tune as accompaniment to her thoughts of death.

Suddenly, she opened her eyes and tensed. Blackness prevented her from seeing anything, but she thought her father had moved. Oh, was it her father or that the ship now rocked normally? She could hear the rain, pelting rain, but sensed no lashing of the ship.

Again, Arttarna stirred.

"Father, Father." She leaned over him, felt for his wet garment and wiped his face.

"I am dying," he said.

"No," she almost shouted, hope returning. "You are going to live. We all will live. It's only raining now."

After sitting and considering the situation, she said, "You need sleep." She squirmed around, trying to push Sebi's legs against the side of the hut.

Sebi cried out.

She said, "Sebi, turn around and move over against the wall."

Groaning, he tried to move.

By degrees, under her guidance, the two men managed to rearrange themselves. Sebi now lay hard against the opposite wall, Arttarna prone in the middle of the mat. Kelu kept her place next to Arttarna, but pressed her body tightly against the door.

Suddenly, it opened. She found herself flat on her back, looking at a candle held by the captain. The flickering flame made his face look grotesque.

He took in the situation at a glance. "I'll send some sailors to sweep all this water and vomit out. We can't do much else until morning light. That won't be long now."

"I'm trying to get my father to sleep," Kelu said limply.

The captain looked exhausted.

"Has everybody been sick?" he asked.

"Everyone except me."

"We're lucky we're not at the bottom of the sea," he muttered, turned and left.

Kelu scrambled unsteadily to her feet. Almost instantly, two sailors with candles appeared. They pulled Arttarna and Sebi out of the hut and pushed them to the side. Deftly, with swipes of long-handled brooms, they cleared out the hut, sending the water and vomit splashing towards the ship's rail. Finished, they laid the two men back inside and closed the door.

Kelu opened it to sit down in the doorway. Arttarna moaned and shivered. She spread her hands helplessly. His robe was soaked; her garment was wet. How could she possibly keep him warm except with her own body? Oh!

She poked Sebi where he lay against the side of the hut.

He groaned.

"Sebi, move over against your master for warmth."

Sebi shivered and started to move.

"Good. Now move closer, Sebi." She watched him struggle. "That's right."

When Sebi reached Arttarna's side, both men sighed.

As soon as Kelu heard their even sleep breathing, she stood up, sore and aching, to go check on Eshtar.

Water still covered the floor of her hut, and the stench

gagged her. Kneeling in the near dark, she felt around until she touched Eshtar's body.

Still curled up, her face covered with vomit, Eshtar was breathing. Using Eshtar's wet robe, Kelu washed her face and tried to straighten her legs.

"No," Eshtar cried, feebly.

"Come on, Eshtar," Kelu said, "lie flat. You will sleep better." Standing up, she pulled the slave around before her own knees crumpled.

Several hours later, Kelu woke with a jolt. Light streamed in the open door. It took her a minute to realize that she lay across Eshtar's limp, sleeping body. Shouts came from the deck. She jumped up and rushed to her father's hut.

Sebi and her father blissfully slept, their faces a normal color. Leaving the door to their hut open so they would breathe in the warm, fresh air, she returned to her own hut, lay down beside Eshtar, and promptly slept.

15

"The storm has blown us way off course," the captain informed a weak, but alert Arttarna. "It will add many days to the trip. And, among other things, you will undoubtedly find food scarce."

Arttarna's stomach churned unpleasantly at the very mention of food. His staff reacted the same way when he repeated the conversation to them. Though Cook tried valiantly to make the remainder of their supplies attractive and tasty, most of it went to the hungry crew.

Kelu walked around the deck each morning, anxious to get onto land. She could hardly contain herself the day their ship sailed into the harbor at Katsambas. From the deck of the docked ship, the warehouses, the brown earth, the buildings, the town looked so inviting that waiting for her turn to disembark brought tears to her eyes.

The harbor inside the long, curving breakwater, seemed to extend as far as her eye could see. All along the high dock, tied broadside fore and aft, ships swayed gently. From ships anchored alongside those, passengers and workmen crossed and recrossed short, wooden gangplanks. Long, low buildings nestled among trees that came right down to the water. Kelu gloried in the trees. She had never seen such lush greenery.

Throngs of men moved around among the ships, in and out of the buildings. Naked to the waist, tight, brightly colored skirts clothed them to mid-thigh. Her eyes bulged. She turned to see her father's reaction.

At the rail, Arttarna's head swiveled back and forth, taking in the whole scene. He showed no emotion. Suddenly, his face lit up. Smiling, he turned to Kelu. "Our guards have arrived," he said.

Kelu searched the crowded wharf until she spotted a small group of men wearing the long belted robes of Mitanni. She stretched her shoulders. The sun felt warm and wonderful on her back.

"Let's go," said Arttarna.

With Eshtar behind her, Kelu followed him across the gangplank.

"Where is Sebi?" she asked her father's back.

"He and Cook are helping Rasi with the horses."

Once they reached the ground, the guards drew near. "The palace is within walking distance, Ambassador," the lead guard said. "The priest-king keeps excellent roads throughout the island."

Rasi brought Arttarna's stallion on a short lead. Arttarna eyed the horse. "He is a bit wobbly." He stroked the animal's soft nose.

"He hasn't got his earth legs yet," said Rasi

"Neither have I." Arttarna smiled. "I will take Kelu on him since we lost her mare in the storm. The rest of you manage on the other two."

"I'll walk, Master," said Sebi.

Eshtar eagerly said, "I'll walk, also."

"Four horses came days ago," the lead guard said. "It's a good thing a couple of us happened to be on the wharf."

"And, Master," announced another guard, "we have a house."

"Excellent all around," said Arttarna. He mounted the stallion. The guard handed up Kelu. Placing her in front of him, he said, "Indicate the way."

"Pass these buildings here on the wharf." The guard pointed a finger. "Then you'll see a wide road bearing to the right. It leads directly to the palace."

Ordering the others to follow him, Arttarna slowly walked the horse through the crowd of people and past the wharf buildings. The road, wide enough for two horses abreast, stretched in a fairly straight line through a lovely wooded area. Kelu exclaimed over the greenness of the trees, the beautiful bird songs, and the constant flow of people.

As they reached the cultivated fields and private homes, she praised the abundance of crops and the dun colored houses with their deep red pillars.

"It is gorgeous," she cried, clapping her hands.

Arttarna agreed.

The road curved around a clump of trees. As it straightened out again, Kelu excitedly pointed her index finger at a large tan building. "Is that the palace?"

"I doubt it," Arttarna answered. "I have the impression the palace is extremely large." He looked around. "Kelu, I think we ought to give the horse to Rasi. Everybody seems to be walking." He turned and beckoned Rasi.

"Help Kelu down," he said when Rasi stood beside him. Dismounted, he handed over the reins. "Tell Sebi to send the guards with you to our house and come to me himself at the palace entrance."

With that, he smiled at Kelu. "Ready?"

"Ready." She glowed with happiness. "How different this place is from Hattusas. The sky is blue, the sun is warm, and lots of people are outdoors."

"It's different alright and I admit it is a pleasant change."

They walked along companionably.

"Oh," Kelu sung out. "There is the palace, that great tan building with red columns. It is the same tan color as the houses. I do not understand it. This road is beautifully laid with large, square, polished slabs, yet the palace and the houses look like"— she hesitated—"mud, as if they were peasants."

"What you think is mud, Kelu, is in reality finely dressed stone. I advise you to withhold your opinion until you have a more solid foundation to judge the people and their building practices."

"Oh, look," gasped a distracted Kelu, waving her hand at two young men rounding the corner of a building. Each rested a hand on the flanks of a magnificent long-horned bull. "Look at their clothes, their tiny waists, and broad shoulders."

"Watch yourself," said an amused Arttarna who had carefully observed the two young men before his daughter discovered them. "That bull is the finest specimen I have ever seen."

"They do not have many clothes on." Kelu ran her hand along her neck to ankle dress. "They only have the band cinching their waists and those short tight skirts. I'd like them to have more clothes on. That embarasses me."

Arttarna could hardly keep from laughing. "I think the

walkway to the palace is on our left where all those men and women are moving up and down."

"All the men are dressed in different colored little skirts," Kelu observed. "And the women wear long bright gowns."

They started along the fine, smooth-stoned walkway, eagerly gazing at the great palace before them. The only occupant of the small guardhouse greeted Arttarna.

He responded, "I am Arttarna, the new ambassador from Mitanni."

"Our priest-king is holding court today. You may enter."

A tall man dressed in a cinch-waisted skirt, a fitted blue hat with a gorgeous feather projecting from the front and arching over his head, said, "Excuse me; I am going in and will be glad to show you the way."

Arttarna nodded graciously. "Kelu," he said sharply as she hung back, watching the colorful crowd of people.

They walked through a retaining wall into a large open court full of people, walking back and forth and talking in groups. Arttarna's gaze swept the people before fastening on the finely fitted white gypsum squares paving the courtyard. What a marvel of skilled workmanship.

The guide threaded his way through the crowd to the palace entrance, an open-fronted-covered lobby. A single centered red wooden column supported the roof. The painting of bull games on one wall attracted Kelu's attention, but she didn't dare speak to her father. Guards opened the double entrance doors.

Suddenly shy, Kelu dropped behind Arttarna as they started to walk along the wide corridor. She gazed at the wall designs. Painted men and women bearing gifts, musicians, and priests, walked beside her. She thought it much more beautiful than the painted walls at home in Mitanni.

Abruptly, the corridor turned left. A short distance further brought them to the central court. Kelu stopped and stared. The open court stretched way beyond anything she had ever seen. Staircases led up to the second story. Doors opened off it. Red columns held up balconies. Red outlined some doors. Buff-colored stone constituted the walls. The whole court was paved with the smooth stones she had been walking on. She felt overwhelmed, breathless.

Everywhere she looked, men and women in bright clothing

moved through the room. She soaked in the elegant cut of the women's dresses, but she couldn't really figure out what she thought she was seeing. Some of the older men wore long robes much like that which her father wore. All the young men had on those skimpy, tight skirts. She fluttered her eyelids and lowered them.

Their guide turned right. Kelu's eyes hit two sets of red pillars, a raised black pillar in the middle. Along the top of each set of pillars sat a row of small double horns. Two large sets capped the square stone pillars on either side of the edifice. Next to that, a wide staircase rose and beyond that, four doors were outlined in red paint.

Kelu saw the guide enter the second door, followed by her father. Afraid of getting lost, she hustled after them, only to find herself in an oblong room full of people and Arttarna disappearing through a door opposite. In panic, she shoved her way between some men and ran to the door.

Just inside, her father dropped to the floor in front of a man in a long white robe seated on a high, straight-backed chair. The man wore the most beautiful crown she had ever seen, all multicolored feathers, mostly blue with several about the length of her forearm, curving out backwards from the top. Seeing Arttarna drop to the floor, Kelu quickly fell onto her knees, dropping her body forward, face down.

"Rise," said the priest-king.

Arttarna rose, Kelu following suit.

"You are from Mitanni. You are welcome here."

Kelu heard that much before becoming engrossed in the wall painting behind the king. Great beasts with curly fur and long curly tails sat on green underbrush and stretched their necks to smell tall, green plants. Unabashed, she stared, fascinated.

Then, her eyes traveled to the group of women sitting a short distance from the side of the throne. She flushed, realizing that they had stopped gossiping to look at her. She desperately wanted to hide. Those women were more elegant and more sophisticated than anybody in the Hittite court or in Mitanni. They sat on the floor in their beautiful puffed-sleeved, full-skirted dresses. She looked sharply. The bodices with the high, round necklines, were made of sheer, sheer fabric. Kelu shuddered slightly. Would she be expected to dress like that?

The ladies' dresses and lovely long, dark, curls cascading from their headbands, enthralled her so that she hadn't paid attention to her father's conversation with the king. She caught a softly whispered, "Kelu, bow," as he went down.

She flattened herself on the floor and thought she heard delicate tittering from the group of ladies. Oh, if the ground would only open up, she would gladly sink into oblivion. Never had she been so mortified.

Arttarna started to rise. She rose awkwardly and edged as close to his back as she dared. He started to back away from the throne and bumped into her.

He stopped, bowed to the king and said, "Your Majesty, please forgive my incompetent daughter. She is not used to such grandeur as we find here."

"She will get used to it." The king smiled at Kelu. Even in her embarrassment, she managed to twinkle back at him.

Her father took firm hold of her arm. They both backed towards the door to the anteroom. An elderly man in a long gown opened the door, and the assembled courtiers swallowed them up. Arttarna turned around, swinging Kelu as he did so by the firm grip on her arm. He rapidly retraced their steps across the central court, the corridor, and the south porch.

The minute they descended the steps, Sebi scrambled off the ground and ran to them.

"We have the use of the house left by our last ambassador," he said when he reached them. "It's been vacant since he died so it needs a thorough cleaning, but will adequately fill our needs. Eshtar, Rasi, and Cook are there, and I have hired some servants."

"The guards?" Arttarna inquired.

"They live there, too. It's very large." Sebi sounded apologetic.

"Good." Arttarna nodded in agreement.

"It is within an easy walk."

"Lead on." He looked at Kelu. "Do you think you can keep your mind off the local atmosphere enough to reach our new home?"

Kelu blushed. "Yes, Father."

Soon, her feet tapped out eager staccato on the stone pavement as she kept one step ahead of Arttarna.

"You now seem anxious to see our home," he said to the back of her head.

"As I run your house, Father, yes I am anxious to see it." Kelu turned a bright face to him.

"And a good mistress of my house, you are," he said, smiling at her.

"This is our house," said Sebi, gesturing at a round, tan, sandstone house on their left.

All three stopped to observe the house.

"It has those lovely round red pillars against the tan and a second story," Kelu said, her eyes aglow.

"Being round, it should give the rooms an interesting shape," said Arttarna. "Let us go in."

Sebi opened the door for them.

Kelu stopped just inside the door. "There is only a long hall," she objected.

"There are seven doors," said Sebi, using his forefinger to count down the doors. "Each door leads to a group of small rooms. The door number is specific to the rooms. Number one is the storage area." He moved to the door on his right and placed his finger on the number one.

"The doors all have different colors," observed Kelu, looking down the hall.

"What is number two?" Arttarna walked slowly along.

"Cleaning and upkeep."

"The blue door, the color of water." Arttarna nodded. "And three?"

"That is the central room with the shrine," answered Sebi. "Go on."

"Four gives access to your private quarters."

"The green door. Nice." Arttarna turned the doorknob. "I assume one of the others is the kitchen area."

"Six. Five leads to the second floor. And seven is the sleeping area for your servants. The guards are in there along with all the others."

"Very good." Arttarna pushed open door numbered four. "It is another corridor with two doors," he said in surprise.

"The one on the left leads onto the large stairwell going to the main living rooms of the house. They're rather luxurious."

Sebi lowered his eyes as he said this. "The hearth is on a raised platform. And a window looks out onto the light well. The other door opens onto the stairwell going to the latrine."

Though determined to let Arttarna see for himself, Sebi couldn't resist a description. "It has a wooden seat with a round hole and a little extension. A removable bowl lies just under the hole. Towards the top in the corner, two abutting slabs have little pipes. Water jets out and drains away through outlets in the wall." He sounded absolutely ecstatic.

Arttarna opened the left-hand door and ascended the wide staircase.

"Well, well," broke from him as all three entered the large, beautifully furnished reception room.

"I love this room," Kelu crowed, running to the light well, an open space within the structure of the building that let sunlight stream in as delicately as a fountain. "Oh, look, there is a little garden down below."

Arttarna followed her. "And there's a door leading out to it."

"Can we go down?"

"Right now, I want to see the latrine, then we better find Eshtar and the servants Sebi has hired."

He turned to his slave. "This is a rather large house, Sebi. It is going to take me some time to find my way around."

"You'll spend most of your time here, Master. You have a whole suite of rooms all around the light well."

"Oh, the bedrooms." Kelu skipped around the light well.

"You will set up one room for my office, Sebi?"

"I will, Master."

They descended the stairs. At the base, Arttarna opened the the latrine door. Sebi waited.

"You are right, Sebi," Arttarna said from the doorway, "that is quite an establishment. I will bathe before dinner." His eyes sparkled in anticipation. "I would like to have a look at our kitchen." Arttarna started for the door to the corridor. "Kelu," he called up the stairs, "we are going to the kitchen area. You may want to come."

"Yes, certainly," she called, jumping down the stairs two at a time.

"Careful," he snapped and followed Sebi.

Sebi opened the red door, numbered six. Instantly hustle

and bustle greeted them. At a table covered with cooking pots, a scullery maid sorted vegetables. The heady aroma of cooking food pervaded the room. A burly young male entered carrying two buckets of water. Eshtar in conversation with Cook, immediately broke away and hurried to Kelu.

"Well," commented Arttarna, "it looks as if the whole staff were in the kitchen."

The scullery maid dropped to her knees, as did the youth and three others, two women and a man, who hurried in from different rooms.

"Sebi, are these your hires?"

"Yes, Master. The two women are for the housework, the man for heavy work. These two,"—he motioned at the scullery girl and the burly boy—"to help Cook."

"That sounds reasonable." Arttarna raised his voice. "You have been told by my man Sebi what your jobs are. He will be your overseer in all things." Momentarily, he hesitated. "Rise and go on with your work."

Turning back to Sebi, he said, "Where is Rasi?"

"There are no stables here. Rasi went off with the horses and a guard to show him where they stabled the other four horses."

"Very well." He looked at the burly young fellow. "Have the man build a fire in our hearth to take the chill off this long empty house."

"Kelu," Arttarna called as he started to leave.

Deep in conversation with Cook, she said, "I will follow in a moment, Father."

Arttarna nodded and returned to the delightful comfort of his private quarters, Sebi behind him.

Before many days had passed, a messenger appeared at their salon door with an invitation for Kelu to attend a gathering in the queen's hall.

"So, it has started already," commented Arttarna, undecided whether to be pleased or angry.

"I am going to wear my own clothes." Sitting across the fireplace from Arttarna, a determined set to her mouth, Kelu moved to the edge of her chair.

"There is no reason you should not," he said. "You are not a Minoan. You are not required to follow their fashion."

Kelu let out her breath, eased back in her chair, and relaxed, the tension gone from her face.

Arttarna studied his beautiful child and wondered how many sons this queen had.

At the appointed time, a royal guard appeared, young, muscular, and wearing the skimpy skirt that embarrassed Kelu. She walked stiffly behind him, thanking her gods that she didn't have to talk to him.

The guard led her across the central court from where they had originally met the king and up the grand staircase. The broad, shallow treads of the gypsum steps made ascending easy. The gorgeous red columns that she adored followed the staircase on a stepped parapet. She walked up the middle, feeling like a queen herself. Light streamed across her from the well, casting her shadow over the red columns.

On the first landing, the guard motioned Kelu towards a door, bowed, and hurried down the stairs.

Kelu walked into an elegant, long room flooded with light. Her mind barely registered the predominantly blue and white decoration before a smiling court lady greeted her. "Please come with me to meet our queen."

The queen sat on a straight chair rather than the sloping chairs that everybody else used. Her ladies surrounded her. Kelu gracefully dropped to one knee and bowed her head.

"Rise," said the queen, "and come over here by me."

Kelu advanced slowly until she considered she was the proper distance from the queen and stopped.

For a few long minutes, making Kelu uncomfortable, the queen stared at her face. Finally, she said, "You are the most beautiful young woman I have ever seen. I would be pleased to have you grace my court." She indicated where she wished Kelu to sit and picked up her conversation about the latest bull-leaping trials.

Kelu looked at the exposed breasts of the ladies and quickly looked away. That fabric was extremely sheer. She studied the painted walls. The ceiling had white concentric circles against a blue background. The wood around the doors was painted the opposite, blue circles on white. Large blue bottle-nosed fish cavorted in a whitish sea. Little orange and yellow fish swam around them. Every once and a while a long, plump fish with what looked like a gourd for a nose stared at her. She wiggled in delight.

On another wall, dancing girls in long billowing skirts moved gracefully towards and away from each other.

Witty, happy conversation flowed around her, which she didn't understand. All the talk of bull-leaping left her confused. Did that big animal she had seen the first day in Knossos jump up and down? Did the animal leap over something? Was it a contest? She simply didn't know what they were talking about.

At the end of the afternoon, as she was leaving, the queen said, "You must come with us to the trials next week. They are held in the large temple."

That evening, sitting with her father after a simple meal, she asked him about the bull-leaping.

"The bulls do not leap," he said. "Apparently it is the young men and women who grab the horns and leap or somersault over the back of the charging bull."

Kelu's eyes became as big as spindle whirls. "They could get hurt," she gasped.

"I am told some do, yes. They get gored."

Kelu's hands covered her face as she saw the young guard who had escorted her to the palace gored and bleeding. "How terrible." Then she added, "There are, what the queen called trials next week. She invited me to go with her."

"Very well, you may. I intend to go also and find out what this is all about. Somehow, it is tied in with their religion."

The subdued talk of people drifting toward the large, main temple expressed excitement and tension. Arttarna in his long lightweight deep rose-colored wool robe, belted with an exquisitely embroidered fabric, entered with a group of ambassadors and Minoan officials. In a long, pale green gown embroidered at the hem, Kelu walked with dignity, her father noted, in the middle of the queen's ladies. Inside the large, rectangular bull court, the ladies veered to the right side, the men to the left.

Handsome young men in their nip-waisted skirts walked slowly around, smiling at the crowd. A few charming young girls, as scantily clad, mingled with the young men. Kelu couldn't help but notice what beautiful bodies they had: strong, athletic, healthy, without being obviously muscular. Their long black hair curled softly. In spite of her embarrassment, Kelu thought them beautiful.

Suddenly, everyone stopped talking. Led by a young man, a huge, superb bull walked into the court. In the middle of the court, the young man stopped. A young woman took her place about a man's length in front of the bull and a young man stepped behind it, careful to be a man's length behind. In the hush, Kelu could hear her heart beat.

The man who had led the bull into the court took a few quick steps toward the rear of the animal, slapped it on the rump and instantly moved out of the way. The bull charged. The young woman standing quietly some distance from it, gauged its speed, ran towards it, grabbed the horns and vaulted over its back, landing on her feet behind it. A swoosh of exploding breaths sounded and then applause.

One after the other, the young men and women vaulted over the bull. One young fellow started awkwardly and landed on the animal's back. The bull pounded his hoofs in the dirt. A tall man wearing a feathered hat subdued the animal by grabbing his horns and forcing his head down. The youth quickly slid along the bull's flank and hurried away.

An excited, titillated Kelu rushed to their salon when she got home to find Arttarna already there.

"That was so thrilling," she gushed, her face aglow. "I would love to be able to do that."

"Kelu," said a startled Arttarna, "do not even think about it."

In the year that followed, Kelu took great care not to defy her father, but pushed to the limit. She hung around the bull court, became acquainted with the young men and women active in the bull-leaping. They seriously told her that they were serving their god through this dangerous activity. Conscious of the way they felt, Kelu sat quietly in the temple contemplating their god. She talked to the priests.

"The horns of consecration, or of plenty as they are called, are the symbol of the bull god," one priest told her.

"What does it look like?" said Kelu.

"Great gods, child. You mean you don't know? You see

horns of consecration everywhere. They sit on the tops of doors in the palace."

"You mean," stuttered Kelu, "that white stone that is flat on the bottom with the two arms that stick up and the big scoop in between?"

"Exactly."

"So you are worshiping the bull god all the time. He is your most important god?"

"Well, he's one of the most important. The double axe symbolizes Potnia, the great lady goddess. And you see that all around, too."

"Oh, yes, I do."

"When a bird sits on the double axe, it means the deity is present."

Kelu looked around uncomfortably, trying to remember if she had ever faced the goddess and not known it.

"She is also the snake goddess," the priest continued. "We have a beautiful statue of her in that small room off the bull court."

"I have seen that. She is beautiful." Kelu decided not to mention her dislike of snakes.

"There is also a god called an earthshaker. Every so often, he gets angry and shakes the earth. That causes much destruction and even death. Then all the people in the palace and the temples meet for a day of prayer, trying to placate him. But after a while, we get lax in our prayers, and he causes more damage." The priest rubbed • his chin. "It's hard to know how to make him happy."

Kelu made a mental note to say some prayers to the earthshaker for the safety of her home and those in it.

That evening, Kelu repeated to her father everything that the priest told her.

"On the surface, this country looks peaceful and contented, but I am not sure that is true. I have an ominous feeling that there is something dark and sinister that goes on here. I have not been able to find out what it is," Arttarna said.

He got up and paced the floor. "The society is complex. Somehow I do not think their king has much power either as king or priest. He has an important group of courtiers around him for security and support. You and I see those people all the time. The other classes are almost invisible except for our servants who are free citizens, and I do not see much of them. The remaining group consists of serfs. Some of them have rights; the rest are simply chattel."

Arttarna resumed his seat. After a few minutes, he said, "I guess I have told you this because I am uneasy and have not expressed my concerns to anyone. Excuse me for burdening you, Kelu."

"Father dear, do not excuse yourself. We used to share our knowledge in Hattusas. I am almost twelve now, so why should we keep our concerns from each other?"

"You really are becoming quite the young woman. And you handle yourself well at court." Arttarna smiled. "You spend almost as much time with the queen as with me."

"She is very good to me, though I must admit, Father, I like your company better."

"Well, that is wise." He beamed at her.

"Hattusas has the same kind of social structure with slaves and agricultural laborers, does it not?" Kelu asked.

"Yes, but everything was presented openly, none of this dark, foreboding undercurrent."

"I do not sense a dark undercurrent. You have met most of my young friends, the ones who come here. Then there are the gentle, kind priests. They seem anxious to teach me about their religion. I am almost ready to join them, except I think I would have to participate with the bulls."

"I think it would be best to pray to Teshub, our storm god, and Vishnu. You can trust them."

Kelu gave him a startled look. The comment had been uttered in great seriousness, his voice authoritarian.

"The chief priest has invited me to go with him and some other priests and young people to the Elleithyia Cave. It is very old and very holy. The daughter of Zeus and Hera was born in this cave. Her name was Elleithyia, hence the name of the cave. The sacred stalactites in the cave have a low wall around them, the priest said. The sacrifices take place on the altar outside. The bull is Zeus' symbol. Isn't that amazing?" She looked him in the eye, hers wide and intense, but went right on talking.

"The priest said that cave is the main temple of their great female goddess and therefore dedicated to women and children."

"The Minoan religion is very foreign to us. I do not like

your getting too involved in it, Kelu. You may go to see the temple this time, but let it stop there."

Kelu unhappily bowed her head, letting Arttarna see her irritation.

"Take Eshtar with you tomorrow."

"Oh, Father, I do not need her company."

"Kelu, your slave's job is to care for you and protect you. You do not take her to the palace, and now you start visiting the religious caves alone. I prefer that you take her with you."

"None of the Minoans take a slave," Kelu objected.

"You are not a Minoan."

Kelu rose and went to her room. She found Eshtar pacing. Surprised, she said, "What's the matter, Eshtar?"

"Nothing, Mistress. I'm just restless tonight."

"I have been neglecting you. Father thinks you should come with me tomorrow to the Cave of Elleithyia."

Eshtar eyed Kelu sidewise, aware that Arttarna didn't like her being constantly with the priests, and also aware that Kelu didn't want a slave tagging along. "I will willingly go, Kelu, and try to keep withdrawn from you and your group of friends."

"Very well." Kelu flopped onto her bed and lay staring at the ceiling. Eshtar nervously ran her hands up and down her arms and finally left the room.

In the meantime, Arttarna fumed. He hated to outright deny Kelu her friends and interests in Minoan culture, but somehow the priesthood with the king at its head disturbed him. He wanted his daughter to be independent, but he was finding her a little hard to handle.

He became aware that Sebi lurked in the background.

Without turning his head, he said, "What is it, Sebi?"

Sebi hurried to his side and dropped face down on the floor.

"Get up, Sebi," Arttarna said briskly, a bit taken aback. Immediately all his attention focused at the sight of Sebi's tense face. "What is wrong?"

"Master, I'm your slave and I beg you. I want to take a wife."

"Take a—There is nothing distressing about that. Why are you upset? Did you think I would object?"

"Yes, Master."

"Why? Do you want me to buy her?"

"That is not necessary, Master."

"Your duties will not change, Sebi, but of course, you may take a wife." He observed Sebi. "Who is this woman?"

"Eshtar," Sebi managed to whisper.

"Eshtar! She is Kelu's slave. You have to ask Kelu."

"Do you think the young mistress will object?"

Arttarna looked away and ran his fingernails back and forth on his knee. Kelu didn't seem to be interested in having Eshtar around anymore. She probably would find marriage a good way to get rid of the slave. "No, but you must ask her."

"Yes, Master." Sebi silently left the room. He headed straight for Kelu's room and found Eshtar walking the corridor. She ran to him. "What did he say?"

"I have to ask the young mistress for you."

"She's in a bad mood, lying on her bed."

"Come in with me." He took her hand and drew her to Kelu's door. They stood side by side. He knocked.

"Enter," came Kelu's voice. Then a surprised, "Sebi!"

"Mistress," Sebi said, going to one knee, "may I take your slave to wife?"

Kelu's eyes jumped to Eshtar. "So that is why you were so nervous."

Turning to Sebi, "Of course, you can, Sebi." Kelu bounced off the bed and flung her arms around Eshtar. Then, on second thought, "What did your master say, Sebi?"

"He said I still have to do my job, but that I had to ask you for Eshtar."

"Then it is settled," she burbled. "How exciting. We will give you a fine wedding."

Eshtar smiled, the stress gone. "We'll talk about it tomorrow after we return from Elleithyia."

At the cave temple, next morning, the high priest himself informed Kelu that because she worshiped with them, he had brought the most beautiful rhyton in the palace collection to pour the libations.

Standing in the forefront of the group around the holy stalactites, as the high priest wished, Eshtar behind her, Kelu eagerly awaited the appearance of the promised rhyton.

Slowly, the high priest walked from the dimness at the back

of the cave into the candlelit area around the stalactites. A ritual headdress of lilies and waving peacock plumes crowned his head. In front of him, facing the group of worshipers, he carried a bull's head rhyton. The golden horns glittered in the flickering light. The black head glistened. Its clear eyes pierced Kelu's heart at the same time that the white nostrils seemed to flare. Trembling, she stepped back against Eshtar.

A hushed, breathless silence pervaded the temple as the high priest poured wine from the cup, known as the rhyton, over the stalactites, then walked outside, followed by the reverent worshipers, and poured the wine remaining in the rhyton's cup over the altar at the entrance. Dramatically, he recited ritual poetry.

After the sacrifice of a small goat, the high priest let Kelu examine the rhyton closely. "It's carved from one piece of black steatite," he said. "You see the rock crystal and jasper eyes? The nostrils are mother-of-pearl, and the wooden horns have been gilded. Wine is held in the hollowed-out interior, accessed through the mouth."

"I have never seen anything so beautiful," whispered Kelu.

The high priest smiled serenely at her, lifted the rhyton from the table and disappeared into the back of the cave.

The young Minoans burst into low, excited chatter at the unusual mystery and effectiveness of the service they had just witnessed. Kelu kept silent, subdued and overwhelmed. She stood quietly beside the fig tree in front of the entrance and faced the east, an expression of serene intensity on her face.

Eshtar watched Kelu, worried about her reaction. Kelu remained withdrawn all evening and announced earlier than usual that she was going to bed

"I'll bring you some hot broth," Eshtar said.

Leaving the kitchen, hot broth in her hand, she met Sebi on his way in. "Sebi, Kelu has forgotten all about the wedding plans."

Sebi nodded. Eshtar walked on toward the green door.

After giving the broth to Kelu, she headed for the main room. Arttarna, sat in his chair gazing into space, his hands knotted under his chin. Eshtar went down on one knee. He jumped.

"What is it, Eshtar?"

"Forgive me, Master, but I don't think it's wise for Kelu to be exposed to this local religion all the time. There was something scary about the ceremony in the cave. She turned pale and fell back against me when the bull's head appeared from the dark."

"Whether she likes it or not, you—perhaps even Sebi or Rasi—should accompany her at all times. I do not know how else to handle this without outright denying her. And I do not want to do that."

Alone, having spent considerable time in thought, he got up and walked to his desk. Picking up a piece of papyrus paper, he sat down and penned a letter to his king.

Your Majesty, in the year and a half since coming to Knossos, I have estimated the strength of the army, but I think the Minoan king is more likely to use his army to conquer other kings on the island rather than help Egypt in military enterprises. The Egyptian king seems to have lost interest in military exploits. However, the Minoans trade heavily with Egypt and also heavily with Mycenae on the mainland. Myceneans are beginning to infiltrate the island. Warfare in that direction appears inevitable. Wherever Your Majesty thinks best to send me, I will go, but suggest that Egypt might be a good place to start.

After sealing the letter, he called Sebi.

"See that one of my messengers carries this on board a boat in the morning. He is to deliver it to King Tushratta in Mitanni."

16

Master," yelled Rasi.
Hearing the panic in Rasi's voice, Arttarna jumped from his desk chair and rushed into the main room. He found Rasi nervously twisting his hands, his face anxious.

"What is the matter?" Arttarna tensed. Fear gripped him.

"I was watching Kelu," Rasi began, "and one of the priests distracted me—actually pulled me into an alcove to show me some treasurers. When I was able to get away from him, Kelu had gone."

"Gone where?" he said, in sharp staccato, pushing down panic.

"I don't know. I overheard some young men mention a cave temple. On a whim I asked where it was. It's at the other end of the island, the wild crags above the sea that face the Egyptian realm."

"Long, hard riding." He glanced around the room, judging time.

"You'll go there even though it isn't certain?"

"Of course, I will go. And you will lead the way. You have a quarter of an hourglass to bring horses and supplies."

Heavy footed, frantic, Arttarna entered his elegant red patterned bedroom, flung back the earth-brown drape secreting his clothes, yanked out a lightweight coat, pulled a blanket from the bed as he passed it, and exited the house. While impatiently waiting, he folded the blanket and tied it in his coat. The high, rocky coast was always cold. And when they found Kelu—his mind refused to face defeat—the blanket would be useful.

He looked up at the sound of horses' hoofs. Rasi appeared, leading the sturdy big bay horse that Arttarna liked, and a small, fast, black animal for himself. In his other hand, he carried a little basket with bread and bits of cheese.

Arttarna leapt onto the bay and started to gallop, then stopped to wait for Rasi. Together, they galloped along, slowed the horses on rough spots in the road, and returned to a gallop. The sun sank. Arttarna called a halt. Setting the horses to graze, he said, "We'll eat something while we wait for the moon to rise and light the forward trail."

Jittery, nervously munching some bread, Arttarna scanned the sky. "There it is," he suddenly shouted, pointing at the rising moon.

Quickly mounted, they galloped along the shore, having both the moon and the reflection from the sea to light their way. The trail started to rise, rocky and uneven, slowing their progress.

Finally, Rasi yelled behind him into the wind, "Master, we must stop."

Arttarna pulled alongside him.

"If I am right, we are not far from the location," Rasi said. "We had best walk the horses a short distance and shackle them. Their hoofs clicking off these rocks would herald our coming."

Arttarna nodded. He gazed out over the sea. Even at this great height, he could hear the pounding of the waves against the rock. "Any moment, the sun will rise. Do you know the time of their sacrifices? That must be what they came for!"

"No, Master. But we can hide ourselves where we can see the temple entrance."

"Lead on."

They moved forward slowly, trying to mute the sound of the horses. A gray line appeared where the sky met the sea.

"Here," Rasi whispered. He dismounted, picked up a rock and used it to fasten the reins of his horse. Arttarna followed suit. Exposed now on the crags against the lightening sky, the two men, snuck catlike ahead, Rasi in the lead. Suddenly, he dropped to the ground in a small crevasse behind a jetting rock. Startled, Arttarna couldn't see him immediately, then dropped beside him.

"Where is the temple?"

"Over there." Rasi pointed to a slit in a great bolder, barely visible behind the usual fig tree at the entrance.

Arttarna stared at the slit, turning over in his mind the maneuvers of storming it.

"We wait."

Rasi shifted his weight for more comfort.

The sky turned orange. The lip of the sun appeared. Arttarna kept turning his head from the entrance to the sun. It burst from the sea into an array of deep orange clouds on the horizon and turned the rock slit to orange.

His ear detected steps. He poked Rasi.

Rasi's finger pointed to a path coming from the opposite direction. A man wearing a long white robe and a tall, feathered hat appeared. He carried a small round pot in one hand and a knife in the other. Behind him a woman in the long, full robes of a priestess sang softly. Behind her, two priests supported a boy, also in white. Behind them came two more priests, each gripping one of Kelu's arms. Arttarna bit his tongue hard to prevent a cry. Five men and one woman. He only saw one knife.

"Kelu and the boy are drugged," he whispered. He felt for his own knife; he knew Rasi also carried one.

The lead priest stopped and said something to those behind him. He then entered the temple, followed by the priestess and the two priests with the boy.

"We will give the others time to settle down before we rush these two," Arttarna whispered. "Surprise is on our side." He started to count, taking his time.

Suddenly, a great rumble came from way below them. The earth gave a violent jerk, throwing him from behind the rock. Astonished, he looked back. The rock had disappeared, gone, nothing but air where it had been. Arttarna clutched at the trembling ground beneath him. He couldn't get up. His stomach heaved. Deep, nervous fear churned through his body.

Screams came from inside the temple. Two bloody priests staggered out of the entrance, grabbed the rock at the slit, fell flat, rolled over, and remained motionless.

The two priests holding Kelu fell, drawing her down. All three tumbled a few feet before being stopped by underbrush. Arttarna attempted to crawl toward them, but the trembling of the earth kept him flat, vainly clutching at air. He cried out as a hurtling bolder grazed his leg. Ignoring the pain, he tried to crawl on. Gods, he had forgotten about the tumbling rocks. Where was Rasi?

Suddenly feeling more secure, he moved his hand over the

ground. All motion had stopped. He jumped up and rushed towards Kelu.

She sat dazed, shaking her head.

"Kelu, Kelu," he yelled.

With a cry of joy, she scrambled to her feet. One of the priests clutched at her robe, but she yanked it from his hand and, wavering wildly, ran to her father.

At the cave entrance, Rasi stood over the other priest, a rock in his hand, ready to bash the man's head in if he moved. A second later, he shrugged his shoulder, and kicked the dead priest onto his back.

"Look inside for the boy," Arttarna called.

Cautiously, Rasi slid through the widened entrance. Almost instantly, he returned. "They're all dead." He shook his head. "The boy lies naked on a slab, the priest over him, crushed by falling rock. The dead priestess sags in a corner." Glancing over the bodies of the three dead priests, he said, "The other priest who held Kelu seems to have disappeared."

"We cannot worry about him now." Tightly holding Kelu's arm, Arttarna started along the path.

They found the horses bloodied and screaming, stamping around a small, flat section of rock, having bucked loose from their bridle stones. At the sight of Arttarna, the bay let out a pained whinny and stampeded him. Arttarna quickly sidestepped the horse and grabbed the bridle. Talking softly, he continually shortened his grip on the bridle until the quivering animal stood still under his soothing hand.

Rasi had trouble catching his mount. He no sooner got near the horse than the animal skittered away. Finally, Kelu managed to catch the bridle when he was snorting and pawing the ground in defiance of Rasi.

"We will walk them to the closest little cluster of houses where we can commandeer horses. These two are too bruised to ride far," Arttarna said.

"If there are any, they'll be pretty awful nags."

Arttarna laughed gently at Rasi's disgusted look. "The best we can find. I'll take Kelu back. You care for these two. I'll send someone back with the nag."

He placed Kelu on the horse. The bay whinnied and tried to turn around. Arttarna steadied him.

"Kelu, can you manage to stay on his back?"

"I do not know. I am dizzy."

"Lean forward and put your arms around his neck."

They walked for some time, descending from the rocky coast towards the center of the island. "Master," Rasi said, "I think we need to turn off this path to the right to find some habitation."

Arttarna looked at his pale, drawn daughter. "Rasi, in spite of the bruised state of the horses, I think we better mount. You lead. I hope it is not far."

Rasi helped Arttarna onto the horse then handed him a limp Kelu. Taking a firm grip on Kelu with his left arm, Arttarna pulled her against his chest. His right hand held the reins.

"I do not feel well," she said.

"I realize that, dear. Lean against me and try to sleep." He nodded to Rasi. "That horse is still skittish."

"Too many cuts. My legs bother his sides."

Arttarna shrugged, much as to say, "We cannot help it."

As soon as he noticed a track, Rasi turned right. "I'll gallop ahead a little to see if I can find any houses."

Again Arttarna nodded and continued his easy, slow walk.

After a bit, Rasi returned. "I found a farm. The whole family stands in the road, terrified. The wife won't go in the house. There has been some damage."

"Does he have horses?"

"One pretty poor specimen."

"That will have to do."

"The farmer whined, but brightened at the money I offered him and the promise of the quick return of his animal."

At the farmhouse, Arttarna transferred to the nag and took Kelu up in front of him. "It may be three days before this animal comes back," he said to Rasi, while observing the farmer's careful examination of the bay.

"Yes, Master." Rasi's nodded.

Arttarna stopped at one of the settlements he passed through to get food. Kelu wanted nothing but liquid. "Wine," she announced.

He refused her wine, asking water and a liquid gruel for her.

They reached the palace of Malia by late afternoon. Arttarna explained that he was the ambassador from Mitanni, that his daughter was ill, and begged some accommodations for the night. Though he didn't say so, he himself could barely navigate from exhaustion.

Shortly after noon the following day, they reached their own home. Looking quite ill, but in her right mind, Kelu rushed to Eshtar as she might have rushed to her mother, clinging to her neck and crying.

"Put her to bed," Arttarna ordered. "She has been heavily drugged."

"Kelu!" Eshtar exploded. "How awful." One arm around Kelu, her other curled under Kelu's elbow, shaking her head in disbelief, she gently steered her young mistress towards the bedroom. Every few seconds, she let go of the elbow to pat the wet cheek.

In her bedroom, Kelu tumbled onto the bed. Eshtar stripped her and pulled the light blanket over her. "Do you want to sleep or talk?" Eshtar sat down on the bed, her hand running up and down Kelu's arm.

"They frightened me," Kelu whispered. "It happened so fast."

Eshtar rang a bell for a slave.

As soon as the door opened, without turning, she said, "Bring a hot herbal drink for our young mistress."

"A priest asked Rasi to look at some heirlooms. The minute he disappeared, two priests grabbed my arms, lifting me off the ground, and ran out a side door. They handed me to a priest on a horse. I struggled. Another priest gave the one holding me a bowl of some awful smelling liquid that they forced down my throat. I could feel myself weakening, unable to move. He held me like a sack, half over the horse. We started. I passed out."

"My poor darling," murmured Eshtar.

"The next thing I vaguely remember, I stood in a grove, dressed in a long white robe, and a young man in a long white robe stood next to me. Priests surrounded us."

"One of them said, 'This won't hurt. You won't realize what's happening.' Two priests took the arms of the young man and started slowly along the path. Then a priest on either side of me took one of my arms. 'Walk,' one of them said. With their help, I managed. I did not know where I was or where I was going. Everything was fuzzy, and I started to weave. The two priests fell and pulled me down. Then, like the end of a bad dream, my father called."

With a knock on the door, the slave handed a steaming bowl of liquid to Eshtar.

"Sip this," Eshtar said, taking the bowl from the slave.

Kelu tried to hold the bowl. "I cannot," she sobbed.

"Never mind. I have a good grip on it." Eshtar rose. "I'll sit behind you to brace you and hold the bowl." She laid the bowl on the floor, propped Kelu up and settled herself behind her mistress, then picked up the bowl. Sliding her arms around Kelu, she managed to guide the bowl to her lips.

Kelu sipped in silence. Every few sips, she emitted a groan. Finally, she said, "That is enough. I am tired."

Eshtar laid her flat and tucked the blanket around her. After making sure Kelu slept, she wrapped herself in a blanket and settled down on a chair to watch through the night.

Once, at an extremely light tap on the door, she whispered, "Yes?"

Arttarna entered and hung over Kelu.

"She's restless, but she sleeps," Eshtar said.

For a few minutes, he watched Kelu sleep. "If you need me, call Sebi," he said and left the room.

"Eshtar, wake up. You must be terribly uncomfortable." Long-faced, sad-eyed, dressed in a loose white robe, Kelu stood in front of her slave.

Eshtar struggled with the blanket, trying to stand up. "Forgive me, Mistress. I watched your restless sleep most of the night, then dosed, I guess."

"It doesn't matter. I am not going anywhere." She pointed to Eshtar's mat at the foot of the bed. "Lie on your mat and sleep. I will call for some bread and yogurt."

"I'll tell Sebi. He's right outside the door."

"My goodness," Kelu said quietly. "I am receiving a lot of attention."

Eshtar went to the door while Kelu climbed back into bed. She pushed her head bolster behind her back and sat up with the blanket tucked across her chest, hands folded on top, her face still and serious.

Turning to face Kelu, Eshtar sucked in her breath. The harrowing experience had deepened Kelu's beauty.

"Lie down, Eshtar."

"No. I'm awake now. I'll eat breakfast in the hall with Sebi."

A knock, and the door opened. The cook stood before them holding a large, flat basket covered with food.

"Cook!" said a surprised Kelu.

"I wanted to see for myself that you were all right, Mistress."

"I am fine. Thank you, Cook." She beckoned, "Come in and put the tray on my bed."

Arttarna appeared at the door. "Well," he said, surveying the room, "we do have a family gathering."

"Sebi," he said loudly, "join us."

"Excuse me, Master, I brought Mistress food." Cook cringed and would have slipped away.

"I am not scolding you," Arttarna said. "We are all worried. Your concern is appreciated."

"Now," Arttarna examined the food tray, "bring me some vegetables in sour cream."

"Yes, Master." Cook smiled at Arttarna and hurried out.

Arttarna advanced towards the bed. "My child, do you feel like getting up? It is a beautiful day. You might enjoy a short walk."

Kelu drew back under the blanket. "I don't want to go out. I do not want to be seen."

Silently stroking his neatly trimmed black beard, Arttarna observed his daughter. "Well, you have had a very traumatic experience. We will let that go for the time being. You can sit in the light well garden." He turned to go. "Eshtar, when Kelu is ready, have Sebi place two chairs and a little table. I will sit with her a while."

"Yes, Master."

"Eshtar," Kelu said when the others had left her room, "I'm just beginning to realize what those priests intended to do to me. That must be why they have been so nice all along." She hid her face in the blanket and shuddered. "I don't ever want to see any of them again. I don't want to ever leave this house as long as my father is ambassador here."

Eshtar raised her eyebrows. Only three days had passed

since her abduction. Kelu needed more time before she could put the experience behind her.

"The whole earth shook. It made my body tingle unpleasantly I clutched at air."

Eshtar's eyes widened. Was this true or Kelu's imagination?

"The priests holding me staggered around and fell, pulling me to the ground. I sat there on the shaking ground trying to scream, but no sound came. One priest fell against me. I pushed him off. He toppled over. The other priest simply disappeared. I could have run away, but I didn't know that then. Besides, I couldn't get up. I heard my name. I couldn't tell where it came from. Suddenly, the earth was still, and I knew my father was calling me." Kelu started to cry. "I was so relieved."

"Kelu, Kelu." Eshtar took the girl in her arms and rocked her.

Eventually Kelu stopped crying and got out of bed. "I will dress."

Thinking hard, Eshtar helped her dress. As they finished, she said, "Kelu while you are recuperating might be a good time for Sebi and me to marry."

"That is right. So much has happened we have not had time to do it." She paused for a second, her face frozen, before her normal color returned. "Good idea. I will speak to my father."

With that, Eshtar led her to the garden in the light well. Once Arttarna joined her, Kelu said, "Father, we need to have a small wedding here in the garden for Eshtar and Sebi."

Arttarna's brow rose. "You are right. I will arrange it." He smiled at Eshtar. She flushed, knowing full well that he realized she had mentioned it to distract Kelu.

"As we have no priest from our temples here, I will officiate as the representative of our king and marry you properly."

He put two fingers above his right eyebrow. "Let me see. We shall have the ceremony four days from now, late in the afternoon when the direct sunlight has disappeared and there is coolness on the flowers. Tell Sebi, Eshtar."

"Yes, Master." She went down on one knee and bowed her head.

"That is enough of that. You may go."

Bowing profusely, Eshtar backed into the house.

"Now, my dear, I have something else to discuss with you."

Kelu widened her eyes and watched him intently.

"A message came from the queen this morning expressing sorrow that you had died in the sacred temple when the earth god struck. I am frankly surprised that she knew you were there. From what she said, apparently many others died, either by being hit by hurtling stones or by falling down the embankment. I have never experienced the earth trembling like that before."

"One of the priests once mentioned to me that the earth god did that, and they don't know what they have done or how to appease him."

"They better find out. It is very unnerving." Arttarna examined his fingernails. "Be that as it may, Kelu, I intend to tell the queen that you survived."

"No." Kelu jumped from the chair. "Please don't, father. I don't ever want to go out again while I live here. I don't want to see those people. I'm afraid." She landed on her knees before him.

"Oh, my dear child." He gathered her close. "The queen will find out. It is better that we tell her." He stroked her hair while he thought. "I am going to bring Rasi in to guard you when I am busy. And Eshtar will be with you always. You do not have to go out for the time being. At least until you get over some of the horrid experience you have been through. Then, we will see what happens. In the meantime, we have a wedding to perform."

Near sundown four days later, Eshtar and Sebi were married in the garden, attended by Kelu, Rasi, and Cook. To officiate, Arttarna wore a costly formal dark blue wool robe and gold lapis lazuli loops in his ears. Not to be outdone, the kitchen staff trundled three tables and an elaborate meal into the garden.

Looking at the beaming staff lined against the wall, the happy faces of Kelu, Rasi, and Cook, he ordered Eshtar and Sebi into two chairs placed beside a small table. "Serve them," he said to the assistant cook. "Now I invite all of you," he swung his arm across everyone, "to take food and sit down."

Hesitantly, a little embarrassed in front of the master, they edged towards the table, then eagerly helped themselves. With sly glances at Arttarna, but looking pleased, they grouped themselves around the food table and one other table, sitting as close together as possible.

Arttarna slowly, sedately, walked from table to table, speaking to each one. Sitting between Rasi and Cook, Kelu watched him with admiration.

The reaction of the court to the news that Kelu had survived was instantaneous and unexpected. The king sent a long, flowery epistle, exclaiming over the fact that she lived. She had met with favor from the god. He intended to have a formal ceremony and present her at court. Perhaps she would use her influence with the god to help appease his anger. How fortunate the palace was to have such a gifted person.

Arttarna laid the letter on the garden table and watched Kelu, the shiny black hair, the exquisite loveliness of the pensive face folded within itself, showing no reaction. Ten days had passed since her return home. She still refused to set foot outside the house, had little to say, wrapped in her own replays of what had happened.

"Kelu, I would like your reaction to this letter from the king." Arttarna tapped the letter with his forefinger.

"I will not go," she said in a small voice, looking at the ground.

His eyes narrowed. He pulled at his beard. Then, folding his hands in his lap, he said, "I have put up with this moping long enough. Life goes on, and you are lucky to still have a life. Has it ever occurred to you that I survived that violent earth shake along with Rasi and the two horses? We were there to rescue you because I love you dearly and want you to develop into the fine woman I expect you to be."

Still, he saw no reaction.

"Whether you like it or not, you will go, and you will behave appropriately."

"No," she screamed. "Somebody will spirit me away. Those priests will not stop trying."

Arttarna swallowed hard. So, she feared another attempt. She probably had a good grasp of their thinking. That meant careful guarding, but she had to go out. This sitting around in the garden had to stop. Minoans couldn't be trusted to guard her and his staff was too small to care for her and do their work. His mind ran over the different people he saw at the palace and at the port. Myceneans. He'd hire Myceneans.

"You will be well guarded. I shall hire young, strong Myceneans. They are not loyal to the Minoan king. And I will be with you. Sebi and Eshtar also."

Kelu flung herself forward, covered her face with her hands and sobbed. "I am afraid."

After a few minutes, Arttarna said, "My dear child, I will do whatever I can to help you, but you must face the future." He waited until Kelu sat up and squared her shoulders. "Tomorrow, we two will walk a short distance towards the harbor and back with our escort. The public will get used to seeing you with an escort."

He rose. "I will send Eshtar to you. I must do something about this escort."

She watched him, erect and walking rapidly, enter the house.

Late in the afternoon, Sebi came to Kelu and Eshtar who were playing a board game in the social room. Bowing before Kelu, he said, "Master wishes you to come to the room at the entrance hall."

Kelu's eyes widened. She looked at Eshtar in consternation.

"I'll come with you," said Eshtar, rising.

Kelu rose and slowly walked along the main corridor, followed by Sebi and Eshtar, to where her father waited. She looked at Arttarna then one after the other at the six muscular young men dressed in long Mycenean skirts who stood in a row looking at her.

"These six young men," Arttarna swung his arm in an arc to include the six, "will guard this house while you are in it and guard you with every step you take outside it."

"My father, I appreciate your care for me." Kelu bowed.

He took her arm, and they walked along the corridor together.

The morning walk turned into a parade. Kelu walked beside her father, two men in front, two behind, one on each side. People on the road stared and gave them wide berth.

On their return, Eshtar noticed Kelu's heightened color, bright eyes, and head held up. Eshtar wanted to shout for joy.

* * * *

Each day, the length of the walk increased. Kelu obviously enjoyed her parade. She returned rosy cheeked to the delight of the staff. Again, the house hummed.

One afternoon, a messenger from the king arrived. He wished to have Kelu presented at a formal court in the throne room. After that, Kelu, the queen, and the highest court officials would offer prayers in the inner sanctuary behind the throne room.

Arttarna responded that he hoped the king would include him in the group going to the inner sanctuary as he, too, would like to offer prayers for his daughter.

The return message agreed to his request with the comment that his presence would be unusual. Only because the two of them were from a foreign country was the king allowing Arttarna's presence.

Arttarna instructed the six guards. "You are to place yourselves right in front of the door to the inner sanctuary. At any cry from me, you are to force your way in. Do you understand?"

All six nodded and flexed their muscles, ready to take on the whole Minoan army for Kelu.

The question of what dress to wear at the presentation required hours of discussion between Kelu and Arttarna. Finally, they called for Eshtar to join them.

"We want to talk about the design with you, Eshtar," said Kelu, "because you must make it."

"I'll do my best, Mistress." Eshtar sounded unsure.

"It is basically simple, Eshtar," Arttarna said. "You will do fine."

"We have decided I should wear our Mitanni style for this presentation, something more priestess-like," said Kelu.

Eshtar nodded, her eyes moving back and forth in thought.

"Because even very thin wool would be too heavy for this hot climate, we have decided on linen."

"That will drape nicely," Arttarna added.

"This afternoon, Eshtar, you and I will go shopping for the cloth. We will walk to the little stores at the harbor."

"Good." Eshtar nodded. "We don't have much time: about a day and a half."

"We can begin as soon as we return." Kelu looked at Arttarna for approval. "I want something very pale in color. Pink, I think. That looks well with my light-brown skin."

"It does." Eshtar smiled.

A happy, enthusiastic Kelu returned from the shopping expedition with Eshtar and a large package carried by one of the Mycenean guards.

"Take it to my room," Kelu ordered the guard.

"Where is my father?" she asked Sebi, who met them at the door of their private quarters.

"At court."

"Ask him to come to my room as soon as he returns."

Kelu and Eshtar hurried to Kelu's room where they quickly spread the fabric on the floor, then stood surveying the pale pink, medium weight linen.

"It's so beautiful," sighed Kelu.

"Let's see how much we need for the skirt." Eshtar picked up an end and held it at Kelu's waist.

By the time Arttarna arrived, Kelu and Eshtar were happily draping and snipping.

"Beautiful!" he exclaimed.

At the appointed time for the presentation, Kelu walked into the throne room, her father at her side and the six Myceneans behind. Her long-sleeved pink linen robe draped softly over her entire body, leather sandals peeped from under the hem as she walked. Eshtar had pulled her black hair tightly back, plaited and twisted it at the back of her neck. Her priestess-like robe and beauty drew uncontrolled stares from the seated queen and ladies.

Kelu moved slowly towards the king and dropped to her knees, head bowed. Arttarna, slightly behind her, did the same. The six Myceneans behind him also bowed. They had spaced themselves across the room between Arttarna and the Minoans present, both priests and officials.

"Rise," said the king. "We have asked you here today to honor you for a life favored by our earth god. None of us have ever been able to appease his fury. You have. We would make you his priestess." Arttarna raised his eyebrows. He needed to think that through. "We request that you pray to him in his temple, ask his forgiveness for our actions and guide our nation concerning his wishes."

The king, wearing an exquisite short skirt and a gorgeous

feathered headdress, the plums arcing over his shoulders, rose. "Follow me into the inner shrine, where I, as chief priest, will install you as a priestess."

He walked through the narrow door, Kelu behind him, followed by Arttarna. The six Mycenean guards moved close to the door, preventing the entrance of anyone else. A small group of priests and officials gathered right behind the guards and acted as if they would force an entrance. They stood together fidgeting and looking annoyed.

Through the partially open door, everybody could hear the priest-king intoning a long induction rite, then a few minutes of silence before the king led Kelu from the inner shrine, moisture from the libations dripping from her hair.

They continued into the central court, now crowded with courtiers and slaves stationed around a great feast. The crowd joyfully fell to their knees before their new priestess, knowing that the earth god would be appeased.

Later, sitting across from each other in their social room, Arttarna said, "You handled yourself with aplomb today, Kelu. I was extremely proud of you." He beamed at her.

She blushed and hung her head, a smile lighting her face and softening the blush.

"Your dress was perfect for the occasion."

Kelu ran both hands down the skirt. "I love this dress."

"After today, you have nothing to fear. The Minoans stand in awe of you. So I think we can dismiss your Mycenean guards."

"No, please. The public is now used to seeing me with them. I think we should continue the guard force."

"Well, if you say so." Arttarna tried to hide his amusement. She adored all the attention. "But don't get carried away with your importance, Kelu. That is something new in your character."

Momentarily, she stared at the floor in front of him. "I guess you are right. I do like being surrounded by those handsome young men and adoring crowds of people."

Arttarna flipped his eyes over her. She was developing nicely. "Well, the Myceneans can remain for now. We will reduce the number of guards gradually." He recrossed his legs. "Changing the subject, I have something of importance to discuss with you."

"Yes, Father?"

"The queen mentioned going to the earth god's temple to pray. I suspect you are expected to pray out loud and that there may be more than the queen present."

Kelu's hand flew to her cheek. "Oh, my."

"Exactly. You need to be prepared. I suggest you write out a prayer suitable both in content and length and memorize it."

"Will you help me, Father?"

"Of course. We'll start tonight as I have no idea how soon the queen will want this done."

They labored over the prayer until late. Kelu finally went to sleep repeating portions of it. By morning, she added gestures to the prayer.

"Very effective," said Arttarna, repeatedly nodding his head. "Your gestures set the prayer off to perfection."

Each day, Kelu rehearsed the prayer. By the time the queen summoned her, she felt completely at ease and prayed with feeling.

Dressed in her pale pink robe, she walked sedately into the temple beside the queen, followed by the queen's ladies. Two chairs had been placed in front of the altar table. The queen sat in one and motioned Kelu to sit in the other.

A priest of the temple made a short speech then asked Kelu to pray.

She rose, stood directly in front of the altar and prayed in a loud, clear voice.

As she returned to her seat, she looked at the queen. The lady had a beatific smile on her face and tears running down her cheeks. Kelu sat down with a thump, amazed at the effect of her prayer on the queen. Goodness, she thought, I hope she doesn't expect me to do this often. I better ask father to help me prepare.

Between them, they prepared four more prayers. Kelu asked Sebi to put a small table in her room. She lined up the prayers on the table. Each day, she went over them, but concentrated on memorizing the first one to perfection. After she delivered that one, she told herself, she would perfect the next one.

The queen frequently invited Kelu to her suite, but said nothing about another public prayer.

Arttarna reduced the Mycenean guard to four. Surrounded by the four, Kelu again took an interest in the bull-leaping, but without any desire to do it herself.

After the second public prayer, which the king attended, Arttarna reduced the Mycenean guard to two men. "I think," he said, "I'll leave you those two men permanently. Having them seems to be appropriate."

Kelu became quite a sought-after celebrity. Parties failed to be successful without her presence. Arttarna attended to his ambassadorial affairs and stayed out of her limelight, though he gloried in her popularity.

Soon members of upper class families began to approach Arttarna on behalf of a son who wanted to marry Kelu. Each time, Arttarna called her to their social room and asked her about her feelings for the young man and whether she wanted to marry that particular Minoan aristocrat.

After giving serious though to each man, she said, "Father, I think the man is delightful, I like his company, but I do not want to marry him. Besides, I do not think it wise for the priestess of the earth god to marry."

Arttarna wasn't sure he liked her last statement because he wanted her to marry a suitable man. However, he didn't want to leave her in Knossos. He wanted her to marry a man of Mitannian aristocracy. As no eligible Mitannian males lived in Knossos, he found himself in a quandary. She was of an age where she could marry at any time. Should he send her back to Mitanni? To whom? The King? Would their queen find a husband for her among the nobility?

He worried about her marrying each time he was approached. Arttarna never dwelled on the subject with Kelu, though. He had never seen her so happy.

One morning, with all this on his mind, he walked as usual to his desk. There in the middle of the desk where he couldn't avoid seeing it lay a letter from his king.

17

Momentarily, unable to face the probable contents, Arttarna sat at his desk staring at the communication from his king. Tushratta, King of Mitanni, had sealed the papyrus with his favorite personal lapis lazuli cylinder seal. In his mind's eye, Arttarna could see the beautiful polished seal as Tushratta meticulously rolled it across hot wax to leave this exquisitely sculpted seated figure of the god Teshub, his feet on a lion, behind him a heraldic griffin and before him two Mitannian warriors. The motif repeated itself three times around the cylinder, about half the size of his thumb.

Many times had he seen that seal since his arrival in Knossos. This time, he dreaded the contents. He had written his letter in a state of fear for the safety and sanity of his daughter. Now, titular queen of Knossos, the letter would destroy her happiness.

His own ambassadorial activity over the past two years as a resident of Knossos passed before his internal sight. Right from the beginning, he had been amazed by the administrative techniques of the island. The palace at Knossos controlled everything in the country—extensive mining, the wool industry, agriculture, making of pottery for export, art objects, shipping. The shipping alone overwhelmed him. What a cosmopolitan industry. The Minoans dominated the sea traffic. The ships were owned by Minoans, usually captained by Canaanites, carrying raw materials to Knossos and moving the finished products to the cities of their world.

The Minoan style of central management even extended down to the herdsmen. The palace placed one hundred sheep with a herdsman, making him responsible for their care and having him report directly to the palace. Many, many such units existed throughout the country. The same sort of organization held true for the weaving of wool. No wonder the country was so rich. Even the temperature of the island and the quality of the soil added to their success.

The island had extensive mines. He had watched the metal workers, men, nude because of the heat, stand in front of each furnace, changing copper and tin into bronze. From there, he had gone to the artists who painted concentric circles and octopi onto huge vases that were shipped to the peoples of the Euphrates valley. One of these gorgeous, vibrant, vases rested on a table in the Assyrian palace at Nineveh. Many times, he had admired it.

Able to delay no longer, Arttarna picked up the papyrus and pushed his thumb under the seal. The hardened wax cracked. The first sentence sent ice through his veins.

My brother has left Nineveh and returned to Mitanni.

Rapidly, he read on. *He is already stirring up trouble for me. I need you here, and I need you in Egypt to push their king, Akhenaten into sending an army to help me in any Assyrian strike. Egypt is the more important at the moment.*

That was all. He didn't say what Artatama was doing, what kind of trouble he was stirring up, or whether his son, Suttarna, had come with him. Arttarna pulled at his beard and bit the inside of his mouth, trying to make sense of what he read. From the sounds of the letter, he should transfer his diplomatic efforts to Egypt immediately and try to needle Akhenaten into sending his army on a military swing through all the territory on the Mitannian side of the Great Green Sea that owed allegiance to Egypt. The whispering that reached him about the Egyptian king made him realize that that would not be easy. The man apparently was lazy, his only interest his palaces and his women.

Well, so be it. As soon as possible, one of his messengers would leave for Mitanni with a letter informing Tushratta that he would transfer to Amarna, the capitol of Egypt, as soon as he could draw to a close his work in Knossos. He admitted to himself that he had discovered about everything he needed to know about Knossos, everything of use to King Tushratta. His only dread was breaking the news to Kelu.

He shrugged. It had to be done.

Pulling a piece of papyrus towards him, he rapidly wrote to his king, sealed it with his special seal, called Sebi to his side and said, "Send this with my messenger as usual on the first boat leaving Knossos."

Arttarna knew the minute Kelu walked into the room that something had happened. Eyes down, she started slowly towards the corridor leading to her bedroom, changed her mind, and veered towards a chair. Halfway there, she turned again and came to a halt in front of his desk.

He pushed aside the report that he had begun to write to the king and waited. She didn't look at him. She drew the forefinger of her right hand along the edge of the desk. He observed the way the pale pink robe she wore complimented her flushed cheeks. Her dark hair curled in tendrils over her ears in the Minoan fashion.

Finally, she looked at him, her eyes somber, without their usual sparkle. "The king reprimanded me today."

The totally unexpected statement made Arttarna grab the edge of his desk and lean forward. He quickly controlled himself, simply saying, "Why?"

"A messenger came to the temple, announcing that the king wanted me to appear in the throne room immediately. The minute I presented myself, all conversation stopped. Everybody looked at me." Tears started to moisten her eyes. She blinked them back.

Sitting still, Arttarna watched the little frown gather between her eyes.

She swallowed. "The king informed me that I was not praying to the god properly because a minor rumbling of the earth occurred on the edge of the island towards the mainland. I thought quickly, fell down on my face, and said, 'Great King, the god did not send a huge shaking so he must have heard most of my prayers. I will go over my prayers carefully to find the portion the Earthshaker did not like or where I might have neglected something.'

"The king scowled and said, 'You do that. If we have any more upheavals, I will strip you of your position.'"

Tears tumbled from her brimming lids. "I was so mortified that I just lay on the floor. He told me to get up and leave his presence."

Stretching out her arms towards him, she said, "Father, I do not know what to do more than I have already done." Her head swayed from side to side as she passed one hand over her wet cheeks and dried it down the side of her robe.

Arttarna sat motionless, his eyes closed, his hand covering the lower part of his face. When he opened his eyes, he laid his hand in his lap. "I think I have a solution, Kelu," he said. "First, you must know that I received a message from King Tushratta yesterday. He wants me to go to Egypt."

"Egypt," gasped Kelu, placing both of her hands flat on the desk. "That's where Tadukhepa is." She wrinkled her forehead. "You will take me with you?"

"Of course, Kelu. Whatever made you think I would leave you here?" He drew his eyebrows together, his mouth becoming a straight line.

"I'm their priestess," she said in a small voice.

"Good. My thought is that Egypt does not have these earth upheavals. They probably have a god to make sure they never do. So you will suggest to the king that you should visit Egypt to consult the Aten, the great god of the Egyptian king, to find out what the Egyptian priests do to prevent these eruptions and learn their rituals. Naturally, I will accompany you."

"How perfect, Father. I will tell the king tomorrow."

"No, you will write to him, saying that you are in prayer on the subject and will inform him of what the god wishes you to do."

Kelu laughed. "Then in a day or two, I will let him know that I am instructed to visit Egypt to consult their priests?"

Arttarna nodded. "Yes. We will write the message together with details of when and how we intend to travel. I also must write him, excusing myself from my duties at his court so that I may accompany you. All our staff and belongings will go with us because it may take a long time to achieve our purpose."

"All your guard force, too?"

"A few of them will leave for the port of Memphis tomorrow with instructions to wait for us. The others will return to Mitanni to remain there until they are needed in Egypt.

Four days later, the king sent for Arttarna.

In the throne room, he bowed to the solemn, but pleased looking priest-king.

"I assume," said the king, looking down at the prostrate figure of Arttarna on the floor, "this suggestion is yours."

Arttarna touched the floor with his forehead.

"A brilliant solution. As a result, I am putting one of my fastest ships at your disposal. As I understand from your letter, you think this search may take your daughter some time. Therefore, the ship will return after depositing you and your daughter on Egyptian territory. Naturally, you are to keep me informed of your progress."

"Your Majesty, you are most gracious. I pledge to you that my daughter will write to you as soon as we learn what you are to do to stop this scourge on your country."

Arttarna left the palace feeling rather smug. The idea that had flashed across his mind with sudden brilliance while facing his stricken daughter had made their departure so smooth that he had to admonish himself on his rising pride.

None of his household saw the royal family again. Three days later, Arttarna, Kelu, his four servants, and his precious horses, boarded the king's swift ship and were rowed out of the Katsambas harbor.

18

Their ship floated slowly along the dock at Memphis, the ancient capital of Egypt. As soon as slaves finished tying the ship fast to small stone pillars with thick hemp cords, the Minoan captain hurried to where Arttarna stood at the rail with Kelu.

"Ambassador," he said, "if you will excuse my suggestion, the Egyptian riverboats would be swift and comfortable for the trip to Amarna."

"My thanks to your king and to you," said Arttarna.

Placing his hand on Kelu's elbow, he guided her down the gangplank into the swarm of people on the dock. "We will wait here until Rasi brings the horses off the boat," he said as Eshtar, Sebi, and Cook joined them.

Kelu stood mesmerized by the huge warehouses, the people, the Egyptians' dress, the great seagoing ships.

Her father cast his glance over the buildings and the noisy crowd, expecting to see one of the three guards he had sent ahead to Memphis. His eyes slid over one man then quickly returned to him and came to a halt.

The guard ambled close by, his eyes on the Minoan ship, and said, "Master, we have found lodging for the night."

"Excellent. Where are the other two guards?"

"Resting. We have been taking turns waiting on the docks, watching for ships coming from Knossos so we would be here when you arrived."

"Good. Take Sebi with you to our accommodations and bring the other two back here. We will wait."

Sebi and the guard disappeared into the crowd

"Here comes Rasi," said Kelu. "He's having trouble with your horse."

Arttarna immediately went to Rasi's assistance.

"He keeps shying at all the people here on the dock," said Rasi.

Taking the lead from Rasi, Arttarna whispered softly to the horse, and stroked him. The stallion whinnied and pressed against him, but soon walked along.

Almost immediately, the guard returned with the other two.

Arttarna pointed to the first guard. "You go immediately to Amarna and tell the chancellor that we will leave Memphis early tomorrow morning by fast riverboat to come to Amarna."

"Yes, Master." The fellow slipped away.

He dispatched one of the two remaining guards to Mitanni. "Tell King Tushratta that we have arrived in Egypt and then wait to see if he has any instructions for me. In any event, come to me in Amarna and bring the other guards with you."

The man turned and left them.

Arttarna addressed the last guard. "Reserve two riverboats for tomorrow morning, one large and one small. But before you do that, lead us to our accommodations. You and Cook help Rasi with the horses as we go."

"Yes, Master."

Rested and well fed, the group again joined the crowd on the docks the next morning. The guard led them along the river, away from the great seagoing vessels, to where the riverboats moored. He pointed to the two boats he had reserved.

"Quite satisfactory," said Arttarna after looking them over.

Standing alongside the smaller boat, he called out to Kelu. "We are going in this one." As she moved to his side, he took a firm grip on her elbow, helped her over the side, and watched as she seated herself under the awning, in the center of the boat.

"Eshtar," he said, pointing to the area behind Kelu.

"All the rest of you get into that big craft."

Sebi, Cook, and the guard helped Rasi board the horses. Having made sure everything suited him, his horses secured and his belongings stowed out of sight, Arttarna seated himself beside Kelu and ordered the boatmen to push off.

Kelu watched as the Egyptians, in their short linen skirts, swiftly poled the vessel into the middle of the river. The long, narrow boat skimmed over the water. To her amazement, she hardly had time to focus on a farmhouse, a lush pasture, or a group of cows before it disappeared and something else came into view.

"This, too, is a rich country," said Arttarna, noting all of the fields of waving grain.

As they approached Amarna, Kelu sat up straight and leaned over to grip the side of the boat. "Look at the mudbrick houses. Look at that large stone building. Oh, this is so exciting."

Arttarna smiled. He also thought it exciting.

Their boat slid silently alongside the wharf.

The guard he had sent to Amarna stood near an Egyptian official surrounded by a whole retinue. Arttarna sat back contentedly. "That is probably the emissary the chancellor has sent to receive us, Kelu. He is very elegantly dressed in that multipleated white linen skirt that angles stiffly out from his body."

"Father, you really think that funny garment is elegant?"

"Remember, my dear, this is Egypt. You will find many things different from Mitanni as well as from Hattusas and Knossos."

Kelu sank back in her cane seat and tried to avoid staring at the official's skirt.

The boat slowed to a stop. Immediately, many hands grabbed the sides. After pulling the boat to the wharf, workmen tied it securely to the small pillars.

The group of men surrounding the official broke apart. Those who appeared to be slaves raced towards Arttarna's boat while the official followed sedately under the large fan his slave waved over his head.

A bowing servant took Kelu's hand to steady her as she stepped from the boat onto the dock. She stood aside and turned to watch her father. He dexterously stepped from the boat and moved towards the Egyptian official. Kelu followed.

"I have the honor of greeting Ambassador Arttarna, the famous representative of King Tushratta of Mitanni?" The Egyptian smiled and lowered his head in greeting.

"You are gracious. Yes, I am Arttarna of Mitanni."

The official bowed. "I am Head-of-Household of Nakht, the Chancellor of Lower Egypt, at your service, Ambassador. The chancellor hopes you will accept his hospitality until we build you a house."

"His great kindness is humbly accepted." Arttarna bent slightly from his waist. "I have my daughter with me."

"She will be well cared for in the suite of the chancellor's young daughters." The official snapped his fingers at the slave to bring the chariot. "We will ride together to the chancellor's home in the southern suburbs."

To Arttarna's utter amazement, two prancing white horses pulled a gilded chariot to a halt right in front of him. The dark-skinned, hairless, and slender head-of-household stepped into the chariot behind the driver and signaled Arttarna to stand beside him. Kelu squeezed in close behind her father and clutched the sides of the chariot. Off they trotted.

"You must let us know how much housing space you will require for yourself and your attendants. It only takes a day or two to build a house once the site is chosen."

Arttarna lowered his eyes. Interesting comment. He wondered how that was possible.

Noticing Arttarna's reaction, the head-of-household explained that they could build houses that fast because they used mudbricks. "We have so little stone in Egypt," he said, "that we reserve that for our temples." The Egyptian smiled. "But our houses are quite comfortable inside with inlaid floors, plastered, and beautifully painted walls." He leaned towards Arttarna. "The chancellor has ordered one of the city's best painters to attend you and paint your house according to your desires."

"I am anxious to meet your chancellor and offer my thanks," said Arttarna.

The horses sped alongside a high mudbrick wall. Arttarna narrowed his eyes in approval as he watched the animals trot, their heads held high, feathers waving, bells jangling.

"This is the chancellor's property." The head-of-household pointed to the mudbrick wall on their left. "The entrance is just beyond."

The driver pulled in the horses and turned them through the gate. Glancing around, Arttarna estimated that the numerous buildings must include kitchens, servants' quarters, outhouses, stables, stalls and pens for the flocks, granaries, and produce storage areas. The enormous main house had a flat roof. Useful, Arttarna realized, when the weather turned very hot. One of the buildings even looked like a private chapel. Quite an establishment, he mused.

The driver drew up to the forecourt of the house. Servants immediately ran out to escort Arttarna and Kelu into the large reception room with cobalt colored pillars holding up the roof. The blue of the ceiling, and the red and yellow of the floor, overwhelmed Arttarna's senses. Down a long hall, he could see another pillared room with a lofty ceiling and gaily colored walls. Probably the dining room. He surmised that the family's private rooms surrounded these two public rooms.

A slave bowed. "Ambassador," he said, "please follow me. Your daughter will go with the woman to the children's area." He indicated the female slave who stepped from behind him.

"Come this way," the woman said to Kelu.

Arttarna watched her go to the left; he followed the slave to the right. They passed through a small family living room, the chancellor's workroom off of it. From there, they entered the sleeping quarters. Bedrooms with bathrooms and closets amazed him. Whichever way he turned his head, he saw bright colors and elegant furniture.

Kelu followed the Egyptian woman down a corridor. Before she had time to look around, she found herself whisked to the upper floors and ushered into a reception room in the children's quarters. A girl of about her own age rose languidly from a chair and smiled. Kelu swallowed hard, hoping her face didn't show the shock she felt. The girl wore an intricately pleated sheer linen garment, draped over her arms and ruffled around the bottom, with absolutely nothing underneath. Her head and body were shaved except for a long lock of dark hair that covered each of her ears. Kelu cautiously pressed her hands against her thighs to feel the fabric of her long pink linen robe, feeling certain the girl couldn't see through it.

"Hello." The girl greeted her with a happy, bubbling voice. "I'm Merenaten. My father is Nakht, the king's chancellor."

"I'm Kelu. My father is Arttarna, the Ambassador from Mitanni. We have just arrived."

"Oh," said Merenaten. "I know about that. You are staying with us until your house is built. Come along. I'll show you around." She led Kelu down a corridor. "My two brothers and three sisters, and I all live here in this area. We each have a bedroom, plus a couple of common rooms. And sometimes, we are allowed part of the roof when the weather gets too hot."

She opened a door. "One of my brothers sleeps here."

Kelu made a polite gesture of acknowledgment, but refrained from expressing her true opinion of the horribly small room. The bed took up all of the space.

"Do you have any brothers or sisters, Kelu?"

"No. I'm an only child."

"That's too bad. It's fun having brothers and sisters. I'm the oldest. Of course, the two youngest still have nursemaids. They live here, too."

Merenaten opened another door. "You'll probably sleep in this room."

"What pretty walls," said Kelu, her eyes shining as she gazed at the small boats on a quiet lake, black and orange birds fluttering around the reeds along the shore. The blue lake, set against the darker blue of the sky, made the bed seem to float in a watery bower.

Merenaten laughed. "I'm glad you like it. One of the best painters in the city did our rooms. And Papa let us choose the subjects. My youngest brother chose the theme for this room. He likes birds and fish and alligators."

Merenaten led the way up the flight of stairs to the roof. "You'll have a good view of our garden from here," she said, sweeping her arm around to indicate the house's garden and pool below them. "My father ordered all kinds of exotic plants and had them brought here. I don't know what a lot of them are."

"Oh, there's my father," said Kelu, pointing to two horsemen coming at a slow canter from a building behind the garden.

"The man on the right is the king's architect. They are probably going to make a decision about your house now."

The girls watched Arttarna and the architect ride towards the main exit. Kelu saw her father turn to the architect and say something. Sure that he was telling the architect what he wanted in a house, she wished that she, too, could hear what he said.

"As to where I would hope to have this house built," said Arttarna, "I prefer a plot of land close to the administrative center of the government."

"That's understandable," said the architect. "I'm sure we'll be able to find you a spot for your home that will be fairly close to the palace. There are some parcels of land available at the edge of these southern suburbs, a bit close to the workshop of Tuthmosis. But with a surrounding wall, that won't matter."

"Who is Tuthomosis?"

"He's the king's official sculptor. All of the statues of the royal family are made in his workshop." The architect reined in his horse.

"There is the workshop." He pointed to a large, low building on the right of the road ahead. "You could build on this empty space next to it. The plot runs all the way back to those brown hills and the southern tombs."

Arttarna studied the area. "I assume that large building just beyond the workshop is the king's palace?"

"Exactly right. And beyond that is the Great Aten Temple."

Arttarna turned his attention to the layout of his house. "I need an elegant, but comfortable, design with large enough accommodations for my daughter and me, stables for my horses, housing for my staff, kitchen, and sanitary facilities."

"Very good."

"Situated so close to the Nile, your water supply here must be plentiful."

"Yes, that's true," said the architect. "And having so much water also makes it possible for us to have fresh produce year-round. Our food is grown in the gardens across the river. The produce is rowed over each morning. Will you need animal pens? Or don't you plan to raise animals for your table?"

"I don't think so, provided there is a public market."

"There is."

"Fine."

"Then, Ambassador, I'll go ahead and draw plans for a traditional Egyptian house. The main door will lead into a rectangular hall with wooden pillars, the public reception area. Beyond this, you will have a few semiprivate family rooms, including dining room and your sleeping quarters. I imagine you want two bedrooms."

"Yes. Each with it's own private garden."

Smiling, the architect agreed. "The laborers will start making the mud base for the first layer of mudbrick early tomorrow morning. I'll mark off the outline for them tonight." He added, "After we lay the bricks, we pour more mud over them and then slam down another line of bricks on top of them to force the mud up through the seams. I'll also have my men put stretchers over these headers to bind them."

"Will the roof be flat, as with most of the houses here?"

"Yes, we make them of boards, covering them with durra stalks to protect them from the sun while they dry out and congeal. It's very efficient. Your house will be finished tomorrow. The next day, the plasterers and painters will finish the inside, and you will be able to move in the following day."

"Amazing. Absolutely amazing," said Arttarna.

The architect smiled. "While the plasters work on your house, the laborers will construct the other buildings you require and the surrounding wall. How do you want the walls inside the house painted?"

"I find the blue ceiling and the red-and-yellow floor in the chancellor's reception hall impressive. But I think I would prefer garden greens with trees and floral designs over the columns and walls instead of solid colors."

"It shall be as you desire," said the architect, bowing.

"I will leave you to your work and ride through the city center."

"Very good, Ambassador. As you look around, you may be interested to know that the king laid out the city himself. He came here from Thebes and drove his chariot around the area he wanted for his capital. He gave the workmen exact instructions for everything from the Great Aten Temple to the dwellings of the shopkeepers."

"Phenomenal." Arttarna wagged his head in astonishment. "He must be very talented."

"Our king is truly impressive."

Again, Arttarna bowed his head.

"You will find the king's house behind the great palace, between the Great and Small Aten Temples. Then, further along," the architect continued, "you'll come to the northern suburbs where the majority of the people live. Most of the city's merchants make their homes in that section of town because they have easy access to the quays from there. On the other side of those suburbs, you will see the North Palace, the North City, and the North Riverside Palace, all of them strung along the river."

"In easy reach of the boats."

"Exactly."

In profound amazement, Arttarna rode off to investigate this city King Akhenaten had raised up from the sand.

As Arttarna reached the palace complex, also housing the two temples to Aten, he slowed his horse to a walk, both because of the crowds of people and to get a better look. That large building ahead on his left must house the harem. How many women does he have? He inherited all of his father's wives, plus those he had himself. Added together, he could have a thousand wives. Arttarna shuddered at the very thought of so many wives.

Certainly Gilukhepa, King Tushratta's sister, if she were still alive, and Tadukhepa, were lost in that horde. They were only minor wives.

He counted out the number of years since Tadukhepa had come to Egypt. She was a woman now. It occurred to him that she must be about the same age as Queen Nefertiti, the king's principal wife. How could he get in touch with her? As children, she had been his daughter's closest friend, though five years older. A sweet child. Perhaps the chancellor might have a suggestion.

The head-of-household met him as he returned. "Ambassador, King Akhenaten has sent word that he will receive you tomorrow. So Chancellor Nakht needs to see you promptly at four by the clock this afternoon."

Promptly, as requested, Arttarna presented himself at the dining room door. The dark-skinned, beardless man sitting on a cane chair rose and came towards him. Tall, with a considerable paunch, he wore a round green hat and the usual stiffly pleated white linen skirt, along with a gorgeous gold and jeweled necklace over his shoulders and chest. About six thick fingers in depth of gold and gems, Arttarna judged. It blew his breath away.

"Chancellor Nakht," said Arttarna bowing, "I am deeply honored."

"Ambassador Arttarna, the honor is mine. You are welcome here for as long as you need to stay."

He gestured towards a door leading out of the dining room.

"We will go to a small private room where I will instruct you on how you are to behave in front of the king."

Arttarna followed the chancellor. The room they entered had beautiful garden scenes painted on the walls and no furniture. Nakht closed the door.

He turned to Arttarna and said, "On entering the great public reception room, you will have to make a deep bow, doubling over at the waist. It's rather uncomfortable, but it is prescribed by royal etiquette. While remaining in that position, you will then have to walk slowly towards the throne at the other end of the hall. Now, try it."

Arttarna doubled over.

"Further." Nakht put his hand on Arttarna's back and gently pushed.

"Ouch." Arttarna straightened up. "I can't do that."

"Yes, you can. Do it slowly, and keep trying until you are able to do it."

After three tries, Arttarna bowed properly.

"Now, walk to the end of the room," said Nakht.

After the first step, Arttarna gasped and stopped.

"Take a deep breath and try again," Nakht said encouragingly.

The practice took time, but Arttarna finally succeeded in walking while bowing. Straightening up, he said, "I find this performance degrading."

Nakht shrugged. "As you walk towards the king, be sure not to look at him. He is a god, and the public can only look at gods on special occasions."

After retiring to his room for the night, Arttarna practiced bowing time after time. Because his bedroom was tiny, he could only walk a few steps, but as he made the bows, he tried to figure out how he could look at the king without appearing to do so.

In the morning, Nakht and Arttarna stood in front of the great open doors of the king's reception hall. A rigid soldier in full battle dress guarded each side of the door. Arttarna caught his breath at the size and color of the huge rectangular hall with its red and green pillars.

A few men fanned out on either side of the two identical thrones. Nakht doubled over, making the formal bow required in the king's presence. Instantly, Arttarna doubled over. Together, they walked towards the far end of the hall. He stopped when Nakht stopped.

At first, because of his awkward position he had difficulty finding Akhenaten. Finally, the throne came into his vision. The king slouched on the throne. His sandaled feet rested on an ebony and gilt footstool. On his head, he wore the double crown of Upper and Lower Egypt and held a crook and a flail across his naked chest. Arttarna stared at the king's unexpectedly well-developed chest, amazed because the rest of his body looked soft and flabby.

A skirt of sheer pleated linen, tied around his waist, covered his genitals, but did not hide his heavy hips and thighs. The thought flashed through Arttarna's mind that this king seemed almost feminine.

Raising his eyes slightly and discreetly, careful not to make eye contact, he studied the king's face. His heavy, sensual mouth rose above the prominent chin from which hung the false beard, the sign of Egyptian royalty. The king's long, narrow, pasty face so flabbergasted Arttarna that he had to exert himself to listen to what Akhenaten was saying. That face bore no particular good for Mitanni or any other country.

Fortunately, the king was saying nothing that required a reply, only the usual formalities, welcoming him as the representative of his brother king, Tushratta of Mitanni, followed by many, many sentences extolling the friendship between their two countries. Akhenaten expressed his pleasure at having King Tushratta's ambassador be a resident in Egypt's capital city.

Arttarna's back began to hurt. He closed his eyes and wondered how long he was expected to hold this position. He opened them again when a lovely female voice added her welcome to the king's. She sat up straight on her throne, a footstool under her feet, the blue crown on her head, and had an exquisitely beautiful face. A wide gold and jeweled necklace also covered her chest. Otherwise, her shaved body, visible under the sheer linen garment, was nude.

Finally, having completed the ceremony of welcome, the royal couple dismissed him. With Nakht, he backed out. In the vestibule, in an agony of pain, he couldn't straighten up.

You're not the first person to suffer this," said Nakht and motioned to a masseuse, who hovered nearby, ready to be summoned in case of need.

"I leave you in capable hands. As soon as you are able to

mount your horse, ride back to my house. I will see you this evening. I think you can be pleased with yourself. Your interview went very well. King Akhenaten spoke to you longer than he does to most of the people he sees."

"Your king was most gracious, and I am a fortunate man to be so honored." Arttarna controlled his tongue, making no uncomplimentary remarks about Akhenaten or the bowing custom that was the cause of his pain.

With that, two slaves picked him up and followed the masseuse.

An hour later, Arttarna ordered his horse brought to him. On his way back to Nakht's house, he stopped to inspect the progress on his new home. Already, internal partitions were visible. The public reception room and three semipublic chambers had been marked out. Excellent, he thought, noting that the two bedrooms had been placed on opposite sides of the semipublic rooms. The green stone inlay on the plaster of the reception room floor pleased him. It gave a lovely spring feeling to the room. Six pillars had been set into the foundation, only waiting the roof to make the room architecturally complete. Delighted, he rode on.

Over dinner with Nakht, he broached the subject of Princess Tadukhepa. "The princess and my daughter lived and played together as children. Kelu hopes to renew their friendship. Can you help her?"

Nakht remained silent, his head bowed, for what to Arttarna seemed a long time. Finally, he said, "Probably the only way Kelu could see Kiya, which is Tadukhepa's Egyptian name, would be for Kelu to live in the harem as her assistant. I will contact her and ask her if she will receive your daughter."

Three days later, before the lingering heat subsided, Sebi hurried through Arttarna's bedroom into the lushly green private garden and immediately felt the slight coolness away from the stifling heat.

"Master," Sebi went down on one knee at Arttarna's elbow.

Arttarna raised his eyes from the government manuscript he was studying. Sebi held a slender papyrus roll in his outstretched hand.

"From the harem, Master."

"Tadukhepa," exclaimed Arttarna, taking the roll from Sebi.

He untied the bit of linen ribbon, unrolled the papyrus, and read it over quickly.

"Do you know where Kelu is, Sebi?"

"In the public audience hall, Master."

Kelu was walking around, inspecting the building when her father entered.

"Kelu," he said, waving the papyrus, "this note from Tadukhepa says that she has ordered a room prepared for you in the harem and longs to see you soon."

Kelu clapped her hands in glee and started to dance around the room, singing a little song that she and the princess had learned as children.

Arttarna laughed. "Well, it won't all be fun. I'll want you to do some work for me."

Kelu looked at him in surprise.

"Come along to my garden, and I'll tell you about it."

Once they had seated themselves in the garden, Sebi brought iced drinks, which he set down on the narrow table between their chairs, and left them.

Arttarna told Kelu that Tadukhepa now went by the name of Kiya. "What I hope you will be able to do for me is to gather information about Egypt that might be useful for Mitanni. The women in the harem won't be as guarded as the men in Akhenaten's court. The chancellor is a closemouthed man. He has only told me things that I already know or could observe for myself. King Tushratta has sent me here to find out if the Egyptians might help us if we are attacked. You may be able to learn more about this than I will at court."

He sat quietly, thinking.

"Perhaps Akhenaten has no intention of aiding us or anybody else on our coast. My own impression is that he is not interested in his eastern territories, or even in other parts of Egypt. I think he is an eccentric aesthete who is only concerned about this city, the Aten, and his women."

After further consideration, he said, "So far, all I have learned is that Egypt is the world's most fertile country because of the yearly flooding of the Nile. Grain grows here almost without effort. The Egyptians' main crops are wheat and barley, which they use to make the bread and beer most of the people live on. The supply of grain also pays the wages of the country's well-trained and efficient civil service. The Nile teams with fish, and the land all around it supports small game, fowl, fruits, and vegetables."

He sipped his drink. "Even the country's desert yields wealth. Gold and precious metals are abundant there, mined by the slaves. The richness of this country is overwhelming. The courtiers here at Amarna seem to have everything they want. But do they stay in this capital city of their own free will, or are they prisoners, unable to leave because of Akhenaten? They are isolated from the great centers of Thebes and Memphis and from the rest of Egypt. It's like living in a nutshell."

He turned to Kelu. "What did those girls you saw at Nakht's say about the rest of Egypt?"

Kelu drew her mouth down and snickered. "Nothing. They talked only about young men and clothes."

Arttarna snorted. "I've never seen such nudity among the aristocracy."

"It shocked me at first, too, Father, but I'm getting used to it."

"Well, don't let me catch you dressing that way."

Kelu tittered. "Don't worry, Father. I'd constantly be trying to cover myself."

Looking at her, Arttarna broke into a loud guffaw.

"Anyway," added Kelu, "I'll find out what I can while I'm at the harem. I'll try to get the princess to talk. I haven't seen her for so long, I don't know what she's like now."

"She was a gentle, charming child, and probably is a gentle, charming woman. How much power she has in a harem of a thousand women, I'll leave to you to find out."

"Will Eshtar come with me to the harem?"

"No. I want her to stay here to run the house."

"But Eshtar is mine, Father," said Kelu softly, with knitted brow.

Arttarna observed her. "You are right, of course. But if you will allow me, I think an Egyptian, maybe a dwarf, who knows this city well would better serve our purposes."

In silence, Kelu thought over his reasoning. "All right," she said finally.

"I will buy you a dwarf. However, there is one important thing. Too frequent communication will draw attention to her. So bind her to you and use her wisely."

"I will, Father." She fussed with her long braid before saying, "I'm pleased and honored that you have asked me to do this. I will try to do it well."

He leaned over and patted her shoulder. "My darling child, having lived with me in so many places around the world, by now, you are well schooled in this business. You will be a credit to me."

He straightened in his chair. "Let's go eat. Cook must have supper waiting. Sebi hasn't come to summon us. Now that he is married, he isn't constantly anticipating my every move."

19

On a warm bright morning a week later, accompanied by an ugly, dark-brown skinned dwarf twice her age, Kelu presented herself at the harem entrance.

A stately eunuch, dressed in the usual sheer white linen skirt, a gold chain around his neck, opened the door. "Princess Kiya awaits you," said the eunuch. He bowed. "Follow me."

He led Kelu and her dwarf to the harem's enormous, color-overwhelming, high-ceilinged reception room. Scenes from the lives of the Egyptian gods, elegantly painted in blue, green, yellow, and red, decorated the walls and gilded chairs lined one wall.

Kelu tried to judge the size of the room. Was it big enough for the one thousand wives her father said Akhenaten was supposed to have? Only a handful of women moved about in the room. Their small number made the room look huge by comparison. Some wore sheer robes in the semi-nudity style her father objected to; the others were dressed in the more traditional white linen sheath. All had perfectly hairless heads and bodies.

Her reverie turned upside down when she heard a lovely voice call "Kelu." And suddenly, she was caught in the strong arms of Tadukhepa, Princess of Mitanni.

"How wonderful to see you, Kelu. You haven't changed a bit except you are taller and older." Tadukhepa chatted happily, still hanging onto Kelu. "Come to my suite." She led Kelu down a corridor and into what Kelu considered a small room, painted in soft purple, blue and rose designs.

Kelu gulped at the exquisite workmanship, the luxury. Two carved and gilded stools on either side of a square gold-inlaid ebony table occupied the center of the room. Hundreds of polished pink and gray stones set in plaster and smoothed to perfection created a stunning floor. A tiny alcove to the right of the entrance door contained Tadukhepa's bed. The carved headboard and footboard, inlaid with ivory, stood on gilded legs in the shape of lion's paws. Next to the bed, an ivory-inlaid ebony dressing table with matching stool squeezed against the wall.

Kelu looked at Tadukhepa admiringly. An embroidered, fitted cap covered her head. Never fat, her body had rounded into that of a charming young woman. A large turquoise and gold pin just under her breasts held her pleated linen dress together. To Kelu's relief, the dress covered Tadukhepa's body.

"Tadukhepa, you are beautiful," exclaimed Kelu. "But you are hairless like all those other women?"

"Yes, of course."

"Why?"

"Because of the heat, the dust, and the bugs here. All the women at the court depilate their bodies as do a lot of the men."

"It looks funny, Tadukhepa."

The princess laughed. "I'm called Kiya here in Egypt. You must learn to address me that way."

"I'll try, but I may not always remember."

"Never mind. You'll get used to it." Kiya led Kelu to the table in the middle of the room and pointed to one of the stools. "Sit here." Taking the opposite stool, she leaned forward, placing her arms on the table.

"I have found much favor in the king's eyes, Kelu. I have born him two daughters." Kiya's face broke into a happy, delightful smile. "I think I'm with child again."

Kelu stared at her, amazed that her childhood friend was already the mother of two.

Kiya glowed with happiness. "I'm not quite sure yet, but I've told the queen."

"How wonderful." Kelu clasped Kiya's arms across the small table.

They sat gazing into each other's eyes. Looking at Kelu, Kiya felt the same happy companionship she had felt when the two of them lived together in the royal nursery in Mitanni. What a pleasure to have her back. "Let me show you your room. It's off a tiny corridor next to mine, making the two rooms a suite." Kiya rose. "Queen Nefertiti gave me a gorgeous golden bed for you."

"May I please have a mat for my slave?" Kelu pointed to Tefnut lurking in the doorway.

"Of course. She can sleep at the foot of your bed."

"Her name is Tefnut," said Kelu. "I have given her permission to go into the street whenever she needs to buy something for me or for herself. Is that all right?"

"I will alert the guards that she is free to come and go."

Kelu turned to the dwarf. "You heard what princess said, Tefnut?"

"I did, Mistress."

At that moment, Alala and Lesser Slave who had cared for Kelu in the royal nursery entered the room. Alala carried a white linen dress draped carefully over her extended arms.

With a cry of delight, Kelu jumped up and ran to Lesser Slave. The slave caught her shoulders to hold her and look at her. "Kelu, I can't believe it. You have grown into a beautiful young woman." She hugged Kelu.

Alala stood close, her big smile covering her entire face. "Kelu, how wonderful to see you—"

Kiya interrupted her. "You'll have time to talk later. Right now, I want you to help me dress for the afternoon reception, Alala. Put the dress on the bed." She turned to Lesser Slave, "Show Kelu her room then return to your duties." To Kelu, she said, "Get settled then come back to me."

Lesser Slave led the way to another tiny room containing the golden bed along with the same furnishings as in Kiya's room on the same polished pink-and-gray flooring.

Kelu felt honored when she saw the golden bed. "This really is beautiful," she said to Lesser Slave, touching the footboard.

"It's gold leaf," said Lesser Slave, secure in her knowledge of Egyptian artistry.

Again, she hugged Kelu. "I really must leave you for my other duties. But now that you are living here, we will see much of each other."

Kelu watched her hurry down the corridor.

Turning back to Tefnut, she said, "Lay my cosmetics on the dressing table."

As Tefnut was about to put her jewel case down, Kelu took it from her and opened the lid. She picked up a coin from its painted wooden square, holding it between her thumb and index finger. "I want you to look carefully at this gold coin, Tefnut. It is stamped with my father's seal."

Tefnut took the coin from Kelu's fingers, and, holding it close to her eyes, looked at the seal, turned it over to gaze at the intricate design on the back, and returned it to Kelu.

Kelu placed it back in the jewel case.

"If I am ever in trouble," she said, "you are to take that coin to my father. He will know what to do. He gave it to me for that purpose." She closed the lid of the jewel box. "Do you understand, Tefnut?"

"Yes, Mistress."

"Oh, and get yourself a mat, Tefnut," she said as she started for the doorway. "There is room at the foot of the bed."

On reentering Kiya's room, Kelu saw an elegant elderly woman sitting on one of the gilded stools, Kiya on the other. Before this regal woman, Kelu felt shy. She sat with grace, her back straight. Beneath her fitted, embroidered hat, elaborate gold and carnelian earrings hung to her white-draped shoulders. A large sunburst gold pin fastened the pleated linen gown.

"Aunt Gilukhepa," Kiya said, turning happy eyes on Kelu, "this is Kelu, my dear childhood friend, the ward of Arttarna, the Mitannian Ambassador."

Kelu gave Kiya a startled look at the term "ward," but remained silent, remembering the conversation she had had with her father in which he told her that Tushratta had asked him not to reveal that she was his daughter.

A smile crossed Gilukhepa's face. She had even, yellowish teeth. Kelu particularly noticed her teeth because so many of the older people she had seen here in Egypt had lost either several or all of their teeth.

"Kelu, this is Aunt Gilukhepa, my father's sister."

Kelu automatically fell to her knees.

"Rise, child," said Gilukhepa. "My niece has told me much about you, and I wanted to greet you." Gracefully, she rose. "I must return to my duties now."

In shy wonder, Kelu watched her glide from the room.

"Sit down, Kelu," Kiya said, indicating the other stool. "We have a short time to talk before we go to the great hall. The queen is coming to the harem today."

"Nefertiti," gasped Kelu.

"Yes." Kiya smiled at Kelu's breathless awe. "You'll love her. She's so beautiful, kind and clever. She helps the king in his work."

"Really? Does he have a lot of work?"

"He has a lot of correspondence to deal with. Other kings are always begging him for ivory and gold, mainly gold. They all want gold. Sometimes, he fusses to me about the amount of gold my father wants. But my father isn't any different from those other kings. They all want gold because it helps keep their countries wealthy and stable. He sends them some, but nothing like what they ask for. Then they send a letter back complaining about the amount of gold he sent." Kiya laughed. "They even ask him for Egyptian princesses to marry their sons. Isn't that incredible?"

"But other kings send their daughters here. Like you."

"True, but we are to some extent hostages, a bond that our fathers will remain loyal to Egypt in case of war. Egyptian princesses are never ever sent abroad. That's unthinkable."

Kelu raised her eyebrows.

"Does the queen help him write the letters?"

"I think she helps him word them. He has many scribes who do the writing."

"Of course. I forgot." Kelu blushed.

"Mostly, she helps him in the temple. She conducts many of the rituals for the Aten."

Kiya jumped up from the stool. "But enough of that now. You must dress for the queen's appearance. It's very formal."

Kelu hurried to her room to change her dress. "The pale yellow robe, Tefnut," she said. Tefnut helped get the robe over Kelu's head then surveyed her. "That sets off your golden brown skin nicely," said Tefnut.

"How lovely you look," Kiya exclaimed when Kelu again presented herself in Kiya's room. "You are all grown up and no longer the little playmate I remember. Thank goodness King Akhenaten doesn't come over here with all of his wives and children." Kiya laughed in gentle amusement.

Kelu blushed furiously.

Then Kiya really laughed at Kelu's embarrassment. "Don't worry; he stays in the palace behind ours with the queen."

Rising, she said, "Let's go see if my aunt has entered the reception hall by now. I expect slaves are already bringing in the children. My younger daughter is still a toddler and lives in the wet nursery, but you will see my older daughter," said Kiya, pleased.

They started slowly along the corridor towards the reception hall, walking side by side, having picked up their relationship right where it left off.

In the audience hall, Kelu was surprised that so few women had arrived. The room still looked empty in spite of the happy sounds of women greeting each other.

"Do the women who live in this harem stay in their rooms all the time?" she asked.

Kiya smiled. "You have much to learn. We don't sit around perfuming ourselves all day long, as I understand the king's wives do in Assyria. We have responsibilities. For instance, we are in charge of weaving all the linen used to wrap the bodies of the dead. That is a great honor. And it also requires tremendous amounts of linen."

"Do you receive pay for that?"

"Not as such. The king gives each of us a small amount of gold every year, plus we have private income and our own estates. We personally administer those. The king doesn't touch any of that."

Kelu's eyes were wide as serving plates. "You mean all his wives are independently wealthy?"

"Well, not all, but most of them, yes. My father sent all sorts of valuable gifts with me when I came here to marry the king. I was allowed to keep most of that. And if this new baby is a son, Akhenaten will shower me with even more gifts." She was silent for a minute. "It's unfortunate, but some of the women have never even seen the king. All they have to live for is their weaving and the administration of their estates. They are prisoners here, albeit prisoners with a lot of freedom."

She stopped talking and thought before saying, "Take my Aunt Gilukhepa, for instance. She's very wealthy. But now that her husband, the old king, is dead, she just lives here without any power. She's happy to be occupied doing the weaving and overseeing her properties."

"I suppose there are many others like that," said Kelu.

"Of course. All the women my king inherited from his father plus some of his own that he never sees."

"At least the ones he inherited got to be wives to his father. How sad for his own." Kelu suddenly felt aggrieved, thinking about the fate of all those women.

Kiya shrugged. "They're busy."

Abruptly, the reception room started to ring with laughter and the squealing of children, the overall buzz of many chattering women. The little children were all nude, the long hair locks over each ear proclaiming their youth. Mainly, the women wore the white see-through linen garments, allowing Kelu to see the variation in the color of their bodies. Some had golden tan skin like hers, some black, some white and all shades in between. The vibrant colors of the walls and the dark blue pillars flecked with gold added to the vivid scene.

Kelu stood transported and stared and stared until Kiya took her arm, saying, "Come along. I see Aunt Gilukhepa."

In front of Princess Gilukhepa, Kelu again fell to her knees and started to lay her head on the floor. Princess Gilukhepa caught her shoulders. "Stand up, Kelu. Don't ever do that again. As Kiya's friend, you are now my friend."

Kelu stood up, but kept her head bent. "Thank you, princess," she whispered.

"And we were good friends," Kiya said. "Then, of course, I came here, but we wouldn't have had much more time together anyway. Ambassador Arttarna would have been assigned to some foreign capital and taken Kelu with him."

She turned her head as a little girl, running pell-mell, yelled, "Mama, mama," and flung herself onto Kiya.

She stooped and kissed the dark-haired, black-eyed little girl.

"Kelu, this is Ankhesenpaaten-the-younger." She stroked the child's head. "Say hello to Kelu, darling."

Ankhensenpaaten-the-younger dropped onto one knee and bent her head.

The bow brought back such memories of bowing before Queen Inui in Mitanni that Kelu smiled broadly and patted the child's shoulder.

"Darling what—"

Hushed whispering, whipping through the room made Kiya break off and turn around.

"The queen. The queen is coming." Amid the hubbub, an elderly, plump, but regal woman hurried past them. "With three of the princesses," she stage-whispered over her shoulder.

"Oh my!" sighed Kiya. "You are lucky to be here on the day the queen honors us with a visit, Kelu."

She leaned over to hug Ankhensenpaaten-the-younger. "Run back to your nurse, darling."

"I want to stay with you."

"Not today, darling." She gave the pouting child a little push.

"You stay with me, Kelu," said Gilukhepa, "while Kiya greets the queen." Leaning forward slightly, head down, she backed towards the nearest wall. Kelu mimicked her.

With her back against the wall, Kelu stared at the tiny woman standing in the center of the room, three young girls standing in a row behind her. Through the sheer white dress, she could see every line of the queen's nude body. A large gold, gem-studded sunburst held the flimsy dress together just under her breasts. On her head, she wore the blue, flat-topped crown, well balanced above her long, slender neck. Her light brown skin glowed. Kelu thought she had never seen anybody so beautiful.

Kiya glided across the now empty center of the room and went down on one knee before Queen Nefertiti. "Your Majesty, we are deeply honored."

"Rise, dear Kiya," Nefertiti said. "I came to congratulate you on your hoped-for confinement and to tell you that the king and I have received the ambassador from your country."

"You are most thoughtful to tell me, My Queen. And his ward, my dear childhood companion, is here with us." She smiled at the three princesses in their pleated linen dresses, heavy make-up, and side locks of youth hanging from their otherwise hairless heads.

"How delightful for you," said Nefertiti. "I should like to meet her." The queen's large, soft black eyes, surrounded with kohl, swept the room.

"She is standing against the wall beside my aunt." Kiya gracefully waved her hand, summoning Kelu.

"This time," whispered Gilukhepa quickly, giving Kelu a little push, "you go face down and stay down."

Kelu couldn't move, bedazzled that this graceful, beautiful woman waited for her to approach.

"Move." Gilukhepa nudged her again.

Kelu hurried across the room and dropped flat instead of going to her knees and dropping her head.

Kiya said, "This is Kelu, my dear friend," and pointed to the body on the floor.

Queen Nefertiti smiled, shaking her head slightly, her eyes amused. "Rise, Kelu, and meet my daughters, the royal princesses."

As Kelu awkwardly scrambled off the floor, Nefertiti turned to her daughters. "Meritaten, my eldest at twelve years, has her own palace and staff."

The queen introduced each of the young princesses before saying, "My other three daughters are in the palace with their nurses."

She has six daughters, thought Kelu, surreptitiously eyeing the queen's body, slim except for some thickening around her waist and thighs..

"We are pleased to welcome you among us, Kelu," Nefertiti said.

"Kiya, will you attend me as I speak to some of the other women? Then, I must meet with my mother-in-law, Queen Tiy, in her rooms."

"Off course, Your Majesty." Kiya took her place, slightly behind, but still at the queen's side.

Standing beside Princess Gilukhepa, Kelu turned pink and stared after the queen. Her body through the linen glowed a pale golden color. Streamers inlaid with red, blue and green gems hung from the back of her blue, flat-topped queen's crown. Kelu licked her lower lip at the thought of that straight nose, delicately arched black eyebrows and full lips. She felt limp before such beauty.

While Alala and Lesser Slave bathed and perfumed Kiya the following morning, Kelu sent her dwarf for papyrus paper and black writing liquid. She simply had to pour out to her father the wonderful thing that had happened yesterday and her poor behavior, how Princess Gilukhepa, King Tushratta's sister, had instructed her afterwards on kneeling and behavior before Queen Nefertiti.

She wrote that her little room was comfortable, that Tefnut slept on a mat at the foot of her bed, that Kiya had produced two daughters and expected another child. She talked about the management of the harem, and the independence of the king's many wives, the freedom they had in dealing with their own affairs.

Then, unable to resist, she added some of the gossip about Akhenaten. The Aten took most of the king's time. Apparently his only interest was his religion. He left the running of the government to the queen, his mother, his chancellor and the other government officials. Kelu closed the letter with paragraphs of flowery, ecstatic descriptions of Nefertiti's beauty, but couldn't refrain from commenting on her fat lower abdomen and thighs.

Before she had quite finished writing, Alala appeared in the doorway. "Kelu, Princess wishes you to accompany her to her sunshade to offer prayers to the Aten."

Kelu sent Alala back with the message that she was honored to be asked and would be ready to go to the sunshade within minutes.

"Tefnut, take this to my father." She deftly rolled the papyrus and tied a small strip of linen around the middle. After a few brief toiletries, she rose and rapidly covered the few steps to Kiya's bedchamber.

"Good morning." Kiya kissed her, looked closely at Kelu and laughed. "You are absolutely glowing today."

"I'm so enchanted, I'm beside myself. I've written my fa—" She gulped, put her hand over her mouth and coughed. "—my guardian, telling him about meeting the queen yesterday."

"That was really lucky. Nefertiti doesn't come here often, and when she does, she rarely has the princesses with her. So I thought we should go to my sunshade this morning and thank the Aten."

"Don't you worship the gods of Mitanni?"

"No. The Aten is serene and wonderful. You'll see."

Carrying an armful of flowers, Kiya led the way across the polished, inlaid floor of the reception room, taking Kelu to the rear of the building. As they exited the harem, a soldier standing stiffly by the door doubled over in a bow. They crossed in front of the royal palace to reach the Great Aten Temple. The guard at the door in the wall surrounding the temple dropped onto his hands and knees, jumped up, and opened the door, seemingly all in one motion.

"Why are there so many soldiers here at the palace?" asked Kelu as they entered the temple grounds.

"The king doesn't believe in war so he keeps his army occupied as guards." Kiya waved it off as fluff. "Didn't you notice the two soldiers at the entrance of the harem when you got here?"

"No. I guess I was too interested in seeing you again to pay any attention." She smiled. Kiya gave her a quick hug.

After a short silence, Kiya said, "My sunshade is a small, one-room building in the first courtyard of the temple. The Great Aten Temple is a series of open courts connected by big pylons, which are sculpted like lotus buds. The altars are set up in the open courts, very different from the great temple in Thebes. The chief altar here is in the center court on the steps where the king and queen pray to the Aten. My aunt says the shrine for Amun-Ra in Thebes is very dim and mysterious. It made her nervous. She used to attend festivals there when Amenhotep III was alive. During those festivals, she had to walk from the riverboat to the inner shrine behind the king and some officials, going past a whole row of sphinxes facing each other. The priests brought the god out and showed him to the crowds of people. Here, the rays of the sun represent the god."

Kiya brushed Kelu's arm affectionately. "Here are the sunshades."

Kelu gazed at the little houses in the courtyard, three in the center and five surrounding those three. "Which one is yours?"

"The king's is the one in the middle with the queen's on the right, and mine is on the left. I'm the only harem member who has one." She turned to Kelu. "The king gave it to me after I had my first daughter."

Kiya walked through the open door of her sunshade and beckoned to Kelu to come along.

Kelu followed hesitantly, not sure that she should enter since she worshipped Teshub and the other Mitannian gods.

The morning sun lit the tiny room. Kiya laid the flowers

she had been carrying on the altar before raising her arms towards the golden sun disk painted on the wall near the ceiling. Spreading sunbeams from the disk reached towards the two women. Kelu jumped on seeing a hand on the end of each sunbeam. Some of the hands held the ankh of life. She stepped back, not quite afraid, but definitely uneasy. Were those hands going to grab her? She looked behind her, wanting to run from the sunshade.

Kiya dropped to her knees, keeping her hands raised, and gazed up at the sun disk. "Glorious," she said, "You rise on the horizon of heaven, O living Aten, creator of life. When you have arisen on the eastern horizon, you fill every land with your beauty. You are gorgeous, great and radiant, high over every land. Your rays embrace all the lands that you have made."

Kelu knelt down behind her, but didn't raise her hands. She mumbled an apology to Teshub and asked for help against this strange god.

Kiya bowed her head and remained silent for what seemed an eternity to the wary Kelu. What was she thinking back of that still, serene face? Kelu didn't dare move.

Finally, Kiya rose, again raised her arms to the spread hands of the sun disk, dropped them to her sides, turned and smiled at Kelu, a soft, beautiful smile.

Having risen when Kiya did and backed to the door, Kelu returned the radiant smile without realizing that she did so. How beautiful Kiya was. Not like Queen Nefertiti, but wondrously beautiful.

Kiya passed before her, and they left the sunshade.

20

Kelu sat gossiping with two young women in the main hall. She had made several friends during the time she had lived in the royal harem.

The two women suddenly hunched over, scrambled to their feet and, trying to look invisible, scurried behind a lapis blue pillar. Kelu blinked. What had she said? Then she cringed as a short, plump, disgruntled-looking woman, wearing a Nubian wig, sailed right up to her, coming to a dead stop not two fingers away. Kelu reached for the wall behind her to keep from falling backwards.

In the past, she had peered at the woman from behind a pillar. She knew all the young women were afraid of Queen Tyi, the king's mother. Without warning, her knees knocked.

"Who are you and what are you doing here?" Queen Tyi's sharp, crisp words caused Kelu to flush.

In the abrupt rigid stillness that replaced the happy chatter, every eye focused on Kelu.

"I—I—"

"Don't stutter."

Gilukhepa glided to Kelu's side and dropped gracefully to one knee, head bowed. "Great King's Mother, forgive this incon-sequential child. Do not let your displeasure fall on one so igno-rant, so uneducated. She has been brought up in foreign courts, which cannot possibly equal the elegance and grace of your royal court here in Egypt. This non-entity of a child is the ward of the ambassador from Mitanni, here at the instigation of Kiya, who wished to see her childhood playmate again."

"The Mitannian Ambassador, you say?" Tyi took a hard look at Kelu. "You have been here for six months?"

"Yes, Great King's mother," said Kelu. She managed to get onto her knees and bow her head.

"Well, your guardian is an intelligent man, a good ambassador. I have had dealings with him."

Tyi's eyes shifted. "Gilukhepa, knock some grace and knowledge of how to address me into her head."

The queen brushed past the two kneeling figures.

"Follow me," Gilukhepa whispered into Kelu's ear. She hurried from the reception hall, Kelu at her heels.

In Kiya's room, she sat down on one of the gilded stools. "You sit on that stool across from me," she said. "It's about time you learned some palace politics. So listen carefully to what I have to say. You are not to get into that kind of trouble again. The next time you see Queen Tyi, you are to go down on the floor, not just hands and knees, but face down. If she asks you a question, you are to answer her without looking up. Most of the time, she will simply pass you by, but you are to stay face down until she has moved away from you. Do you understand?"

"Yes, Princess." said a chastened Kelu.

Gilukhepa reached across the table and patted the folded hands resting against the edge of the table. "Queen Nefertiti, as beautiful, charming, intelligent, and capable as she is, is nothing more than a brood mare. The king desperately wants and needs to have a son to follow him on the throne and maintain the dynastic succession. But Nefertiti only produces girls. While Akhenaten loves his daughters, if Nefertiti doesn't have a son, and soon, he will replace her."

"Oh, no. How sad for her and the princesses."

"Yes, but that was a digression from Queen Tyi. I think you should know something about her background."

Gilukhepa shifted her position on the stool.

"Born into a family of Egyptian aristocrats, Queen Tyi was thirteen years old when the king saw her, fell in love with her, and married her. She turned into a strong-minded, dominant woman and ruled King Amenhotep as well as the country. Now, she rules her son. Though she no longer has the power she once had, she lives here in seclusion instead of at the great palace in Thebes."

The princess added that both she and Queen Tyi lived in the royal harem in Thebes when Amenhotep III was king. He had many other wives besides us—too many for one harem. Hence, there are harems all up and down the river. He would stay at the various harems when he traveled around the country, supervising the economy. Most of those harems still exist, though Akhenaten doesn't visit any of the harems outside Amarna. He doesn't even come here. His wives have to go to him. They pass through the Window of Appearances, which connects the harem with the royal residence."

"Have you ever been in the royal residence?"

"Yes, once. Queen Tyi asked a small group of us to accompany her to see Queen Nefertiti when she was confined with her last baby."

"What's the residence like?" Kelu leaned forward, eagerly.

An amused little smile crossed Gilukhepa's face. "It's just on the other side of the main highway, a vast walled compound with storehouses, gardens, a nursery for the young princesses and, of course, a large and luxurious apartment for the king and queen. You have never seen anything so splendid. All of the walls, columns, and floors in their apartment are painted and inlaid with colored stones, glazed earthenware such as faience and other types of pastes. You can't imagine the beauty of the color effects. Every piece of furniture there is exquisitely carved and covered with gold leaf, and is either made out of ebony or some other beautiful wood."

Kelu repeatedly wagged her head in utter astonishment.

"Nefertiti lay on her bed wrapped in blue covers, her favorite color. Slaves surrounded her. Anything she desired, they brought."

A sigh came unannounced from Kelu. "I wish I could see that apartment."

"Don't even think that," said Gilukhepa sharply.

Her tone silenced Kelu. After a long pause, she said, "What exactly are the king's duties? What does he do?"

"His duties and what he does are two different things."

"What do you mean?"

Gilukhepa squinted and pressed her lips together. "Well, he is supposed to meet with his chief dignitaries on a regular basis to get oral reports from them on such things as the collection of taxes, the level of the river when it floods every year, and the condition of the harvests grown on its banks. But he lets others such as Nakht do that. He also has to read the many, many documents he receives and decide what to do with them. Nakht has to do that, too. Besides that, he is the country's chief justice. But he delegates that. And frankly, so did his father. However, Amenhotep used to travel around the country to inspect things like the irrigation systems along the river. Akhenaten doesn't even do that. His only interest is worshiping the Aten."

"My goodness, Aunt Gilukhepa," said Kiya from the open door, "what are you filling Kelu's head with? She's not interested in that."

"Oh, yes, I am," said Kelu. "This court is so different from the others I've been in, I'm fascinated."

"Incidentally," said Gilukhepa," I have heard through palace gossip that you told the priest-king at Knossos that you would let him know what god Egypt has to prevent great movements of the earth. I hope you told him that Egypt doesn't have such a god, that we don't need such a god."

"I did," said Kelu, blushing. "I wrote to him about it soon after we arrived, but have received no reply."

"You probably will not either. He has to look for some other way to stop the earth from shaking."

She turned to Kiya. "I hear our chancellor scolded him in no uncertain terms for the last shipment of large painted pots he sent here."

"That is true," Kiya observed. "Nefertiti complained that she asked for one to put near the door of her bedroom, and the workmanship was so shoddy that she sent it back. Even King Akhenaten complained about having such a poorly made piece in the room."

"Oh, my," said Kelu.

"Nakht was furious," said Kiya. "He sent the pots back on the next ship."

She laughed.

"Well, no more of this, dear Aunt. I'm sure Kelu would like to come into the garden and sip a cool drink." Kiya turned to her friend. "Wouldn't you, Kelu?"

"Sounds enticing," said Kelu, smiling.

She looked at Princess Gilukhepa. "I appreciate all you have told me, Princess. I didn't know how to bow properly to Queen Tyi and made an idiot of myself."

"You did?" gasped Kiya. For an instant, she stared at Kelu.

"You see, there was a reason for the lecture." Princess Gilukhepa smiled at Kelu, rose, and walked to the door.

"I better check the weaving rooms."

Kiya and Kelu followed her. "Kelu will keep me company for a while," said Kiya, beaming at Kelu. Hand in hand, the two friends sauntered towards the main hall.

Hours later, before getting into bed, Kelu asked Tefnut for papyrus and writing liquid. She wrote almost word for word the conversation she had had with Gilukhepa.

"Tefnut," she said, rolling up the papyrus, "deliver this to my father first thing in the morning."

"Yes, Mistress."

As she crawled into bed, Kelu felt a pang, recalling that Gilukhepa had introduced her to Queen Tyi as "ward."

Restless and lonely, Arttarna laid Kelu's letter on his desk, wondering if her stay with Kiya would ever end. He missed her terribly. How could he fill up his time? His eye landed on Sebi, squatted in the corner of his office.

"Sebi," he said, "perhaps at noon, I shall take the riverboat to Thebes. I want to see the former capital and compare it to the fantastic luxury in Amarna."

He drummed on the desk with his fingers. "Have Rasi bring my horse around. I'll go see Nakht and ask him for a place to stay. We"—he looked pointedly at Sebi—"may be gone a week, more or less."

"Yes, Master." Sebi knelt in submission then ran from the room to tell Rasi to bring the master's horse.

In Nakht's red, yellow, and blue reception room, Arttarna listened as Nakht ordered a scribe to write a letter to the administrator of Akhenaten's palace in Thebes and request palace courtesy for the Mitannian Ambassador during a short stay in the city.

"You should be quite comfortable there," said Nakht. "I suggest you wait until morning when the sun isn't so hot to board one of the swift riverboats."

"I am grateful to you." Arttarna bowed low.

Early in the morning, he seated himself under the awning in the boat he hired.

"Sebi," he said, without turning his head, "I expect you to

observe how the people outside Amarna feel about their king, including their attitude towards his god and the capital he founded. I will do the same. We will compare our judgments when we return."

"Yes, Master."

Long before the riverboat reached Thebes, Arttarna became aware that they were approaching the old city. Commercial passenger boats, produce boats, pleasure boats, skittered along the river or idled in the marshes. The activity on the river far surpassed what he had seen in either Amarna or Memphis. Vegetable gardens started to appear along the riverbank, extending right down to the water. All along the shoreline, scantily clad men bent over hoes or squatted in the thick, nurturing soil, their hands busy with plantings. Nude children paddled in the muddy river's edge.

Soon, spaced mudbrick houses lined the shore then narrow lanes separated the rows of houses. The occasional stone temple, standing a little apart from the houses, also began to increase in number as they neared the city.

Suddenly both Arttarna and Sebi grabbed the right side of the boat and leaned over. Human-headed stone sphinxes faced each other across the wide paved walkway from a beautiful small stone temple up to a soaring temple set in an extensive complex behind mudbrick walls.

"That must be the great Amun-Ra Temple," said Arttarna, completely overwhelmed by its grandeur.

Almost instantly, their boat slowed. Arttarna swiveled his head around to look at the dock a short distance ahead. A portly dark-skinned man, dressed in the stiff pleated linen skirt typical in Egypt, and three slaves stood on a platform at the top of four stone steps. Behind them rose the royal palace.

The slaves jumped down the few steps to grab the riverboat. The official stepped forward.

"I am the Palace Administrator." He bowed. "Chancellor Nakht informed me that you wished to see something of our great city."

"Yes," said Arttarna smiling. "The chancellor is most gracious."

"Please follow me into the reception room."

In the palace, Arttarna stared, amazed. The huge reception

room extended across one side of the palace, an entrance at either end. Magnificent pillars that glittered with gold and gems held up the ceiling while polished green stone covered the floor. Elaborate painted battle scenes decorated the walls.

"Our great king, Amenhotep III, held court in this room."

"How elegant. The court here, with this room full of people, must have been a wondrous sight."

"Yes, it was. We miss having our king live here."

Arttarna detected the dissatisfaction in his voice.

"Is there anything in particular you wish to see today?"

Bowing slightly from the waist, Arttarna said, "This afternoon, I would like to visit the commercial area of Thebes."

"Excellent idea. Most of the merchants are still there. The produce market is already closed for the day, though. To see it, you will need to get there early in the morning."

"Very well, I will do that tomorrow morning and will see the rest of the market today."

"As you wish." He bowed his head. "The slave will show you to your room, and I will have a boy put at your disposal to guide you as you go to the market. When you return to the palace, tell one of the slaves to prepare some supper for you. And any other time, if you wish to eat, don't hesitate to order the slaves in your quarters to fetch you food."

He signaled to one of the slaves to show Arttarna to his room.

Aarttarna, along with Sebi, followed the slave along exquisitely painted blue corridors. He admired the gorgeous shades of blue on the walls, his practiced eye noting the variation in the color of the blue paint.

From the closeness of the area to the palace reception room, Arttarna guessed that the rooms off the corridor were meant for foreign ambassadors and their staffs. They entered one of the luxurious rooms painted in the same brilliant blues as the corridors.

"Sebi," said Arttarna after examining everything in the room with care, "I am used to luxury, but the luxury in which the Egyptian royals live is almost beyond comprehension. Look at the ebony wood, the gilded headboard on the bed, the inlaid top of the dressing table. I suspect every room on this corridor is the same."

"Very possibly, Master," said Sebi.

"As we leave, tell the slave to place a mat for you."

"Yes, Master."

Arttarna walked out the door and along the corridor lead-ing back to the reception room.

Having reached it, Arttarna found a small nude boy wait-ing for him. The child's black eyes looked up at the two men quizzically.

Arttarna smiled at the boy. "Take us to the market," he said.

The boy nodded.

They climbed into a riverboat and poled along the river until they reached an area crowded with people of all descrip-tions—men on horseback, matrons followed by slaves, children around a squatting vendor of confections. Arttarna walked with care around the items spread over the ground. Cookware, handcrafts, lamps, covered a large section of the market.

Taking his time, he inched along, fascinated by the number of objects the vendors offered for sale and the bits of silver that changed hands. He walked in and out of several little shops to assess the handwork of the objects traded. As in other markets he had visited, he found a wide variation in the quality of the goods, from sloppy and cheap to superb and expensive. The color, the vibrancy of the market, enthralled him.

After he had gotten a good sense of the city's commercial area, he turned to the boy and said, "Where do the officials live?"

"In the southern suburbs."

"Do we get there by riverboat?"

"Yes," said the boy, shrugging.

Cruising along the southern suburbs, Arttarna understood why the boy had shrugged. High mudbrick walls surrounded every house, making it difficult to see anything. However, he could judge the size of the house by the length of the wall around it. Behind those homes on both sides of the river, other estates existed. The wealthy suburb stretched as far back as he could see.

Arttarna mused. All the rich owners of these homes had chosen not to follow Akhenaten to Amarna. They wouldn't show him much allegiance if his power were ever threatened. Though, of course, some people such as judges needed to stay no matter what their feelings.

After a reasonable cruise along the river, seeing little because of the walls, he turned to the boy. "That's enough for today. Take me to the produce market early tomorrow."

The boy bowed assent.

Shortly after dawn the next day, they reached the produce market. Arttarna found it much like the one in Amarna—crowded and noisy, with the occasional screaming altercation as the people bargained over the beautiful fresh produce. Arttarna shook his head and laughed.

Later, at the entrance to the Temple of Amun-Ra, he said to Sebi, "Keep the boy with you. Wait here until I get back."

Slowly, he advanced between the great papyrus-budded pillars, staring in disbelief. How small and puny they made him feel.

A tall, immaculately groomed priest in a starched white linen skirt walked towards him with sedate, measured steps, a gentle smile on his bronzed face. The smile spread to his almond-shaped eyes. "May I be of assistance?"

Arttarna smiled in return. "A tour of your famous temple would be much appreciated. I find myself overwhelmed by its beauty and grandeur."

"You are a stranger here?"

"Yes, from the Kingdom of Mitanni."

The priest's smile broadened. He half turned and extended his hand, sweeping it across two rows of seven columns with beautiful papyrus-bud capitals. "These pillars were placed here by our king, Amenhotep III, the father of the current heretic king." He spit out the last two words.

Arttarna lowered his eyes.

"The wall decoration in this area of the temple illustrates our god, Amun-Ra, traveling on the river from our temple, which is his home, to the nearby temple of the goddess Mut. He goes there at the time of the Opet festival."

"What is that? Forgive my ignorance."

"Please, no apologies. The Opet festival celebrates their union and happens in the late summer. A great procession of priests escorts Amun-Ra's bark as he sails from this temple to Mut's temple so that he, Amun-Ra, can unite with her. After a great feast, he returns here in an ecstasy of joy."

"The procession must be an impressive sight," said Arttarna.
"Yes. It is glorious."

They moved slowly forward. "We now enter the Solar Court
of King Amenhotep III." A double row of magnificent columns
with papyrus-bud capitals of the most elegant workmanship
surrounded the court on three sides. Arttarna stopped to savor
the beauty of the temple. The priest gave him time to look
around.

"On that far side," said the priest, "is the entrance to the
great hall of our king. Amenhotep III would lead his court through
here with great solemnity on his way to offer prayers and a
sacrifice at the main altar." He gestured towards a hall that had
numerous columns.

"As his son has moved the court to Amarna, that ritual is
no longer conducted in this beautiful hall. Unfortunately for us,
he has both defamed Amun-Ra and shown no concern for properly administering Egypt or the territories conquered by our
great military king, Tuthmose."

Arttarna noticed that the priest said all this with quiet dignity, but his eyes were angry and flashing. So, this priest not
only resented Akhenaten's worship of the Aten, but thought that
the king was destroying Egypt's military might. Interesting because he himself believed that ordinary Egyptians missed the
panoply of Egypt's military might.

"We will now enter the great hall of our king," said his
guide.

Standing under the hall's great pylon, Arttarna gasped. He
tilted his head back, his eyes bulging. Eight rows of columns,
brilliantly colored in reds, yellows, blues, and greens, met his
stupefied gaze. All had papyrus-bud capitals except those lining
the central walkway, which fanned out into open papyrus blooms.
Never had he seen pillars so gigantic or so breathtaking.

After letting Arttarna gaze as long as he wanted to, the
priest apologized for not taking him to Amun-Ra's room. "He
lives in semidarkness. It's better we do not disturb him."

Arttarna agreed. "Perfectly understandable."

The priest led him to the room where the two sacred
barks were kept. Only the door through which they entered
and the door to the sacred lake relieved the dimness of the
room. That second door allowed the priests to carry one of the

gilded, lightweight barks sitting on stanchions to the lake for use by the god. Arttarna and the priest existed the building through that door and faced the tranquil, sun-dappled lake fed by the Nile.

"Does Amun-Ra sail his bark on this lake?" asked Arttarna.

"Yes, unobserved by common people. Each morning, Amun-Ra sails and each evening we priests purify ourselves in the lake." He turned. "The great scarab you see on the shore"—he swung his hand towards the opposite shore—"was set there by Amenhotep III to represent the newborn sun."

The priest remained silent for a short time. "We constantly pray to Amenhotep III in his god state to intercede against his son. That individual has made a mockery of our religion. Amun-Ra is angry. We try to pacify him by telling him that the whole thing will collapse the minute the current king dies."

Jolted, Arttarna remained still, gazing across the water and listening. He noted that the priest never called Akhenaten by name.

"The fact that the queen bears only females is Amun-Ra's proof that the dynasty will not continue," said the priest.

Arttarna shuddered internally. So Egypt would not only have a religious fight, but a dynastic one as well. He knew the priests would win. What would happen to Tadukhepa and her aunt?

"We will return to the entrance now. You are welcome to enjoy the peace and godliness of our temple any time while you are a resident in this great city."

Arttarna bowed his thanks to the priest.

He found Sebi squatted in the shade afforded by the size of the temple as the sun slanted off it. The boy who had guided them around Thebes lay curled up beside him, asleep. Motioning to Sebi not to move, Arttarna walked up to the boy and stood looking down at him. "About eight or nine, do you think?"

"Probably eight," replied Sebi.

Arttarna gently nudged the youngster with his foot.

The boy hopped up and dropped to his knees at sight of Arttarna. "Please, please don't tell the master at the palace that I went to sleep," he pleaded, his clasped hands raised.

"Of course not," snapped Arttarna. "Lead on. Where do you propose we go next?"

"My Master suggested I show you the workmen's village of Deir-el-Medina."

"Very well," said Arttarna. That might give him an idea of what the laboring classes thought about their king and his god.

The boy loped ahead. They crossed the river and entered the village.

On a path so narrow that they had to stand against a wall and wait for a laden donkey to pass, the boy turned his head back to speak to Arttarna. "I will take you to my father's house. We live in this village."

So this was an arranged visit for just the purpose he had had in mind. They walked along a row of identical, single-story houses lining both sides of the pounded-earth main road. The flat roofs undoubtedly served as another room—sleeping, cooking, and eating in the summer's heat.

The boy veered left and opened the door of a house halfway down the line of homes. "Father," he called.

In seconds, a thin, light-skinned man in a short linen skirt, banded about the waist, appeared.

"Welcome to my humble home," he said, bowing to Arttarna.

In a quick look around, Arttarna saw several small statutes of deities in the wall niches. Otherwise, the room was bare.

The man led Arttarna to the house's sitting room. "My wife will offer you refreshments," he said.

His small, skinny wife, wearing a simple garment that had short sleeves and covered her from neck to ankles, brought in beer and flat bread, which she placed before Arttarna.

Arttarna slackened his thirst and ate a bit of the bread.

"What type of work do you do?"

"I'm a plasterer and I need to work. I used to work in the nearby tombs, but not much tomb building is going on now. Only some small ones are being built. They are for wealthy men who served Amenhotep and remained here."

"Is that enough work for the village?"

"No."

"But all of you have a home."

"Yes, each family here has a comfortable home with rooms for sleeping, a kitchen, and a roof. But we used to receive regular pay of fish, vegetables, milk, and small cattle. We also got firewood, which we stored in our cellars. But we stopped hav-

ing all those things when the new king moved everything to
Amarna. Some of the families in our village moved there to
work on his tomb in the foothills back of the city."

"I have seen the area."

"The rest of us have had very sparse work since then,"
continued the man. "All the plasterers in the city suffer." Bitter-
ness showed in his voice.

After a little more talk, the conversation lagged, and
Arttarna made a motion to leave.

As the workman preceded him to the door, Arttarna surreptitiously slipped a little gold among the dishes on the floor.
He bowed to his host and left the house, followed by Sebi and
the boy.

Walking back to the river, Arttarna mulled over the sullen
resentment he sensed from the city's occupants. The fury underneath the quiet exterior of the priests boded no good for this
king or for Egypt.

The following day, a fast riverboat returned Arttarna and
Sebi to Amarna.

21

Kiya's voice sounded sharp, unpleasantly pitched. "Kelu, come here this minute."

Trying to fathom the basis for the sharpness, Kelu moved slowly towards Kiya's room.

"Here," commanded Kiya, pointing her finger at the floor directly in front of her. She stamped her daintily sandaled foot then grabbed her protruding abdomen. "Oh, this baby is so active."

"Are you all right? Can I help you?" Kelu braced Kiya with one arm.

"How dare you touch me, you, you slave."

"Slave?" Kelu blurted. "I don't understand you, Kiya. Your pregnancy must be affecting your senses."

"My pregnancy has nothing to do with this. You are a slave. Get that white linen dress and that beaded collar off this minute. And, here"—Kiya threw a short gray garment on the floor—"put this on."

Stunned, Kelu said, "No, I won't. That's a slave's dress."

"You used to do my bidding as a child; you better do it now. I'm queen of Egypt. Move." She started menacingly towards Kelu.

Pale and frightened, Kelu ran to her room. "Tefnut," she called, "come quickly."

The dwarf appeared, seemingly from nowhere.

"Princess Kiya has ordered me to put on this slave dress," Kelu said with a sob in her voice.

"Why?" Tefnut scowled angrily.

"I don't know. I don't know what has got into her." Kelu turned to her dressing table, opened her jewel box, and lifted her father's gold coin, stamped with the seal of Arttarna, Ambassador of Mitanni, from its tiny painted wooden square in the box. "Take this coin to Ambassador Arttarna right now. Give it to him personally, to no one else."

After Tefnut left, Kelu placed her gold, precious stones and enamel necklace in the jewel box, removed her linen dress, and slipped the gray slave garment over her head. Humiliated, she returned to stand before Kiya.

"Down," commanded the princess.

Kelu knelt on the floor.

"You palm yourself off as an aristocrat when you're nothing but a slave. You hoodwinked my father and shamed me. I'm going to have you whipped."

She signaled to the eunuch that the distraught Kelu had not noticed standing in the corner. "Go ahead."

The whip curved in the air and came down across Kelu's shoulders. She screamed in pain and crumpled onto the floor.

"Another," yelled Kiya in glee.

The whip descended across Kelu's back and buttocks.

"Harder."

Again, the whip lashed through the air, coming down with a harsh crack against Kelu's soft flesh. The excruciating pain left her unable to cry out, stopped her breath, made her feel faint.

"Again."

Kelu lost consciousness.

"Two more," commanded Kiya.

As the whip blooded her back, Kelu remained motionless.

"Dump her on her bed."

The eunuch grabbed the unconscious Kelu, threw her over his shoulder, and left the room.

Kiya stormed back and forth in the confined space for a few minutes until her anger subdued. She shook herself and hurried to the main reception room as rapidly as she could waddle.

Lying on her bed, Kelu fell in and out of consciousness. She kept her eyes glued shut. If only the excruciating pain in her back would subside. With an agonizing effort, she rolled over on her side. Ah, that gave a little relief. She wondered if the lash had cut her skin, if her back would be scarred. She heard the door open.

"Mistress, Mistress." Fear reached Tefnut's short legs, causing an explosive rush to Kelu's side. "What have they done to you?"

"The coin?" The effort to speak made Kelu wince in pain.

"Ambassador Arttarna has your coin. I gave it to him myself."

"What did he say?"

"He told me to come back and wait with you."

Tefnut's sharp eyes swept over Kelu, noted the bloodied gown and the welts on her shoulders. She hustled around the bed to get a better look. "Great Amun! Who did this to you?"

"Princess ordered a eunuch to whip me."

"You need a physician." Tefnut rushed to Princess Gilukhepa's rooms. Her slave sat on the floor before the closed door.

Tefnut nervously clasped and unclasped her hands. "Tell princess that we need a physician immediately in Princess Kiya's suite."

The slave disappeared inside. Almost instantaneously Gilukhepa hurried out. Thinking Kiya's pains had begun, she swept along the corridor as though wings aided her.

Tefnut gulped and ran, trying to stay behind her. "Princess, it's Kelu," she panted, "not Princess Kiya."

Gilukhepa halted, turned to stare at Tefnut for a moment then flew on. She glided into Kelu's room, around the bed, widened her eyes, raised her eyebrows, heavily let out her breath, and departed as rapidly as she had come.

"Bring cool, perfumed water and a soft cloth," Tefnut heard her say to someone in the hall.

Seconds later, a slave appeared, a bowl in one hand, a cloth in the other. She handed them to Tefnut and retreated.

As gently as she could, Tefnut start to bathe Kelu's shoulders. Kelu cried out in pain. Tefnut laid the damp cloth across the bruised shoulders. Kelu cringed.

Princess Gilukhepa entered the room, followed by a royal physician. Tefnut backed away from the bed, closed the door and stood against it.

The princess stopped at the foot of the bed where she could observe as the physician treated Kelu. He walked past her to the other side of the bed. Carefully, he raised the wet cloth and bent over Kelu's shoulders, his eyes inches away from her body.

Gentle as a breeze, he passed his hand over the swelling under her bloodied dress, felt her forehead, and noted her breathing. All through his examination, he uttered clucks of disapproval.

In accompaniment, Tefnut emitted little worried sobs.

A knock sounded. Tefnut peeked out the door then opened it wide. Two burly female slaves stood in the doorway. "Ambassador Arttarna has ordered us to bring his daughter to his home," one announced. "He waits at the side door of the harem."

Taken aback by the word "daughter," Princess Gilukhepa slowly nodded assent.

"Bring a stretcher," said the physician. Without a word, the two slaves disappeared.

Shortly, they returned, carrying a strong piece of linen doubled over and stretched tightly between two poles. They laid this on the floor parallel to the bed.

"Lift her gently," ordered the physician. -

One of the women slid her hands under Kelu's neck, the other placed her hands under Kelu's thighs. Barely raising her an inch, the women slid her from the bed and lowered her onto the carrier. She cried out again before lapsing into unconsciousness. Biting her lip in worry, Tefnut carefully draped a clean sheet over her mistress.

Addressing Tefnut, the physician said, "Tell the ambassador that I will collect my medications and meet him at his home."

"I will," said Tefnut.

In the dusty side street outside the harem building, Arttarna paced back and forth frantically. He ran his hands through his hair, pulled at his beard, snorted. What was keeping those slaves so long? All they had to do was grab Kelu. Two strong, burley women could overpower anyone who objected to letting Kelu leave the harem.

The door opened. He stopped abruptly when he saw the stretcher. Kelu needed a stretcher? He rushed to her side. Unconscious. For just one instant, he collapsed internally. Then, "Follow me," he commanded, setting a fast pace. Tefnut marched solidly behind the slaves bearing the stretcher.

At Arttarna's house, the two women carried the stretcher into Kelu's room and placed it on the floor alongside the bed.

"Lay her on her stomach," said Arttarna.

Lifting her with extreme gentleness, the women placed Kelu on her side then rolled her onto her abdomen. They picked up their carrier and left the room.

"Tefnut," said Arttarna, "take that garment off Kelu. I'll send Eshtar to help you." He hurried out of the room.

Tefnut started to pull the bloody garment along Kelu's legs. Eshtar entered. One look at Kelu and tears formed. She hurried to the bed.

"I'll raise her hips and you draw the dress up," said Eshtar. Working together, they pulled the slave garment over Kelu's buttocks then had to stop. The dried, caked blood on her back caused the dress to stick to her body. Eshtar ordered perfumed water and a cloth.

Using the cloth, Tefnut dampened the dress. Eshtar cautiously pulled, Tefnut dampened and Eshtar pulled, tugging the dress ever so slightly until the fabric released. They repeated this process several times until the garment came off. Tefnut tucked a clean, lightweight linen sheet around Kelu, leaving her damaged back exposed.

They looked up at the sound of a single knock and the door opening. Arttarna entered, accompanied by the physician, carrying a large, colorful box.

Arttarna hovered for a few minutes. He couldn't stand it and bolted into the reception room where he vented his anger in loud, wild guesses as to the cause of the beating and threats of vengeance. Only Sebi heard.

After what seemed an eternity to Arttarna, the physician came out of Kelu's room. He smiled. "Your daughter has been badly beaten, but I think she will be all right. I have rubbed a healing salve on her back and shoulders and left sedatives for her with your slaves. I also instructed them on how the drugs should be administered."

"Will there be scarring?" asked Arttarna.

"The salve should help her back heal and reduce some of the scarring. But whether I can prevent all the scarring, at this point, I don't know. It's too early to say." He picked up his medication box from the nearby table where he had placed it while talking to Arttarna. "I'll come first thing in the morning. She will probably regain full consciousness sometime during the night."

"May I ask you to deliver a note to Princess Gilukhepa?"

"Yes, I will see that it is delivered."

"Give me a few minutes." Arttarna hurried from the room, to return shortly with a piece of rolled up papyrus.

The physician courteously bowed and picked up his bag.

Left alone, his fingers curved across his mouth, Arttarna shook his head sadly. Upon reading his note, Gilukhepa would know the truth about Kelu and his promise to her brother, King Tushratta. Giving himself a final shake, trying to throw off his mood, he went to Kelu's room to stand and look down on her, his face drawn and worried.

Kelu lay partially on her side, propped by bolsters, her eyes closed, but color back in her face. Arttarna lingered at her bedside until Eshtar gently said, "Master, there is nothing to do. Tefnut and I will alternate sitting by Kelu tonight." He looked so sad that she wanted to comfort him.

"I know," he said. "And I appreciate your concern for her." He touched Kelu's hand. After a few minutes more, during which he watched her silently, he left the room, withdrawing to his office, where he could be alone and not have to worry about disguising his feelings.

"Tefnut," said Eshtar after he left, "try to sleep for a few hours. I will watch over her first then you can do it. We will take turns so one of us will be awake to attend her when she regains consciousness."

"All right." Tefnut dragged the words out. She didn't really want to share the care of Kelu, but Eshtar was the mistress' senior slave and what she said was wise.

In the morning, Kiya woke with the disturbing feeling that somebody other than Alala had entered the room. She opened her eyes and raised her head to look into her reception area. Princess Gilukhepa, severe and straight, stood in the center of the room. Sensing trouble, Kiya said, "Please, Aunt, send for Kelu to help me dress."

"Alala will help you dress after I leave you. Right now, I have a few questions, and I expect straight answers from you."

Kiya pushed her feet over the side of the bed and sat up.

Gilukhepa didn't move from the spot where Kiya first saw her or change her attitude in any conciliatory way. Tall and slim, dressed in her immaculate formal white linen garment and her exquisite jewelry, her dark brown face tight with controlled anger, she frightened Kiya. "I want to know exactly how Kelu came to be beaten last night, who did it, and why."

Anger flared in Kiya. "She's a slave. She hoodwinked my parents and disgraced me. I have a letter proving it."

Gilukhepa extended her hand. "Hand me the proof."

"Slave!" called Kiya.

Alala instantly stood behind Gilukhepa. Without taking her eyes off Kiya, Princess Gilukhepa said, "I will call you when you are needed."

Alala disappeared.

"Hand me the proof," Gilukhepa repeated.

Realizing that she could be in enormous trouble if the information in the letter were false, Kiya became frightened. The ruddy, angry color faded from her dark skin. Eyes lowered, she waddled to her jewel case on the dressing table, supporting her abdomen with her left arm. Out of the box, she drew a piece of papyrus. "I received this yesterday." She handed the papyrus to her aunt.

"You may sit down, Kiya."

Gingerly holding her protruding abdomen, Kiya sat on the stool.

Gilukhepa turned the papyrus right side up and read the single paragraph plus the signature.

You have living with you as your dearest friend a slave, the daughter of a slave. Arttarna lied to your father when he begged him to take the slave's child as an attendant to you. I know this to be true because I am Arttarna's wife. He gave me the slave as a present. Garadu, wife of Ambassador Arttarna.

"After you read this, Kiya, what did you do?"

"I confronted Kelu with the knowledge. She denied that she is a slave, but this letter from Arttarna's wife sounds convincing, and I believed her. I forced Kelu to put on the slave's garment then I had her whipped to punish her for lying to me and my family."

Without moving any other feature, Gilukhepa closed her eyes. She took a deep breath. "Ambassador Arttarna is Kelu's father. She has been taken to his home so she can recuperate."

Kiya muttered, "Her father! Oh!" Putting her elbows on the

little table, she cradled her head in her hands, uttering little moans.

"A royal physician attends her. The eunuch you had do the whipping has been imprisoned."

Kiya groaned and pressed her fingers into her face.

"The queen is furious and is threatening to tell the king. Ambassador Arttarna has written to your father, telling him what you have done. You are in disgrace. You are not to leave your quarters until Queen Nefertiti has been here to see you."

Gilukhepa turned abruptly and left a frightened, deflated, penitent Kiya, clutching the table for support.

Princess Gilukhepa sent the papyrus communication to Arttarna along with a note explaining that a special messenger had delivered the enclosed letter to the harem.

Standing in the dining area, Arttarna read the letter. So, his supposition that Garadu might be behind the attack had proven true. He went out into his bedroom garden, hoping that the coolness of the air and the sweet fragrance of the flowers and shrubs would calm his anger. This was the fourth time Garadu had tried to destroy his daughter. The first time had been at the court in Mitanni. The second, he now felt sure, was the day Prince Zidantas died. And the third might be questionable, but he didn't think so. That had to be the attempt to sacrifice her in Knossos.

For a long time, he sat in the garden, the papyrus communication limp in his hand. Finally, he called, "Sebi, send one of my guards to me."

"Yes, Master."

He continued to look straight ahead when the man knelt beside him. "You have been with me for a number of years. You know where the parents of my ex-wife live?"

"Yes, Master."

"For the fourth time now, she has attempted to destroy my daughter. I think I need say no more. You know what to do."

"I do, Master."

The man left as silently as he had come.

Sebi hurried into the garden and stood besides Arttarna. "Master, the physician has seen mistress and wishes to speak to you."

"Bring him to me."

Moments later, the physician walked into the garden and bowed before Arttarna. "She is improving rapidly," said the physician. "I put some more ointment on her back and gave her another sedative."

"What about scarring?"

"Maybe there will be a little scarring on her back, but not on her shoulders where it would show."

"Thank the gods for that." Arttarna was silent for an instant before saying, "You will come again tomorrow?"

"In a few days, Ambassador. If she improves as she has already, I think that will be sufficient."

"Very well."

The physician bowed and departed.

Arttarna rose and went to Kelu's room. Propped on her side, munching fresh bread dipped in a beef stew, Tefnut and Eshtar supervising every mouthful, Kelu smiled at her father. "The physician has just left here," she said.

"He says you are doing well," said Arttarna, returning her smile. "Now, I want to talk to you, Kelu."

"Tefnut," he said, turning to her, "Take this food out and both of you leave us."

Tefnut grabbed the nearly empty bowl of stew, put the bread on the dressing table and followed Eshtar out of the room.

Arttarna pulled the stool from where it stood against the wall, placed it by the side of the bed, and sat down.

"Kelu, Princess Gilukhepa had a scribe write me a note and enclosed a letter that Princess Kiya received two days ago. I think it wise that you read that letter. If you have any trouble reading, I'll help you. Then we can talk about it." He handed her the sheet of papyrus.

Kelu shifted her position slightly and read slowly, her index finger stopping at each symbol. Finished, she extended the letter to Arttarna. Their eyes met.

"Was my mother your slave?"

"Only in the sense that I gave a man money for her. She was never a slave in the normal sense of the word. I happened to be in the slave market and noticed the humiliated, frightened girl being offered for sale by a poverty-stricken couple. They were shy and sad and very upset that they had to sell their daughter into slavery. A rough man tried to fondle her. She cried out and jumped from him. The dealer yelled at her and grabbed her arm. On impulse, I raised my hand and called, 'She's mine.' The dealer knew who I was. He told her to follow me. She was probably fourteen years old."

He ran a hand through his hair. "I gave her as a present to my wife. However, before long, I had fallen madly in love with Kelpha. Do you remember her name?"

"Yes. Hepit, Pamba, and the cook called her by that name. But I didn't know she was a slave. Though now that I think about it, I should have guessed. We lived in the kitchen, the servants' quarters."

Arttarna kept silent for a long time, fighting his emotions. "My wife, a jealous woman, sensed my feeling for Khelpa and started to mistreat her. One evening as I passed her, I noticed an ugly bruise on her arm. I stopped and asked how she had gotten the bruise. She obviously didn't want to tell me, but I demanded an answer."

He stopped speaking, casting his eyes on the floor. Silently, Kelu watched him.

"In halting language, she told me that Garadu, my wife, had pulled her arm straight and repeatedly hit the muscle with a heavy metal rod because Khelpa had dropped a bundle that was too heavy for her. Right then and there, I took her to my friend Pamba, the Hittite, and asked him to keep her. And, of course, that's where you lived."

"Your wife never knew about me?"

"No. She realized I had hidden your mother and that I was seeing her constantly."

"Is—is—" Kelu spoke with difficulty. "—the woman who attacked me in the royal nursery your wife?"

"At that time, she was my wife. The day after she tried to murder you, she was no longer my wife."

"Oh, Father, it was my fault," wailed Kelu, trying to sit up.

Instantly, Arttarna jumped to his feet, his hands pushing her back among the bolsters. "My dear child," said Arttarna, caressing her arm, "I didn't want that woman. I wanted your mother as my wife."

He sat back down. "Actually, she was my wife in all but the ceremony. She was the most beautiful woman I ever saw and the sweetest. No other woman could ever match her."

Kelu turned her head away. Unstoppable tears ran down her face.

"Kelu, you are as beautiful as she was. You are my child, as you know, and her child. Are you a slave? No, you are not. The moment I took you into my house and recognized you as my daughter, you ceased being a slave, if you ever were. Your mother was a member of the lower classes. She had that exquisite light brown color that you inherited rather than my dark brown skin."

"Does anyone in Wassukkanni know that she is my mother and you are my father?"

"Pamba does, of course, but nobody in the court other than King Tushratta. I don't think even the queen knows. The king and I talked of your background, as I told you the day I explained that I was your father. To everybody else, your ancestry is a mystery, if they consider it at all after these years. People here might question you about it because of what Kiya did. If pressed, all you need to say is that your mother was a lady of Mitanni. And I don't believe the fact that Khelpa was your mother will cause us any more problems."

Kelu looked at him questioningly, her fingers floating over the papyrus.

"This is the fourth attempt Garadu has made on your life. I have now taken steps to see that it never happens again."

Kelu closed her eyes. She knew what he meant.

Shortly, she raised her eyes to his and said, "What about Kiya?"

"Unfortunately for her, Queen Nefertiti is furious at what she did. Gilukhepa did not say what her punishment would be, but I hope it won't be too severe at the moment anyway with her pregnancy so close to conclusion."

In a sad, soft voice, Kelu said, "I would hate to have anything happen to her."

"Granted. But now, my darling child, we must get you strong and well." He kissed her forehead.

"I think I'll sleep a little then ask Eshtar to bathe and dress me so I can sit in my garden."

"Good idea. Tefnut has gone back to the harem to collect your belongings. On the way to my worktable, I'll send Eshtar to make you comfortable." He gave a little snort. "You have a problem on your hands between the two women, each wanting to be the one to wait on you."

Kelu laughed. "I love them both."

A short time later, from the open doorway of Arttarna's workroom, Sebi said, "Master!"

Arttarna looked up.

"Tefnut waits to see you."

"Good. Tell her to come in."

Halfway to the desk, Tefnut knelt on one knee. "Master, I have brought all my mistress' belongings from the royal harem."

"And?"

"I did not see Princess Kiya. By order of Queen Nefertiti, the princess has been confined to her rooms until her baby is born. She is not allowed to have visitors."

"That will be a hard punishment for Kiya. Do you know when the baby is due?"

"Within the week."

"How is she?"

"Her slave says she spends all her time crying. Princess Gilukhepa has tried to talk to her through the door, and she won't answer her. The whole harem is upset at the harm she has done to the king's relations with Mitanni. They say she should know better, that Kelu is your acknowledged daughter. She is not a slave."

Slowly, thoughtfully, Arttarna said, "I hope her crying doesn't bring on the baby. If it is a boy and anything happens to the child, the king will do some punishing himself." He shook his head. "Poor Kiya."

"I will keep you informed, Master."

"Excellent, Tefnut." Arttarna picked up his stylus to finish the letter he had started to write to King Tushratta.

Much to Tefnut's surprise, Kelu was not in her bed. She laid the jewel box on the dressing table and looked over the three white linen dresses. They all needed laundering. She tossed them on the floor and walked to the open garden door. There beside a flowering oleander bush sat Kelu, bolsters at her back, a blue sheet tucked around her knees. Eshtar stood in front of her.

A happy smile on her face, Tefnut hurried to Kelu's side. "Mistress, you are better." She noted the pink color in Kelu's face and the absence of the agonizing pain wrinkles on her forehead.

"Yes, I'm better. The physician will come again in three or four days, but I think I will be up and around by then," said a confident Kelu.

Tefnut made a clucking sound with her tongue. "Not too fast. You have plenty of time to let it heal."

Eshtar smiled at the tiny slave. She really cared for Kelu. Eshtar shifted her glance to Kelu. Obviously she had learned the treatment of slaves from her father. She herself adored the girl as if she were her own child, worried about her, suffered with her, and complained to Sebi when anything bothered her. Sebi took it all in stride, though she knew he adored Kelu, too. She fervently prayed to both Mitannian and Egyptian gods that Kelu's back would not be scarred. At her marriageable age, she didn't need welts on her back.

The next morning, dressed in a fresh white linen garment, carefully gathered at the front and held together by a great gold sunburst set with pearls, carnelian and lapis lazuli, Kelu breakfasted with her father, a blooming, healthy young woman going on thirteen.

Arttarna observed the glow, the perfection of dress, the happy face. "My dear, you have brought the light of golden days to our home." Before he became maudlin, he applied himself to his gruel and tender beef slices.

Three days later, hanging over Kelu's bed with the physician, he inspected her back. To his relief, he saw no raised welts.

"Those red marks," said the physician, "will fade in intensity, but will probably never go entirely. That is the best we can hope for."

"You have done well. She is not unacceptably marred."

"No. In which case, I will not come again, unless you need me for some other reason. We have our hands full at the moment with Princess Kiya. Her last birth was easy. This one will not be."

"She is due right about now, is she not?" said Arttarna.

"Any day. She continually sobs and paces the floor, begging for the presence of your daughter."

"Oh!" Kelu hid her face in the bedding. "I wish—"

"No, Kelu," said Arttarna sharply. "You are to stay out of the king's harem."

The physician nodded agreement.

Two days later, moving leisurely, Arttarna and Kelu had reached the dock area, prepared to walk along the river when Kelu grabbed his arm in consternation.

"Look at that water! What's happening? Is it going to drown us on this side?"

"No." Arttarna smiled down at her. "This is what is so fascinating about the Egyptian river. It's the basis of much of their great wealth. Each year at this time, the river floods, inundating the land. When it recedes into its channel, it leaves wonderful sediment on the land. The farmers immediately plant. The growth is immense, outstanding. Huge amounts of grain are stored in government bins to feed the public with plenty left over for use against disaster. Egypt has so much grain, they even export some."

"It never floods on this side?"

"It's channeled so, no, it doesn't. It is channeled through the great cities south of us also. Important religious services take place every year in thanksgiving for the great abundance of the river."

They walked slowly, stopping every few minutes as Kelu exclaimed at some marvel.

At one point, Arttarna said, "Egypt has many other sources of wealth."

"Like gold," Kelu announced.

Arttarna snickered. "Yes, like gold."

"I know King Tushratta writes letters to King Akhenaten asking for gold. Kiya told me so."

"Yes, but that's between the two of us," he admonished.

She bowed her head, embarrassed.

"Not only does the government receive gold from the Mines of Kush, the area in the south, but this river makes possible trade with other southern countries which supply ivory and ebony, ostrich feathers and eggs, leopard skins, cattle and slaves. So you see, Egypt is not only rich in what they have here, but carries on a tremendous amount of trade, not just with the south, but all the countries going towards Mitanni and north of us. From a place called Punt, they receive myrrh, all kinds of beautiful plants. Egypt doesn't have trees so they want costly woods, as well as incense and eye cosmetics."

"So that's where we get the eye kohl!" gasped an astonished Kelu.

"They also import monkeys and greyhounds, a form of dog."

"I can't believe this."

"Other countries send sheep, fine oils and honey. Have you seen any elephants?"

"Not that I know of. What's an elephant?"

"An enormous, gray animal with a long, long nose and great ears."

"How funny."

"You may see somebody riding on an elephant at one of the religious parades."

"Oh, when?" Kelu wiggled in anticipation.

Arttarna laughed. "Probably soon. They have religious festivals constantly."

She stopped walking and gazed across the river, scanning all the land as far as she could see covered with water.

Sensing that she was tiring, he said, "We will go home now. This afternoon, we can sit in my garden, and I will tell you about their government. I've written some pointers to our king. He would be wise to institute them in our government."

Kelu's eyes opened wide. She had thought the Mitannian government perfect.

Arttarna read her face. "Well, it is not quite."

"What isn't?" She bridled.

"All our citizens should be like you." Arttarna let out a loud gaffaw. "For instance, King Tushratta is the head of the justice department. Here, King Akhenaten delegates that responsibility. I think our king should do the same. Many men in our government would be excellent at this job."

"What else?"

"Later." He turned her around.

Early that afternoon, trying to get away from the heat, Kelu and her father seated themselves in his garden. The small table between them contained cool drinks. An eager Kelu turned to Arttarna.

"Please, can we talk about the government now?"

"Well, to begin," Arttarna sipped his drink and placed it back on the table, "Egypt has two chancellors. One serves all the northern part of Egypt while the one whose house we stayed at when we first arrived serves all of Southern Egypt. Their powers are determined by a code of regulations that has been in effect for generations. They take care of all the administrative business such as boundary controversies. They write numerous reports to the king about everything that goes on. Another of their jobs is the construction of great temples, so that even the bricks manufactured are controlled by them."

"Goodness, that's a lot of work."

"They are exceedingly busy men. However, the one thing they don't control is the finances. Numerous overseers run the treasury. Their rank is just under that of the chancellors. All taxes and payments in kind are delivered to the treasury."

"What do you mean by payments in kind?"

"Some people don't have money. They pay their taxes or debts by giving a cow or a donkey. Maybe some who have vineyards give wine. That's what I mean."

Sebi came to the door and waited. Tefnut hid behind him.

"What is it, Sebi?"

"Tefnut has information." He stepped aside.

Tefnut moved into the opening. "Princess Kiya has gone into labor. The harem is frightened."

22

With a cry of agony, Kelu leaped to her feet. "Father, I must go to her."

Arttarna looked at his daughter's distressed face and quivering body. "My dear, undoubtedly, Kiya is surrounded by physicians, helpers, slaves, everybody who could possibly be of use and otherwise. You would just be in the way. However, I realize your anxiety. You may go with Tefnut as far as the harem. I do not want you ever again inside the king's harem. Do you understand?"

She nodded, along with a reluctant, "Yes, Father."

He looked at Tefnut. "Tefnut will keep you informed."

"Yes, Master."

Kelu spun round and rushed from the garden, through the house, along the main road, Tefnut trying to keep up with her, and stopped at the harem entrance. "Tefnut," she panted, staring wildly at the closed door, "tell Kiya that I love her, I forgive her. Make her understand."

"I will, Mistress." Tefnut knocked, identified herself and entered, leaving Kelu alone, her nose almost touching the door. For long minutes, she stood there, gazing unseeing at the narrow door with the military guards on either side. Then she turned and scanned the street. The usual crowd of merchants, workmen, townspeople, horses, slaves pulling loaded donkeys, chariots, passed by.

She kept emitting little moans. A tragedy might be taking place in the palace, and they went about their business unconcerned. She moved a few steps away from the door and rested her shoulder against the building façade. How long she stood there, she didn't know.

Suddenly, the door opened. Tefnut stood before her. "Mistress, I begged the midwives to tell the princess what you said, but they would not. She called out for you. I elbowed some of the people and pushed into the room. I had almost reached her when somebody grabbed me. I yelled to her what you said. She turned her face towards me and smiled. Then she screamed and twisted, clutching the bed. I came away." Tefnut's voice dropped and her little body sagged.

"Go back. When she delivers, come and let me know. I'll be right here." Kelu continued to lean against the building, walked a short distance up and down in front, conscious that the guards moved their heads along with her motion, then stood still, watching the sun sink.

An aristocratic looking young Egyptian glanced at her, stopped, looked, started towards her. One of the guards moved between them. The young man heedlessly brushed off his thought and continued lazily along the road.

Tefnut exited the harem. Quietly, without expression, she said, "We will go home now." Tears formed in her eyes.

Kelu grabbed her shoulders and shook. "Tell me what happened, Tefnut."

Tefnut stood rigidly in front of Kelu, lowered wet eyelashes, and said, "Slaves carried the swaddled baby away. Princess is dead. The king is distraught. He tears his hair. Queen Nefertiti tries to comfort him."

Kelu crumpled. She put her hand on the wall to steady herself. Then with tears streaming down her face, she said, "We will go home, Tefnut."

At their light evening meal, Arttarna and Kelu sat at the table across from each other, saying little. Kelu played with her food then pushed the bowl away.

Head bent, eyes on his own bowl, Arttarna said, "I shall write a note to Princess Gilukhepa asking her what she wishes me to do about telling King Tushratta."

"It's so sad." Kelu ducked her head, trying desperately not to cry. Suddenly, she said, "I don't want to have any babies. That could happen to me."

Taken aback, Arttarna had to collect his mind. "You don't necessarily have a choice, my dear."

She lowered her head and pouted. "I'll ask the old women what to do."

Arttarna observed her through narrowed eyes, but said

nothing, expecting time to take care of the matter. This might be the moment to bring up some changes in their household arrangements to get her mind off Princess Kiya.

"Kelu, with your consent, I am going to free Tefnut and send her back to her family."

Kelu's head went up, her eyes intently on him.

"Eshtar will take her proper place at the foot of your bed. I want you to run our home the way you ran it in Hattusas. That pleased me."

She smiled weakly at his praise, not sure she wanted to lose Tefnut.

"I will tell the dwarf in the morning."

"Suppose she doesn't want to go."

"I cannot imagine any slave not wanting to be free."

After breakfast, Arttarna sent for Tefnut. Then, sitting behind his desk, with Kelu seated nearby, he gave her her freedom.

Tefnut's face lit up like the sun.

"I will send you back to your family a free woman," Arttarna said.

Tefnut fell to her knees, her hands clasped in front of her. "Please, Master," she begged, "I have always wanted to work on the riverboats. A free woman, I could do that and earn some money to help my family." Then, lowering her eyes to the floor, she added, "We are very poor."

Quietly, Arttarna said, "As you wish, Tefnut. Do you want me to help you?"

"If you would tell the captains I'm free."

"I'll give you a piece of papyrus stating that I have given you your freedom."

"Thank you, Master." With bowed head and lowered eyes, she said, "You have both been good to me." Fleetingly, she looked at Arttarna before letting her eyes linger on Kelu.

Later in the day, she returned, to stand before Arttarna who sat working at his desk. "I have found a boat," she said. "The captain will hire me, but he wants to see the papyrus you said you would give me."

He glanced at the top corner of the desk, picked up a piece of papyrus and handed it to her. With a formal bow, Tefnut went in search of Kelu.

Fifteen days after Princess Tadukhepa's death, Sebi placed

a package from Princess Gilukhepa on the desk in front of him. "A royal messenger brought this," said Sebi.

"Open it."

With great care, Sebi unwrapped layers and layers of linen. First, a rolled papyrus addressed to King Tushratta appeared. For some minutes, Arttarna held it in his hand. Then slowly, he said, "I'll send this by personal messenger. It relieves me of writing the details about Tadukhepa's death." He laid the letter down and looked at Sebi who promptly continued the unwrapping.

Watching, Arttarna breathed heavily as gold started to appear followed by jewels. Finally, an exquisite collar lay on the desk. "For Kelu," he said, his eyes devouring the beauty of the workmanship.

Sebi nodded and again began unwinding. The last of the linen fell away. In his hand, he held a beautiful glass drinking cup. "For you, Master."

Arttarna reached for the glass and carefully turned it round and round. A glittering blue predominated, fading into a warm, glowing red at the bottom. Flecks of other colors spattered through the blue. "Gilukhepa has been more than generous." He kept turning the lovely glass around to watch the color change. At last, he handed it to Sebi. "Put it in my bedroom where light catches the glass so I can see it from my bed."

The household began to settle into a routine. Each morning, Kelu haunted the markets along the river, accompanied by Cook. Though she and Cook discussed menus, commented on the produce, and made their daily purchases, Kelu missed Tefnut's company. She searched each boat that sailed by, hoping for a glimpse of her dwarf. At that final parting, she and Tefnut had hugged each other and cried. Afternoons, she found boring and wished for the gossipy, happy chatter of the harem. That didn't last.

Merenaten, the chancellor's eldest daughter, introduced her to a diverse group of young Egyptians. They fished in the marshes, hunted lions in the western desert, and partied away the evenings. She started curling her heavy braid of black hair around the top of her head like a cap.

Arttarna watched, glad to see her enjoying the company of other young people again. She had seemed so sad lately. He spent his time as usual, writing in the morning and socializing in the afternoon, trying to glean information useful to Mitanni.

At sundown, one evening, Arttarna sat in his garden enjoying the coolness when suddenly the messenger he had sent to Wassukkanni so many months ago knelt before him.

"Master, I have returned."

"And?"

"The matter you sent me on is concluded. Your daughter will never again be bothered. I went—"

"That's enough. You have done well."

The man hurried away.

Weeks later, sitting with Kelu in his garden, a worried expression on his face, Arttarna said, "Another letter came this morning from King Tushratta. His brother stirs up all kinds of problems. I don't trust the man. And this Egyptian king is no use at all. He cares nothing for his brother kings who have given him their loyalty and depend on his strength. Suppiluliumas of Hattusas keeps up a steady incursion into the territory of his neighbors and receives no rebuff from Egypt."

Arttarna sat silently, looking blindly at a delicate young fruit tree, then said, "Suppiluliumas has eyed Mitanni for a long time. And one day, he will be back. This time, he will be victorious, perhaps with the help of Suttarna, King Tushratta's nephew."

"Why would Suttarna want to destroy Mitanni?" demanded Kelu, moving forward in her chair.

"In the hope that Suppiluliumas would appoint him as vassal king."

"He couldn't, he wouldn't." Kelu leaned forward. Her fist came down on the small table at her elbow, making her glass of beer jump.

Arttarna passed her comment off with a wave of his hand. "Who knows what he's doing?" He looked at his fingernails. "Whatever it is, it means trouble for Mitanni. An unscrupulous man, his only interest is in furthering his own ambition."

"Our poor king," Kelu lamented. "First, he ordered a great celebration for the coming marriage of Prince Mattiwaza to an Amurra princess, then the bride died before she reached Wassukkanni. Second, he recalled his brother from Nineveh, and his brother is undermining him."

Looking at her, Arttarna smiled, his eyes adoring her.

"The whole business is just awful." Kelu slid back in her chair.

"And the sad thing is that in spite of everything I've written him, King Tushratta still thinks Egypt will come to his aid." Arttarna wagged his head. "It's useless."

Kelu caught her breath. "While we sit here talking, King Suppululiumas could be attacking."

"No, my dear. It's winter. King Suppiluliumas doesn't go to war in winter."

"Oh! I forgot."

He rose. "Enough of that. Let's go to the king's audience in the Window of Appearances."

Kelu jumped up. "He will open his audience by leading the public in a beautiful hymn to the Aten."

"How do you know that?"

"Princess Gilukhepa told me. She taught me the hymn."

Kelu started to sing in a high, sweet, young voice.

"Thy dawning is beautiful in the horizon of the sky.

O living Aten, beginner of life!

When thou risest in the eastern horizon

Thou fillest ever land with thy beauty.

Thou are beautiful, great, gleaming and high over every land

Thy rays, they embrace the lands to the limits of all thou has made

How manifold are they works

They are hidden from before us,

Thou art afar off, yet thy rays are on the earth;

Thou did'st create the earth according to thy heart

While thou wast alone."

She shyly looked at her father with a little smile.

"Lovely," Arttarna pronounced and started into the house.

A crowd had already assembled in the street below the bridge between the harem building and the royal residence, the center of which, high above the street, formed the great Window of Appearances. In silence, the crowd waited, every eye fixed on the window.

Arttarna and Kelu stationed themselves against the harem-building wall across from the residence. Shortly, the main road under the bridge became packed solidly way back to the building's edge. Uncomfortable in the dense pushing crowd, Arttarna worked his way gingerly around a well-dressed fat Egyptian who pressed against him. That was better. He could breath in the space against the wall behind the man. Next thing he knew, Kelu shoved the man.

"Kelu, come around him," Arttarna said, stretching out his hand towards her.

"That's better," she said, facing Arttarna.

A cry went up. Kelu jerked her body around and raised her head. "Oh, there's the king," she yelled. "And here comes the queen with three young princesses." She jumped up and down, grinning excitedly.

"Look," said Arttarna, "the king leans way forward towards the people, shaking a sistrum, making it rattle."

"The queen has one, too, and the little princesses tiny ones." Somehow, that pleased her.

As they watched, the princesses hugged their mother, pushed each other playfully, and smiled down at the silent, mesmerized crowd.

The audience over, the people dispersed.

"The queen has a younger sister called Munodjimet," Kelu observed as they walked along.

"I have not heard talk of her," said Arttarna, looking down at his daughter, "only of the six princesses."

"That's because she's not royal."

"Explain yourself."

"The queen isn't royal either. Her parents, like the parents of Queen Tyi, her mother-in-law, are wealthy aristocratic Egyptians. The king saw her and fell in love with her. As his father had done the same thing when he saw the thirteen-year-old Tyi, he couldn't object when King Akhenaten wanted to marry Nefertiti."

"Well, you are full of information. Where did you learn all this?"

"Princess Gilukhepa told me all about the royal family one day when she was instructing me in court etiquette."

"What else did she say?"

"The king's mother, Queen Tyi, lives in the harem and owns slaves to care for her numerous agricultural holdings. She doesn't like it because the queen only produces girls. She wants the king to put Nefertiti away and marry some important royal princess."

"He has plenty of royal princesses in his harem."

"He won't do it. Besides, he likes beautiful women."

"Nefertiti is certainly beautiful."

"She's artistic and charming, too. She designed that blue crown she wears all the time."

Arttarna raised his eyebrows. "Not only is she a strong, competent queen, but a talented artist. Very impressive."

Absent-mindedly, he scratched his head. "Other kings are married to strong-minded women, but their behavior is destructive. I wonder if their behavior would be different if the women had more freedom. Egyptian women have more personal freedom than our women."

"You give me a lot of freedom, Father."

Arttarna reached over and patted her shoulder. "True, because I need your help and you are intelligent. However, you notice I do not leave decisions to you."

Kelu opened her mouth to refute his statement.

"—except in our home," he quickly added.

They both laughed.

Three months later, Kelu woke thinking about the afternoon's large dinner party. She kicked the linen sheet off. Already, she felt unbearably hot. "Eshtar," she called.

"Good morning." A smiling Eshtar appeared in the doorway.

"Three buckets of water. I'm already perspiring." She followed Eshtar to her bath where Eshtar slowly poured three buckets of warm water over her. Kelu squirmed in delight. "I'm thinking about shaving my body. All this hair is constantly wet with perspiration."

"You better consult your father before you do that. I don't think he would like you to lose your beautiful long, black hair."

"Then we'd see how much freedom I have."

Eshtar eyed her strangely.

Later that day, the half-expected, the talked about in the privacy of a bedroom, happened. Queen Nefertiti left the royal quarters for the palace in the southern suburbs, accompanied by the young boy Smenkhkare. No outward reaction occurred in the city that day or the next day when King Akhenaten married

Maritaten, his oldest daughter. Kelu and Arttarna discussed it at dinner.

"It's disgusting," Kelu pronounced. "His own daughter."

Arttarna shrugged. "The Egyptian royal line descends through the women. The king by law is obligated to marry his sister or daughter, though many do not."

"I think it's terrible." Kelu screwed up her face in anger.

"That's because you are partial to the queen." Arttarna ended the conversation.

Kelu pouted.

Many months later, hot and tired, Arttarna plumped into his garden chair. "Sebi, have Kelu join me here as soon as she returns." He sighed and leaned back. The letter from King Tushratta that morning amounted to a command.

He looked up as a radiant, excited young woman flew into the garden. She rushed to him, dropped onto her knees and placed a hand on his arm.

"From the looks of you, that must have been quite a party."

"You'll never believe how wonderful." She sighed. "Nefrititi's parents, Ty and Aye, are absolutely charming. The house, the furniture, is so beautiful. The dinner had seven courses and was perfectly delicious, the service incredible. Musicians entertained us and even dancing girls."

Laughing, he held up his hand. "That's enough. I gather the party was successful."

She nodded, her eyes and face sparkling. "But there is news that made everybody speechless for what seemed forever. Then everybody whispered wildly."

"Well, what is this astounding news?" he prodded as Kelu hesitated.

"Queen Meritaten has borne a baby daughter."

Arttarna's chin dropped, leaving him speechless.

Kelu laughed. "See. That's just the way we all reacted."

"Astonishing." He shook his head.

Kelu hopped up and went to her own chair.

After a few minute's silence while he mulled over the ramifications of the new royal baby, Arttarna said, "I also have news which is more disturbing to us that your news."

"What could that possibly be?"

"We are ordered home."

"Home!" She clapped a hand over her mouth.

He nodded. "We've been away more than six years."

"It doesn't seem that long, yet it seems forever. I left," she hesitated, "practically from the royal nursery. That is a long time ago."

"You go home an accomplished, beautiful young woman of marriageable age."

"To meet nice men, appropriate men, of my own nation."

"Appropriate aristocrats," he said pointedly.

She looked at the ground beside her chair. He had said she could have a say in whom she married. A little shiver went through her. "Will you hunt somebody right away?"

Having noted the tremble, he studied her before answering. "No. We both need time to renew acquaintances and observe the eligible young men."

Her chest rose in a relieved sigh.

They sat in silence, each thinking of the Wassukkanni they had left behind.

With a sigh of his own, Arttarna said, "Mitanni will be a change after four years in these hot climates. So prepare yourself for the cold, the ice, the snow."

"Along with the blazing fires, cuddling up before them. I'm ready."

He smiled. "So am I."

23

For three days, Arttarna haunted the dock area, searching out any ancient army man he could find. To each of the few grizzled old men in Amarna, he said, "Did you fight in Amenhotep III's wars against the Canaanites and Philistines east of Egypt?"

Most of them said, "Yes."

"What's marching across those sandy wastes like?"

"Terrible. Terrible."

All the old warriors said the same.

Standing on the quay, he called to the riverboat captains. "Is Mendes the best starting point on the route to Kantara?"

The answer quickly blew back on the breeze, "Yes."

The fourth day, sitting at his desk, going over his notes, he raised his head and his voice. "Sebi!"

Immediately, Sebi bowed before him.

"Send Kelu to me."

"My dear," he said when Kelu appeared, "sit down."

She raised her eyebrows in surprise, but sat on the chair Sebi magically placed behind her.

"In spite of your hesitance about the Great Green Sea, I think the wiser course is to go part way by ship."

A frown appeared on Kelu's brow.

"Once we leave the vegetation alongside this great river, the way consists of long days across sandy wastes. We would have to join a caravan to prevent our getting lost. The heat is terrible. And while there are the occasional oases, there are no accommodations."

"I know what that's like," she said.

Arttarna smiled, remembering the escape from Hattusas. "That was reasonably comfortable compared to the trip we face now." He shifted his position. "I suggest we sail north as far as Mendes."

He pushed a drawing he had made of the river and the route of their travel across the desk. "Here is Mendes." He placed his stylus on a round blob. "We then travel"—the stylus moved—"across sand to Pelusium on the coast. That should give you a sense of what days of sand and heat would be like. It won't be pleasant. We'll go together, including the guard staff with me at the moment. They will walk so progress will be slow."

"And take a ship from there?" Kelu said through a drawn and tense mouth.

"The ships sail along the coast. It's summertime. The boatmen say heavy storms do not occur at this time."

She still showed unease.

"It is best, Kelu. The other way is long and hard. I don't want to subject any of us to that."

Kelu bowed her head in acceptance.

On the day of departure, Arttarna organized his crew with his usual efficiency. "You, guards, hop into this large boat. It will hold all of you."

As they climbed into the boat rocking gently at the quayside, he said, "Rasi, get the five horses into that one where you see the captain beckoning. Sebi will help you."

He looked around. To one side, a short distance from the river, a group of young Egyptian men and women surrounded Kelu.

"Kelu," he raised his voice, "it's time to go."

Amid tears of sadness and promises to remember each other forever, Kelu dragged herself away from her friends.

"In here," he said when she reached him.

"Eshtar, in the back." He took his seat beside Kelu and motioned to the captain.

From the dock, Cook waived good-bye to them.

"I wish you were coming with us," Kelu called.

"No, Mistress. I've had enough of ice and cold."

"Cook will be all right," Arttarna said as the boat slid away from the dock. "I found him a good position with wealthy Egyptians."

Kelu settled back. "I love to ride in these riverboats. My

friends and I used them when fishing in the marshes." She looked wistfully at the shore as they passed the boundary of Amarna. "Actually," she said, turning to her father, "I'm a little afraid."

"Why?" He gazed at her with concern.

"I was a child when we left Wassukkanni. I knew nobody except the royal children. Now, I have to face the whole of Mitannian society."

"My dear, you have faced the society in every country where we have lived. This will be no different."

"Yes, it will," she insisted. "I have to find a husband."

Startled, he caught her hand. "Kelu, we go into this together. You may not realize it, but this is going to be as traumatic for me as for you."

Slightly parting her lips, she stared at him in amazement, read the loneliness in his eyes and understood. She depended on him, yes, but he also depended on her. In silence, she placed her other hand on his clasping hand. For a long time, they sat without moving. Finally, withdrawing his hand, Arttarna said, "Well, we are making good time."

They spent two days in Mendes then joined a caravan crossing the sandy waste to Pelusium. The sun beat down on them, burning sand struck Kelu's eyes, got in her clothing, irritated her skin, insatiable thirst gnawed at her. She glanced at her father, thankful that he had insisted on the shorter route.

In the great seaport of Pelusium, Arttarna easily found a ship loaded with grain sailing to Ugarit where they disembarked. There, he purchased horses, and they headed for home.

As they closed in on Wassukkanni, Arttarna could feel his excitement rise. Pictures of the rooms in his elegant palace apartment kept circulating through his mind, his furniture, talks with his king. Pounding up the slope toward the palace gate, his heart stopped for a moment when he passed the spot where Khelpa had been struck. Maybe one of these men had done it. They rode at the same breakneck speed on the sweating horses as his guard force had ridden that day. Those behind struggled to keep up.

The palace gate opened for Ambassador Arttarna. They cantered through, the guards swerving to the left to their quarters. Slaves appeared, seemingly from nowhere, to help him and lift the tired Kelu from her horse.

"Your quarters are ready, Ambassador," said the guard standing in the entrance doorway.

He couldn't wait. He rushed along the corridor, Kelu almost running behind him, Sebi trying unsuccessfully to take the lead. Then, in quiet dignity, he stood in the middle of his reception room and surveyed everything.

"Sebi," he said softly, "we are home."

"Yes, Master," said Sebi, beaming.

"Kelu, you know where your room is."

"Yes, Father." She sent him a loving smile. "Eshtar!"

"Yes, Mistress." Contentedly, Eshtar followed Kelu toward the back of the room.

"First thing in the morning, Sebi," Arttarna said, "Send word to King Tushrata that we have returned."

"I will, Master, but he may already have received word through the guards at the gate."

"True. However, I intend to have a peaceful dinner and evening in my own home before the cares of state descend upon me." With that, he started for his bedroom. "Four buckets, Sebi," he said, savoring the feel of the water pouring over his naked body.

In the morning, Arttarna had only half consumed the mush made of local wheat and goat's milk when a slave dressed in the royal livery arrived to escort him to the king's private rooms.

In swift motion, he gulped down the remains of the mush, wiped his mouth clean, straightened his beautiful morning robe, and signaled the royal messenger to lead.

"You arrived last night, and you didn't contact me," King Tushratta accused the face down prostrate figure in front of him.

"Your Majesty," said Arttarna, "after days of hard riding, sweat and dirt, in no decent way could I appear before my king."

"Oh, stand up, Arttarna. I can't hear you when you mumble into the floor."

Hearing the irritation in the king's voice, Arttarna leaped to his feet. With bowed head, he said, "You would not have been happy with me, dirty and sweaty as I was, Your Majesty. I told Sebi to notify you first thing this morning."

"And he came, not too early," grumbled the king.

Arttarna stood in silence, head down.

"Well, I had a chair placed here by me. Sit in it."

Meekly, Arttarna slid sideways into the chair. He hoped Tushratta wouldn't continue to castigate him. For the first time, he raised his eyes and looked at the king. The sight shocked him. In six years, Tushratta had aged. Worry lines crossed his brow. A nervous twitch kept his lips in motion. His hair showed gray and had thinned. The sight of his friend worried Arttarna.

"Your Majesty," he said quietly, "I gather all is not well here in Mitanni."

"Far from it," Tushratta blurted out. "My brother and his son keep an army around the country which stirs up the people. The Egyptian king sends me no gold, for which I have continuously asked. Plus, he has not returned the gold statue of the goddess Ishtar of Nineveh which I sent to his father as a curative when he was ill." Tushratta fell silent then in anger, he said, "The Egyptian doesn't even answer my letters."

"Your Majesty, I tried to warn you by my personal messengers as well as by letter that the Egyptian king lived inside a bubble, surrounded by his family and a few loyal subjects, his only interest his god. The rest of the country waits in anger, watching the destruction of old temples. There is much unrest, particularly among the priests of Amun-Ra, but all is a turbulent river underground. The king does not move out of Amarna. What army there is guards him in his capital city. He and his family live in unbelievable luxury. Other than those who serve him, no one lives in Amarna."

Tushrata gasped. "You paint a devastating picture"

"I intend to, my king. I traveled around the country to judge the people myself. Other than those in the capital, the country is desolate and open to any predators."

"I had no idea." Tushratta looked at the floor and slowly shook his head.

"Expect nothing because that is what you'll get."

Tushratta's hand went to his forehead. "And my problems here are unbearable. I need the help of the Egyptian army."

Arttarna raised his spread hands in helplessness. Finally, he broke the ensuing silence. "What is your brother doing other than spreading his army around?"

"For one, he steals valuables from my palace, silver plate, Minoan vases. Suddenly, I discover that some article is gone and that he has sent it as a gift to the King of Assyria. I can't stop it."

"Great Teshub," exclaimed Arttarna, sweeping his eyes around the room.

"My honest and efficient chancellor came upon some of my nephew's people trying to remove that silver and gold door which I took as booty when we were victorious over the Assyrians."

"Not that!" Arttarna almost fell off his chair.

"Naturally, the chancellor sent the men running, called some of my guards who removed the door. I have placed it in my personal quarters." Sadly, he said, "Arttarna, what shall I do?"

"A difficult question. If you refuse him entrance to the palace, he might lead his troops against you."

"I think he will anyway."

"The only thing I can think of quickly is to forcibly confine your brother, your nephew and their retainers, to a specific part of the palace."

"Frankly, between us, I have considered having him eliminated. I may come to that."

"Where is the queen?"

"She is here with me. Why do you ask?"

"I wondered whether she might be in danger."

Tushratta's face took on a startled look.

"Just a thought, Your Majesty. I assume you have taken precaution for yourself. You may remember, you did away with some members of your family when you became king."

"Yes, I have thought of it." Tushratta sighed. "I have sent my younger children, along with their nurses, to safety in case of hostage taking. The queen and my other women are here."

Arttarna whistled under his breath. Things had come to a strange state, brother against brother and nephew, as it turned out. "Has Prince Mattizawa gone, also?"

"No. Prince Mattizawa stays with me, of course."

"As it should be." Arttarna nodded his approval.

"Well, what do you think I should do?"

"Perhaps send the prince out, with appropriate armed guards to make himself known to the people, make himself liked by them, as their next king."

Tushratta nodded agreement. "I'll send Mattizawa out today."

"And bring Prince Shaushtatar back to help you while Mattiwaza is away."

"Well, I'll think about that."

Arttarna continued. "Add to your army. Train it well. Use the great parade ground in the rear of the palace to do this. March them around every day. Let Artatama see it."

"Good thought." Tushratta looked straight at his friend. "Arttarna, it's a joy to have you back. My chancellor is a superb administrator, but he has no ideas."

Arttarna smiled at his king.

Tushratta smiled back. "You may go now, but have dinner with me and the queen later."

The interview over, Arttarna bowed himself out.

On returning to his apartment, he sat at his desk and thought. Six years ago, he had known every aristocratic family in the city. Undoubtedly, he could quickly move back into their circles, but he had to find out which ones had eligible sons. He drummed his fingernails on the desk as his thought raced.

Suddenly, he brightened. The queen. He could stake his fortune on the fact that the queen knew every eligible aristocratic male in the city. Smiling to himself, he went to his stables to check on the horses they had so mistreated yesterday in the push to reach the palace.

Rasi wasn't there. The stable boy informed him that Rasi was riding with young miss.

"Saddle me a horse. While you're doing that, I'll look over the horses that were brought in yesterday. Where are they?"

The boy indicated.

Arttarna was rubbing his hand over the mare ridden by Kelu when the boy returned with a big brown stallion.

Quickly mounted, he trotted off, wondering where he might find his daughter and Rasi.

A short time later, three people walking their horses came into view in the distance. Strange. The woman certainly looked like Kelu, but who was the man beside her. He kicked his horse into a canter. As he drew near, Kelu waived. Arttarna squinted. They had been home less than a full day, and Kelu rode beside an extremely handsome, dark-skinned young man. He snorted. And he had intended to introduce her to the young aristocrats! Maybe he didn't need to talk to the queen after all. So what! He'd question her about the eligible males anyway.

During the conversation at dinner, Queen Iuni asked him

about Kelu. "She must be quite grown up by now. You have not married her off in one of those wild countries?"

"No." Arttarna laughed. "But she is quite grown up. I had intended to ask you about which of our families has an eligible young man."

The queen smiled. "Many families have fine young men, the one named Zike probably the most sought after by the mothers."

Again, Arttarna laughed. "This is absolutely amazing, my queen. I rode out late this morning, looking for my equestrian daughter, only to find her with a young man who apologized for riding along with her without a proper introduction. He said his name was Zike."

Queen Iuni smiled graciously. Arttarna had the distinct feeling she didn't like the implications of that.

24

As Eshtar dressed her the following morning, Kelu discussed the possibility of doing some supervising in the palace wearing rooms or setting up a small establishment of her own. Both of them jumped at the knock on the door. Eshtar opened it.

"A message from the queen for mistress," said Sebi.

"From Queen Iuni!" cried Kelu, pleasure lighting up her face.

"Yes." Sebi smiled. "She has asked you to present yourself in her private audience hall mid-afternoon today."

"My gracious," said Kelu. "She's treating me like an adult."

"You are an adult," said Eshtar.

Kelu hurried to tell Arttarna. Dressed for court, he was heading for the exit door, preparing to circulate among those attending and renew acquaintances. Kelu stopped him.

"Wonderful," he said, and wondered if the queen were gagging her adversary. Zike might make a good catch for one of the lesser princesses. "Bow before her the way you did as a child."

"That was a child's bow," laughed Kelu.

"I think it would do well with the queen to continue that. She favors you."

Kelu took her father's advice when admitted to the queen. She went down on one knee and bent her head.

Queen Iuni laughed. "You were so cute, Kelu. Come sit on this cushion by me." The queen indicated a large red wool cushion on the floor.

Kelu rose gracefully and walked with elegance to the cushion. The queen scrutinized her every motion, noting the exquisite beauty of her bone structure.

The minute Kelu sat down, she burst out, "Your Majesty, I
lived with Tadukhepa until just before she died and saw Princess Gil—Are you all right, Your Majesty?"

One of the queen's hands clutched her breast, the other
covered her mouth. She looked pale and had closed her eyes. In
a second, she managed, "Tell me all you know about Tadukhepa
and the king's sister."

Kelu moved to the queen's feet and laid her head in the
royal lap. Hands locked together, the two talked and cried,
cried and talked, until the king came in after his audience.

One look at them, and he said, "You have got to stop this."

He clapped for a slave. "Bring some warm water for these
ladies to have their eyes bathed. And send two of the queen's
ladies here."

The slave ran from the room.

"I thought you intended, Madam, to discuss with Kelu—"
He stopped short, stunned by Kelu's beauty as she turned her
eyes up to him. "—what she might do to help you," he ended
lamely.

Two female slaves entered, each with a basin of warm water.

The queen and Kelu separated so the slaves could lay compresses on their eyes. Under the king's fascinated gaze, they
discussed how Kelu could help the queen.

On his pronouncement that they both looked better, Kelu
left the queen's chamber and walked along the corridors until
she reached her own suite. Arttarna was standing in the middle
of the reception room and turned as she entered.

"Have you been crying?" he said sharply.

"Yes, and so has the queen. We both cried and cried until
the king came in and stopped us."

"In other words, you spent the time talking about
Tadukhepa."

"Yes. She wanted to know everything. And she promised to
tell the king what I said about his sister."

"I gather the interview went well," he said with slight
sarcasm. "Now, Queen Iuni won't object to young men around
here."

Kelu fluttered her eyelashes. "Why would she object?"

"Because, my innocent one, she has young daughters who
won't all go to royal houses."

"Oh." Kelu raised her eyebrows and slid her eyes to the side.

"Also, I have spent a busy morning. I have invited the best young people, men and women, in the city to a dinner next week to introduce you to Mitannian society."

In a twitter of excitement, Kelu flew to her room to discuss her wardrobe with Eshtar. She pulled three elegant robes from her tiny dressing area and laid them across the bed. The two women stood before the bed, Kelu with an index finger across her cheek. "Nobody here in Mitanni has seen any of these," she observed. "So whichever I wear doesn't matter. However, this sheer white linen isn't appropriate."

"Agreed," said Eshtar.

Kelu ran her hand over the bright red wool. "I like this. The color is happy." She skipped the white linen, taking one step sideways, and said, "I think I'll wear this." She picked up the pale green wool, the color of spring foliage, with multicolored wide embroidery all around the bottom and held it against herself, turning towards Eshtar for comment.

"An excellent choice." Eshtar nodded. "It sets off your light brown skin beautifully."

Kelu smiled happily. "That's decided."

The day before the dinner, Sebi supervised the slaves as they moved long tables into the reception room. Their new female cook pulled in extra palace slaves to help in the kitchen. Preparations and cooking spilled over into other palace domiciles as well.

The party day dawned cool and bright. Ambassador Arttarna's quarters hummed with activity. Sebi and Eshtar ran hither and thither, supervising the additional slaves. Delicious smells flowed from the kitchen area. Neighbor slaves hustled back and forth, carrying great pots of food. The long tables in the reception area gleamed. Beautifully painted pottery bowls lined each side of the tables; great platters of three different kinds of bread lined the middle. A slave busily set a beer goblet behind each bowl.

Arttarna stayed in the quiet of his office, away from the hubbub unless Sebi came to him for advice. Just before the appointed hour of the guests' arrival, the slaves magically vanished. Arttarna, dressed in gorgeous red wool covered with embroidery, took up a station near the reception room door. Sebi, wearing his new blue wool skirt, manned the door.

Glowing, Kelu entered, dressed in her lovely green wool, her hair braided around her head the way she had done it in Egypt. Tadukhepa's fabulous gold and gem sunburst sparkled on her left shoulder. She walked slowly up to her father and stood at his side. He swallowed hard, trying to control his emotion as he looked at her and quickly looked away, concentrating on the door.

Accompanied by two young women and a man, Zike arrived first. His eyes devoured Kelu. Suddenly, the room swarmed with young people. Kelu moved gracefully among them, speaking to each one, trying to remember their names. They drank toasts, planned parties and picnics.

Arttarna looked over the crowd as they sat down to supper. Delighted with what he saw, he told himself that his choices had been good; any one of these young men would make an acceptable husband for Kelu.

Immediately, huge caldrons of food arrived and disappeared. In one corner, a slave plucked a harp. One young guest sang along in a pleasing tenor. Others joined in. Arttarna swelled with pride at the sight of these fine young Mitannian aristocrats.

Much later, when the door closed on the last three guests, an ecstatic Kelu fell into her father's arms.

"They are nice, Father. I'll find a husband among them."

"Any one of them would be an excellent choice. We'll wait and see what offers you receive." Personally, he thought Zike the best of the lot. From his observation, the boy was smitten.

He turned to survey the mess. One of the slaves ran around the table, grabbing up the breadbaskets from all over. Another slave meticulously picked up the wine goblets while others reached for bowls and dumped uneaten food into the round wooden tub near the kitchen door. Only then did the slaves wash off the debris on the tables.

From then on, younger people constantly filled their quarters. Kelu frequented the greatest homes in Wassukkanni as well as other palace quarters. She spent time helping the queen with the weaving rooms and some of the king's social functions. She wandered through the empty royal nursery, looking with nostalgia at the tiny closet where she slept and the room she had shared with Tadukhepa. She hadn't even seen Mattiwaza before he was sent away to travel throughout the empire. And with the other children in hiding out of the city, the nursery seemed forlorn.

At breakfast one day two months later, Kelu said to her father, "I'm surprised that we haven't had an offer from Zike yet."

"I am also. Would you accept him?"

"Yes, I like him."

Arttarna stored the comment. She had not discovered love. However, it would be a good match. Love would come.

Two weeks passed. Three families contacted Arttarna with bids for marriage between Kelu and their sons. Arttarna hedged, non-plused about Zike, always a constant, attentive guest.

Oblivious to the offers, waiting for Zike's offer, Kelu walked along the corridor in the royal quarters one morning, headed for the queen's private audience room. The door a few steps ahead of her had been left opened. A young man dressed in an elegant purple robe, authority in his bearing, walked out. His shiny black hair hung just below his ears and gold rings dangled from the lobes. He glanced casually around, stopped short and almost yelled, "Kelu." Instantly, he stood in front of her, taller than she and broad shouldered, his face eager.

"Prince Shaushtatar," she stuttered.

"I didn't mean to shock you." He laughed gleefully.

"It's quite a surprise."

"I arrived two days ago. My father decided that he wanted me here since Mattiwaza is away on a trip around the empire. I had heard that Ambassador Arttarna has been called back to Wassukkanni and assumed that you came with him."

"Yes," said Kelu, flustered. "We arrived one night and Prince Mattiwaza left the next day."

She shifted her feet. "I must hurry to your mother now, but I'll tell Father that I have seen you."

"Your father? Who is your father?"

"Ambassador Arttarna."

"You never called him father when I knew you."

Kelu smiled gently. "I didn't know he was my father. I guess he got tired of hearing me address him as ambassador and instructed me to call him 'father'; in fact, he is my father."

"That's wonderful news. I thought you were just his ward."

"I really must go. Your mother is waiting for me."

As he didn't move, she walked around him.

He turned with her, his eyes following her as she walked away from him. "I'll see you soon," he said to her moving back.

Later, in her own quarters, she told Arttarna about the encounter. "Can we invite him to dinner?"

"That is not our place. He must do the inviting." Arttarna didn't like the flush on her face. As he needed to discuss Prince Mattiwaza's trip with the king, he better have a good look at Prince Shaushtatar. He knew the king had finally called him back.

The following morning, he entered the king's audience court before any others. The prince sat just below the king. Arttarna made the appropriate bows then personally greeted Prince Shaushtatar.

Obviously glad to see Arttarna, the young prince smiled.

Surveying the now half full hall, the king announced to the assembled crowd, "As you people know, we have brought Prince Shaushtatar back to help us while Prince Mattiwaza is out visiting the people of our empire." After that comment, he opened the morning session.

When the audience broke up, Tushratta motioned Arttarna to his side. "I wish you and your daughter to dine privately with us today."

"We are much honored, Your Majesty." Arttarna glanced at Prince Shaushtatar and knew from his intent expression that he had been paying close attention to the exchange.

After that dinner, Kelu and Shaushtatar had many opportunities to see each other. Their meetings continued even after Mattiwaza's return to the palace. Arttarna waited nervously to hear Kelu's comments after seeing Mattiwaza for the first time in years.

"He is a very handsome man," she said indifferently.

"You used to think you wanted to marry him," said Arttarna.

"I was enamored with getting married," Kelu responded thoughtfully. "Princess Tadukhepa was getting married and Prince

Mattiwaza said he wanted to marry me. Actually, he was a very kind, gentle little boy. But now I see a hardness in him that I do not like."

Arttarna nodded. He, too, had sensed something unpleasant beneath the prince's elegant charm. On the one hand, he was pleased that he no longer had to worry about any involvement on Kelu's part with Mattiwaza, but as he watched her in Prince Shaushtatar's company, he became sick at heart. She loved him.

He also knew that Zike loved her. Still, Zike's family had not contacted him. Would Kelu consent to marry him now? But she understands that she cannot marry the prince, he argued with himself.

The question of Zike solved itself the day the boy came to him and asked for a private talk. Pleased, sure Zike intended to offer, yet surprised the offer didn't come from his parents, Arttarna led him into his office and closed the door. He pushed the only chair in the small room up to his desk, motioned Zike into it, and sat down himself behind his desk.

For a minute, Zike nervously twisted his fingers. Arttarna sat still, letting the boy collect himself.

Finally raising his eyes, Zike said, "Ambassador, I love your daughter to distraction, wildly. I have never loved anyone else. You must have wondered why I did not ask my parents to contact you."

"Yes," Arttarna said quietly.

"My parents are as upset as I am."

Arttarna's eyes sharpened.

"Our queen has demanded me for the second princess."

Arttarna soundlessly let out his breath.

"I have met the girl. She's nice, but she's not Kelu. What can I do?" Zike asked diffidently.

Sensing what Zike had in mind, Arttarna looked at him with sadness in his face. "Zike, unless the princess dies, there is nothing you can do. It is best you not see so much of Kelu. She only goes to an honorable marriage."

"I'm not surprised at your answer and will abide by your wishes." Without another look, Zike rose and left the room.

Arttarna sat for a long time. One problem solved, but a larger one loomed on the horizon. He reported to Kelu at dinner what had transpired between him and Zike. "In no way will I allow you to become a second wife to anybody."

"Neither would I accept him that way, Father." In a second, she added, "Actually, I would not accept him now anyway. I love Prince Shaushtatar."

There the problem lay on the table.

"And he loves me," she added.

"So you have discussed it," he said, his voice hard. "What was your decision?" He expected to have to ship her to Pamba in Hattusas, which he would do if necessary against her will.

"Nothing," she said matter-of-factly. "We both know the rules."

"Oh, my dear child." He closed his eyes in agony.

"Don't feel badly. He's here. We see each other. But I could not, I cannot, marry any of the others."

His own experience all over again, unable to marry the woman he loved. But he had been forced into an unhappy marriage. "You don't have to marry any of the others," he said softly.

Both Kelu and Shaushtatar were discreet. He knew they rode together and met at other times when they could. Many a late afternoon, alone, without attendants, he entered their quarters to eat with them. He escorted her to parties in the town, but took care not to get themselves talked about.

Arttarna agonized as he saw no future for them. He also knew that Tushratta continued to search for suitable wives for his sons among the daughters of his brother kings and that Shaushtatar expected to accept his duty.

He sat alone at his desk, unhappy, fretting, the day he suddenly became aware of a great undercurrent of noise throughout the palace. He rose and went to the door. The sound of running feet and continual screaming came from the section of the royal quarters. Closing the door behind him, he hurried that way. Terrified slaves started to pass him. The door of the great audience hall stood open. No guard stood beside it. Loud hysterical sobbing coming from inside the room met his ear. He ran the short remaining distance.

Just inside the door, he saw the bloody body of King Tushratta lying at the foot of the throne. The wildly sobbing queen, covered with blood, lay on top of him. The chancellor knelt beside the king, trying to comfort the queen.

Arttarna's horrified glance met the chancellor's as he knelt across from him.

"Prince Mattiwaza stabbed him," said the chancellor

Arttarna gulped. How could he have prevented it?

At that point, Prince Shaushtatar ran into the room, Kelu behind him.

With a cry of horror, he flung himself to the floor beside his father.

Arttarna quickly rose to leave the space for Shaushtatar. He put his arm around Kelu and held her close.

"Mother dear," Prince Shaushtatar said after a few minutes. Using his strength, he pulled her into his embrace.

She sobbed on his shoulder. "Your brother did this."

Shaushtatar's head jerked up from its nest against his mother's hair. He glanced rapidly around.

"Where is my brother now?" His jaw clenched as his eyes swept all the faces in the room.

No one spoke. Finally, the chancellor stepped forward. "He has disappeared, Your Highness. I have sent the guards to look for him."

"Search every corner of this palace."

"Move," Shaushtatar yelled as the guards hesitated.

His stern face and commanding stance galvanized the guards into action. Grabbing their swaying swords, they rushed from the room.

The queen raised her head at Shaushtatar's command. She glanced over the crowd in the room. Then, her son supporting her, she rose unsteadily to her feet.

"Kneel," she cried in a quavering voice to the crowd, "before my son Shaushtatar, your new king."

For a moment, as everyone dropped to the floor, Prince Shaushtatar stood startled. He looked around, trying to judge the mood of the courtiers. He supposed he was king now, but Mattiwaza should be king. He really didn't want to be king. He had watched his father struggle. He didn't want the responsibility. However, as he thought about it, he realized that being king could at least have some advantages at the moment.

Shaushtatar looked around again. Everyone was waiting

for him to do something. All right, he'd do it. He stepped towards Kelu. Taking both her hands, he pulled her to him and turned her around so she stood beside him.

Still holding one of her hands, he raised his other arm for silence. "I take Kelu, daughter of Ambassador Arttarna, as my queen."

25

As he passed his slave in his quarters, Arttarna said, "Sebi, Kelu will spend the night with the queen. She needs Kelu with her for comfort."

A few steps later, he turned on Sebi. "Do you know how to escape from this palace and Wassukkanni unseen, unfollowed and uncaptured?"

Sebi stood motionless, facing his master blinking rapidly. When he stopped blinking, he said, "Yes."

"Good. As soon as possible, do the palace part, judge the city part and return to me."

"Now?" said Sebi, mystified.

"Now." Arttarna spun around and went to his office. After some minutes of drumming on his desk with his fingernails, drawn brow and eyes unseeing, he rose and casually wandered to the main palace gate. Unable to find Mattiwaza, guards milled around, uneasy, noisy. Cries were starting to rise in ever-louder volume demanding the appearance of their new king.

Arttarna mentally checked each person that went through the gate. He spotted two members of his messenger/guard force. Surreptitiously, motioning them to follow him, he spoke to the guards at the gate, passed through, and sauntered down the main road. At a sufficient distance from the gate to be unobserved by the palace guards, lost in the crowd hurrying up and down, the two men following him drew alongside.

Without looking at them, Arttarna softly said, "Have the entire force spread out over the country. I wish to know the moves of Artatama's troops." With his jaw hard, he whispered, "If it's too dangerous to come back here, don't. I'll know what your absence means. That is all." Arttarna turned into the tiny temple from which he had buried Khelpa.

The two guards walked on.

As he left the temple, he heard shouts of joy. Rapidly walking back up the incline, he reached a spot where he could easily see the palace gate. On top of the right gate tower, Shaushtatar stood waving to the crowd, Kelu beside him. To his disgust, he felt moisture seeping into his eyes.

The queen's head appeared. Shaushtatar stooped to help her up, placing her between himself and Kelu.

Arttarna hurried to his quarters. Sebi waited. "All is as you wish, Master."

"Excellent. Tell Rasi to be at a safe spot—which the two of you decide upon—with four horses within four days and be prepared to wait there until instructed further by you or me." After a second, he added, "Rasi may need a horse for himself. Let him be the judge."

"Yes, Master."

"I don't know what will happen here. Instinct tells me there will be trouble. You and Eshtar are to be prepared to leave along the route you have just covered at a moments notice."

Leaving a stunned, stupefied Sebi, Artttarna went to his room and stayed there, sending for something light to eat after dark. He then dismissed Sebi. Once he felt sure all was quiet, silent as a stalking animal, hugging the corridor wall, he hurried to the royal quarters. Absolute quiet reigned there, too. He observed the two guards stationed at the entrance. To the one in charge, he said, "It would be wise if you ordered two more guards to walk up and down in the corridor here in case there is trouble."

The thought simmered slowly through the man's mind. Arttarna watched the expression on his face. At last, he said, "That is a wise idea, Ambassador. I will do it."

Arttarna nodded approval and returned to his own bedroom where he spent a restless night. The horror of Tushratta's assassination haunted him. His best friend had left him. Just from one minute to the next, Tushratta was gone. He put his hands over his face and groaned.

Sudden thoughts of his happy childhood surprised him. He folded his hands across his chest. A picture of the large estate outside the city where he had lived with his parents and siblings and many other relatives rose in his mind. The only mistake his adored parents had ever made, as far as he was concerned, was choosing Garadu as his wife. But it was during that unhappy experience that Khelpa had come to live with them. Her death was still an agony to him. His days were busy, but when night came, alone in his bed, the look of surprise in her eyes when he last saw her, lying on a mat, her body crushed, haunted him. He groaned again and rolled over onto his stomach, breathing her name.

Putting his arms around his bolster and resting his chin on it, he thought about Kelu. Their little daughter, like a ray of light, had come into his life. He had brought her up as a Mitannian aristocrat. As the gods had willed it, she had turned out well and was making a good marriage. She loved Shaushtatar, so she would undoubtedly be happy. As her father, he could have done no better for her.

First thing in the morning, he would send Sebi for the high priest. He would see to it that Shaushtatar married Kelu immediately. No matter what objection Shaushtatar or Queen Iuni might make about rushing the marriage ceremony, he wanted to make sure that Kelu was properly wed, especially during this time of great danger, when anything could happen. They could always have a magnificent public ceremony later.

His happiness for Kelu was mixed with sadness. He had done all he could for her. But the moment she became the king's wife, her status would change. She would immediately be surrounded by fawning courtiers and ladies in waiting. She would have responsibilities around the palace. He would play less of a role in her life. In the meantime, he intended to do everything possible to get them safely out of Wassukkanni if such drastic action had to be taken. But he had no desire to escape with them. He sighed.

His life! What was his life now? Tushratta was dead. Although he would be the father of the king's wife and still have prestige, he would no longer have the same position at court. He had been ambassador for so many years that he had no intention of leading a merely decorative existence.

He got up and walked to his dresser to drink some of the beer Sebi had left there for him. After satisfying his thirst, he paced back and forth in the room. If the Assyrians got hold of him, Artatama and Suttarna would probably have him flayed alive. He balled up his fists. Never!

Arttarna stopped pacing. He suddenly knew what he would do. Calmness spread through his body. He lay down on his bed. With a smile on his lips, he whispered, "Khelpa," and promised himself a short nap. The dawn was at hand, and he needed to see his adored child married to Shaushtatar.

On returning to the royal quarters in the morning, he found arrangements for cremating the king's body and conveying the ashes to the temple well underway. He cornered a harried Shaushtatar.

"Your Majesty, while sympathizing with you in all the pressures of the day, please grant this wish to a worried father. I have sent Sebi for the chief priest of the great temple of Teshub to marry you and Kelu. It will only take five minutes."

Shaushtatar opened his black eyes wide, a delighted grin on his face. "Ambassador, that is the best thing you could have done. Let us do it quickly and get it over with before somebody objects that she is not royal."

Now, it was Arttarna's turn to look gleeful. Wonderful. Shaushtatar was on his side. "I wish to see the two of you married, Your Majesty, first, because she is my daughter, but also because I just do not know what is going to happen here in Wassukkanni."

"What is going to happen is that we are going to bury my father and have forty days of mourning."

Shaushtatar called a slave. "Ask my mother and Kelu to come to our private audience hall immediately."

The two ladies, a bit flustered by the haste appeared just as Sebi arrived with the chief priest. Shaushtatar caught Kelu's hand and drew her to a spot beside him right in front of the chief priest.

Arttarna moved between the chief priest and the door. "Sebi, stay with me and watch this marriage."

Standing behind Kelu and her son, the queen looked confused. She scowled, opened and shut her mouth, preparing to object, admonish, stop the proceedings. Before she could verbalize her objections, the five minutes ended. A broad smile spreading across Shaushtatar's face, he stooped and kissed his wife.

"I actually feel much stronger having you by my side now with all we have to face." His eyes full of love swept over her. She smiled and brushed his cheek with her fingertips.

Arttarna heaved a big sigh of relief and motioned to Sebi to leave. The queen loudly fussed over the informality, the swiftness, the lack of witnesses. Shaushtatar apologized and promised her a grand royal wedding the minute the forty days of mourning were completed. "I will invite the whole city," he said. Kelu giggled.

Then the business of the day enveloped them.

Arttarna sat at his table and ate a prodigious amount of bread, yogurt, cucumbers, wheat gruel, boiled fish and drank milk. "Sebi," he said, "the minute you reach safety with the other three, you are a free man."

"No, Master. I don't wish to leave you."

"Just remember what I said."

Scowling, Sebi stood behind his master counting out the people and horses. Kelu and the king must be included. He couldn't make it add up. After a minute, he realized that Arttarna needed more food. Later, he commented to Eshtar on the amount Arttarna had eaten, as if he hadn't eaten for days. She, in turn, wondered if she should go to Kelu.

"I think Kelu will come for her clothes. So wait," he said.

Kelu didn't come; she sent a slave to tell Eshtar to come to her. "You are to particularly bring the red wool for the service of the ashes on the elegantly embroidered garment and the offered food," the slave said.

"I better hurry," Eshtar told Sebi. "She is queen now. I am her slave."

"She still depends on you. However, when the signal comes from the master, be sure she obeys. But regardless of what she says, you are to come to me. Do you understand?"

"I do, my love. And I promise you, Kelu and Shaushtatar will both come."

Sebi gave her an approving look.

Eshtar departed so quickly that she left a surprised, speechless husband.

After the formal service where the old queen, Shaushtatar and Kelu sat side by side before the heavily decorated chair holding the garment and the jar of ashes, Arttarna cornered the new king. "Your Majesty, send your mother immediately to her younger children."

At Shaushtatar's incensed look, he quickly said, "Please do

not take my advice the wrong way. I mean this only for her safety and think it imperative enough to speak to you this way."

"She will object. Why is it so important?"

"Frankly, I don't know specifically, but all my bits and pieces of information tell me for her own safety, it is wise."

"Ambassador, knowing how much my father depended on what you said, I will do that, even though I don't like it. This is mourning time for my father."

"Better she live. Which brings me to another point. If I send to you suddenly to come to my quarters, no matter what you are doing, drop it and come. Do not question, just come."

Shaushtatar frowned at him. With bowed head, Arttarna dropped onto one knee.

"Please excuse me, Your Majesty. My concern for your welfare made me overstep my place."

"What do you think is going to happen?"

"From minute to minute, I don't know. However, I do know that your uncle Artatama with his troops are headed toward our city. I can't prove this, but I think Assyrians are with him."

"Assyrians!" gasped Shaushtatar. "We could handle my uncle with our own troops, but the Assyrians—" He left the comment in mid air.

"Go about your daily business and hope that I am wrong. I don't want to upset the whole government and have it dissolve. But please be prepared."

Shaushtatar stood quietly for a few moments, eyes lowered. Raising them, he said, "I will follow your advice."

True to his fears, his mother objected violently. "Mother, as king, I command you to do as I say."

"Since when do you have the nerve to order me from this capital?"

"Unfortunately, just between us—and this is not for you to spread around, dearest mother—great danger lies ahead. I want you out of it."

"Danger? I intend to face any danger with you."

"That is not your choice."

"You just try."

In the end, Shaushtatar had slaves pick her up, screaming and fighting, and place her in an ordinary chariot drawn up to the private royal entrance. In the gathering dusk, sadly, standing alone, he watched the entourage, guards before and aft, leave the palace grounds. One female slave climbed into the chariot with her. As he turned back into the palace, he wondered if he would ever see her again.

Arttarna knew the chariot had departed because, he, too, waited in the disk for the return of any of his men. None came that night. The trouble was still at a distance. Did it mean that the Assyrians were not a party to the uprising?

Each day, Shaushtatar trained his armed forces behind the palace. He held long conferences with his chancellor on the state of the empire, without mentioning the danger in the back of his mind.

By the fifth day after Tushratta's death, Arttarna's men started to straggle in. Each bore the same message. Artatama's army marched on Wassukkanni. Two men said that the Assyrians were marching from the west.

Arttarna shuddered. "You," he said coldly to the men after they reported, "leave the area and never come back."

"Master, I don't understand. I want to stay with you. I have worked well," each said in turn.

"How dare you argue with me? Get out. Go to another country—now."

The men looked at his hard face and left. Unhappy, hurt, they drifted around the palace courtyard and talked together. Suddenly, Sebi appeared among them. He handed each man a small sack of gold and turned away. The guards left Wassukkanni, heading north to look for work in the small states along the coast east of the Hittites.

Every day, Arttarna had Sebi check the escape route. Sebi said, "Master, there is nothing there." But Arttarna waited, nervous, unable to work or eat, though Sebi placed delicacies before him. He debated with himself. When would be too soon, when too late?

Hoping to relieve her husband's worry, Kelu suggested that he invite four of their closest friends to the mourning palace. The city seemed quiet. She knew he had heard nothing from her father and was beginning to fret. At night, he held her in his arms and forgot his worries; they forgot everything, except their love for each other.

"Thirty more days of mourning," he said to Kelu one morning. Hand in hand, they walked slowly from their private quarters towards the reception hall. Suddenly, Sebi fell on one knee before them.

"Ambassador Arttarna begs you come at once, both of you." He glanced behind them. "Where is Eshtar?"

"In my room," Kelu said.

"You go with the king. I'll get her."

"But I have people to see," said Saushtatar, frowning.

"Please go, Your Majesty. The Assyrian army has reached the western part of the city. They are looting, burning, raping and slitting everybody's throat." Sebi cast Shaushtatar a frantic glance as he raced towards their sleeping quarters.

"My love, we better go to my father. Obviously he has something in mind that is urgent." Kelu started for the door; Shaushtatar followed. Swiftly, they made their way to Arttarna's office. He sat behind his desk, three brown goatskin sacks before him on the desk. Sebi and Eshtar entered.

"Sebi," Arttarna said, "take this sack"—he proffered the smallest of the three—"and wait with Eshtar in the corridor for Kelu and the king. Then you know what to do."

The minute Sebi closed the door behind the two of them, Arttarna turned his attention to Kelu and Shaushtatar. The new king looked pale and shocked, Kelu wide-eyed and terrified. To steady himself, he picked up a second sack and handed it to Shaushtatar. "You will need this. Sebi will lead you to safety. Work your way to Hattusas. Search out Pamba. Kelu, you still remember where he lives?"

"Yes, Father."

"Pamba will present you to King Suppiluliumas."

"No," cried Kelu.

Arttarna ignored her.

Eyes closed, agony in his face, Shaushtatar listened.

"The king will set his army against the Assyrians and put you back on your throne, albeit as a satellite of Hatti."

He picked up the third sack.

"But, but—" Shaushtatar started.

"There are no buts now, King Shaushtatar. You do as I say." Arttarna brought his hand down flat on the table. "Kelu, take this sack and guard it well."

Kelu put out her hand to take the sack and almost dropped it. "What's in this?" she exclaimed. "It's heavy." She pulled it close to her body for a better grip.

"Never mind now. You must hurry. Follow Sebi."

"But we can't leave without you," cried Kelu, flinging herself upon her father, her free arm going around his neck, tears starting to stream down her face.

He kissed her, held her tight and turned pleading eyes on Shaushtatar. "Take her. I can do no more."

Shaushtatar gripped Arttarna's shoulder. The eyes of the two men met and held in perfect understanding.

Banging and screaming suddenly sounded in the distance. With a sad smile, Arttarna tried to push Kelu away. "Go, my darling."

Shaushtatar grabbed her arm and forced the sobbing Kelu from her father's embrace. Holding her arm in a firm grip, he pulled her from the room.

Arttarna hurried to the door to watch them. Sebi led, running along the corridor. The others followed, Shaushtatar bringing up the rear.

His body sagged. He closed the door. Somehow, he knew they would reach Hattusas. Slowly, he walked through his palace rooms, lovingly touching favorite furniture. Using both hands, he raised a beautiful alabaster lamp high above his head and shattered it on the smooth hard floor. A few small family pieces, he had stowed in the sack Kelu carried, along with a fortune in gems and gold.

From his bedside table, he picked up the container of beer and the drinking glass he had received from Gilukhepa in Egypt. He took them to the reception room and laid them on the table he had moved to the center of the room. After placing a chair behind the table, he sat down facing the door into the corridor. For a few minutes, he shifted his body in the chair, deciding what seemed the most comfortable position.

That decision made, he poured beer into the glass, retrieved a small cloth packet hidden in his robe, and emptied the powered contents into the beer. Deliberately, he swirled the liquid, watching the play of light on the surface.

The awful noise of terrified people screaming had become louder and continuous, running feet, slamming doors. He cocked his head and listened. The sound, still distant had increased considerably since Kelu left. So, he thought, the Assyrians have entered the palace and are slaughtering everyone they find.

For a short time, he listened. As the screams and noise grew closer and louder, he smiled, lifted the glass to his lips and drank the contents. He slowly turned the glass round and round, admiring its beauty. Suddenly he gave a yell of victory, crushed the glass in his hand, dropped the fragments onto the floor, and settled into the position he had chosen.